TRUELIGHT BRINGER BY BR PAYNE

Cover Illustration by Aleksandra Klepacka
Map by Karin Wittig

To my parents, without your endless support, this book could not exist.

"There are no ordinary people. You have never talked to a mere mortal." – C.S. LEWIS

CONTENTS

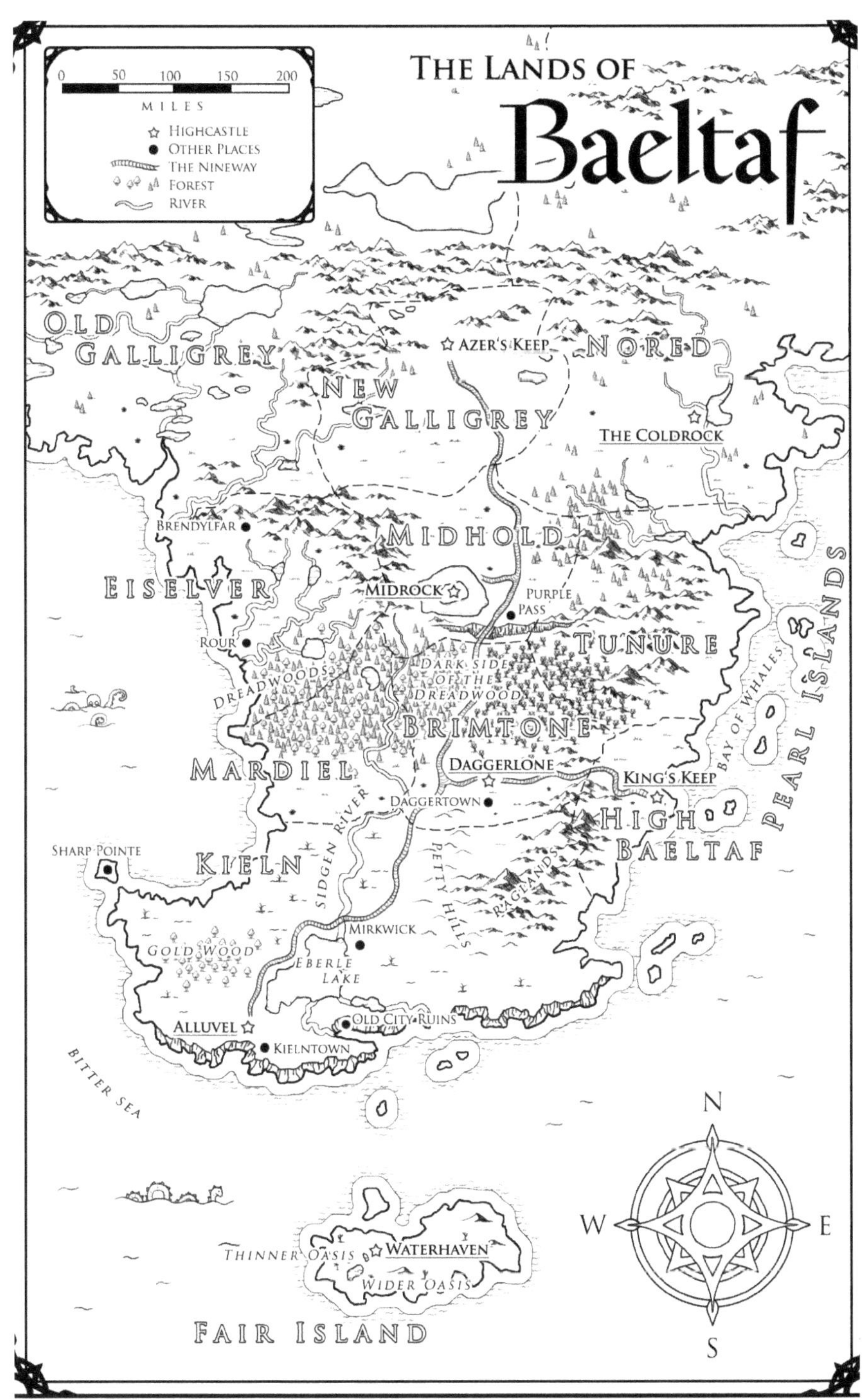

THE LANDS OF
Baeltaf
0 50 100 150 200
MILES
HIGHCASTLE
OTHER PLACES
THE NINEWAY
FOREST
RIVER
OLD GALLIGREY
AZER'S KEEP
NORED
NEW GALLIGREY
THE COLDROCK
BRENDYLFAR
MIDHOLD
EISELVER
MIDROCK
PURPLE PASS
ROUR
TUNURE
DREADWOODS
DARK SIDE OF THE DREADWOOD
BRIMTONE
PEARL ISLANDS
BAY OF WHALES
MARDIEL
DAGGERLONE
KING'S KEEP
DAGGERTOWN
HIGH BAELTAF
SHARP POINTE
KIELN
SIDGEN RIVER
PETTY HILLS
RAGLANDS
MIRKWICK
GOLD WOOD
EBERLE LAKE
OLD CITY RUINS
ALLUVEL
KIELNTOWN
BITTER SEA
N
W
E
S
THINNER OASIS
WATERHAVEN
WIDER OASIS
FAIR ISLAND

PROLOGUE

translated from The First Book of Amina, II.1-5:

"[Truelight] is alive, unlike the rest of life. [Void] is dead and working. No one else sees the sharp vines? More real than I am.

One day, all will see. When the next bringer meets that hollow born, it will be too late."

Bile, sour and hot, rose past the knot in Santir's throat. He swallowed, continued with his slow, heavy breaths, and kept his eyes on the gray sky moving toward him. It wasn't that he disliked flying, in fact he loved it— the way clouds broke against the front glass, the gentle and constant hum of the vessel, the violet lights illuminating the control room. It was all glorious for a simple man like him.

What made him ill was the speed at which the vessel flew, more so his brother's reckless steering. Santir felt better when he steered his own vessel, but Yeroen never allowed it when they crossed the Line. They'd exhausted all debates on whether this measure was protective or domineering.

Santir was also wary of the destination; no matter how many times he traveled to this Eastern kingdom, the same nervous tension built in his stomach as the winds developed their own mind. This third time across the Line, he knew the turbulence would get worse from here. His knuckles popped and whitened, bone tight against brown skin, gripping the side of the copilot's chair.

"You haven't hacked up your last meal on the controls yet," Yeroen barked. The air vessel rocked with his boom of laughter. "We are making good time, don't you think? Better than last. Back thrusters three clicks up."

"Three? Not in unwielded winds. I told you— recordings

showed storm signs just a few panes north. You can't go faster than this." *My poor ship.*

His brother shouted, "Three clicks for God's holy luck!" and nodded his head once, staring straight at whipping gray clouds in front, the strong forces of air long uncontrolled.

"This is my ship," Santir said.

"Fixed how many times with my money? That's what I thought. Three clicks!"

However lucky the number, this was still Santir's ship. He reached across the control desk and turned the closest dials two clicks to the left.

The vessel lurched forward, and Yeroen shifted into the correct gear. They were soaring then, flying so fast that Santir could hear the pressure of the sky beat against the paneled siding.

A loud *bang,* a *boom* came from somewhere in the tail, and both brothers looked at each other worriedly just as the control panel lights started blinking. Alarm windpipes screeched and echoed.

Santir slowed the vessel four clicks and checked the blinking control panel of the thrusters, the airshoots. He cursed as the scribe mechanism stopped recording, its beetle-like hum stalled.

"A water source?" he yelled over the blare of the windpipes. Yeroen looked affronted by the question.

"I checked them myself in Talosa, and never again—" he said but got distracted by something Santir could not sense.

Yeroen unclasped the buckle at the front of his harness and bolted straight through the door behind them, towards the tail of the ship, and the craft tilted, jerked left then right. Santir unclasped his own restraint, leaped for the steer as fast as he could, gripping it tightly, and realized with despair that the vessel was losing altitude. He felt a terrible shudder toss the ship to one side, and he turned the steer forcefully to the other, and then he smelled the heavy fumes curling into the control room. The sirens stopped. It was too quiet. Santir cursed as the vessel dipped and then they were falling freely. The steer jammed. The violet lights stopped blinking, and the control room darkened. He clicked in his harness, securing himself tightly to the pilot chair.

Santir finally hacked up his last meal onto the steer and gear shaft as the vessel sped downwards toward the sea below, so quickly that he could not think to move. Smoke billowed forth, obstructing the view out of the glass front. He felt another strong pull in his stomach, and he thought he might be sick again. Santir closed his eyes and prayed to First-One that he be accepted into Paradise.

Forgiveness, I should ask forgiveness.

Here I come, Klo.

Thunder boomed and metal groaned. The vessel crashed and every bone rattled.

At first, Santir couldn't breathe. The metal of the ship hummed loudly around him, and he blinked away the black as best he could, gray color smearing the corners of his sight.

It was too painful to swallow as he opened his eyes, feeling cracks in his ribs when he straightened and coughed. The control room was dark, but light faded in and out from... *somewhere*. His head tottered, too heavy for his neck. It took time for Santir to notice anything but the taste of metal in his mouth and the pain in his sides.

From the glass front, he saw they crashed on a haggard beach, the gray plumes of wreckage rising higher than the few palm trees he could see. *An abandoned beach, hopefully*, he thought, imagining the outcome of explaining an airship to Bilers. *They'd try to burn us living.*

"Are you hurt?" he heard his brother yell from the back of the vessel. Besides a cut on his head and a cracked rib, he was fine.

"No," Santir called back, wiping the thick blood off his forehead and brow. It clung to his coarse hair. Beyond the door, he heard the ship's entryway open and fall with a loud smack upon the sand. He released his belt and staggered out of the control room, past his bedroom and to the entryway. His lungs burned, and each cough felt like crashing again. He exited the vessel slowly, turning to see the full extent of the damage.

The airstone held and had not been crushed upon impact, and he gave three silent thanks, coughing. He gave a fourth to Yeroen, because his brother must have raised the sea to save them.

The sky was a searing white gray, and the ocean around them a mottled reflection, both turbulent and stirring. The beach wrapped behind them in both directions.

An island. There must be hundreds of uncharted Biler islands.

Santir's ears rang. He turned on the beach and noticed a short distance away a boat, two large wooden oars laying against its side. Without Yeroen's sense, it would take both of them rowing weeks to get to the Biler lands, but Yeroen could get them there in days. *It is a convenient coincidence,* he thought, staring at the boat, *a blessing she would say. Never a coincidence. Thank you, Three-One for the blessing. It will have to do.*

And it would do miserably.

The full sound of the world re-emerged. Yeroen had his hands in the salt water, yelling; his arms were badly burned. Santir could finally hear Yeroen cursing the man who sold him the vessel, cursing the guilt that kept Santir from selling it and getting a better, sleeker model, and lastly cursing Three-One for making both of them poor men with a mountain of debt and only one plan. When Yeroen finished, Santir rolled up his sleeves, preparing for the long task at hand.

He sighed and asked, “Smell that?” Yeroen acted as if he didn't hear. “You shouldn't have trusted a Southach nobody with the repair. Only a real descendent can tune refined firestones for these vessels. They're delicate.”

Yeroen tied his curling hair in place on the top of his head. “Could you have afforded that? How long shall this take you?”

“See,” Santir said at the steaming tail, “I will know more when I open the panels. If I find that our energy sources have gone to shit, what then? We are hundreds of panes from the Blessed Lands."

"Something is wrong with the fire source," said Yeroen. "An airstone panel burned me. If we have all we need, and nothing is ruined, how long will this take you?"

"Two, maybe three days," Santir replied, pulling open the outer shell of the vessel's tail, which released a puff of thick exhaust into his face. He was glad he overestimated how much time he'd need. Coughing up the smoke hurt his chest, and as he undertook revision of the back thrusters, he wondered how many ribs were cracked.

"After this trip, we will be able to afford dependable Canyai service. I'm excited," Yeroen said through bared teeth. Fresh blisters tore open on his hands and he rinsed them a last time in the salt water. "How far are we?"

"At the last reading, over thirty panes away. It will take more time than you think. You cannot glide into their port on a commandeered wave. But I had my own business in the Biler's place. I can go with you and return to fix all this," Santir said, stepping away from the damage.

The Great Fire dipped low on the horizon, scattering pink and golden light through thick cloud, dim color across the sloshing grays on the shore. Almost pretty, though Santir wouldn't admire it.

"That adds too much time. You stay, fix the vessel. I will take care of your business." Yeroen grinned smugly.

"You don't know what to find," said Santir.

"Rae told me all about it. I know what to find."

He didn't want to argue, though he doubted Yeroen knew exactly what he had to retrieve from the Biler Dominion, because not even Santir knew *exactly* what it was, even with Rae going over her request a fourth time. He rubbed the back of his sore neck and thought he'd rather not run tasks for anyone, least of all Rae.

So, Santir agreed.

In silence, the brothers unloaded their illicit cargo onto the small wooden boat, stacking the woven boxes and cramming them where they did not fit. Yeroen removed the oars from the boat's side and tossed them to the sand before dragging it to the water's edge.

"I will return in three days, give-take," he said as he settled in the boat. Yeroen leaned over and placed his left hand in the dark water, the muscles of his forearm tensed. "You better have all this sorted by the time I return. We need a win, brother."

The sea crawled up Yeroen's arm and stretched into two playful curls before carrying the boat off to the East.

Part 1
Baeltaf
Kieln, the 10th Dominion
702 A.C. (After Cleansing)

1. BAD BEGINNINGS

Tisinda's children weren't safe here. With yesterday's news, she couldn't deny it. The desert-call, the gift of her people, like a cold sheet wound tightly around her chest, pulled her to Waterhaven's Oasis. She never felt safe on the Mainland, but Kieln was her children's home. She thought they'd have more time. But yesterday, the dire message came.

The Hollowborn was found. Truly found.

Found by one, found by one thousand— it would soon be the same. The Hollowborn, her son, would be named.

No matter what she thought.

He's just a boy.

Tisinda rose from bed, tip toeing on cold floor and old threshes. She let her mind wander with her eyes, out the window. Behind dirty glass she saw the distant Bitter Sea, Kielntown's slanting roofs and chimneys smoking.The Sun's warmth touched her face, white.

Almost like home, though it was nothing like home. She allowed herself to imagine sands rolling out as far as she could see, and the searing, dry heat. If she closed her eyes she could feel herself there, Fair Isle, running across the dunes with her younger sister tumbling after, coloring their skirts with sand.

She fought rust to open the creaking window and felt breeze too damp.

She heard the Calling across the water. Felt its frantic tug-tug-tug in her heart. Ancient and unsettling.

Clouds covered the Sun, dimming the world, and Tisinda opened her eyes. Still cold.

Wet air blew in, sending a sharp chill down her spine. Gathering her garments, she retreated deeper into her chamber. *I am not a child of summer.* She was of the Abandoned, untamed now.

Brown autumn arrived to Kieln in full force and would spin into winter with quick ease. Nights seamlessly turned to days, days to nights, but the relentless pounding of rain would fall forever, the sky gray. Never-changing.

This dry morn was an omen.

Tisinda knew that she should be out in the highcastle, as it was already approaching midday. Her husband would notice her absence. He always did. Tisinda stared at her pale face in the looking glass that hung beside her wardrobe and thought back to a time when her skin had been kissed by light.

Her fine, blonde hair clumped in knots around her head. With a sigh, her fingers went to work, pulling apart wispy strands. She thought back to her childhood. The Fair Isle, though not long a journey from these most southern shores, seemed like a different world to Kieln.

Tisinda had visited six of the eleven Dominions of Baeltaf after marrying Tagnar Hwaelin. While the capital offered enticements to a young and naive girl, she found the others severely lacking and unprepossessing. And before that, when she was still small with the most innocent hopes, she had gone with her father to the true West, long forgotten by this part of the world.

Abandoned, she mused as her fingers methodically twirled white strands into their place. *The West was wise to abandon this place. And now*, Tisinda thought, plaiting her long hair at the top of her head, *the lords of the northern Dominions squabble about territory and kill their own countrymen, and everyone else is about to lose their minds. Hollowborn, Other, Hasyal. He's not, he's just a boy.*

She called for one of her handmaidens to come empty the chamber pot, and for the other one to dress her, but her mind wandered back to her life before Kieln, when she had taken simple pleasures for granted. Vision glass, protection, privacy within court.

Like little mice, the servant girls entered the chamber, making sure not to lift their eyes too high or say a word too soon. The older servant picked out a heavy blue dress from the wooden wardrobe, one meant to bring out the little color in Tisinda's pale eyes. The maid, red hair falling carelessly from her bonnet, anxiously waited for the High Lady's rejection of the dress.

Tisinda looked the dress over in the woman's fat hands, reaching out to touch the true gold designs woven into the bodice. Fine Kielnish gold. The embellishments swirled around one another atop the celeste linen, curling across the midsection, reminding Tisinda of powdery earth carried on a hot breeze.

"This one, High Lady?" asked the younger maid, holding the white and gray dress Tisinda would never wear. It reminded her of the white dresses she wore after her mother died.

"Shall I get one of the others?" The older maidservant was anxiously tucking sleeves back to their places.

A day wanting to dwell in memories. Her strange desire for reminiscence pulled Tisinda from her present. The Calling. *This loud? I must go. Tomorrow.*

The simplest decision of the day. *Blue and gold, white and gray...*

"The blue," Tisinda said, and the older servant stayed to help her dress.

Today Tisinda's ears had little to report, but she expected nothing could compare to yesterday's letter from the Deep. Her maid could not understand the weight of yesterday's message. Words like Hasyal and Hollowborn meant nothing to her, nothing to Baeltaf.

The pull gripped Tisinda's gut— not the corset, the Calling. She needed to journey home, especially now that the Deep's whispers had come to her.

Tisinda thought of her three children, imagining their faces soft and vulnerable as when they were babes. There was no safer place than with her family in the Fair Isle. On the whole Rock, only the Fair People could know the truth. Her family, Rooj, was richest and honest enough to know everything. Tisinda would take her children with her, she decided long ago when she first heard the whispers of yet another war in Baeltaf. She might never return to the Mainland, but there was still chance she might come back as the greatest of them. Perhaps Queen of Baeltaf, while Baeltaf lasts.

She didn't believe in end day prophecies, even knowing what they would call her son. Perhaps she didn't believe for that very reason... she couldn't believe, or sooner they'd come. But Tisinda hedged her bets.

Her husband's position was frailer than he knew. *Only the cunning survive the coming years*, she thought wryly, *and there are none more cunning than the Rooj.* She sucked in harsh breaths as her maid pulled the strings of her corset tighter and tighter still. When she had finished with her dressing, her chambermaid left her. She had a knack for knowing when Tisinda wanted to be alone.

She did not know how long she stared out her window to Kielntown and the sea, clinging to old memories of dry winds that tasted of salt and endless summer. A knock on her chamber door pulled her eyes away from the fog, which now had begun to form atop the marshy beaches miles away. She hoped it would not rain today. "Enter," Tisinda called out, expecting her husband to walk in and berate her absence from castle life. She felt like a ghost in Alluvel, waiting.

A sigh of relief escaped her when she saw her eldest son walk through the doorway. *He is so tall. Like my father.*

"Jonnere." Tisinda looked up at him. "You are early home."

"I returned after dawn and meant to surprise you." His voice reminded Tisinda of her father's, clear and gentle, higher than most men's. She was not surprised but smiled all the same, her heart content for the first time in weeks. *When was the last time I was surprised?*

Jonnere smiled and the High Lady could see him as a little boy again, his legs fat and wobbly, that sweet smile always on his face. Now before her stood a man grown of twenty-one years, less confidence in that smile.

"I thought that you'd like to walk in your garden with me today. Perfect time, first dry day in so long," he said, rubbing his hand across his beard. She would have preferred if he shaved, like any civilized man, but her husband mocked her preference and taught his sons that true men grow hair on their face. Jonnere's beard matched Mainland fashions, a shocking pale eyesore on his tanned skin.

Tisinda looked back out the window, feeling her son's worried eyes on the back of her head. Jonnere was always the one to worry: for her spirits, for his father's approval, for everything. So unlike Mittrik who only cared for swords and hounds and hunting.

She agreed to walk with Jonnere so that she could see the youthful smile on her son's face once more. She missed him while he traveled across the moorland to East Kieln, thirty days and nights gone.

He extended his arm to her as they approached the alabaster columns that aligned her garden, and he led her atop the path made of Island sailing stones. Tisinda's glass-sheltered garden was nothing short of glorious by all Mainland standards, though that was not saying much. Some called her extravagant, her second son among them. Others expected nothing less of a Rooj. Hers was unlike the gardens of the Dominions to the north, not containing any sort of green shrubbery or trees inlaid in darling morning-roses, hers was clear of pleasant smells. No, the garden of the High Lady was a gift from the High Lord after the birth of their first son, and it was meant to remind her of home. The stones turned to fine sand beneath their shoes as they walked, and the desert palms of her past rose amongst the sharp and spiny root plants. Large lilies grew across the sand, lining a winding path to a small oasis-like pond at the heart of the garden. The white flowers smelt like metal. Like blood.

Tisinda and her son walked in silence. On a day dry as this, it was almost pleasant to be in the little space her husband allotted her, a quarter acre within itself. But when the rains heaved themselves upon the bitter chill for countless days in gray fog, the sight of the pitiful desert made her want to weep. She wished for the sun to come down harsher on her face and hands still, bathing her skin and calming her mind. The Sun wasn't hot enough to ease her worry.

Never hot enough, this shrouded Sun.

"Anon, I shall return to Fair Isle. These days of wet seem without time. I crave nothing more than good days in the Sun with my sister."

"Yes, Mother, I thought you would feel that way." Jonnere bent down to pluck a white flower from the ground, rose and handed it to her. "It is your custom now. Declined winter altogether for the past three years, you have. That's why I thought you might want to walk with me tomorrow if it doesn't rain. I never know how long you'll stay on Fair Isle, and I never know when Father sends me out again."

Tisinda frowned at him, twirling the flower. It did not look like the waterlily she favored as a child, but it had long ago become her favorite for all the times her children would pick them from this too dark sand.

"I want you to join me this time, with Mittrik and Leonara. My father and sister miss you all dearly, and I am no less excited for them to see the sort of man you are. It has been a very long time since you visited your mother's home. You should miss it. They'll hardly recognize you—" she smiled, added—"but you will shave that face before we go."

"I was nine the last time I set foot atop those shifting sands." He wouldn't be excited for the voyage.

Tisinda felt the familiar pang of bitterness directed at her husband, who always spoke poorly of the unforgiving heat and dry of Fair Isle, and even worse of the Islanders, no doubt tainting her children's opinions of it all forever.

"When you spend enough time in the dunes, you find footing," she said and touched Jonnere's face, one so much like hers, so much the face of her people. His skin tanned to the palest shade of gold, his blonde hair flat over his ears and above his broad brow, a beautiful slender nose, and eyes like ice. "It is my greatest desire you all join me, Jonnere. Someone must help me contain Mittrik. You know how he wanders and gets himself into trouble."

He chuckled. "Speaking of Mittrik," her son deflected the topic with his token gentleness, "I have yet to see him or Leo and I've looked about the whole castle and yards. His absence is never a good omen."

There are no good omens.

"No. They aren't in the castle to greet you, sadly. They weren't expecting you as I was. Your brother tricked your priestess, and now he and Leonara are at the lake, no doubt enjoying this clear day," she replied, sitting atop the bench made from southern beachwood. Sunlight dulled atop the waters of the little pond, the sound of toads croaked in the reeds. Hideous creatures.

"The High Lady's ears abound," Jonnere repeated the words that had become so popular in Kieln, a playful twinkle in his eyes. He was unaware of how many ears Tisinda had. She herself was unaware.

"Say you'll go with me," she began, standing from the bench. "The desert is calling for us, trust me." He could not understand what her words meant, but Jonnere heard the truth. They were in danger, the Calling pulled them, though he couldn't feel it.

Jonnere could never say no to her, so he simply smiled and bowed before he left toward the great hall. Tisinda hoped he would not resent her for stealing him away before his war, but she would not let him stay.

Mittrik swung off his destrier, landing in the course ground and clay with a soft crackle beneath expensive boots. He lifted his little sister from her saddle and set her firmly on the beach. Lake Eberle twinkled under cloudy light; trees and large boulders scattered across the damp land, dry leaves rustled in the heavy wind. Unseasonably good weather.

Leonara ran to where the water met the pebbled sands, stopping before she got her precious shoes wet.

Mittrik saw his sister pinch her little arm. The scraggly beach of Eberle too good to be true for the poor girl. She probably thought she would wake back in the confining study room with the modaire. Leonara closed her eyes and the cool breeze that came off the water swirled her pink colored skirts about her.

"Mittrik!" she exclaimed, opening her pale eyes to him. "This is the most wonderful day. The gods are smiling at us, I know it. I can feel it. Thank you!" She started skipping along the edge of the lake. "I'm so happy Nexitha believes all your lies."

"You think she'd have learned by now."

Mittrik finished tying the horses to the large gailwood tree, making sure to pat Ilder on his head and stroke his braided mane before he walked beside Leonara. He inhaled crisp lake air, humid and chill, still clinging to the salty smell of the rain. They watched the lake change as it pushed upon the shore, the clouds folding and unfolding over the Sun. Gray on gray on gray but beautiful. Leonara took off her golden gloves and set them atop a large rock. She looked at Mittrik, alight with mischief and wonder.

"I shall not tell the modaire, don't you worry." Mittrik laughed. "I spent most of my childhood learning how to fool the old crone."

"How can you do it?" Leonara questioned, searching her brother's eyes for something he did not know. He shifted his gaze back to the waters of Lake Eberle.

"I do not know what you mean," was his curious response.

"You lie. So, so easily you lie. To anyone. Can't you teach me?"

Mittrik did lie easily when it suited him, though he understood his sister's religious nature. She never lied, never the smallest fib could he remember. *She fears the wrath of our father first, unreachable gods second. Or perhaps it's the other way around.* Mittrik picked up a flat stone. He wound his arm back before flinging the stone across the great lake, let out hollowing breath as it skipped once, twice across the water.

He ended up telling Leonara that he would do no harm to her innocence, could never teach her deception, and that their father would call Mittrik quite Fair indeed if he discovered he did such a thing.

"Are you having difficulty in your lessons, Leo?" Mittrik asked.

She rolled her eyes. "I hate memorizing names. I can remember the dates of big battles and changes of power because those matter. I can understand anything I read, the ideas of great thinkers, and I'm good with figures, but a lot of history is just memorizing long names of long dead people. It's tedious. I hate it. My mind does not keep all the Jonnithers and Edgars untangled. When I have sons, not one will be an Edgar."

"A terrible name, I agree, but long dead Jonnithers built Kieln. That's why those men matter."

"And Jonnithers not yet born may break it. Yes, I know why it matters. Doesn't make it easy. It's easier for you when you're so good at everything. I excel at nothing, and Father yells at me for the difference. He will yell at me today for running off, but I've already promised myself to confess. You can come with me to temple and listen beyond the door. I always do."

Mittrik was unlike his sister, who believed in the gods so steadily. She would pray to the gods every night before falling asleep, every morn wishing blessings upon the Dwellings Hwaelin. To Hetten's temple for the smallest sin to receive penance, to the Sisters' for every fear, and Leonara sang loudest of them all on Crestdays. Mittrik did not remember when he stopped believing that the gods answered prayers, but it had been years since he recited the Sister's Sanctions or bent a knee to Hetten in the morn.

"My birthday is only two moons coming," she said once the silence became unbearable, dragging out the word *only.* She persisted flipping a smooth stone between her thumb and fingers.

"No time at all."

"What will you get me?"

"What do you want?"

"From you? Blue flowers from the ruins and a song. Also, a new saddle, one of white leather like Princess Rexanne's. When she came two years ago during her Courting tour, do you remember it? You might not remember what she sat, or perhaps you did take special attention to her seat. It's the most beautiful saddle I've ever seen. Clean, bright. Decorated in suns."

"And you'll want golden swords instead of golden suns on your white leather saddle?"

"Of course, golden swords! I asked Father months ago, but he hasn't said a word about it. I won't ask again. I think he has forgotten but I don't want to sound spoiled. So, make sure I get my saddle. Remind him. Say you will, and do not lie."

"I will, and I don't lie to you," he told her, and together they listened to the crows in the gailwood and the lake on the rocks.

"Do you think I could learn how to swim? I think I could if you taught me," she sounded very sure.

Mittrik sighed. "Leo. If I could teach you as I taught Jonn, I would, but Father would have Baynard whip me if I brought you home dripping lake water Underheel. You should not concern yourself with swimming."

He could tell she did not like his answer. "What if, one day, I am on a ship that wrecks and find myself drowning because you were scared of old Baynard? Shall I concern myself while I drown?"

Leo would get her way, always knowing how to convince him. If born a man, she would make a finer lord than Mittrik, he believed. "Fine, one day, I will teach you. This summer, when it's not so cold."

She beamed out to Eberle, and Mittrik turned to the water, remembering the day his older brother took him to this very spot and asked to be taught to swim in the icy waters. Mittrik always loved to swim, no one had to teach him, but Jonnere was more fearful. He would wade out after Mittrik but panicked if his feet did not touch the silty ground. Mittrik was fifteen Sisters' passes younger than his brother, just over a year, but first to do many things as children: the first to pick up a sword, the first to hit the center of a target with his arrow, and first to jump headfirst into the freezing lake. Jonn had nearly drowned, but if not for Mittrik's teaching he most certainly would have on the next Sister's Greeting when their father threw them both into the water and told them, "Swim like men or meet Hetten."

Leonara's too delicate for such things as swimming, Mittrik thought decidedly.

Her bony elbows poked out at her sides as she dug in the sand. She looked like the twig dolls he would make as a boy. He wondered how a young child was supposed to move in heavy clothing such as hers. How she managed to bend down, let alone ride her horse as well as she did, Mittrik had no idea.

The wire in her skirts forbade her from squatting low, and the high collar of her dress was no doubt choking her skinny neck. She often complained of how her collars itched, tickled and bothered. Still, women could become used to terrible discomforts, when deemed necessary. Leonara hummed as she scooped wet sand up with her hands, pouring it all into a pile on her left, her pale blonde hair nearly touching the ground.

In the quiet, Mittrik thought of his mother. Imagined her laying in her chambers, wrapped in pelts, sheltering her fair heart from Kieln's cold breezes. *At least it has not rained today*, he thought. *That should put her in better spirits.*

Mittrik looked out across Lake Eberle, wishing it was the Bitter Sea. Roaring, violent, secretive but just as gray. His mother once told him, when he was a boy, that the longing in his heart to cross the sea was his calling to Fair Isle. He did not know if he believed that a part of him was so connected to the lands of his mother, but he always wondered about the beyond the Bitter Sea, beyond the Eleven Dominions of Baeltaf. The Westlands were forbidden and forsaken, he knew. They were filled with creatures of magic and horror, yet the promise of danger only excited him. *What else is out there, beyond mines and petty hills of Kieln?* he'd marvel when he stood before a large body of water, intent on the gap in between them.

In truth, he was unsure if he believed in the legends of Old —magic, daemons, and fortune-telling groles. Surely what was out there was strange, but not impossible. *Surely…*

“Are we all going to become more and more like strangers as we get older? I mean, Jonn is so different now than last autumn,” Leonara spoke, startling Mittrik out of his own thoughts of fancy. “Before he left, he told me he’ll likely be going again as soon as he returns. He’s spent little time in Alluvel this year. It’s been just us, hasn’t it? You and me, and sometimes Mother, if she can get out of bed. Father always gone to High Baeltaf to sit on Dawnburst’s council, Jonn now practically High Lord. I don’t think I know Jonn anymore. Not as a person, just as a brother.”

“Certain courtesies will make us seem more distant when Jonn is actually High Lord and you are a lady of your own pretty dwelling. But, no, we will never become like strangers, Leo. I will always call you names and you will always pick fun at my expense like brother and sister, and Jonn will always try to act like Father and scold us for anything. It will always be the same, even as it changes, you and me and Jonn.”

“He doesn’t scold us anymore. Or smile. He just stares out windows, thinking. He goes away to Brimtone every month visiting Lady Ritra, or to deal with the petty politics of underlords in the east. I feel like I haven't spoken to him since he started courting Ritra, but even when he is with us, it is like he is far away in his head. When was the last time you saw him laugh?"

"He hasn't forgotten us, Leo, do not be troubled. Forgotten how to laugh, perhaps, but Father is throwing him into the thick of it to see how he goes. It's good the underlords see him. Kielnmen need to see him as his own man, less our father's son. Jonn will do anything not to disappoint." Mittrik sighed again. "And you know he visits Brimtone to negotiate with the High Lord about the renewal of the steel trade; courting his lovely daughter is simply a reward for the dull affair."

Leonara giggled, covering her mouth with a pale white hand.

"Do you think Jonn and Ritra will be wed very soon?" She smiled and spun her thick skirts around her, splattering the hem in dirt. Mittrik thought she might be imagining weddings how little girls see them— true love, songs of bells, a bride in her silver gown under the marble arches of a sun temple.

"Father could not hope for a better match for him." Mittrik continued throwing leaping rocks across the lake.

"I think one of the princesses would have been a good match as well. There's enough for him to take two if he wanted and the price was right. His sons could have had a high place in the succession of the crown if he married one of the Osbur princesses."

"That would have been a good match as well. He still could take one."

Her face showed she was more than appalled. "No princess would be second wife to a *Gilgar*, Mittrik! Who do you think I shall wed?" Leonara asked, rising on her toes to see his shocked face.

"Leo, you are only three and ten. You have less than three Sister's passes until you need to worry yourself with the vanities of women and the eagerness of lords. Until your Courtings, you should think of childish things, while you can.

There will be sufficient time for the rest, a lifetime or more."

"But I wasn't taught to be a child, I'm taught to be a lady. I'm told to mature and think of my future."

"Lucky for you, since becoming a man, they tell me I have a talent for childishness. I can teach you how to be immature, if I cannot teach you to lie. Here," Mittrik picked up a smooth stone from the sand, "I'll teach you to make it leap atop the water."

He flicked the stone with his wrist across the lake, and it skipped once, twice, three times before settling with a plop of finality and sinking. Leonara picked up a stone and tossed it sideways, trying to imitate his graceful movements. The rock struck the water with a heavy splash and dropped to the bottom. Mittrik placed a second smooth stone in her hand.

"All about the movement of your wrist, quick and straight. Like this." He showed her how to draw her arm back, telling her when to let go of the stone. It *clonked* and sunk into the water. "Turn a bit more when you release it."

On her third attempt, the stone skipped once, causing Leonara to squeal in delight.

"So, who shall you wed? Has father told you?" She asked, breathless from her giggling.

Mittrik fumbled his stone.

"If I'm to marry soon-like, no one has spoken of the woman or date to me," he responded truthfully. He indeed preferred the company of trulls to that of proper ladies, they understood all his jokes, but he wasn't going to tell his sister that. A breeze lifted his hair off his shoulders and sent shivers down to his toes. He decided to sit in the sand, exhausted with thoughts of silver gowns and temple bells.

"Have you never seen a lady worthy of you, is that the difficulty?" She japed, and he knew how she loved to tease him. "Or are you hoping for your own Osbur princess? You danced with Rexanne when she toured, I remember your face even though she was intent on Jonn. You are old enough to start looking more closely. It will soon be time for you to marry some beautiful lower lady as father might intend."

"Kieln finds itself lacking the crowds of beautiful ladies from which to choose," Mittrik joked, but his sister was right. He would be expected to take a wife to ensure good standing with another Dominion or, more likely with one of his father's bannermen, but the High Lord had not mentioned Mittrik's marriage yet. Jonn's wedding to Lady Ritra Gilgar of Daggerlone was first. As second heir to the richest of the High Houses, Mittrik could have his pick of younger daughters of all his lowerlords, though the ones he'd met were not to his liking. If he did not mention a lady first, his father would decide.

Mittrik's fate, like his clothes, was laid out neatly before him everyday, and he'd known since he was a small boy. He would marry a lady, his father would give him his birthright which included five hundred acres, as many serfs, and a small castle along the Sidgen, and he would choose to live in whichever castle was grander: his or his wife's. He had seen the castle called Rosewell Bend, however, and so assumed the latter would be his circumstance.

He added, "Certainly whatever I do, it will not please Father."

"You, the favorite child?" said she, her tone dramatic. "You could never displease Father, Mittrik. Do you have a clue of his idea of a good match for you?"

"He hasn't brought it up, thank the gods. You're right to think he will, though. I fear the day. What if I don't want to marry a noble lady?" His sister's brow furrowed in confusion. "What if I don't want to marry at all?"

She paused, considering. "I'm sure there's still time for you to be ordained as an aidaire, if that were true. Though Father might hang himself with your prayer cord, and I can't quite imagine you in an Overseer's hat. Are you willing to shave your perfect hair?"

"I'm serious, Leo. Why should I be happy to marry someone I haven't chosen, who could be brainless as easily as she could be conniving? Perhaps I have read too many legends and tales of Old demigods, but I wish to find a real purpose. Something more than love."

Leonara laughed. "More than love? But what else is there? You may be hopeless after all. You're not a son of Hetten, you're a son of Hwaelin which is rather great. And you'll be knighted, only to die singing songs of Old demigods in some Mardielan lady's castle." She wouldn't stop giggling.

"I'd rather die singing songs of my own, remember. If there is to be real purpose to my life, I need a great one. If I have to love, I want a consuming love, the like of Gerdwill and his Rosette. A love you'd give up everything for." Giggles erupted from both of them. "A grand thing, you know, honorable as Caeth on his quest—that's what I want, some kind of *something* more than this."

"You act a romantic at your best." Leonara looked down upon her brother before managing to topple into a sitting position next to him. "You find consuming love and honor in those debauched dens in Kielntown?" she asked, and Mittrik chortled, his voice thrown across the lake farther than any stone. His sister was much more perceptive than he thought.

"No, I find other things there," he conceded, "but perhaps I'll travel west one day. Find my true venture. And magic and groles."

"You go too far, Mittrik," her little voice remarked. "Anyone who goes to the Forsaken West is Doomed by Hetten, you know that, and it isn't just something they say in temple. A grole would eat you. You'd lose your soul to magic."

He knew what was said. Uncertain if priests had the truth of it, he decided to let her think he was joking.

"So, am I not permitted adventure and romance in life, as well as you?" she insisted, staring hard into his eyes.

Mittrik placed a hand on hers and looked away. "Leo, do not be so naive to think we're permitted anything. What's said in temple? Gods have their way, and usually the most willful men."

The High Lord's heavy hand landed hard on Jonn's back. He hid his discomfort, glad to be a head taller than his father, so he could lift his chin and save face.

Alluvel's gray stone paled in late evening, and enticing smells of bread and meat spilled into the dining hall as servants carried large trays to the golden table.

Jonn's mouth watered. A tiring day; as he sat, he felt soreness in his legs from every galloping stride. Days on horseback, East Kieln and back. Jonn's father, High Lord Tagnar Hwaelin, sat to his right at the head of the long table. A servant silently entered the room with two gilded goblets, pouring wine and hiding his face.

"And your brother, Jonnere?" The High Lord didn't meet Jonn's eyes before he drank, face stuck between the binding of an old book.

Jonn took a deep drink and scoffed. "I should know? I've not seen him since returning. It would be quite the job to always know his whereabouts."

"Your brother has the spirit of a great lord," was all his father's response, a browned page turned.

More like the spirit of a wild horse. Will it always be like this? Jonn wondered. Would Mittrik always do exactly the opposite of what he is told and be praised for his tenacity, while Jonn rode weeks through the marshes and settled disagreements between underlords, only to be met with his father's stale convention of derision?

Yes, he imagined it would be like this until he took the place fate marked for him.

Until then, his father would give him such tasks as settling disputes between Jarles and Bluers, forever feuding over a century dead stolen warhorse. Jonn's father had given him more duties than scolding Bluers, but he used that face of displeasure while he did, as if Jonn wasn't worthy of these small tasks. He couldn't help but feel as though his father expected him to fail. Jonn knew that he could not fail; he knew what was at stake, what they'd be risking next year. He would do all that was asked of him to prove his worth. *Wherever,* Jonn wondered, *wherever have I failed him before?*

Jonn had been a timid child— undeniable. But he had long ago become a man worthy of his father's respect. He blamed his Fair appearance for his father's disapproval. The High Lord looked at Mittrik and saw himself as he once had been with broad shoulders, curling brown hair and eyes the color of the Bitter Sea. He looked at Jonn and saw a Fair Islander— too tall, too lean, too blonde and entirely untrustworthy.

Jonn's father could not find it within himself to love and trust the same son. Mittrik could keep the love, because he did not have the trust. But for his looks, Mittrik was wholly their mother's child.

But Tagnar trusted Jon; Tagnar's plans required it. And Jonn was first son, first trusted. Greatest comfort in times of war.

Tagnar Hwaelin had warned Jonn of the artfully devious ways of the Fair, where vanity and scheming were taught to Island children while Kielnish highborns learned to read. He wondered how much his mother retained of her Fair upbringing after living most of her life in Kieln. *Enough to grant her every secret south of the Sidgen,* Jonn mused. His mother's ears were notorious.

His brother and sister walked into the dining hall at a leisurely pace, chuckling about whatever was whispered before they entered. Their father set the journal he read on the table to survey his youngest two children. A rushing servant spotted the large book and replaced it with a plate of dried Island figs. Jonn looked to his siblings and could see Leonara's skirts splattered in mud; she was gloveless, and Mittrik still wore his riding boots. Jonn wished detachedly that he was born a second son. *But you cannot change the path the gods design.*

"Jonn!" Leonara shouted, running when she saw him. She

barreled into a hug. "Thank gods you're home. I prayed for you and your company. Torner says you fell into the mud, and they had to pull you out."

He thanked her for her prayers and did not acknowledge the squire's account. His sister stopped and curtsied for their father, "Good Night, Father." She took her seat at the table, placed to the right of Mittrik who sat across Jonn. Mittrik smiled at him, and Jonn returned it because he should.

"And where did you ride this morn?" Their father asked sternly, looking past Mittrik and staring at Leonara.

"Mittrik took me to the lake today," she exclaimed, practically rising from the seat, fluttered from the thrill of her day. "It was so beautiful, like a portrait. And I have some pink in my face, look! And I did forget my gloves, but Mittrik said he would ride to get them tomorrow if they're still there. Modaire Nexitha said today could be the one dry day this week, so we had good luck."

"And why did you take off your gloves?" High Lord Hwaelin looked unimpressed, folding his large marred hands. Warrior's hands, and Jonn looked down at his own unscathed skin. His father shifted gaze to his second son. Mittrik looked unabashedly at their father, and Jonn waited for any kind of chiding but knew he would be disappointed.

The High Lord spoke to silent children. "Your sister should focus more on her readings, son." To Leonara, "Your modaire tells me you cannot recite all your kings even still. Is it your desire to be simpleminded?"

So Leonara would be the one to receive a lecture, Jonn supposed. He would never blame his sister for their brother's reckless erring, and he almost said so, but— better their father reprimand her than him.

Leonara's head dipped, earlier exuberance all vanished. She picked at the skin around her nails as their father commenced his speech. "Five centuries our dwellings and name have remained, and we have ruled Kieln, which is why this family is so revered. Ours was among the First. Ours is fundamental to the ruling of Baeltaf. Our gold supplies the capital, our rubies glitter in the king's crown, our ships provide the Bones with fish. You are my daughter, a Hwaelin, and you shall do better in your studies or I shall take over your instruction." His loud voice entombed the dining hall, emptied of bustling servants.

Their father had taken over Jonn's instruction when he refused to learn geography at nine. Jonn nearly shuddered remembering his father's scorn and the way he cracked the backs of his legs when he could not remember the name of a Northern town. Mittrik stared at him, and Jonn wondered if his brother knew he was remembering it. Mittrik had always done better in his studies and took to the great old books as easily as everything else. Mittrik lowered his eyes to the table teeming with Alluvel's best fare.

It all was carefully set, a large portion of ham and an assortment of breads displayed on golden platters decorated. The smoked quail called out to Jonnere most and his stomach growled in anticipation. For a week he had been eating hard bread and pickled fish as he traveled to the Eastern-most castles and holdfasts in Kieln. He was thankful when his mother walked into the dining hall, hair flowing long behind her like a veil. The three men stood from their seats, and all but Tagnar bowed respectfully to the High Lady.

High Lady Tisinda strode into the room slowly, taking her place at the other end of the long table. Distant now, and always. High Lord Hwaelin looked on at his wife with a slight grimace and sat abruptly as she did. Jonn often heard his father admonish his mother for her long absences during the rain, and he knew that the High Lord's temper was already wearing thin.

"Shall I pray?" Leonara's soft treble was thunderous over the silent tension. Tagnar nodded, and she started. "Oh Hetten, giver of warmth, light, and life, thank you for your presence with us today. Thank you for supplying the crops that we eat, and for nurturing the animals we consume. Bless the daughters as they watch over the children of the realm. Bless the sons as they honor the gods and the king through the strength you supply. Oh Sisters, lovers of the Divine, please be at peace and quiet so that we may remain in the calm. Be it so, amen."

Mittrik began stacking slices of ham on his plate before Leonara finished her short prayer, but their father said nothing. In silence the family ate, listening to the sounds of cutlery scraping plates, Mittrik's incessant boot bouncing beneath the table, and the coming storm. Soon, however, his mother approached the subject of a voyage South, all of them going together. Jonn knew the answer before his father spoke it.

"Leonara will go with you to the Oasis whenever you desire to go, but Jonnere and Mittrik must stay here."

"My father would be overjoyed to see our sons now as men grown. He could not come for Mittrik's tourney for that rotten illness, but he has recovered. It has been too long since all my children have been on the Isle."

The High Lord humphed in response as he chewed at the ham.

Mittrik leaned back in his chair, taking a deep drink from his goblet. "Now at Waterhaven there are crowds of beautiful ladies. I would love a stay on the Isle. I think it is exactly what we need. Don't you agree, Jonn? I think entertainment is due before you tie yourself to Gilgar's daughter."

"I am sure you think so," Jonn said, ignoring Mittrik's villainous smile. Mittrik would choose entertainment over any course. Jonn didn't care to visit the Fair Isle, and he cared even less to follow his brother around as he whored and drank across the villages by Waterhaven.

Their father at last said, "On the Sisters' Greeting, my men and I ride to Brimtone to meet with Gilgar and his. Jonnere must go. He is at last set to wed Gilgar's daughter. We shall sign the papers to end her Courtings on that day, with a wedding upon your return from the island. You must make it a short trip as I want them wed before winter ends."

Jonn swallowed quickly, the boiled squash burning its way down to his stomach. It was sooner than he expected. The full moons were a week away, then they would ride to Brimtone and Jonn would be truly engaged. The time did not matter much, in the end, only he thought he would have more of it. He knew he would wed the young lady because his father demanded it of him. She'd make a satisfactory wife. She was not unintelligent and laughed at Jonn's attempts at humor. The young Ritra was pretty in a plain way, her brown hair always pulled back and plaited at the very base of her neck to mimic capital fashion. He'd convinced himself her brown eyes were not the color of mud.

"It was a fine day," said High Lord Hwaelin, clearly keen to change the topic, "your children managed a ride to the lake to soak in the heavy light." Leonara perked up at the mention of her small adventure, and looked at her mother with a smile.

"I could have guessed for the color on my daughter's cheeks," the High Lady noted, her pale eyes lifted to meet Tagnar's deep blue. "But I was informed."

"Your ears abound and heard it? What else have you heard going within Kieln?"

Jonn did not understand his father's inquiry but said nothing. *Does he expect her to know his plan? Will he tell her, after all?*

His mother sighed, "If there was more than gossip, do you think I would not tell you?"

Jonn remembered something his father once told him, concern yourself when Islanders answer questions with more questions.

Tagnar smiled. "That's all you've heard? Pointless chatter?"

"Mm. Mainlanders rarely have a point, and I have heard enough chatter for all my lives. Am I supposed to have heard something specific, my dear?"

Jonn looked to his father, who placed more slices of ham onto his plate. The High Lord supped the rest of his meal in silence. Jonn understood his parents' way of silent argument with their eyes, the traditional war of mealtimes. His siblings avoided it.

Leonara and Mittrik made a game of catching grapes in their mouths when their father wasn't looking, and soon that game turned into pelting Jonn with grapes until he joined.

Their mother said nothing of it.

The moment Tisinda entered her chambers after supper, she set to write to her sister. Talia Rooj remained on the Fair Isle, allowed to marry an Islander with whom she fell in love. The man was dead now, but not for any curse like Mainlanders believed. Tisinda's sister was allowed to keep her family's old and worthy name, as was Islander custom. She tried not to covet her sister's position, because it was Tisinda's duty as the eldest daughter, her brother's duty as eldest son, to elevate their family's position.

Rooj must always rise. These were the words her father, High Lord Rooj, told her the day she realized she must marry a Hwaelin. She was first betrothed to Tagnar's eldest brother, and when he died in the Owner's War, she was then betrothed to the second son. And by the war's end, only the youngest Hwaelin survived, so she married him. It saddened her at the time on account of both older brothers having prettier faces and better attitudes than Tagnar. Still, through cunning and nerve, Rooj would rise, even when it felt like lowering herself.

She sat at her table and dipped the plume into the inkwell, not knowing where to begin. With her deception? With the threat of the Hollowborn? Her husband's pointed questions lingered over these. *Why is he so curious now?* She pondered, uneasy. Since she heard the news from the Deep, danger seemed to lurk everywhere. Perhaps she was unduly suspicious. Perhaps not.

She wrote quickly, letters looped across the parchment. Tisinda wondered if her daughter would ever write as neatly as a proper young lady. Had she been raised on the Fair Isle, she would write better and speak more eloquently than the boorish Mainlanders. As of now, she was one of them. Stupid, no matter how truthful. Leonara should know how to use her gift to her benefit, and she should be known to the rest of the Rock as a beauty of the Isle. Despite her daughter's indifference toward studies, her softness, Leonara was a true Fair child—born in the water, in the Thinner Oasis. A true Fair Islander, and soon she would understand what that meant. When her first blood came, Tisinda would tell her.

She signed the bottom of the page, reading it twice over before blotting the excess ink. She would tell the redheaded servant girl to take it to the rookery and attach it to her golden sparrow. Her sister would receive it in one day and night. Such things took longer in the East. *If only I had married that Canyai prince,* she thought not for the first time as she poured gold wax on parchment. She did not seal it with the symbol of her husband's dwellings, but instead with the impression of her ring, embossed with the image of the desert palm.

Suddenly, she heard heavy footsteps approach up the corridor. She looked around before stuffing the letter snug between the mattress and the bed frame.

A demanding knock sounded through the chamber, and she knew it was her husband. She bid him enter, and Tagnar glided into her bauer. *Mittrik walks just like him*, she noted. Both always made sure their movements appeared fluid and effortless but of course it was as intentional as anything else they did. She lowered her eyes to the floor as he walked to the center of the room.

"You think I am here to chastise you," he said, walking over to the table and pouring wine into one of the gold goblets. "I'm not."

He drank slowly and carefully, his eyes never leaving her. They made silent demands, and she could almost remember a time when she might have loved him— when they were both young and before she realized how drenched he was in his animosity for her people. She felt something unpleasant shift in the room as he set the goblet down and poured himself another drink, then one for her as well. He offered it to her and she took it without a thank-you. She sat in her chair wishing instead she could taste the much stronger sweet rums shipped to the Isle. Soon she'd indulge in those tastes, she told herself.

She needed to calm her nerves and decided to drink half the wine in the cup. Her nose scrunched involuntarily; she had never liked the Mainland's wine. Tagnar paced in front of her, and he reminded her of a growling jakiza behind a cage. She attempted a smile.

"You know something, Tisinda," he said and stopped, standing with his shoulders squared and his chin stiff. "Tell me exactly what you know."

Exactly? Why act clever? What does he think he means? She would never tell him of her dealings in the West, lest she be condemned by his cruel false gods. Burned at a stake for her sins. And she would not tell him about her dealings with Fair Isle lest he kill her himself. *He is not clever enough, as ignorant as any Mainlander, and he would not know what to do with all that I know.*

The Oasis. I must go home. She could no longer deny that she felt it in full: the oldest song of Fair Isle— loud, undeniable. Too loud, and she fought to keep her expression calm when she answered him.

"I know much. I'm an educated Island woman. Shall I enthrall you with a song from my home? I know many of those. Do you want fresh gossip of who spends the nights in Kensgood's bed beside his lady? I would not speak of it at your table in front of your servants, my lord. Ah— perhaps I can recite the old histories of Baeltaf, though I know less of these things." She lowered her gaze and smiled playfully.

He smiled back, and perhaps it was the wine, but tonight she liked the way it lifted his cheeks. The smile looked youthful although it sat on a weathered and darkly bearded face. His hair curled, the strands of gray reflecting in the dim candle light. She took a deeper drink. He had been kind and gentle to her long ago, she could almost remember. She could almost forget.

"You mean to hide something from me," said Tagnar. "Some secret."

"My secret? Or yours?" *So many, you stupid man.* She drank and smiled at him, sweet and seductive. Eyes clueless, mouth knowing, both wanting, just as her mother taught her to appear before men at war. Tisinda could have been an actress had she not been a Rooj.

My Oasis, I must go, the thought would not leave her suddenly, repeating itself over and over again in her head. Nothing else mattered.

Go, go.

"We are not different from each other," she told him. "You meant to hide an entire war from me. There is your secret. Can you guess mine?"

She shouldn't have said it. She'd lost control— and why?

Tagnar did so much to keep his secrets from her.

"Who can hide from you?" he asked.

Go, go home. The Oasis. She wanted to answer, say anything to wound his pride, but her lips wouldn't shape words even if her mind could form them. She needed control. She needed to *go, go, go*. Her throat felt too tight in her worry, and she held in a cough, making both her stomach and eyes burn. She wished to cry, though she never cried. *High Ladies do not cry.* Tisinda contained the tears, allowed the cough.

Her husband resumed pacing. "You Islanders think yourselves ahead of me, but you're not. I knew that I could not keep anything from you past the year. You long ago chose your enemies, but you won't be able to stop this, nor will your family. That is what you meant to do, wasn't it? You meant to stop me for what foul reason? It all could have been *yours*."

The Oasis. She coughed again, again, then could not stop coughing. Her throat felt swollen shut and her stomach set on fire. She clutched her midsection, tearing at the gold sequins on her gown, the awful blistering in her gut growing quickly. *Waterhaven.*

"Why would you want to stop me? I am doing this for ours, Cinda, for our children. Always a stubborn bitch," Tagnar went on, and she coughed, blazing lungs aching for air and reprieve. Neither would come, she realized as she dropped the goblet to the floor. "You never knew what was good for you. This… is good for our children. Is it very painful? I did not intend for that, I swear. I never wanted to hurt you."

He lies, they all lie, she thought. He wanted her to hurt. Always had.

She sputtered, fell to her hands and knees, tried to bring up the poison within her. Clamped was her throat. Her vision darkened. *Why had they not foreseen this, of all threats? Or they did. They did. Blood wasted. Wasted.*

She tried to call out for someone, for Baynard. Her voice failed. She wondered if the knight would help her, or if he waited outside the door on Tagnar's orders. She would never decide if she trusted him. *I should not have trusted one.*

Tisinda stared up at her husband, and he stared, too, weak smile never faltering but growing on his horrid face. Always quiet in his anger. *I hate him,* she thought, and then sweet flashes came of her children, her poor children left with this man, of her home and sunshine, and at last of her vengeance before she faded against the floor.

The Calling rang until the end, those words in her head useless: *go to the Oasis.*

Go

Home.

2. WHERE THEY GRIEVE

At dawn, Alluvel woke to the scream of their mother's red headed servant. The maid found her lady hanging from the rafters by her neck, still dressed in the blue and gold gown from the previous night. Mittrik was the first to the room, sword ready.

When he took in the image of his mother swaying there, he dropped to his knees. And wailed. Her mouth yawned open and slant, empty eyes stared lifeless at him, and he could not look away. He'd never seen anything so horrible. It seemed a terrible dream— could not be real, and he waited for the floor to swallow him, save him, so that he may wake in his chambers. His father eventually lifted him off the floor.

For Mittrik, the next few days passed in a blur of Leonara's cries and the High Lord's taciturn remarks. Mittrik held his sister as she wept for hours through the first and second night, feeling only a numb, hollow pain he could not put to words. He did not care that Leonara wiped her snotty nose on his tunic. He combed back her hair and told her it would be alright, but he did not know what he meant by it. Mittrik did not see Jonn, did not know where he was, nor did anyone in the castle. The heir was missing three days, and the traditional mourning days began tomorrow.

"Your brother disappears to weep where no one would see him, soiling himself at the revelation he will never again find refuge behind your mother's strong will," Tagnar told Mittrik on the fourth night after his mother's suicide. His father was angry at his mother, and Mittrik understood the anger. He knew he would be angry when he felt anything, when he stopped feeling empty. The sunlight hung low in the sky, dark in the castle, and the birds outside sang pleasantly unaware of the sorrows within Alluvel.

"When does a man become greater than a man?" his father

asked as he finished signing a letter and stamping it with his ring, the crossing swords leaving their mark in the gold wax. Mittrik knew he wasn't meant to answer.

They were in the High Lord's private study room, and Mittrik stood beside the case of old handwritten books, written by his ancestors. Tagnar asked his son if he felt alright.

Alright, a l r i g h t, he considered the word, rolled it over in his head and took it apart. Mittrik could nod his head, that motion easy. He ran his fingers across the old leather bindings, silently reading the words and forgetting them in the same instant.

His father said, "Your great grandfather was a brilliant man, with distinguished hopes for our dwellings. My father was weaker, but greatness does not always skip a son. You shall be proof of that." Tagnar gave Mittrik a weak smile, and then poured them both a drink. Mittrik grabbed for the chalice, gulped the wine down and set it back on the table. He clutched his fist as he realized his hands were shaking. His father's voice sounded far away.

"The North has been breaking for the past century, victimized grumblers the lot of them." Tagnar stood and walked toward the east-facing window. "My brothers and father, uncles and cousins, all dead. All to bring the North back into the fold. And now that peace has settled, the North fights itself. King Ornund hasn't sent any men to help, and he won't."

From the table, Tagnar plucked a short rolled writ, green seal broken, and extended it to Mittrik. "The siege on Veiltar started some twenty nights ago and is already over. But the North isn't done," he added more quietly. "You can always count on Northmen to bleed and sing about bleeding in these worst winters, but this year it will be different."

"Veiltar fell? Aze retook it?"

Mittrik now attentive grabbed the little message, scanning it quickly. Such big news in such a small note. As simple as his father said, Mittrik almost dropped the writ to the floor. He grew up on stories of his father's siege of Veiltar, of that day the northern castle fell to a host of southern heroes. The day the Last Hwaelin won despite being the youngest commander. That victory now came undone, and his father seemed calm.

"This is true? Wallace Aze has retaken Veiltar? What of High Lord Osbur?"

"Veiltar is not as impregnable as she looks." Tagnar poured two more drinks. "They have Derrik Osbur in chains. Wallace Aze died from a wound after the battle. His son takes his place leading the Northmen. Now young Aze reclaimed his grandfather's dwelling. He has the support of Old and New Galligrey's lowerlords. Over twenty thousand men. They're moving."

"Into Nored?" Mittrik repeated the last line of the message, unbelieving. Or could it be worse? "Or South?"

"The green banners march North next. You and I will ride to meet with Dorgrey and Aze in Midhold before they do. Aze has his eyes for the Coldrock. We will help them take it."

Mittrik's mouth was dry despite the drink. In the years before he was born, the Free North had Olav Nagan as their king, and his son Bruse after him. In those years, war had crushed the north's rebellious legacy with steel and all the blood of Mittrik's kin. Uncles, cousins, great men he never met.

"You want to fight with Azes?" Mittrik asked, feeling a bout of southern pride. "They have Ornund's heir hostage. We will be traitors to the crown."

"Yes, traitors to that crown of Kielnish gold, mined from my lands— that crown of Kielnish rubies taken from the hands of our fathers. Yet I count on the king's inaction for a time. Derrik Osbur cannot press a claim if he melts in the tar pits."

Northmen would kill High Lord Derrik Osbur, heir to the throne. King Ornund VI had only daughters, seven of them by his many wives, and so his cousin was heir. Derrik was favored by the people, much to the king's frustration, for he fought in the Owner's War.

"And so, we should side with northmen against appointed Higher Lords, against our king?" Mittrik asked. "You've always told me Hwaelins are men of honor."

"Yes, but for consequence. We do not side with northmen, not with Osburs or Mardielans or Brimmen or Islanders or even damned notions of honor. Kill them all before dying, son. That's how *I* lasted. Since heathens and monsters fled West, Hwaelins have invested in our own power. You pledge loyalty to no one else."

Mittrik emptied his glass again. It could be so when Hwaelin was a large family. Not now, not since the Fourth.

"Once our king," Mittrik reasoned, and his father turned. "You knelt to Ornund."

"Hwaelins might kneel to powerful men, son, for consequence. Ornund has no power. Not now. The crown owes our house near one million gold suns and thinks to pay me off with the risen taxes he gets from mine own lords. If it were any other man robbing me as he does, he'd hang. But today, Osbur is king. Tomorrow, however..."

He's a man without heir or financing. Mittrik needed to drink much more with how the conversation was going. "How many southern men will march north to fight for Aze's glory?"

His father laughed and poured another round of drinks for them. "Even Bluers and Jarles would behave long enough to riot against me if I sent men north. If Auber wishes to sacrifice thousands to the ice he may, but Aze will receive Hwaelin gold— enough to ensure victory. And it will be returned with greater interest. The North has a mutinous spirit. Vengeance keeps them warm, and they won't rest until either Aze or Dorgrey is seated on the Coldrock."

Mittrik drained the wine in the goblet.

His father took his strong thirst as encouragement to continue, "They will succeed in taking the Coldrock, North's Head, all Nored and then our time will come. Now the Rooj arrive for the grieving day tomorrow, and there is nothing I want less than three Islanders in Kieln, but these things must happen, no matter the inconvenience. You won't trust these Islanders, promise me." He filled Mittrik's goblet again as he spoke. Mittrik heard this before and promised for the hundredth time. Never trust an Islander, they are all rotten liars, they do not take pleasure in winning games but rather in cheating at them.

Mittrik felt his stomach lurch in response to the wine. Had he eaten these past days, he was sure he would retch. He looked at his father, returning his stare, nodded once. He did not speak, for fear tears may begin to fall. Mittrik had not cried since he was a boy. He would not spare them on his mother, never in front of his father. His mother chose to take her life and would not know if he cried. His father would see it now. Mittrik struggled to breathe in rhythm.

"You are tired. Rest tonight, for tomorrow we receive desert snakes." Tagnar slapped a hand on Mittrik's back and walked him to the door. "I need you to ready yourself, Mittrik. Your mind, will, and steel must be ready. Just because we don't war against Nored does not mean we are without enemies. We have battles to come. I will speak more with you when the Rooj are gone."

"Good Night, Father," Mittrik said, his mind turning to gray fog and memories.

"Good Night."

Mittrik did not turn right however to walk up the stairwell and to his chambers. His feet carried him left, out the main walls, into the lower bailey and to the stables where Ilder waited. He tied and mounted his saddle and ran through the night, colorless on the back of the black beast. He ran the horse southeast as fast as it would take him. As Ilder's hooves pounded into the muddy earth, Mittrik finally found his breath again, though it stung in his chest. When Hetten's light rose from the horizon hours past, he arrived at the ruins of the Old City.

A wintry gale surged from the sea below, and Mittrik slowed Ilder to a canter as they approached the cliff's edge. He breathed in the sharp air and tried to forget why he had decided to run through the night. His left hand was sore and stiff, and he stretched out his fingers. He dismounted Ilder and pet down his forehead, and the horse grunted at him.

"Good job, my friend, excellent time," Mittrik whispered before walking back toward the precipice, keeping his footing sure atop the white rocks.

The cliffs hung around a once glorious city of Old, now unreachable except during the lowest of tides. He had seen a very faded drawing of the city once, in a book hidden away in Alluvel's library. Towering creations of architecture, white as first frost and as daunting as the cliffs themselves. Now only the tips of the tallest turrets could be seen peeking up above the high tide. *When did the waters begin to rise to such heights*, he wondered. A harlot had once told him, or perhaps it had been a kitchen wench, that the gods of the Old civilization cursed the city so that no man would be able to live in it, and the waters would never recede long enough to build. Doctor Petrard said that the waters rose long before the daemons fled.

Mittrik peered across the gap, to the other side of the cliffs where the monumental carvings stood through time's erosion. Carved into the face of the opposite cliff, thirteen Old gods, taller than any castle he had seen, stared with hollow eyes back at him. *How could men build such things*, Mittrik sighed loud across the expanse. The high tide rose to the hips of the great rock figures, spumes crashing high and curling back against them as if pleading for them to wake and move.

When he was four and ten he would often come to the Old ruins to escape trite lessons, to stare across at the blank faces of dead Old gods, imagining what their names may have been, over what they ruled. It changed each time he visited, like a game. Gods of war turning to gods of spring and love when he desired. He liked these gods better than Hetten, who oversaw all and cared very little, and the Sisters who cared over all but favored chaos and jealousy.

Chilled rain fell from the gray space above him, but Mittrik didn't bother moving. He knew he should be at the docks back in Kielntown, welcoming his foreign family with sympathetic smiles, tearful eyes. He should be there for Leonara, who would miss him most throughout the first mourning day. He could not, however. Mittrik could not weep in the Sister's temple beside his family when all he wanted to do was scream or take his sword and run it through something. He yelled to the sea, or to Hetten, to the stone faces of Old gods, whatever listened. He did not know.

The rain beat harder against his shoulders, the cold biting his face and he cursed it, feeling rage heat him enough to stand wet and shivering for hours. The wind pushed the breath into him and sucked the breath out of him unreliably. *This rain killed her, drowned her*, he thought, spitting into the mud. *She killed herself.*

He picked up a stone and flung it far, aiming for a god's face and missing by yards. If not for the rain, he'd have noticed how fiercely he wept.

In Kielntown, the heir woke between two barrels of ale in the alley behind a tavern, The Golden Burg. Jonn spent the previous three nights drinking himself into a stupor. When that could not contain his grief, he had laid with a beautiful woman at Tula's den, though he could not remember if she was truly beautiful, nor could he remember her name, just that she had soft, round cheeks that he bruised.

Life of a second son, he bemused tiredly as he stretched his neck, sounding cracks. He rose from the ground, feeling ashamed of himself, feeling his toes cold like ice. *Wine, whores, and wander. A life lacking for honor. Mother would have words*, he thought, but stopped thinking because his heart felt shredded, and he made his way back to the castle.

Luckily the morn lingered in the dark gray hour, and many town folks still slept shuddered inside their thatch roof homes, safe from the dawn's chill. Jonn walked, head down, thankful to avoid any disparaging glares from a crowd; he could not imagine how poorly he looked or how awfully he smelled of gutter and brew.

The men at Alluvel's walls bowed lowly as he approached and entered, but he could hear their sniggers behind him as he walked through the courtyard. By the well, he passed redheaded Sir Elrik and Sir Baynard, the old knight, neither acknowledged him as he passed their hushed conversation.

Jonn walked up the steps and into the Great Hall of Alluvel, morn's light cracking through the windows and toppling gray onto everything.

"Ah, Jonn," his father peered up from the old book he held, holding Jonn's tired eyes with his stare. "Where were you hiding?"

"Yes," he replied, dipping his head. "I apologize. I... was in town." He hated how quiet his voice sounded in the hall.

His father nodded and looked curiously at him. "Very well, get washed. You smell ripe."

Jonn bowed once more before heading to his bedchambers, where a bath was already hot and waiting for him. *Bless the dwellings' servants,* he thought as he lowered his body into the steaming water. He scrubbed harshly at his skin until it was a bright red, and then he scrubbed some more. He wanted to rid himself of the past three days, of every thought, tear, and every spilled cup.

The day was still new when he walked into the dining hall, dressed in the heavy red and black garments of mourning. The table was already set, breads and porridges barely warm. Jonn felt no hunger, instead a terrible emptiness.

Leonara walked into the hall then, her long crimson gown draped like fluid around her. She wore a feathered hat that was almost too large for her childish face, and her collar and hems were matched in intricate beaded black lace. Her skin appeared translucent in the light of Hetten. Jonn noticed her puffy eyes and rubbed-raw nose.

"Good Morn, Leo," he said as he tucked a wispy strand of hair behind her ear. She looked up at him, and her eyes brimmed over with fresh tears.

He pulled her into a tight hug, and her little body shook as she sobbed into his dark coats, her head tucked firmly into the space between his side and elbow. "It is the day to cry, my girl." Leonara sniffled and pulled herself away from Jonn's arms, wiping the tears away with balled fists.

"I hate crying."

Tagnar approached the two with, "Have you broken your fast? There is no more time." He wiped away a tear clinging to Leonara's chin. "The Rooj are early, and we must leave for the port now."

"And Mittrik?" Leonara faltered. She clicked her small heels beneath her dress and fretted with the skin around her nails, already red and fresh.

"I do not know," their father said. "Put on some gloves and we shall go."

All the way to the port of Kielntown, Jonn distracted himself by being mad at Mittrik. *How could he not be here to receive Mother's family?* Jonn wondered, *Where in Doom could he be? Not at The Golden Burg, or I would have seen him. Though most likely inserting himself where he does not belong, one way or another.* He rode his horse beside his father's, two of the dwelling guards in front, Sir Osmond's squire plodding along with them, and Leonara sat in the pulled carriage behind them. The wheels creaked along the cobbled streets of the fishing village, and Jonn tried to focus on the distant sounds of the high tide mills sloshing and turning with the rising water.

He smiled at the laughing children that trailed at their back, thinking themselves sneaky and unseen as they hid behind crates and ducked into alley streets. The townsfolk prostrated themselves to their High Lord as they saw him, and those that didn't were sure to hear Sir Baynard Torde's deep bellowing, "Clear the way! Clear the street for your High Lord!"

Sir Baynard was as constant as autumn rain; he'd been knighted in the years before the Fourth Great War and fought alongside Jonn's father in the siege of Veiltar. He'd crossed tar pits and the cursed Deadwood to win against the North. Sir Baynard had been a high knight of Dwellings Hwaelin longer than Jonnere had been a son of it.

The day was beginning to warm, and the smell of Kielntown again so close reminded him of his past nights, tangled in ill-fitted sheets with the brown-haired woman and dripping in tavern ale. Jonn swallowed dryly and prayed to Hetten.

He did not make it a habit to pray since his life was filled with blessings before, and one mustn't tempt the gods when life is filled with blessings, but he recited the Sister's Sanctions on Crestdays and spoke to Hetten when he thought the god might care to listen and grant a kindness. *Hetten*, he prayed, *let my mother be reborn as a bird, a golden sparrow like her own, or an Island macaw, so that she may fly and see things as wonderful as anything. Let her be free, please. Not a lady again. Sisters, have mercy. Be it so, amen.*

He caught a tear as it slid down his face and turned to see if his father had seen. He had not; the High Lord kept his narrowed eyes toward the docks of the Bitter Sea, where the blue sails of the Rooj ship, emblazoned with the white symbol of the desert palm, flapped against the evergrey sky.

Jonn remembered very little of his mother's family, only that his grandfather was peculiar and spoke in endless riddles. *Why can some birds sing false songs? And why do we care to listen the same?* Rhinere Rooj had asked him so many times when he last visited the Fair Isle— so many times that all the words lost meaning, not that they held any for Jonn in the first place. He dismounted his saddle and stood tall, preparing himself.

The three Islanders walked down the wooden ramp from the ship and onto the dock, Jonn's grandfather Rhinere leading his aunt and uncle in languid steps towards the waiting Hwaelins. They all wore white for the grieving day, a peculiar Fair custom. He could not see his aunt's face behind a gray veil, which was elaborated with pearls and designs of drooping white lilies. Jonn could see his father tense at his side as they approached. They stopped two feet away, faces blank of expression.

“My children,” High Lord Rhinere hugged Leonara and Jonn, who stiffened involuntarily. “The mouth salts on unexpected sea journeys. Nothing savors without some salt, but open wounds still burn.” Jonn and his sister shared a look as he released them.

“Our dwellings are welcome to you, High Lord.” Jonn bowed politely.

Their aunt, still veiled, drew Leonara into her chest and whispered into her ear. Jonn strained to listen.

“What a terrible thing that we reunite like this, neice, nephew,” declared his uncle, Sir Rhion, tall in front of them, with a bow to Tagnar. “And to you, High Lord.” His face was clean, his eyes paler than any Jonn had seen, like the off angle of a glass shard.

“An egregious time,” Jonn heard his father say. “Shall we head straight to the Sister’s temple?”

“The other one,” his aunt grumbled, “your younger son, shall he meet us there, High Lord?”

“Mittrik had to ride east this morn, my lady.” The veiled woman audibly huffed. Above them, the gray clouds darkened, and the cordgrass soundly shook in the wind.

“Then we go before the toad’s call,” said his grandfather with authority, and the three Rooj entered the wheelhouse with Leonara and rolled up the winding road to the temple of the Sisters.

“Do you think they are insulted that Mittrik has gone?” Jonn asked his father.

“Perhaps.” Tagnar shrugged. “Your brother knows why he does what he does.”

Inside the sharp sanctuary of the temple, Jonn’s mother’s body lay at the front on the square stone altar. His father stood a distance away while the Rooj wept behind him. The Sister Moons were carved into the front of the altar, their faces beautiful, painted and etched into waning sides. He had seen their smiles many times before on Crestdays, but now the altar looked more treacherous than before, like a warning of the Sister's cruelty.

Jonn looked at his mother's face, peaceful as if in sleep, but not quite; she was so obviously empty. Her cheeks sunken at a severe angle, the high pleated collar of her dress covered the horrible red marks the rope had left, and her lips frowned. The stained windows cast a multicolor array of triangles on his mother's skin. None of it looked good. Jonn's vain mother would hate the sight of herself.

His mouth tasted like acid, like death, so he breathed through his nose.

Leonara reached out a gloved hand and stroked their mother's powdered forehead.

"She was beautiful," she whispered. "And so, so loving. But very sad, wasn't she?"

Jonn cursed Mittrik once more for his absence, then cursed himself for holding onto the hope that his brother would arrive at the last second.

"She is happier now, Leo," he eventually managed, turning away from the corpse.

"Yes, she must be happier now. Or she is Doomed."

They exited the temple of the Sisters as soundlessly as they entered, passed the line of humming modaires in their prayer shawls and penance chains, passed the paid mourners. Out in the temple courtyard the dwelling's high-knights awaited to escort them back to the highcastle; the four men were dressed in matching gray cloaks lined with white furs of ermine, the Hwaelin crossed swords in gold threading, family sigils stitched into their gambesons of darkest gray. Sir Arne Osmond walked a bit ahead, his black hair waving upward at the nape of his neck, and Leonara kept looking at that neck and not her uncle's looming stare beside her. Rhion Rooj wouldn't stop looking at her.

The comely knight opened the carriage door for her while Jonn and her father mounted their horses.

"Thank you, Sir Arne," she said, tired eyes rising from her shoes to the red bear standing upon Arne's chest, and then finally to his dark eyes. She entered the carriage while she heard him whisper a soft, "My lady."

Leonara's eyelids burned. She needed sleep. She'd woken from a horrifying dream of dangling brides and spiders while it was still dark and had not slept after that. In the cold, she had first gone to Mittrik's chambers, hoping he could calm her. He was good at making her laugh when she wanted to cry. When she could not find him there or in the stables or in the kitchens, she looked for Jonn, but he also had disappeared. She ended up roaming the damp corridors, freezing her toes on the autumn chilled stone until the servants woke, and she returned to her chambers where Modaire Nexitha's scolding waited.

She was exhausted, bones heavy within her skin. She watched her strange lady aunt dip into the carriage beside her. Leonara wished she could be out riding a horse with her brother, father and his men. She wished she could walk back up the hill to Alluvel. Anything would be better than sitting in the carriage with her foreign family.

The humid day picked up the smells of dung and morn dew, and through the slats Leonara could see the procession of commoners looking onto the carriage and waving at their High Lord and heir.

Her grandfather and uncle sat across from her, the shadows doing nothing to soften their features of harsh lines. Their mourning clothes were bright, strange, with delicate and feminine lace around their sleeves and collars. Her aunt's gown was long and made of the thin kind of lace made in the Fair Isle, piles of it white and layered so that it covered her like a swanling's fluff. Her sleeves were cut above her elbows and she wore no gloves, something the village people probably looked at with a shock. Leonara folded her hands in her lap and traced the stitched pattern atop her fingers.

"My beautiful girl," Lady Talia took one of her hands in her own, "you are quite a precious lady of Baeltaf, and you look so like your mother though you have your father's nose." She gave it a pinch. Leonara startled and bowed her head.

"Leonara," Rhion Rooj said, voice booming, and she flinched. He scowled. "You are an elfin little girl, aren't you? Meeker than a mouse, I daresay. In this life you were born a lady at least, but if you act as a mouse, I wonder what Hetten might think of making you next round. Wisen, or you will become nothing more than a plaything for some High Lord. Eventually a mother. There isn't honor in that, if there's no risen blood."

Leonara almost laughed for the bubble of anger that popped in her chest. She stared at him, eyes wide, heart hammering. Only her father, and at times her priestess, had rebuked her so. This man talked as though he knew her—as though he knew her well, speaking so familiarly and discourteously. But if he truly knew her, he would know that she never 'acted small', as he put it. He saw her now, when her grief was so much larger than she. Though he was her mother's brother, Sir Rhion was a stranger to Leonara, and she felt her anger burn into her pride, most wounded.

"Close your mouth, blossoming girl," her aunt whispered, "it makes you look dimwitted."

She snapped her jaw shut and felt fresh stinging behind her eyes. *I will not cry,* Leonara told herself. *Not in front of them.*

Her aunt kept speaking, her gaudily ringed fingers slipped through Leonara's loose hair. "It was quite the speech, but it is true, you are an Islander and that means something. Four centuries ago, you would have been called a princess. You would have held secrets. And been protected."

Leonara didn't think she liked this foreign family. She was not just Rooj, but a Hwaelin first and always. There was honor in being a Hwaelin, and in the histories, those long and boring lists of years and nobles that the priestess and her father promised she would need to know, her father's name went back to the First, to men who fought against evil. The same could not be said of any Fair Islander. The Fair Isle was Forsaken four hundred years ago.

"Quickly wisen, yes. If you wade into waters of glass shard and drink, you cannot reclaim any spilled wine," said High Lord Rhinere, looking at her sternly. "You cannot expect a bloody thing from such lofted pursuits, only blood in the throat."

"I do not understand," Leonara projected and lifted her chin to meet her grandfather's stare, but not her uncle's.

"Most won't, sweetest sparrow. That is the fun." And though the High Lord laughed, there were tears in his eyes.

"Your mother spoke to you of *triewthblood*, did she not?" Lord Rhion inquired in a low voice, a different accent punching that peculiar word, rolling it. He looked out the wheelhouse window to Kielntown, disinterested. There were mourners in the street, but not as many as there should have been.

"I beg your pardon, Sir? I do not know the word."

Her uncle looked at her aunt, his eyes somehow colder.

"Leonara," her aunt called her attention, "will you show me your mother's garden when we arrive? She wrote to me about it and I would like to see it for myself just once."

If mother had spent more time in her garden, maybe she could have found a little more happiness in this life, thought Leonara as the carriage rocked over a great bump in the path.

"Of course, Lady Talia," she answered.

"You will call me aunt from now, Leo."

Leonara almost laughed again. *Jonn and Mittrik call me that. They're alone permitted. Nerve of Islanders!* The rest of the road to the castle was ridden in silence.

In the evening before they were to dine together, Leonara walked from her chambers and toward her mother's garden where she had agreed to meet Aunt Talia. The Island woman was already standing tall at the center, near the pond and white wooden bench, a large spiking plant in one hand. Her face scowled in disapproval before she tossed it to the ground. Her pale hair, which was braided around her head to look something like a crown, caught Hetten's sunlight. Kept it trapped, coveted. White ringlets fell from her temples.

"This garden is a hideous joke," she said as Leonara's shoes dusted sand. "It is clear why your mother hated it."

Leonara rather liked the little square garden within the castle, and when she was younger she would daily come to sit by the green pond and look down into its depths. She used to believe the pond had secrets to keep from her, and so she would sit and tell it some of her own in the hopes of gaining nature's trust. *Silly stupid girl*, she remembered. It wasn't even a natural pond.

"Has your first blood come to you?" her aunt asked, really saying, Are you a woman yet? Though her aunt was not a Mainlander, she was still a lady, and there was nothing older ladies liked more than asking this of the younger. Leonara resisted rolling her eyes.

"No, it has not."

"Your mother has not told you all truths," Lady Talia's tone was suddenly harsh. She walked beside the pool, grazing her tanned fingers across the reeds. They shifted and brushed against each other, almost whispering. "She has not spoken to you about our gift. Tell me, what do you know of the Fair Isle?"

"Of valuable things like the salt trade or shipping, or of its contracts within and throughout the kingdom, I admit very little. I know some Fair dances, but not many. Though I do know the names of all the Islander lowlords and its history within Baeltaf if it pleases you."

"It does not. Do you really know so little of your mother's home? Has she not told you how long our people have dwelled there?"

"She would sometimes tell me stories of dune spirits, and things of ancient saltmen and the desert-call; she used to sing me Isle songs before I slept."

"What do you know of the desert-call?"

"It will call me to safety when I need it."

"To Waterhaven. And what was your favorite song?"

Leonara didn't hesitate. "The song of Deadriver, and the Lady of House Qoii who ran to the Oasis for refuge. It is so pretty, but my father heard it once and forbade it. He did not like the bit about her paramours."

Her aunt sang in the same waifish tone her mother had used. It carried out the garden, into setting day, drifting Fair melody.

Pale was the lady of Deadriver ran,
Pale feet cross crying dead river sand,
To the heart of the Isle,
Fair truth is in wind,
And to catch with a smile,
No man who has sinned.
Where's my Oasis? Where's my trove?

Leonara grinned at her aunt and took a seat on a large rock, taking caution to avoid bumping the spiny plant beside her. "You sing like my mother, that light airy way."

"Your mother was radiant, and the Rock is a worse place without her."

The Rock? Does she mean the Mainland, or the Isle? Leonara didn't understand but said nothing. A single tear fell at her aunt's feet. Talia wore flat slippers instead of a lady's heels. *Perhaps because she is so tall without them, like my mother, or because they are so uncomfortable, and highborn ladies are allowed some autonomy on the Isle.*

The woman's eyes darted about her quickly before she spoke again. "She meant to tell you of the triewthblood once you were ready, when you would not feel so guilted to tell your father. You already know you cannot lie. You must know that, of course. Have you never wondered or asked why you cannot push false words from your lips no matter how hard you might try?"

Leonara stood, fresh hope bubbling in her chest. This was everything.

She'd sat in front of her looking glass until the sky turned black, until her eyelids closed of their own volition, trying to force out a single lie. 'My eyes are brown; I am lowborn; I love oysters,' all she tried to say because it should be simple, but the third word of every phrase made her gag and cough and would not come, no matter how she struggled. Once she had tried to lie to her father about a broken heirloom, a white shell vase with patterned blue stylings that once belonged to her great grandmother, Anetta Hwaelin. Anetta had been an Osbur princess, loved by Kieln for her wisdom and beauty. Breaking the precious ornament brought Leonara to tears at once, but she had tried to lie through the crying; she had tried to blame it on the gust of wind, and then on one of her brothers, and then on a servant but couldn't manage one word against them. She'd really retched and been sick that day, and her father had pitied her for it and sent her to her chambers with barely a reproach.

Leonara's dry tongue clicked against the top of her mouth. "Mittrik says I am too devout to the gods to lie."

"Your brothers are fools, sweetest one. All liars are fools, lords and kings among them. But Islanders have never been deceived by foolishness, never in our long history. We are above the rest. We cannot lie, my dear girl. Not I, your uncle, your grandfather or mother. Any Fair Person born on the Isle is blessed with triewthblood. It is our gift, for we have developed the sharpest wits. It takes special cunning to deceive with truth."

Leonara felt as if a heavy stone had been removed from her gut, and another placed on her shoulders, at once feeling lighter and heavier knowing she was not alone in her burden. *Mother was like me, she never lied either,* she bemused with a smile, but a burn hit her eyes and suddenly tears spilled. Her aunt wiped them and held Leonara's shoulders firmly.

"Cry because you realize how great you can become. Do not cry for your mother, for she no longer feels pain. This world is more spectacular than you can begin to fathom, my dear girl. You should return with us to the Isle, so that you may begin to learn the truths of other worlds. You could learn many things there, of language and science and culture. Baeltaf will entrap you, and I want to see you free. I want more freedom for you than your mother had."

"My father would never allow me to go without my mother," Leonara plucked a lily from the ground and pulled the white petals apart. "Perhaps if Jonn or Mittrik comes."

"They may follow, but there is no home for them on the Isle. They may have the blood of the Rooj, but they are not Fair. Lying fools belong on the Mainland." Leonara did not have it within her to defend her brothers tonight, and Mittrik was a bit of a liar. Still no one had seen him in the highcastle since yesterday. As soon as Jonn appeared, Mittrik went.

Lady Talia sat on the beechwood bench and took off her slippers. A Mainland lady would never do that. She dipped her bare golden feet into the cold, imported powder of the sand and sighed. *Why is Mittrik not here?* Leonara wondered. *Why does he prefer to mourn with small folk, drunkards, and trulls instead of his own blood, who suffer same as him? Sisters curse him, then,* she scorned, but took it back as quickly as she thought it.

"Aunt Talia," Leonara said, "the night after my mother's body was found I saw a light of color violet fall from the heavens in the west. It was so bright, and it came down so quickly, but not like a falling star." Her aunt turned to her, eyes attentive. "And I thought, well, that perhaps it could be Hetten casting my mother down to Doom."

Scoffing, the tall woman answered, "You could think it, for she had no faith in him or any other god for that matter. The light falling was not your mother. Hetten is a false character, my child, one made up by those who are incapable of divine truth. They created their gods to excuse their savagery, and by every god this continent saw blood like nothing else. The god you must serve is the one within your own heart."

Leonara held back her gasp. *The gods are not false*, she fumed. There were ways to prove the Sisters existence. Who took the sacrifice of rubies before cannon-fire and war if not the Sisters? Who could make the cannons blast? Hetten could be called upon and proven real. Who took the sacrifice of blood before springtime if not Hetten? Who made the crops grow? But her aunt who could not lie said the gods were false, so what could she call false or true?

Leonara turned to the small pond and tried to see the bottom. She thought of Fair Isle, a whole Dominion of people just like her, bound to be honest all their lives.

"Leo," her aunt whispered, "your mother wanted to share this with you herself, to tell you what a treasure and burden being a truthspeaker is, especially as a Rooj. The triewthblood is a secret. The greatest secret the Isle has kept from the Mainland."

Leonara matched her aunt's shining eyes and nodded her promise. She would not tell anyone this greatest secret. She promised to carry it with her as her mother did— to the grave.

Jonn was drunk again by supper. He broke off a large chunk of bread, dug out a second trencher, piling it with the minced boar pottage, and ate to avoid talking. His sister's small picked portion was cold now, though she didn't seem to mind, talking more than usual.

The rhythmic pattering of rain did not relent, nor did the claps of thunder miles away. Rain pestered, oncoming, though autumn's end neared. The hails of winter would be disastrous if autumn rains were indications, as aidares said. Jonn tried to focus on that sound of thunder and not on the rest of Leonara's strange behavior. She spoke fast and looked anxious, rocking back and forth and tapping her foot under the table. This action reminded Jonn of his brother, whose absence from the small feast was sourly noted by the Rooj.

"What is Fair Isle like, aunt?" Leonara asked. She hadn't been since she was born. Their father gave a stern look to silence her, but for once it did not stop her. "I imagine it so lovely. I'm sure it does not rain as often."

"It all but never rains, dear girl. Perhaps every two years or so." Lady Talia's food remained untouched.

"Mercy does not come from the sky," High Lord Rhinere's voice was just above a whisper. Jonn kept control of his face, trying not to look quizzical. His sister, however, nodded grimly. Like she understood.

"I say the men retire and refresh together now that we've ate enough," his father spoke clear, standing from his seat at the table. "Let the ladies rest without us. What say you, High Lord Rhinere?"

His grandfather stood and nodded.

"Good Night, ladies," his father bowed before walking out the room. Jonn rose then bowed as well before following his father out. But before he left, he followed Lord Rhion's stare back toward the table and saw his sister move her chair closer to their aunt, whispering something. Jonn didn't like the way the golden man's eyes lingered before they walked out into the corridor.

Inside the High Lord's solar, Jonn warmed himself by the fire, feeling the life coming back into his stiff fingers. His father poured four drinks from a thin blue bottle. Mardielan wine, the richest of the Mainland. Jonn had been drunk too long, since that morn of his mother's suicide, but he wasn't ready to be sober.

He looked nervously at the silent Island men. Their proud stare and their curious eyes, roamed the stone room and fur rugs. His uncle's face remained expressionless, while the curl of his grandfather's lip gave away his discontent. He thought about crib tales of tall, wicked elves and thought they resembled such mythic creatures of Old legends. Jonn wondered, and then dreaded the idea that he too looked so otherly.

The cold rains fell harsher, and his father passed the mulled wine as they took place by the fire.

"High Lord Hwaelin," his uncle said in a calm voice, "we thank you again for your dwellings' hospitality. I am sorry for my sister, and I regret that she was so forlorn to do this thing to herself and her family."

"I wish there was more I could have done." Jonn's father raised his goblet. "To our houses."

"To family," Rhinere Rooj said, raising his goblet but not touching the rim to his lips.

"To Tisinda," Jonn's uncle said before he drank.

Jonn gulped down most of his wine.

"Salt returns to salt, smoke to smoke, it is said. It is," said Rhinere; Jonn watched his grandfather set his cup down without drinking.

"What does he mean, Lord Rooj?" His father was too harsh, with the imposing voice of a greater Lord. Not of a brother-by-law.

"My father feels troubled, High Lord." Jonn's uncle's voice was warm. "A priestess at your temple informed him of your plans for Tisinda's body. My sister's bones belong in the salt crypts of Waterhaven, those in our ancient city. It is what my father wants, and I believe it is what she would have wanted."

Jonn could not help but agree, though he waited to say it. He knew his mother would be wroth at the idea of her remains set to fire on the stained gray beaches that brought her so much misery. Jonn stayed quiet; looking into his lap, he drank. He wanted to drown.

"Your sister was my wife, a Hwaelin on her death day. She shall receive a passage honorable in the eyes of the gods."

High Lord Rhinere huffed in response. "Your gods are nothing to me," said he, "poked high in the mountains to be lost, is all. Suns and moons above me. As threatening as smoke, and how you would burn her. My daughter is of the sand and the scorching sun, of salted land and sea. Her body should be buried with the bones of our ancestors, with the saltmen of Old."

"My wife will be burned by the Bitter Sea for the Sisters' Sake." Tagnar's voice rang steel-like. Cutting.

Jonn looked up, confused. All his life his father spoke little and cared even less of rituals and gods. He performed his Crestdays but nothing else. *He does it to spite them,* Jonn realized, and he tried to fight the anger that surged. He tried hard to think of anything but how his father mistreated his mother, talked down to her so many times just for spite. Spite, the cruelest seed to sow. He'd said the most terrible things to her.

But it was Jonn who remained silent through it all. He was silent right now.

"I shall retire for the night, I think," Jonn said as he sat his glass down before bowing first to his father than to the other High Lord. He wished to say more. "Until the morrow, Father, High Lord, Sir Rhion. Good Night." He avoided his uncle's pointed stare as he retreated from the room.

Jonn walked up the stairs and down the hall, the anger toward his father growing. His father had called his mother torpid, a frail heart meant for featherbeds and silks, a snake meant for Doom, and that is only what he had said in front of others. Jonn shook his head as he stalked. His father had called his mother a lady with the mind of a horse and the ambition of a harlot. And Jonn had said nothing.

His mother had been strong, even after their infant brother's death. *Keelan,* she had named him though he was taken by a fever within the first week. His mother. Resilient and strong in a womanly way.

His mother had been courageous in a purely defiant way, as well. She had loved things that southern ladies were not expected to, like shooting arrows, playing in the lake and in the snow, and hawking. When they were boys, Mittrik loved the hawks but Jonnere was frightened by them. His father mocked him for it, but his mother held his hand and pet the bird with him. He learned to love them once she made him feel unafraid, safe.

He found himself in her chambers when his anger subsided, and he looked to the tall ceilings. *Mittrik found her hanging just here,* the thought choked him.

He looked to her wardrobe and remembered how long it took her to choose her dresses, and thought Leonara would never grow tall enough to fit them as they were. He looked to his mother's bed and remembered all the times he hid underneath as a boy, from his brother's annoyance, from his father's wrath. He was tempted to crawl underneath the bed now.

He could not be in the chamber longer, nor could he understand why he came here at all. He resigned himself to walk onto her balcony to feel the autumn chill, to clear his head, and then he meant to go by the castle's forge to get his new sword. It would be good to find something to take up time. The blacksmith, a portly man named Alden Sterke, had promised Jonn the blade would be fit for a High Lord at wartime, perfectly balanced and ornate. Something that had excited him five days earlier now gave him no joy.

Outside, rain fell on his face, softened in the night time, but soon there'd be no rain . Autumn would end and bring winter to its time, and ice would fall from the heavens like a warship's cannon fire. If he had been here more, been with his mother during this time of year, then she might not have felt so hopeless. He would have traveled with her to the Fair Isle; he would have spent all the winter there if it brought her happiness.

He turned to walk back into his mother's room but caught the sight of a crooked stone jutting from the wall to the right of the entryway. He removed the worn gray brick easily, and saw a damp piece of folded parchment. Jonn took the note and opened it, recognizing the curling letters as his mother's and the date as the night she died. His heart ached, his head spinning the room, but he read quickly, the words begging to be read a second and third and fourth time.

Dearest,

I intend to make the trip back to the Isle with my children within the week. It is no longer safe in Baeltaf.

Whispers have come to me. We live in Shadow Times, according to changers and prophets. The Bringer has reached age, and the Other is undetected by most, but before long the world will be leveled when they meet. They will meet soon.

I fear the dangers closer to me. Our Oasis is loudest in Alluvel. I am unaware of some plot in Kieln, and my husband's recent intrigue in my affairs has me anxious. But you, dear sister, fear nothing— I am coming. I will keep us safe. The war of gold is about to start, and I will leave with mine. I will uncover the rest from Waterhaven. Even from the Isle, my ears linger here. For sons to rule, fathers die.

We trust no one now. Not any Mainlander, least of all Tagnar. Deal with caution.

Rising,

T

His legs went weak. Jonn's throat, wet with wine, choked. His stomach turned in knots, knots on knots, as he read the letter once more. He made to return to the bauer but stopped a hand's breath from the door as he heard his father's voice boom from the corridor.

"I said, search everything again. Tear it apart. See how Rhinere looked at me, he knows. Find out what she knew. I don't need the Rooj squealing like desert rats before I've reached the vein of our efforts."

Jonn turned, barely hearing Sir Arne saying, "Yes, High Lord."

Guilt made his feet shuffle. He didn't want to be caught in the room by his father's knight. Jonn swung over the edge of the balcony's balustrade, holding himself on its ledge. He heard the chamber door open and footsteps fall heavy. The night's wind was cold on his back and pushed him against the stone.

Jonn swung his lower body so that his foot perched atop the window sill below him, and then he dropped back into a castle room with little grace. It was the Doctor's room, but it was empty, and Jonn thanked Hetten. He closed his eyes and breathed twice with effort before leaving, panicked.

Be still, he told himself, but the words of the letter burned into the backs of his eyelids. He read it over once more as he walked. Again and again like the words might change.

His mother had planned to go to Fair Isle, so why would she kill herself before a planned journey? Fragments swam across the page the longer he stared. *Shadow times... Trust no one... least of all Tagnar.*

His mother knew of the High Lord's plans. Jonn shuddered, remembering his father's earnest opposition to sharing anything with the Fair, even his own wife. *Fair Islanders won't fight with you. Blood means nothing to them,* Tagnar would say. Did he suspect his wife knew? Had she told her family? Had he silenced her?

Jonn walked the corridor looking down at his feet, thinking of his father, of Sir Arne's effort to search his mother's room. He did not notice Mittrik's broad form in his way until his brother smacked a hand on his chest.

"Watch yourself, Jonn," Mittrik's voice sounded strained.

Jonn's own breath had become thin.

"Why do you look so pale?" Mittrik did not sound concerned. "Speak, will you? Mind, I'm not in the mood to quarrel about missing the mourning."

Jonn composed himself, harshly whispered, "Grab all the coin you have in your chambers, *all* of it, and meet me in the stables at once. We're leaving." Mittrik started his witty retort, but Jonn said, "Now, quickly!" and spun, racing toward the stairwell without looking back.

Despite himself, Mittrik did as his brother instructed. With the gold he had, he arrived first to the stables. Ilder slept, fatigued from running to the ruins and back, so Mittrik decided to saddle Leonara's mare, Jonn's pale courser next. The stable boy came out to help, yawning and scratching himself, but Mittrik sent him back to sleep. He'd get them readied for whatever Jonn intended. L*eaving?*

Jonn had said, but that didn't make sense.

Mittrik's sword was girded around him, as was his bollock knife, and he waited impatiently for his older brother. He had questions about Jonn's abruptness and expression—what he could only describe as horror— but he would receive no answers.

Jonn entered the stable, cloak around him and new sword at his side.

"The guards at postern gate are paid to look away. We go now," was all Jonn said before mounting his horse and exiting the stable.

Following, Mittrik asked, "Who took a bribe?"

"Let's go."

The brothers left the castle and ran in the direction of the southeastern beaches, leagues from Alluvel and Kielntown. The sharp wind ripped them as the horses crossed the marshes in sloshing, often clumsy steps. Mittrik kept his brother's pace, saying nothing of the mud Jonn's horse threw up in his mouth. Once Mittrik called to him in the light of the Sisters, asking again why they ran.

"Be silent for now," Jonn's voice was pained, so Mittrik remained quiet until they slowed, the Bitter shoreline glinting before them. "Let me think."

"Can you tell me why you are acting so crazed?" Mittrik struggled with the temper of Leonara's mare, coughing out his own agitation. Jonn did not look at him. He stared to the sea as its tide rose up the sand. Every breath came out white, ragged, tired. Mittrik thought if it rained they would freeze to death.

Leonara's mare let out a fatigued noise that broke the silence again.

"Our mother didn't kill herself," it was barely a whisper in the cold.

Mittrik pulled the reins involuntarily. "What are you talking about?"

Jonn handed Mittrik a folded page of parchment. His eyes scanned it, and he felt his stomach drop to his groin.

"Not a suicide note," came Jonn's voice, louder this time and angry, but Mittrik heard it far away. He still could not make sense of the words on the page, dark in the Sister's light. "We can't stay. Father had something to do with it. I could kill him." And branches of ugly chill grew up Mittrik's spine.

"What? Why would you think that?"

But Jonn didn't answer, his eyes were set down the beach at the sound of something dragged across the sand. Mittrik followed his gaze— half a mile down he saw the silhouette of a fisherman, lit by midnight's glow, carrying a small boat to the Bitter Sea, dragging it out the last length to the middle tide. An odd time to set off.

"Jonn, say something I can understand, please," Mittrik tried to regain his brother's attention. "Why would...? Where did you find—*Jonn*?"

Jonn had set his horse running in the direction of the fisherman, wet mud and sand flung up behind him. Mittrik cursed his brother but kicked the mare's sides to follow. *He is going mad with grief*, he thought as they drew close to the fisherman and his little boat.

They approached the fisherman with a start, for he was like no man Mittrik had ever seen. He was black and large, broader than he and taller than Jonn, with arms and legs marked with thick paint. His dark hair coiled about his head in all directions, like heavy ropes in the wind. *He must be cold.* The fisherman wore what looked like a jerkin of thin boiled leather, with cut off trousers of the same material. He turned to them with an amused look on his face. The man was not from

Baeltaf.

He might be a mage. In which case, they should turn and run.

"Jonn," Mittrik whispered.

"Stop there. Who are you?" Jonn asked from atop his horse.

"I do not take an order from Biler," the man spat at them in a strange accent and turned again to his wooden boat.

Mittrik interjected, his hand tightening around the grip of his sword, "Kneel, man. You are speaking to Jonnere Hwaelin, heir of all Kieln."

Jonn looked gratefully at him in the dark. The man before them did not kneel but extended his marked arms before them, revealing more intricate patterns in the Sisters' light.

"And you are speaking to me, heir to some sixty trees. I am leaving," he said and smiled past a smoky beard, teeth white like pearls. *A savage westerner,* Mittrik thought as he continued to stare at the man, who moved with strange grace toward the sea, long arms swinging at his side, singing a loud song. Western wildness was no lie. *Western magic?* he wondered.

"Wait," Jonn dismounted and walked toward the man. Mittrik glared at the back of his head before joining him, flatfooted, ready to run. "My brother and I must leave Kieln tonight; can you help us?" Jonn produced a small pouch from his cloak. "I would pay you for your service and your discretion. Will you take us to Fair Isle?" He handed the man the smallest red stone from the leather bag.

"You took *rubies*?" Mittrik tried not to shout. He stared at his wholly noble brother, who had without doubt gone mad. "Our Fair family is in Alluvel. Why go to the Isle?"

Jonn didn't answer.

The marked man looked at the tiny gem in his hand with a pinched face. He rolled the ruby between his thumb and forefinger gently for some time before splitting the night in a bellowing laugh.

"Keep your raw-bees, Biler." He chuckled, tossing the gem to the sand. Jonn quickly dived to pick it up, but Mittrick could not take his eyes off the man as he splashed into the Bitter, dragging the shoddy dinghy into thigh high water.

"I have gold," Jonn said desperately. "You can have it. We need to leave." He pulled out another purse and shook it. This caught the foreign man's attention. He looked at the heavy bag Jonn carried with a crooked smile.

"Yes, then," said the westerner. "Get in with your gold."

Jonn moved to do just that, but Mittrik grabbed his arm.

"Are you mad? What are you doing?" Mittrik wondered what end his brother sought, if he was determined to go beyond return. From the westerner's gold lust and savagery, they might not return. If they did, they might carry a curse. Be Forsaken by the gods. If they existed.

"If I stay, I'll do something I regret. Trust me, brother," Jonn said, and Mittrik could smell sweetened wine on his breath.

He considered Jonn's white, torn face. *He needs to get out of Kieln, he needs to heal away from Alluvel. It is... understandable. Unlike him. Wholly like me.* "Very well."

The boat dipped as they entered side by side across the strange man. He was still smiling a smile too large for his face. It made Mittrik nervous. *This is the most foolish thing Jonn has done in any life,* Mittrik thought. In this life, Jonn never did anything foolish.

Mittrik considered what their Lord father will say when he discovers them gone. He looked around the rocking boat, spotted a clunky canvas sack. The wild haired man moved it closer toward himself when he caught Mittrik's eyes on it. The man leaned back and clapped his hands together. The clouds overhead cracked as if in response.

Mittrik heard the gray water ripple in the dark, and the skiff moved toward the open sea, rolling quicker and quicker over the incoming tide. Jonn searched the water, his hand went for his sword. Mittrik felt queazy.

"What are you doing? Tell me," Jonn ordered. The boat picked up speed as the waves tossed against them— against any regular current— carrying them into deeper waters.

"Bilers," the strange accent sang in the darkness, "at this

time you sleep. Easier for me." The stranger lifted his face, and then tilted his left palm toward midnight sky. The boat dipped to one side, and Mittrik held on to the wooden bench of his seat. *I was right, he's a mage,* he shuddered.

"I command you to stop this, at once," Jonn shouted, but the boat knifed through smacking waves. The mage swung his left arm, and to Mittrik's right, a form rose tall out of the sea, bending toward him— it seemed to fall. *A mage and a monster.* Too dark to see, Mittrik drew his sword, fast as he could. Breath and sensation fled lungs and body. Surely he was drowning.

A presenting darkness took him under.

3. THE FORSAKEN WEST

Santir sat on the beach, drawing designs in the coarse sand with a stick, squinting at the irritation in his eyes. The hard winds hadn't stopped since last night. Santir wished he had extra sense for wind, to stop the constant pinpricking of the sand.

The Great Fire rose in front of him, blooming the gray sky in yellows and pinks but no birds sang. As far as he could tell, there was no life on this island on which they crashed, only a small circumference of tall, stripped palms bent northeast by years of unwielded wind. The black sand between Santir's toes was cool, and he sunk his feet deep. He looked on the horizon, dreading Yeroen's return.

The vessel lay dormant, no longer smoking but still unable to fly. Santir delicately flipped the cracked stone of Yett in his hand, willing it to warm, but his hands were useless, without sense. He was the Senseless Detunae, the might-be-bastard of his family. *Du* didn't ring in him, certainly *hak* didn't.

The expensive disc was broken, deep veins splintering in all directions within the crystal. It hadn't shattered by the grace of First-One.

Santir envisioned Yeroen's anger and prepared himself for it. There was nothing he could do. There was nothing anyone could do without the right materials or a wielder of flame. Santir could already hear his brother's curses. They would have to voyage back to Canyassor on that miserable, small boat, cramped with whatever cargo they could bring. They would have to leave his air vessel.

Santir groaned as he stood. He walked to the ship, tossing the pricey firestone in the basket with his tools that sat beside the open tail.

He should have gone with Yeroen. It was the third day, and

all he'd done since discovering the cracked stone in the front left thruster was sit pitifully and wait. Worse, Rae trusted Santir with the task of finding helpful books from the Biler's place of worship. She trusted him, not Yeroen. But Santir still let his brother have his way, and he wondered if Rae would be disappointed in him. He wondered if she would tell him so.

The island was small, too small to appear on a map. During his time of waiting and wandering, he'd found the owner of the boat Yeroen had taken. Well, he found the man's bleached bones huddled and picked clean beside a fruitless palm. The man had been an eastern common, that was clear by his simple ragged clothes. Santir had buried him and thought a few well-wishing words, but he wasn't sure of Biler customs.

The sound of his brother's whoops and yells reached him as the boat came into view on the horizon, a dark dot against the gradient of pink sky and gray sea. A curl of water rose white beneath the tiny boat, lifting it higher and higher. Santir watched as the great wave fell fast and sent the boat gliding across the top of the sea in a spin toward the beach. Santir paced beside the vessel as it approached, preparing some sort of speech.

The vessel cannot fly without a fourth fire component, and ours is likely cracked because an Achkan, a non-descendant, tried to tune a firestone. Nothing else is wrong with my air vessel. No, it is your doing, Yeroen. It may take us seven days and nights to boat to the Blessed Lands now, without food, but no, that is not my fault. You were the one who needed to take my vessel to Achka before coming here. Your tasks, your fault.

The boat stopped where the sea met the shore, and Yeroen jumped out laughing. Santir walked toward him, practicing the speech in his head that was sure to dampen his brother's mood. He saw Yeroen retrieve a thin sack from the boat; it looked heavy and unshapely, and Santir hoped for Rae that they got it right. His brother tossed the bag onto the sand, and then released his hair from its knot. His smile was smug.

"Little brother, thank me. I found exactly what she wanted

and more," he said, and Santir felt a little relieved, then panicked when he saw two slumped figures in the boat.

"What did you do?" Santir ran to the pale men, pressing two fingers on one's neck. He felt a shallow thumping beneath the Biler's cold skin. The other man had the looks of a Fair Person, but they both wore the ugly dark furs, animal skins, and carefully stitched doublets that marked Biler nobles apart from their common folk.

"They are not dead." Yeroen was still smiling. "What kind of man do you think I am?"

"The reckless kind. Why bring Bilers back with you? Important Bilers, looks like."

In answer, Yeroen reached into the boat and withdrew a leather bag tied with string, and he tossed it to Santir. He heard the chinging of heavy coin as he caught it.

"You're stealing from them?" Santir tossed the bag back.

"You think I am a true criminal," Yeroen sounded humored, "but these Bilers paid me for a ride. They asked to go to Fair Isle, but I would never go there. I had to knock them unconscious. I had little patience, you know how eastern men are, and they would have soiled themselves at the sight of me wielding."

"They smell like they did regardless." Santir turned up his nose. "This is too stupid, waylaying Bilers."

Yeroen continued smiling and Santir felt his annoyance grow. "There is much gold in their bag, little brother," Yeroen said, but Santir had turned back to the vessel. "I counted enough to get us both out of debt and then extra. We go home rich men. Rich enough to stand in society again. To sit in society at least." Santir knew exactly which society Yeroen preferred. He stopped and realized he could not avoid the matter any longer.

"I did not have all the parts to make the repair." Santir sighed. "The electronics are fine now, but one of the stones of Yett was cracked in a hundred places. We have nothing to finish the combustion, so we will have to boat back to Canyassor."

His brother had stopped listening. Santir clapped his hands in front of him. "This isn't good, Yeroen. We have to return the Easterners back to their land. We cannot leave them here," and he groaned at the thought. *But we* could *just leave them here. Why not add that to our growing list of sins? A sin, but not a crime at least, thank Three-One.*

Yeroen ran back to the wooden boat with the collapsed men, saying something about the ignorance of Bilers.

"Do you hear me?" Santir yelled. "The vessel is not going to fly. I don't have spare stones of descendance lying among my tools. We weren't rich men leaving Achka."

But then Yeroen tossed a small pouch in the air saying, "from the Bilers." Santir caught it. He untied the string and stared with disbelief at the contents. *How did Bilers get so many pure firestones? Pure by their color and shine. How old must these be?* Might be too old. He looked up to Yeroen's grinning face.

"That will do, yes, little brother?" He laughed. "Dozens of stones that warm for the touch of a nonwielder, completely pure. Exactly what you need."

"Purity is not important. I need a much greater stone of Yett to create a perfect combustion. The one we broke was refined." Refined for the specific Abetto airship.

"Pack all those tight for the combustion, could it work?"

Santir picked up a medium sized red stone and rolled it between his thumb and forefinger. They were old and small, but they were firestones and nothing of artifice. At first there was nothing, and Santir wondered if the stone was so ancient and degenerated, only wielders of its energy could revive its power now. Belief only went so far. He pressed his skin harder against it. Harder.

Slowly the stone warmed in his hand, steady light growing from its core. Santir stopped before it caught flame. *I can make this work.*

Mittrik opened his eyes to a blinding gray sky, feeling like his head had been split open. He sat up, and looked out to a near black sea. Jonn was slumped against him, his chest moving up and down in steady breath. *What happened?* Mittrik tried to recall, blinked painfully, taking in his surroundings. *I'm on a beach, but how in Doom did I get here?* He had been in this position, had this very thought, many times before. But he had never been here, at this beach. He was almost sure.

He remembered leaving Alluvel with Jonn in a panic. He remembered his mother's letter. Mittrik hid his face behind his arm at the sunlight as it flooded his eyes, cold and pure white, and coughed up salt water from his throat. He tasted salt and that awful bitter taste that gave the sea its name. He turned to his right and saw a large man laid out next to a great boulder a short distance away, his painted arms folded behind his head, napping.

The mage. The memory of the magic man and his sorcery flashed in Mittrik's mind, and his heart rang. The savage abducted them.

He grabbed his sword and stalked toward the mage, squaring his shoulders. "You! Where have you taken us?" Mittrik called out before stopping at a safe distance, weary and aching from the mage's first attack.

The mage noticed Mittrik and spit something in his strange tongue before standing from the sand. He leaned up against the massive rock beside him and crossed his tattooed arms, dark eyes staring at Mittrik's sword. Mittrik did not lower his gaze, though he had forgotten how giant the man was. In the light of day, he could see the mage's arms and hands were covered in fresh burns and blisters alongside those dark blue designs.

"Some island west of your lands," said the man. Mittrik struggled to make out the words of his jumbled speech.

"West? You are westerners?" He had known.

"I am a *Canyai*. Blessed man." A flash of anger flickered in the wild man's eyes, his face scrunched. "Yasháno!"

A second man, just as tall and broad as the first, came around the other side of the giant boulder, wiping a dark and thick liquid from his hands onto his loose linen shirt. Unlike the mage, this man's arms and legs were bare of any markings, and the sides his hair was cut short to his head, beard not half as full or tangled. His eyes widened at the sight of Mittrik, and then turned pointedly to the marked mage. Mittrik's heart beat heavy in his chest, loud in his ears. *These men are magic. Magic is real. I knew it. I knew it.* Mittrik sheathed his sword. *What good is steel against western mages?*

"Please, I don't mean harm."

"Do not worry, Biler. My brother and I will not hurt you," the mage said before his face broke into a large smile. "Getting caught smuggling is one thing, but to assault an Easterner for true? Ha— I would be locked in fire pits for many passings. Thank you threely, no." He tied his coiling hair in a knot on his head as he said something in an impossible tongue to the other man.

The other man had blue eyes that contrasted his dark hair and skin; it made his expressions very obvious. He said something angrily then turned and walked around the other side of the boulder out of Mittrik's sight.

"You are magic," Mittrik said to the mage. These were the men of Old legends, the sorcerers that King Redbone had slain and drove out of Baeltaf. These were the men who commanded seas and mountains move, and seas and mountains obeyed them.

Again, the strange man's face twisted into anger. "No, I am not magic. I wield waters, yes? Ya du. Du is energy." The man had taken offense. Mittrik stared at the swirling blue designs on the westerner's arms and legs and realized they were depictions of curled waves, piling atop one another, wrapping around his biceps, forearms, and calves.

"You are not a mage?" Mittrik asked.

"I do not know this word, but no."

He had put Jonn and Mittrik to sleep without even touching them, had raised the sea against them. The man's anger dissipated as quickly as it came when he spoke again. "My brother and I are leaving now, Biler. By that tree there are oars for boat to return you to your lands. You should want to start before darkness."

The mage's brother returned from around the rock, carrying in his arms a basket woven from large red leaves filled with small steel objects that glistened in the sunlight. *Weapons.* He set down the basket by his feet before placing his brown hand on the boulder's smooth surface. The space beneath his hand whitened to glow, outlining his palm and fingers. Mittrik stood back, his right hand twitching by the hilt of his sword, the nails of his other biting into his skin.

A piece of the gargantuan rock slowly lowered to the sand, as a drawbridge might be lowered from an enceinte, revealing the boulder to be hollow. The short haired man said something to the mage as he picked up his basket of weapons and walked into the cavity of the stone. Mittrik stared in wonder, his breath catching in his throat. *The West is wilder than I could have imagined. To disappear into rock.*

"You say you're leaving in this stone?"

The mage laughed, turning to leave them. "Not real stone. Hollow. It is flying vessel, Biler. Made of airstone panels. We fly to Canyassor."

A hollow vessel? He stared at the gray stone that was apparently not a stone as the mage walked toward the entryway.

Mittrik had only a small taste of the wonders beyond his world, and he realized, with despair, that it was not enough. These westerners claimed to fly as birds in this boulder. Perhaps they could. Perhaps they were crazed or delusional, or perhaps their magic carried them.

It was a moment that would define him, he knew. A moment that cleared the path he was set to walk, a beginning he could make. Mittrik could not be so close to adventure and let his chance slip away; it was not within him.

"Wait!" The mage stopped and turned, eyebrows lost in his hair. "Will you take my brother and I with you, to the west?"

The man cackled loudly, but Mittrik heard the word "no" amidst it.

He withdrew his purse of gold from beneath his furs and held it up for the mage to see. "You shall have more gold if you take us." Mittrik tossed a sun to the man, who caught it easily. He smiled a crooked smile as he turned the gold coin in the clouded sunlight.

"You Bilers are strange— carrying raw firestones like they are precious, close to your heart, and spilling gold like it is nothing."

"Is that a yes?" Mittrik's heart was overwrought with wild pounding.

"Tufan, why not? Come, Biler. Bring your gold." Without another word, the man walked past him, back toward the boat where Jonn still slept. Mittrik watched as the large man picked up Jonn as if he weighed nothing— Jonn who always stood above the rest—and tossed him over his shoulder before turning back to the rock. And he entered the hollow stone with Jonn.

This was a mistake. Jonn will be wroth, Mittrik suddenly thought. But as he stepped into the hollow stone that was truly not stone, he forgot about Jonn and all other things that troubled him.

Inside, the walls were smooth and white as bone, and a peculiar bright light shone from above their heads. Sunlight, though artifice. The mage carrying Jonn walked down a narrow corridor that opened to their left, and Mittrik followed quickly after. The corridor ended at a door made of gray steel; the large man used his foot to open it wide, revealing more impossibilities.

Mittrik surveyed the room with searching, hungry eyes as the mage let Jonn fall to the silver floor with a thud. Mittrik did not have the words for the wonders inside this room, like nothing he had ever seen.

On either side, the smooth stone walls were lined with hulking things that looked like large wooden cabinets, carved with looping symbols and images of strange beasts. He could hear them click and whir in a bizarre, oscillating rhythm. The wall in front of the room was not truly a wall, but the stone disappeared into transparent glass, brown palm leaves piled on the outer surface. Before the glass window, a table was raised from the stone floor seamlessly, two chairs jutting before it, white and delicate. Large beams glowed beneath Mittrik's boots, painting the room in faint purple light.

To his right, there was a short set of stairs leading up to a knee-height platform that had another white chair, and behind the platform he could see yet another steel door. The boulder looked immense from the outside, but from the inside, it seemed a tiny castle in itself.

"That is my room," the wild haired man said when he caught Mittrik's eyes. "Not for Bilers." Mittrik could only nod.

Then the short haired man walked in the room behind them, and his bushy eyebrows tangled together. He spoke loudly in their language; the two brothers argued back and forth. Mittrik could only watch as they shouted at one another, and the sensible part of him that saw Jonn slumped against a glowing wall hoped that the short haired man would refuse to let them come. But the man threw up his hands and walked to one of the chairs, muttering in a low voice while the mage smiled.

"My brother is not happy," the mage said. "He will be happy when he can buy a new vessel, faster, ah?"

Mittrik nodded. "What is your name?" he asked, foolish for not asking sooner now that he stood in the stone 'vessel' of these foreign strangers.

"I am called Yero." The sneaky way the man answered made Mittrik think he was not called that.

"Very good, Yero." Like everything since Mother's death, the Western name was strange. "I am Mittrik Hwaelin."

"Are you, really?" Yero pursed his large lips together then took his place in the chair beside his brother.

"Sit down, Hwaelin," the mage's brother said in a choppy way. "I will not hear eastern talk for whole journey to ya Canyassor."

So, Mittrik sat on the cold floor beside a sleeping Jonn and watched as the two foreigners clicked and turned things at the odd table before them. Mittrik felt a trembling beneath, and then he heard what sounded like the beating of a hundred hooves. *Horses stampeding here?*

The vessel lifted from the beach, and Mittrik watched with stilled breath and heart as the palm leaves fell off the glass window. His stomach rolled into his groin, and he watched tall palm trees grow smaller beneath them, until they were hovering high in the sky, and all Mittrik could see through the glass was white nothingness. Yero pushed some lever up, and just as suddenly they were hurling through the air. Like a giant picked up their stone and flung them.

He heard a feeble groan escape his brother, felt him stir. He gripped Jonn's shoulder, looking helplessly as the clouds split in front of them, toward the setting sun. *Where in Doom are we going? What have I done?*

What Detached thing are we doing? Santir wondered.

The Great Fire followed its course under the horizon. Santir refused to look at Yeroen. To his brother's credit, he had stopped smiling but Santir kept his eyes on the cloud-streaked sky. They were far enough away from the unbridled tempests of the East that calm was restored to the air around them, water smooth beneath them. The side panels no longer rattled. Inside Santir, nothing calmed at all. *We are bringing Bilers to the great city,* he thought with a shudder. *What will Rae say? She will find out quickly, as she always does.*

Yeroen had always been thoughtless. It was how he gambled

away the winnings he'd earned fighting in the wateryards all those years, and he owed gold to men from Quo'Orinth to Zepey, but *this* was a different kind of carelessness. They risked turns in the firepits of Yettirai if the Talosian guards found they had crossed the Line of Separation without permission. Beyond that, they were smuggling hundreds of baskets of unregulated sweetleaf to the Biler nation, now smuggling people. They traveled with two Biler nobles who knew nothing of the Blessed Lands or the established Rock. Men who fought any difference with steel and war.

It was their way, these Bilers, and it had been since the Old Icemen broke the Rising Wood in half and sent otherkind away. They destroyed the land's connection to magics older than Eerim without thought and killed otherkind for sport.

Seven hundred turns since they isolated themselves, and the Biler lands had been savaged by wars. Even without wielders and magic, without fail every generation had their own cries and battles while claiming to be one united people. How could Santir hide such men in the great city?

Santir turned his head to look at the noblemen, ignoring the stinging in his side from his broken ribs. The one with the Fair looks had awoken, and his pale eyes met Santir's, unbothered to hide his fear. The golden pommel of his great sword was oddly decorated with firestones; he gripped it tightly. The broader of the two men spoke in a hushed tone, so quiet that one would have to strain to decipher. But Santir had no desire to hear ignorant men.

They could not trust these Easterners. Santir had known few, all smugglers and scoundrels. *Yeroen steals noblemen and what else? What end could this have for me?* Santir thought. *If we have the gold to pay off our debts, why does he keep pushing the limit?* But Yeroen was incapable of perceiving limits.

When their course was steadied, Santir unclasped his restraint, stood from the control desk and walked to the instruments on the wall to his left. He opened the wooden panel carved to resemble a papanuj. The recorders spun as they took in the calculations of the wind speeds and temperatures, and the scribings ticked onto the pale longleaf. It would be smooth until Talosa, but the combustion made of little firestones was losing power. Santir ran his fingers down the length of the thin paper, reading the numbers again to distract himself from worrying.

He hated being the responsible one. The role never suited him. It had been Klo, his brother by all but blood, who had been prudent. Rational. Kloennian had been thoughtful and kind and always knew when adventure became foolishness. But that was before the Sfar'Laki's war and his Radicals, before the onset of the plagues. Before the Battle for Coбmak. Santir stopped this train of thought and went to sit in the co-pilot's chair. *Will I have to be the steady one forever? I am not him, I am not a wise or dutiful man. I might sink with the weight.*

As the sky turned to darkness, Santir saw the outline of green earth in the distance— the Blessed Lands. He sighed gratefully as they neared the shoreline.

The aircraft soared over the port city of Léurai, the city in which Santir was born. High spiral towers along the ocean's mouth reflected a rythmic blue across the statues of the First Children, the steady blinking of Leu's crown drawing in ships to the forgiving waters of the cove. Yeroen looked out to the twinkling white-then-blue buildings below, smiling.

"Thirteen gods," Santir heard the dark haired Biler curse.

What a wonder it must be to look upon the sea city for the first time, he thought. Santir cherished those soft memories of his childhood living just outside Léurai, memories of his mother gardening golden mangaes and his uncle taking him and Yeroen to watch the wielding of the tides at the far shore. Santir's father had held tides before he went to search for the lost Onatae. Looking below, Santir tried to catch a glimpse of the white stone home in which his mother slept, but of course it was folly.

"I am near starved," his brother said as the city faded behind them.

"Are you going to be silent all the way home?" Yeroen asked. Santir nodded. "Your dedication at staying angry with me is inspiring. I mean it, little brother, inspiring. Trust me about the Bilers. They will not be a real trouble."

Santir could not contain a bitter laugh.

"These are not men to worry about," Yeroen continued, voice rising. "They smell of fear and wear flowy shirts. Their boots are heeled. Besides, I have a plan half-formed."

"You see how they cradle their swords. If we get caught smuggling Bilers, I doubt even Rae could help us."

"Ah! You do have your tongue. Rae will always help us, Santir."

He shook his head, resigning himself to silence again.

"Fine then, keep sulking. Back thruster one click."

Santir turned the dial.

The vessel sped west inland, over the dark green canopies of the jungle, dark sky around them. Santir wondered what half-formed plan his brother could be plotting. Nothing good, of course. Nothing reasonable. The brothers sat in silence, the faint whispering of the Bilers behind them increasing in volume. They were in an argument. Santir turned to glare at the noblemen, effectively quieting them.

As the moons rose to the center of the night, Talosa became visible. Air ships came and went, like purple stars joining and departing the heavens. The towers of the palace were lit with subtle fires and stood tall over the colorful buildings stacked along every road. Santir looked down and saw in the moonslight the fields of wildflowers outside the city walls, the colors passing below in muted sequences of blues, oranges, yellows, and pinks.

They soared past the capital city and toward the tall mountains behind it, the range of ravines and ridges known as Hahnae's Toes. They circled a familiar mountain ridge and veered upward, and then Santir could see his home.

He would never tire of it.

It was Klo's home, really, but he left it to Santir when he

died. Klo bought his mountain with his small inheritance and the little savings he had at only thirteen turns of age. Klo carved the home into the shorn face of his ridge.

Granite walls peaked out of the mountain and loomed over the great city lights below. Santir remembered the days Klo had spent wielding the ground, rising walls from the foundation and smoothing the many stone steps, going over the layout and plans every free moment he had. Santir shook his head, clearing it of memories that would lead to bitterness. The jungle beneath shook as the hot air of the vessel skimmed atop the trees.

Yeroen guided the vessel to the landing perch to the left of their home as Santir began turning back the thrusters and cooling the combustion, ticking away at the control desk as quickly as he could. All he could think of was how nice it would feel to sleep in his own bed.

The vessel lowered onto the platform with a soft *thunk*. The diligent humming calmed to silence as the soft purple glow of the control room shut off. Yeroen flipped the final switch to lay the aircraft dormant, then unclasped his restraint and swung around to face the Bilers, addressing them in guttural Eastern.

"This is Canyassor, Hwaelin. Welcome to my Blessed Lands."

Both nobles raised their heads from their secret whisperings and stared at Yeroen with stupid faces.

"Thank you," the dark haired one said. The Fair-looking one remained silent but his face gave away his shrewd distrust. Obvious fear. He could not be from Fair Isle with such a face, however blonde his hair. These were Easterners as ignorant as they come.

Santir stood and walked to the measuring instruments, opening the panel with the carved shorefalcon, and scanned the readings on the longleaf for anomalies, more to distract himself than anything. The combustion readings were as he suspected, the back thruster consisting of old firestones misfired a handful of times. If he checked, Santir would see the Biler's firestones as tightly packed red dust. They would have to replace the dust with a true stone of Yett before traveling again.

Yeroen stood and motioned for the Bilers to go with him out of the control room, to the corridor. They stood from their place, hands resting on the grips of their swords, and followed. Santir placed the readings back in the panel then exited.

They walk like wealthy men, Santir thought as he locked the door to the control room behind them. Yeroen opened the door on the right side of the hall, Santir's bedroom on the vessel.

"You two sleep here," Yeroen said in the Eastern tongue. "And tomorrow you are on your way."

"How?" asked the Fair one.

"All questions tomorrow. And maybe answers, too. I want to sleep," said Yeroen.

Both men nodded, though the Fair one's hand still gripped his sword. Santir could have argued about the Bilers sleeping in his room, in his airship, but he thought it better they slept here than inside his home. Yeroen lit the firestone in its small alcove on the wall so that the Bilers would not be left in darkness.

"If persons ask," he said to the shorter of the two, "no one should ask, but it's bad to tell anyone you are Bilers. Your brother passes Fair, and you can have looks of Achkan or Quo'Orinthian or whatever, but do not say Biler. By tides, do not say from where you come, please."

It seemed the Bilers understood the last instruction because they both nodded again, so Santir and Yeroen left the air vessel, leaving wide eyes behind them.

The entryway sighed as it rose behind them and closed with a loud click. The night air was cool and fragrant with the smell of the orange flowers that grew up the side of the stone walls of their home. Free winds shook the heavy branches and leaves around them: the never tired breath of the jungle.

Santir let out his own breath as his feet settled on Blessed soil. They had been gone too long. The nights spent on the deserted Eastern island had been unsettling and altogether too quiet, and before that in Achka, the city screamed all night.

But now Santir heard the soft and steady living songs of the trees around them. The chittering, steady buzz of countless crawling things and the hollers of tree climbers in the distance filled him with a sense of belonging. Alive, free. And at last, he would be able to sleep in his own bed.

Yeroen grabbed his shoulder before he walked up the stairs. “People inside the house,” he whispered. Santir wished he had extra sense. To feel an enemy before he saw them.

The hairs on his arms prickled like gooseflesh as he watched Yeroen close his eyes, feeling *du* beyond the stone wall.

The wooden door swung open.

“Are you just going to stand there?” Teia said from the doorway, hands on her hips.

“Tufan,” Yeroen cursed. “Why are you in our home at this hour, lyaren of Teviona?” He took the steps two at a time and Santir followed.

“Rae thought you might want fresh fruit in your icebox after so many days and nights of travel,” her tone came haughty in response. “Her kindness is wasted on you,” she added to Santir as he walked inside his home, her uniform ringlets shaking atop her shoulders. Her eyes lingered on the dormant vessel behind him.

“It is never wasted,” Santir heard Rae as she ran around the corner, leaning the wooden broom she held against the wall. Both Rae and Teia wore their training clothes, probably having come straight from the Academy. Rae’s dark hair was twisted into thick braids, and as she pressed her cheek to Santir’s in greeting, he smelled the spice of her perfume. When he pulled back he realized she had a red dragonfruit in her hand.

“I know they’re your favorite, so I got many.” They were expensive.

“Thank you,” his voice cracked. Santir coughed before speaking again, his broken ribs protesting. “You are too kind to clean the floors and stock our icebox, Rae.”

“I am glad I did,” she laughed, “or else you two would have gone hungry tonight. There was nothing here. Even your spiders look hungry."

Yeroen scooped her up in a hug, smiling. "You are a blessing to all of us helpless ones, Araeboril," he said as he set her down and pressed his cheek to hers. Santir thought he might have lingered too long. Rae rolled her eyes, then grasped Yeroen by the forearms.

"You are burned," she said, eyebrows pinched together.

"Don't trouble yourself," he said and pulled his arms from her grasp. "I am almost healed." She seemed unconvinced but did not force her hand, though her fingers twitched and sparked with the glow of truelight.

"I can heal you. Please do not be stubborn," she insisted.

Yeroen always smiled when he looked at her. "Me, stubborn? I deserve to feel all of this pain, Araeboril. Don't be troubled."

Santir thought Yeroen stupid and stubborn. Rae would heal his arms in a heartbeat. Santir would have her heal his ribs, and was just about to ask her.

"You brought some cargo. Who is in your vessel?" Teia asked, the eyebrow above her brown eye arching and a smirk tilting her mouth. Santir knew the ruse was over. *She senses them, of course.*

"Friends," Yeroen replied the same time Santir said, "Bilers."

Teia stared from one to the other, fists clenched tight like she wanted to hit them, and Santir could feel Yeroen's burning gaze. But he looked to Rae, her lips parted and her bright eyes wide with shock.

Part 2
Canyassor, the Blessed Lands
Talosa, the Capital City
8913 R.T. (Recorded Turn)

translated from The Second Book of Amina, VI.7-14:

"My children do not see truelight as I do, nor do they have sense to wield it. For this, I have no answer but the will of balance. Xonieren's line is cursed. Mine is blessed.

This middle plane enjoys balance more than its people do. Spirits must lean.

I am something else, without balance, a creature born for one side of the assemblies beyond all space. But there is one out there: my cursed brother. I won that fight between us.

Three-One has shown me this: another time will come and pass. An end of shadow and a beginning of darkness, of creatures I do fear, and the Other, wielder of unholy power, will win. I have seen it in vivid dreams, the next age, the next wielding of the dual spaces and opposite forces. I see destruction waiting in the unbalanced plane. But what good is my fear? I cannot stop the next time they try. That is not my time or space on our Rock, not my task. It is for someone else, and you will know the next Bringer of truelight by name."

4. THE GREAT CITY TALOSA

Jonn walked the length of the small gray room, head throbbing. Mittrik lay on the mat in the corner, one leg thrown across the floor, foot bouncing atop the metal. The clanking beat set Jonn's anxious pace, set the pounding in his head, but it was hard to breathe in such a small room. *This is all my fault,* he thought as his hand raked across his face, stretching skin. *We are in the Forsaken West, and while gods Doom us, this life is short. These mages will kill us given the chance. Then they'll eat us.*

We'll be blessed if it's in that order.

Jonn was sober now, and felt the mistake of leaving Alluvel in every fiber of morality within him. He should have stayed. Fleeing made him a coward. It didn't matter what he believed. It didn't matter what his father did or didn't do.

He clutched tightly at the letter still in the shallow pocket of his breeches, his mother's curving letters coming to haunt. He brought it out to read once more beside the flickering fire in the wall. *Shadow times, she wrote, whatever that means… The West is the worst place for us to find ourselves.*

"How are we to get home now?" Jonn finally asked when the silence felt like it might suffocate him.

"I haven't the slightest idea. I told you, I know as much as you." Mittrik turned on the mattress to look at him. "I woke from the mage's attack, we were in that strange room, flying through the air in this Doomed stone. I imagine tomorrow, after the westerners sleep, we might get home much the same way."

"I am sorry," Jonn said. "This is all my fault. I asked the savage to take us from Kieln with an offer of gold, and now…" He didn't know what to do. Mittrik stayed quiet, turning his back to him.

Knees buckling underneath him, Jonn collapsed and felt shame cling as a shroud might. Declaring for all his Doom. He'd been rash, reeling from his mother's passing, and now they were lost and condemned for it. Forsaken. He thought of the mage conjuring the sea at night, knocking them near death with the force of the waves. The water responded to the mage, bent to his will in some way. How could they stand against magic?

How did men like Hammish the Hammer conquer daemons?

He shook his head, closed his eyes. *Come, you are a Hwaelin,* he chastised himself. *You will find a way home. Would Father hide here if he were in this place?*

A High Lord never would never overreact as you did to a woman's letter, a familiar second voice, not his own, said in

Jonn's mind. It sounded like Mittrik, but had something stern that belonged to their father.

"Do not be sorry, Jonn," came Mittrik's voice in the dimness. Real and tired. When Jonn opened his eyes, Mittrik's dark ones were staring at him. "This is not your fault. Truly, I—"

The metal door behind him opened with a groan, startling them both. The wild-haired mage looked down at them, and Jonn could tell something had changed. The man's large-lipped smile, which he wore throughout most of the journey, was gone and replaced with a grimace near a snarl.

"Come, eat," he said before turning to leave.

Jonn looked at his brother who nodded to indicate they should follow. They walked out of the flying stone, as Mittrik called it, and Jonn turned in shock as the ramp swung up behind them of its own accord with the sound of a soft exhale, sealed the boulder tight like a door. The flying thing did look like a giant, smooth rock. He could scarce believe he walked out of it.

Jonn coughed at the humid air and looked around a shadowed wild. He felt choked in a new way by the dense green in this land; the trees rose tall and doubled over him, blocking any light the Sisters could provide. A howl came from somewhere in the darkness, a chill unfit for the climate cut down his back. His fur coat felt at once too heavy and hot for such a place. The mage marched to the steps of the western home, his dark marked arms swinging at his sides.

The house was as peculiar as it was astonishing, if one could call it a house. Large walls of stone peeked out at odd angles from the bare part of the mountain to loom over the edge of its rugged face, the wall nearest them covered with massive bloomed flowers; the savage's home was carved into the dark rock of the steep, with a dull colored stairway stacked up to a wooden door on its nearest side. Jonn climbed after the savage man with Mittrik behind, feeling his apprehension grow with every step.

When the mage opened the wooden door at the top, Jonn

saw they were not alone. Inside, two women were in the open space, staring at him and Mittrik with curious faces. He imagined his expression looked quite the same. They were unlike any women Jonn had ever looked upon. Immodest and wild.

These savages are all strange and beautiful, was all Jonn could think as he stared at them.

To Jonn's right, the room opened to a grand space with large colorful pillows strewn haphazardly about. The room was dimly lit by sconces of lusterless brown metal, sculpted to look like the faces of fierce creatures, eyes set ablaze with orange fires that flickered soundlessly.

On the left side of the room, one western woman stood behind a wooden table, and she was easily as tall as Mittrik, buxom and strange. Her dark copper-colored arms and middle bare to reveal blue marks similar to the mage's, only hers looked more intricate and perhaps even elegant. They twisted around her arms, legs and exposed middle, winding up and stopping at her shoulders in blue curls, like swells of the sea. A bright blue stone gleamed from above her naval. Her face was comely and oval shaped, framed by many tight amber spirals. One eye was a dark brown, the other a dull blue. Her hand rested on a dagger at her side, and the blade's sharp edge was lined with ocean colored crystal.

Both women had blades strapped and wore men's breeches of a patterned green cloth that fit tightly around their legs, exposing the gentle slope of their hips, stopping just below their knees.

While the first woman was made of soft curves, the second was made of corded muscle and sharp angles. The unmarked woman's arms were also bare, though her breast and midsection were covered with a material that looked like many plated scales, like a fish. *Like strange armor*, Jonn thought curiously. The angular woman was much shorter than the other, little lighter in complexion and strong—with collarbones and arms that looked sculpted of honey colored marble. Her plaited dark hair was unkempt. But her eyes struck Jonn, an impossibly pale shade of green.

"Three blisses. Who are you?" the smaller woman asked, her voice affected by the strange accent with which the mage and his brother spoke.

I'll use a false name, Jonn thought but opened his mouth and said, "I am Jonnere Hwaelin of Alluvel."

He reeled as he betrayed himself, but could do nothing to stop. *She is a witch,* he thought, unmoving in fear. He pressed his lips together.

The shorter woman's dark brows shot up, and she turned to say something unpronounceable to the taller, who straightened to make herself taller still, her shadow crawling up the wall behind her.

The witch said, "You meant to lie," and she laughed at him. "Did you tell them to try to lie to me?" she asked the savage men. Both shook their heads in answer. "I am a child of Amina. You cannot answer my questions with lies, Lord Hwaelin."

Jonn turned to look at his brother, searching for the right words. *There is a reason the west is forsaken.*

"What are you called?" Mittrik asked both women, but his eyes remained fixed on the witch. "I am Mittrik."

"I am called Araeboril by many. By few, Rae," her voice sounded gentle, sweet to hide a bitterness, Jonn thought, like a doctor's medicine. She smiled and pointed to the bigger woman. "This is Teia, one of my closest—my *lyaren.* Welcome to Canyassor, and to the great city Talosa." Her arm extended to the large window that looked over the night's thick wilderness, and beyond that, below and in the distance, a startling city peaked between two hills. Jonn walked closer to the window wall.

The bigger woman narrowed her eyes at them and said, "You are noblemen of Baeltaf." Her voice was deep and accusatory. She said something short in the foreign tongue to the shorthaired savage. A heated argument picked up between the marked woman, Teia, and the mage. Jonn could ignore them as his focus was locked on the sight before him.

From the east facing wall, Jonn could see the city nestled amongst the hills, white walls extending into the sky wrapped around the magnificent sprawl of lights. Above white walls, great curving towers soared to the heavens, tipped with fluttering flags, and millions of windows were lit for the night. The earth seemed to reflect the night's abundance of stars, the lights in either darkness bright and suspended.

"That is the largest, wildest castle I have ever seen," Mittrik said taking a place at his side. "It's so bright."

"That is the royal palace, though some of what you see is the academy's towers," the witch called Rae said to him. She began pointing to the different towers and wide spiraling structures that peaked below them. "The dark colored towers belong to the academy, while the great white structures and that one with the curving roof is the palace of the Tyano."

"The Tyano?" Mittrik asked, staring with glinting eyes at the far-off lights.

"The Great Leader," she answered with a nod. She tossed herself carelessly onto one of the large pillows on the floor. "Father of the Blessed Lands. But that tallest tower there, the sharp looking one, contains the sky eye of the academy. From that place, we view into the farther skies, though not so well as the Confederate sky eye."

The mage crossed his burned arms across his chest.

Jonn had once seen the castle at High Baeltaf, where the king lavished about with his many wives. That castle was great and old, crafted hundreds of years ago out of northern granite and standing tall as anything else in the mountains. The castle below him now, however, was undoubtedly greater. Possibly older. It looked like something that had stood forever, rising from the ground in harmony and defiance, a thing made by gods— the Old gods. So massive was its height and powerful were its walls to leave him speechless. *No man could build that in five lifetimes*, Jonn thought.

"You must be hungry after such a long journey," Rae said,

rising from her place on the floor. "I have fruit cut fresh that we may share, and more in this basket. Teia and I picked them ourselves this evening."

"Rae," the mage said before rolling his tongue off in their lilting language. She shook her head and laughed, walked gracefully toward the taller woman behind the table, and lowered herself to retrieve something Jonn couldn't see.

"We shall eat together," the witch decided, standing and cradling a basket, all but toppling over with odd shapes unfamiliar to Jonn. She tossed one to him, and he stared down at the deep red flesh of the fruit, flecked with yellow and green. "As it is," she said, still smiling, "I never met a Biler, and I have too many questions to number."

Mittrik did not understand how he could be terrified and excited in equal measure, but that was the truth. He sat beside his brother at the table across the peculiar women and at either head of the table sat the foreign men. The wild-haired mage glared at his brother from his seat, dark eyes filled with ire. He poured himself a glass of some amber drink and sipped it quietly as they ate. The mage's brother remained fixed on the green-eyed woman, attention never leaving her, smiling as she spoke. Eventually the woman called Teia poured her own amber drink into a glass. They didn't offer Mittrik or Jonn any.

Jonn made it plain he did not like how the green-eyed woman's questions extracted truth. He tried his best to remain silent during the conversation. He sat with a focused face, struggling to peel back the deep purple skin of a fruit, scowling over everything.

Mittrik did not mind answering her questions, mostly boring ones about the structure of Baeltaf's governance or practices of the Faith, especially since she was so keen to answer his own.

"So, there are High Lords, lowlords, then underlords," she

recounted, ticking them off on her fingers, "positions beyond that within houses and order of faith. But now, that is extensive. And these men serve under one king, you said. Except this Good Thyne that only serves your gods." She spoke like she rushed to stop speaking and plopped a sliced orange fruit into her mouth. "Much has changed for your people in six hundred Rock turns, more divisions. Have you met your king and queens?"

"No, I have never met them." Mittrik laughed when the words were pulled from his mouth. Perhaps pushed out. Either way, he was helpless. "I am sure to, one day, though my father has enough to say about him that I have quite the representation already."

Mittrik was unable to go to King Ornund VI's coronation in the year 686, for he had come down with a terrible fever and could not make the long journey through the Raglands. His mother stayed behind with him. Jonn, however, had gone to bend the knee to the new King Osbur alongside their father and had spoken of the coronation and the delights of High Baeltaf for Greetings' on end after his return. Mittrik had been jealous then, more jealous when his father took Jonn to High Court only the summer next while he was told again to stay in Alluvel.

Mittrik looked about the table at the extravagant colored variety of fruit, then placed a shiny round one in his mouth, expecting it to be as delicious as everything else. The taste was strong and bitter, and he quickly spit it out in his hand. The foreigners began laughing loudly (Jonn visibly stiffened), all but Rae who still failed to repress a condescending smile. She picked one of the round things up herself and used her palms to crack open the shiny yellow encasing, and out popped a small white fruit that appeared fuzzy.

"You eat the meat and spit out the seed," she said, holding it out to him.

He took it from her and tentatively put it in his mouth. The sweetness was not as strong, the subtilty a relief, and the texture something like silk and cream. He spit out an oval shaped seed, black as obsidian.

"What does your father say of your king and queens?" Rae's smile was a radiant thing.

"He's told me he believes the king unfit to sit the throne, and he once referred to his four queens as 'the idiot's flock of fowl. He hates the first Dawnburst queen."

He paled instantly as Jonn kicked his shin under the table. He could envision, even now, his father's anger, but hadn't tried to stop the words that flew from his lips.

"Think before you speak," Rae said with a devious, crooked grin. "It helps but a little. You won't be able to lie but you will not lose your tongue. Much thought and practice keeps the tongue from slipping."

"Yero has told me that he is not magic," Mittrik began.

"Amnotmashee," the mage's words came more slurred than usual.

"Then how is it you can do all this? Bend seas, fly through the air in stones, command truth from a liar."

"All done differently," Rae said while she ate, juice dripping down her mouth and chin. "But it is not magic, not for true. Magic is an old practice. Many kinds of magic have been forbidden since the Separation, here too. Yeroen and Teia can wield waters because they descend from the First Children. Amina was another of the fourteen First Children, and all of her descendants have this ability I have, to ask honest answers."

"Who are the First Children?" Mittrik couldn't track his questions as he tried to keep up.

"The first people born on this land, after it was raised by our god. Teia is directly descended from the first born of the First Children, Leu."

"Which means I am a mighty wielder just as the first Seawoman," Teia said with obvious pride. "Stronger than him," she added with a nod to Yero, who rolled his eyes.

Rae wiped the back of her hand across her stained mouth.

"And we can fly in air vessels because the most gifted alchemists, engineers, and wielders of natural energies strived to make it so. Air vessels are relatively new inventions, though. The first was invented back twenty or so turns. Sea ships were more common turns ago."

"Why did you travel to Canyassor?" Teia asked with sudden curiosity, and Mittrik was grateful to not feel the pull at his lips. Still, for some reason, he did not wish to lie. But he could not tell all of the truth.

"We had no idea what to expect of the West," he treaded carefully, aware of Jonn's harsh stare and ready foot, "and truly we had never heard of Canyassor. The journey was more about leaving Kieln than traveling here."

Rae smiled sweetly and nodded, then stood from her place at the table. Both wild men stood up instantly as she did and looked at her expectantly, palms open at their sides. *They respect this woman a great deal,* Mittrik realized and stood with them. Jonn remained on his arse.

Rae sighed before speaking. "We should go, Teia. Fehatsi should hear what we have learned tonight."

This caused the taller woman to collapse in a fit of laughter, clutching her bare stomach. She said something to Rae in their native tongue. When the woman chuckled, the scales of her armor glittered firelight with the rise and fall of her chest.

"It was exciting to know you, lords. I am overwhelmed with emotion, truly." And then Rae curtsied just as a lady would, though it looked strange with her male clothes and tangled hair. "I hope you enjoy your time in Canyassor. I think we might meet again, but I will pray for Three-One's will."

Teia stood from her seat as well and nodded her head stiffly to them before taking her place at Rae's right side. The one she called Santir said something to them, and soon Rae led him and the woman out of the wooden door and into the cool darkness.

The mage stood, watching them leave the home, and then stretched his marked arms in front of him and yawned. "I was told, bad manners to have you sleep in air vessel. So, you sleep on pillows by window."

"Thank you," Jonn said in a quiet voice, looking pensively at the wall. "And tomorrow we will be on our way."

"What way?"

"Home."

The mage nodded with a smile and disappeared down a corridor behind them, cut deep into the mountain.

Mittrik got comfortable atop two large pillows he placed side by side. The pillows were all different shapes stitched with splotched bright colors and designs of strange flowers, and softer than any featherbed. He lay flat on his back and stared at the cool gray ceiling, head reeling with the things Rae had told him. She had said that there was much more west than Canyassor, different realms, stranger cities and different kinds of people.

The thought filled him with terror and wonder. Jonn sat on a blue round cushion, obviously distressed, his pale face hidden in his hands.

"I will get us home soon," Jonn said as Mittrik grew more tired. "I will make this right, Mittrik."

Not too soon, I hope, he thought before drifting off.

He could not sleep long, haunted by shapeless creatures in his dreams. Jonn snored quietly at his side, but this was not the loudest of noises. The strange chirping and cries of the packed forests flooded the house. When he opened his eyes, darkness uncovered. Nighttime still.

He saw the mage seated at the long table in the room, a wide rimmed glass before him. His glazed eyes passed over to Mittrik, seeming to sense he was now awake. The mage lit a candle and called out.

"Come drink, Hwaelin."

Mittrik rose and took a seat across the mage, scuffing the wooden chair across the stone floor as he did. The mage wore a light linen shirt that covered his arms, and bandages had been placed over his burns. He poured the amber drink from a simple glass bottle and set it before Mittrik on the dark wood. Mittrik gulped it down quickly, but regretted it. It was not a drink like mead or wine. The amber hit his mouth and throat in a sharp burn, with a strong sweetness tickling his nose and the roof of his mouth, and his insides turned hot. He held in the urge to sputter, swallowed the burn again.

"So, is west beyond the Line everything you wanted?" the mage asked as he poured more of the burning drink into their glasses.

How could I have possibly imagined this to want it? Mittrik thought. "It is much more."

His response seemed to please the colored man, but then his smile fell. "You should not have met Rae like this. Santir was right about bad timing."

"Your brother loves her," Mittrik said, taking a smaller drink.

The mage straightened on his chair, flashed white teeth beneath his beard. "You are not stupid, no, Biler? At least not blind." He swirled the multicolored glass in his hand, peering into it as if searching for something, then he picked out a bug and flicked it to the floor.

"Does she love him?" Mittrik asked and laughed at the jealousy in his voice. The mage laughed at him, too.

"Rae loves everyone." Mittrik heard emotion like anguish in Yero's voice. "She must love everyone, every living thing she sees. It is her curse, but no, she doesn't love him same kind." He took a long drink.

Mittrik stared past the glass wall, the night dappled with stars. He did not want to look into the glowing eyes of the wall sconces, their bared teeth and metal looks frightening. He thought of Rae's eyes, for he had never seen any so bright, so pale, not even those of his mother's. He thought of Rae's irresistible questions, of her wide hips.

"You have wanting look, Biler. Not so," Yero said. "She loved most true another man. The brother of Santir."

"You? Or you mean you have another brother?"

"No, not brother like me of same woman and man. *Yaren*, brother but for that. East does not have word for bond stronger than brother."

"What happened to that man?"

"He died in the war. Klo. Mouwat Kloennian." Yero's face folded into something unpleasant and he downed the rest of the contents in his glass.

Mittrik thought to the war raging back in Baeltaf's northern Dominions and felt a sudden guilt for running to adventure instead of duty. His father needed him at his side, he had said as much. Was he craven? Would his father think so?

"That is very sad for her."

The mage considered this for some time before he spoke. "Yes, sad for her. Grieving forever, but she is Rae and knows pain. She does not let pain shame her. Worse for my brother Santir. He does."

Mittrik nodded. He wondered what it would be like to lose Jonn, if he were struck down or taken ill, gods forbid. Mittrik wondered what he would try to do to fill the emptiness Jonn would leave. He felt that brand of emptiness now, a place where the vision of his mother alive had been. He ran west to un-feel the emptiness his mother left. Acerbity and regret reminded him in random pangs. For Jonn? Mittrik would have to run across the world to escape that pain. He would not let himself lose Jonn if he could help it.

"Eh, we have saying in Canyassor," Yero spoke the next words slowly and Mittrik tried to hold onto them. "*Ya Tyano uékan jyare ya Korr*. The Tyano must have the Korr, yes? Tyano is Great Leader of all our blessed lands—" his hands moved dramatically about the whole of the room, "— closest is Korr, second in command. The one who gives advices and fights by side always. Our Tyano is Teviona Iial, yes? His Korr Riambo Rehonan. The relationship of Tyano and Korr must be strong as brothers, they must be yaren." He connected his two fists together. "Santir is Tyano with no Korr now, and I am shit with advices." His fists fell.

Mittrik drank as the mage drunkenly whipped his dark hair around his face, eyes closed. "Tufan, I am watered up and my tongue is loose from time with Rae. Amina's children dangerous. We drink silent, Biler. No talk."

Mittrik was thankful to sit and drink in the quiet. He had seen too much, learned so much, and still knew nothing at all. His head began to feel like fae stuffed it with wet wool and Dreadwood briars— full, busy, painful. Magical. From somewhere in the trees outside, an animal sang out his long, howling song, and Mittrik smiled into the amber.

Santir bolted upright. His eyes opened in darkness, head swimming in currents of dreams that tormented him, dark green eyes accusing.

Breathe in. Hold it.

And out.

His head fell back on his pillow, and he stared up at the high stone ceiling. He was cold, neck and forehead damp. This febrile chill lingered on Santir's skin since the Bilers boarded his vessel, a feeling of wrongness he did not think would fade any time soon.

It was wrong to bring them here, and it was worse that he brought them to Rae with the Selection so close. Bilers in the Blessed Lands, before the royal wedding. It was careless. Rae had always dreamed of the East and its mysteries. He saw the way her face lit up at the sight of the foreign men.

You're just a distraction. The worst kind. She does not need you. Without her, you are nothing. Without you, she is greater, Fehatsi's cruel words that Santir had denied. He was not a distraction, he was Rae's friend, just like Fehatsi. Only her friend. But he recognized that bewilderment in Rae's eyes when she looked upon the Bilers and heard of their home. Almost like when she saw *Santir* for the first time, standing beside Klo. Amused, already distracted. Had he not done just as Fehatsi told him he would? Realizing Fehatsi was right was probably the worst part of this mess.

The Bilers could bring nothing to the Blessed Lands but trouble, and the sooner they were back in their kingdom of whilom thought, the better. Santir scrambled out of his sheets and walked to the washroom, his thoughts on green eyes.

He stretched before opening the washroom's door. The pain in his ribs was gone, the bones perfectly mended. Rae did what she did best and, now master of her craft, Santir did not feel the slightest soreness. He remembered a time when she couldn't heal so cleanly.

The water from the shower was cold as ice at first, but Santir was thankful for the harsh slap of it, the plunging shock in his gut. It distracted him, but only a little. He placed two fingers on the orange glowing firestone mounted in the rock wall, and soon the water that poured from above was warm and gentle. He allowed the water to soothe his muscles and drain his head of ghosts.

After he dried, he walked downstairs and into the space where the Bilers slept before the window, startled to find that the Fair looking one was already awake and seated at the table. Upon seeing Santir, the man stood.

"My brother and I need to get back to Kieln." A night's sleep gave the foreigner confidence. He stood taller and spoke differently than the previous day, like he meant what he said. "Could you take us back to Baeltaf the way we came? In your flying stone?"

Santir sighed, thinking over the words in his head before saying them in the foreigner's tongue. "Our airship cannot fly. It needs repairs that take time."

The Biler nodded, considering. "How much time?"

Santir hated that question more out the mouth of a Biler for some reason. "I don't know."

"We need to return home today or tomorrow. We shouldn't have left. I-Where are you going now?"

Santir turned back to face the man. "My city."

"Then I shall go with you to find a way back to Baeltaf as soon as possible. Will you help me?"

"No." Out of the question. Not a chance. Santir couldn't take a Biler into Talosa, where better ears and false eyes waited.

"If you help me, I will give you twice as much gold as I've already given you," bargained the Biler.

I shouldn't, Santir thought. He imagined having 'twice as much gold' as he had now. *Rae commanded me to help them return to Biler lands, but nowhere in her command did she say* I *had to be the one to return them.* But it was too dangerous. Any Eerim could hear the Biler's thoughts, and any Ku'dur could ensnare his attention. Santir had trouble monitoring his own thoughts in Talosa.

"No. I am going to the city alone," Santir said. "You will not follow."

"Please," the man begged. "I can't just stay here. I need to do something, go somewhere or I'll go mad. If I sit waiting, well..."

Santir knew that feeling. Waiting, without end in sight, brinking on madness. When Yeroen, Klo, and Rae left for war and Santir stayed behind, he learned the pain of waiting. Undue pity came for the Fair Biler.

"Fine," Santir said, "follow, but think nothing. Your thoughts will be heard in the city."

"*What?*"

"We have laws to protect your privacy, don't worry." Because worries were the most dangerous thoughts. "Don't think about your worry. Don't think anything to give you away as Biler. Don't think about yourself unless you have to. Leave your steel and your brother here." Santir pointed to the sheathed sword at the man's hip, then to the snoring Biler in the corner. One Biler would be difficult enough to conceal. Near impossible. In Talosa, there existed few secrets. Santir groaned. *This is as stupid as I'll ever be. Might as well keep going.*

"Men in your city do not carry swords?" the nobleman asked incredulously, his hands hesitated to take off his belt. "I saw a blade strapped on the thigh of a *woman* last night."

"We have swords and all manner of weapons, man and *woman*. We are Canyai," Santir responded. "Our weapons are not like *that*. Your sword will give you away as a Biler and bring attention."

Santir looked at the gemmed, golden hilt of the Biler's sword, the scabbard of decorated animal hide, and wondered what it would be like to grow up a rich Eastern lord. He did not think it would be such a great thing. A shallow life, a puddle of ignorance, unknowing of the Rock's unassailable horrors, therefore willing to create their own. But he imagined many people would prefer such a life, regardless. For the ignorance. A respite.

"Come, then." Santir walked out of his home and down the steps of the steep. Rae and Klo had painted the steps with bright colored flowers long ago, but now the images were faded. The Biler walked down the path behind him and into the trees.

It should be a relief to Santir, that he might not have to take the Bilers back—he could easily pass off the task to another smuggler—but Rae made him feel responsible for the men. Last night, Rae told him and Yeroen to treat the Bilers with respect and kindness, not to lose them. But Rae would ask that for anyone. She didn't know that the Bilers were stupid.

Santir swelled his lungs with heavy Canyai air. He would find the Biler men a way home right after he saw to his debt and traded for a new stone of Yett.

The path from his home to the city road was long and narrow. It curved up and down the mountain slopes, covered by the jungle's rich canopies. Santir walked over the poisonous spike of a plant that had fallen onto the path and told the Biler to do the same. It was almost overgrown and a struggle not to get hit by large leaves that bent over from the dense trees on either side. he hadn't taken a blade to it diligently the past two Rock turns. Yeroen attempted it but quickly gave up on the task.

"What kind of bird is that?" The Biler asked, pointing to

the large winged creature in the green expanse, its red feather mane splayed around its head. The bird's bright yellow chest puffed out as it stared down at the two men with seedy dark eyes.

"A *nenchai,*" Santir answered, passing him. "Do not look at it too long, they are easily offended and could eat you in three mouths." He laughed at the look of horror on the Easterner's face before the nenchai spread its broad wings and took to the sky.

How I'd like to fly with one, Santir thought, trying to distract himself from the Biler's dumb expression. It took some men years to bond with the massive birds, though it was known that nenchai may imprint on particular humans. It was much easier to form a bond with the creatures if you started with a chick.

Santir did not know how he would achieve any sort of communion with this particular beast, who was choosier than most of its kind and attacked Santir twice already. The bird had nested near his home two Rock turns ago and soon would find a mate. *Perhaps one of its nestlings will bond with me if I am careful.* But he knew more likely than not the nenchai would try to eat him if he approached a newly hatched chick. *An empath could do it with ease. Kloennian would have bonded with the discriminating bird by now, had he lived to see it, and we'd both be flying.*

The men passed over the sixth hill, and Santir could tell the Biler struggled in his fur trimmed cloak and leathers. His breaths were short, but the man never complained, only continued trailing Santir with his eyes set in front. They went through streams, over ravines, and Santir thought the man was sure to have fungus on his feet for his sloshing wet boots. The footwear of typical Canyai was open-toed, and the Blessed people were of better hygiene than Bilers.

Sugarflies collided with one another above their heads, fighting over the sweet nectars of flowers. They buzzed by their ears and grappled each other with long spindling legs. As the two walked by a pa bu and its immense white trunk, the leaves and tight petals rippled above them, their long blooms opening in vivid blues and pinks that desired to be seen. Santir heard the Biler's breath catch in his throat.

"What are those?" the man pointed to the tailless tree climbers in the canopy that hollered as if answering his question.

"Papanuj," Santir interpreted for the tree climbers, stopping to turn and look at the man. "Let it be easier than this, Biler. You will not know what anything is, and then you leave. What does it matter if I name everything for you?"

The Biler looked into his eyes and nodded. Santir remembered Rae's advice (order) to be kind to the foreign men. He was hopeless for her, but he was not a tour guide. Her and her constant demands. Still he felt guilt creep up on him as they continued over the rolling hills, the pa bu's wide blossoms closing with no one to see its beauty.

The Great Fire rose in the sky to its highest point as the jungle opened to the city road, the dirt worn down and packed solid from the tread of so many feet. Thankfully, the Biler remained silent as they walked. He heard the river now, and he could smell the mangae farm before he saw the rows of golden leafed trees. It reminded him of the ones outside his home in Léurai. He would climb them at dawn and pick the ripest ones before his mother had the chance. He walked by the farm so often, but it never failed to remind him of his mother and childhood.

A woman yelled from the tallest branches of a tree, her black hair stark against the light foliage. She called for her husband,Tujien, as she tossed the fruit below to him and their oldest son, a boy almost a man. Santir should know the woman and boy's name. Yeroen would know.

Tujien recognized Santir even from such a distance and waved, crooked smile on his face. Tujien was always enthusiastic during a good harvest, and Santir could smell the sweetness in the air.

"Detunae!" Tujien ran to the front of his land, then leaned against the wooden railing of his fence. "Where have you been, young one? I thought you would miss all the good mangaes this season. The city is hoarding them for the union. More than a fourth goes to the city, can you believe? Even visitors will receive a citizen's portion of my produce."

Santir laughed. "The Selection Day will be devourous as this union."

Tujien tossed two of the fruits to him. "I think the Selection Day will be more than anything we are expecting. The city has already given me a number, and I don't think anyone has that many mangae," Tujien said. Santir handed one of the round mangaes to the Biler.

"Who is your friend?" Tujien asked Santir.

Don't think the word Biler. Almost to the city. "Not a friend. He's nobody."

"No one is nobody in Talosa." *Because everyone is,* the saying went. "Well, I shall see you this evening on your return, I imagine," Tujien said. "I'll have a basket for you and your brother. We shall collect until the Great Fire fades tonight."

"Many thanks," Santir said as he peeled back the mangae's flesh and bit into the top of freshest gold. Sweet, but not as sweet as the mangaes Santir's mother grew back home.

Beyond the trees Santir could see Tujien's smallest children playing in the mud with a Ku'dur. The Ku'dur child, antlers barely sprouting, threw a rock at one of the doubleborn but the little girl was a wielder of earth like both her parents, and instinctively raised her small hands in front of her face. The rock stopped midair before her hand and suspended there as the girl grounded her bare feet into the dirt. She whipped the rock at the Ku'dur with shocking speed and struck. One of his eyes would blacken.

"Child!" her mother yelled from the mangae tree. "Honor! Are you going to wield against a defenseless? Pray Three-One and the Select never judge you."

Santir saw the Ku'dur child pout his thin gray lips at being called defenseless.

He stopped watching the children fight as he went down the road, and soon felt the tremor beneath his sandals. Behind, children giggled, but Santir heard Tujien scold his daughter for raising earth during harvest.

Santir laughed at the Biler's face. He did that often while they walked. He hadn't laughed so much in turns.

They passed two women harvesting, and Santir turned to see the Biler's cheeks beaming red and his eyes steady on the road in front of his feet. The women who harvested were topless, their skirts made from the thin fibers of the pa bu's grayish blue leaves, knee deep in green water. Santir wondered what it would be like to live in a world where skin was covered like a scandal. *But he's Fair, Rooj Fair. His face could always be telling me lies, that is what they do. What games does this Island man play? Why has he really come here?*

Santir was a farm boy, but he wasn't stupid. He often behaved stupidly, like this instance, but he was smart enough to know that exposing the Biler's thoughts to Talosa wasn't the worst plan. *What is this man thinking?*

Tomorrow someone would know.

Talosa's walls, and the patches of wildflowers surrounding came into view as the two men trekked the last hill. The towering white walls of the city obstructed the view of anything but the Academy's sky eye. Santir peered across the flowerbeds to the rushing river, churning from the treeline toward Talosa. The River of Ashakai split into three at the city's western wall; one of the streams ran beneath the stone, while the other two wrapped around the city. There were more people in the flower fields than usual, visitors, all anxious to be in the capital for the royal union. It would be a celebration like no other, the first royal union between two of different kind. Human and Eerim wed.

The Biler followed as they walked down the wide road and toward it's gate, across the bridge that allowed entrance. A man atop his oxen-pulled cart passed on the bridge, smiling happily before he saw the Biler and his strange clothes. Santir thought perhaps he should have spared some of his own clothing for the Biler, but dismissed that idea as they entered Talosa. *Most Fair and Quo'Orinthian men dress much the same as these nobles, and there are so many people no one will notice one man. His clothes are not the worry, his thoughts—* My *thoughts. Stop thinking, stop thinking...*

Santir wasn't as thoughtless as he'd like. Bilers had forgotten about better ears by all accounts. Santir worried, but there was nothing he could do to stop Eerim listening if they wanted to. Few Eerim made it a habit to share, but there were vultures in Talosa.

Despite them, Santir loved the clamoring of the city after being away for so long. All of it: the bright colors, the fear of being heard (the thrill that his thoughts were worth repeating), the mingled shouting of vendors next to their high conical piles of aromatic spices or their hand stitched fabrics of traditional design. Warm air sat on the city, heavy, clean. The squeaking flow of carts over cobblestone, airships overhead lit purple trails of fading light.

Wielders juggled fire above their heads, shaping the flames like winged creatures and slinking prowlers that trailed after children's glee. The Biler's shocked eyes were flailing, staring at each colorful building, at people on their stone balconies and all around the street.

Santir looked around to see if there were any Eerim near. Thankfully he did not see any pointed ears. He could only hope that if any were near enough to hear the Biler's thoughts they would not understand the Eastern tongue. To many proud Eerim, learning the Eastern tongue, the tongue of Bilers and Zepeyans, felt equal to debasement.

"Come, and try not to think loudly," Santir said, checking himself, and guiding his companion under a stone bridge that connected the over-road. Squalling children in traditional grass skirts, late for classes, knocked into them. The little wielders juggled airstones from the front to the back of their group as they marched down the street to the Academy.

Santir dragged the Biler by the arm and stopped at one of the shops, a bright purple building with three levels. He bought a bag of candied Quo' Orinthian citron peels from the sweet old woman who lived in the level above. She patted her wrinkled hand on Santir's stubbled cheek and talked of the royal union, like everyone. She let her customers write on her walls, against the purple, paint splattered, "ARAEBORIL WILL SAVE!" alongside "ARAEBORIL WILL FAIL!", "REPENT. ETERNALITY BEGINS." and "GUARD THOUGHTS, GUARD GUNS"

Do Bilers have guns? Tufan, don't think about—

Can't believe my debt will be paid. I am almost free, almost, almost...

Santir wasn't trained in managing thought, simple farm boys weren't, but he kept the Biler close as he wove through the crowd. The Biler's large, bug eyes awed at everything, his head snapping back as a family of Ku'dur walked passed. The Ku'dur child stared with all of his eyes at the strange man in fur cloak, before sticking his little blue tongue out and drawing closer to his mother. The Biler drew closer to Santir.

"Be less of a tourist. Close your jaw," Santir said as he turned right off the main street. "You make people uncomfortable with your face. Is this trait of all Fair men, or is it specific to you?"

The Biler controlled his features to no expression, but Santir noticed how his right hand stretched as if itching for steel.

He reminded the Biler, "Stop thinking of anything. I mean, think nothing. Hum a tune in your head, a bad one, loudly. One more thing." Santir looked straight at the man. "Do not stare long into false eyes of Ku'dur. You'll regret it."

They turned their way down the sprawling mill, away from the main street that led into the city's vendor circles and their crowds. Santir kept his thoughts busy on nothing consequential. He stopped before a black stone building, half the stones deeply imprinted with the face of menacing creatures, the others displayed Ku'dur symbols of peace and good fortune.

Santir opened the yellow door and motioned for the Biler to walk inside; he followed, closing the door behind him. Thank Three-One, there were no Eerim in here. Santir didn't know what he would have done if there had been. Walk out and call the day a loss, he supposed.

Daashana noticed Santir as soon as he walked into the dimly lit bar room. "He is in the back, if you are here to see him." She flipped the fringe of hair out of her eyes, revealing the blood red paint on her forehead and eyelids. Her violet eyes gleamed against the smear of color.

Three men sat at a table near the back door, two plucking the strings of their instruments while the third blew melody into a wind-flute. The harmony cut in half as one man stopped playing to take a deep drink, hiccuping before he continued.

"I am," Santir said to Daashana, pointing to the empty table in the far corner of the room. Thankfully the Biler understood the gesture and sat at the empty table, facing away from the bar and the other patrons.

Santir walked up to the counter, craving a drink before seeing Tar L'Rej, the Ku'dur crook. Daashana leaned over and poured him something bitter, the light fabrics of her dress revealing her slender frame.

"Bargaining for more time on your loan again?" she asked. "Was your airship worth all?"

"Half an airship, truly, but I am here to pay it off." He placed the small pouch of gold onto the bar.

Her eyebrows raised into her hair. "Does that mean I will see you less and less?" She returned to cleaning cups.

"Shana," Santir called her attention. "Do you know anyone willing to take two men to Fair Isle?"

She gave him a stern look and shook her head, "*Fair Isle*? You seek trouble now, Detunae. You are more like your brother than you think." She gave him a wink and shameless grin. She dropped the grin when she looked to the Fair Biler in the corner, his hands folded on the table. "I will have someone get in touch with you. He is going to Fair Isle in two or three nights, and he runs any task if you sell him the right price," she finished and gave her attention and smiles to another man yelling for rum.

Drop them on Waterhaven's steps for all I care. They will receive a family welcome and sleep in featherbeds. Whatever taskman takes them. Santir made his way to the door that lead to the back room; the carvings on the door depicted men at battle wielding fire and winds against one another. These battles were once unheard of; wielders never fought each other on such scale, all Blessed and descended of the same. Until the Radical's war that ended two years ago. Wielders fought wielders, cousins against cousins for their different interpretation of prophecy.

"Santir," Daashana called before he walked into the gambling den. "Tell Yeroen that I am angry with him. He will know why."

"He always does."

Santir dipped his head beneath the frame as he entered the darker room. Immediately his nostrils filled with the harsh peppery scent of Achkan smoke.

Tar L'rej sat at the round moz'daur table with two other Ku'dur and a straight-haired Canyai with red patterned burns atop arms and neck. Child of Tandilyen. The wielder flipped over his stack of three-sided cards and tossed five silver Standard to the table's center before his curious eyes fell on Santir. Behind Tar L'rej, a Takircha taking the projected form of a red-headed man stood with a shortspear at his back, a warhammer in his hand, guarding the Ku'dur. His glowing red pupils settled on Santir, and he grimaced. Tar L'rej looked over the deck in his hand, looked at Santir, and everything else as he placed seven chips at the center of the elaborately carved table.

"Aw, little Detunae. You have what is owed me, yes? Or you would not be so silly to come find me." He held out his long white pipe to the child of Tandilyen, who flicked his fingers gently over the ground herbs to set them glowing.

Santir tossed the bag of coins onto their table, startling them. "Our debt is paid, and all your merciless interest. Fifty-two pure golden pieces equal to thirty gold Standard, all there."

"Funny how you still say, 'our debt' even after these two Rock turns, Detunae. Is Mouwat still paying off his share from Paradise?"

Santir breathed deep, swallowed the acid in his throat. His eyes fixed on the departing coins, not on any blinking eye. L'rej opened the pouch and picked up one of the gold pieces, turning it over in his fingers and pressing his thin wrinkled lips together. Santir imagined what it would be like to hit L'Rej, to see all those eyes widen in shock and then shut tightly in pain as Santir hit him as hard as he could. The eyes on L'Rej's arms and tops of his fingers blinked and narrowed at the gold, while the eyes beneath his brow never left Santir.

"This gold has the impressions of the Biler sun god. You acquired it beyond the Line."

Santir shrugged. "I didn't know that mattered to you."

"It doesn't. Gold is gold, and I will melt it anyway. Just curious, little Detunae. Curious, is all."

Santir waited for the Ku'dur to let him leave, not wanting to spend another moment here. Then a hundred eyes all fell to him at once as Tar L'rej released the orange smoke from his mouth.

"Will Detunae Yeroen ever go back to a wateryard? The Confederation misses him. Might he try his luck in the underground matches, or is your brother too moral for that?"

Santir sighed. "I wouldn't say 'moral.'"

"Maybe I wouldn't either. Quite the devoted follower to goodness and the Law now, I heard. Maybe not the *Law*, exactly, but you know. *Devotion*, your brother has it with more reason than most men."

"He will not fight again," Santir said.

"Not for sport, no. Dueling on the continent has gotten so boring. I do miss watching him ruin a man. There are not many like that Detunae. Few wield with such—*mmm*... as much art as combat." L'Rej turned to the Ku'dur seated at his left, saying, "I was there that day in Achka when he earned his ban, you know. A shame, really. It was more beautiful than awful. So much so that it took the crowd three full breaths to start screaming."

Santir needn't be reminded; he was there. He clenched his fists, time to think before speaking. It would not be wise to upset the thin-skinned Ku'dur, who had more gold than the better half of Quo'Orinth and kept himself surrounded by most lethal company. Santir didn't know how old L'Rej was. Some said he was approaching his six hundredth Rock turn, which meant he was alive when true magic had a foothold in the Confederation. L'rej had spent time in Confederation prison camps, some said.

Before Santir could form any response to the Ku'dur, a loud knock pounded at the back-entrance of the gambling room. Santir jumped, and before any could answer the knocking, six men and women of the city guard barged through, armored from head to toe, faces hidden behind their black masks.

One of the guardsmen kicked the spear from the blonde Takircha's grasp as another grabbed him and turned his arms behind his back. "Laoro Vin Maliot, four-nine-nine-seven-eight-three-three-eight, is this you?"

A snarling scream, as good as an answer.

"You are being arrested for the murder of Shilera Badal," came the voice of the tallest guard. "Are you guilty?"

Another scream.

Santir stood still and watched as the Takircha's eyes flashed fury while he struggled against the chain being locked around his hands. The flesh around his pale face and hands rippled like a moving river during rain, but the guards held him down as he thrashed against the table. Tar L'rej and the other Ku'dur backed away from the struggle, one tripping over his long white robes, while the child of Tandilyen only leaned a bit to the left in his chair.

Another guard grabbed the morpher at the elbows and three

worked to escort him out of the back door as he yelled curses. He vanished from Santir's view as they walked the street.

"How can we help you?" Tar L'rej asked and bowed his thin body toward the remaining four guards in the gambling room. His Ku'dur companions bowed as well.

A lithe woman stepped forward, removing her mask to speak. "Are you Tar L'rej?"

"I am," he said as he rose, delicately folding his long arms in front of his chest.

"You and your company will follow me for questioning."

"We would be delighted," he whispered and licked his lips.

She led the way for them out the door, and the fire wielder at last rose from his seat. She led them away from the bar, up the street, turning out of sight beyond a vendor's shop.

Santir knew this murder would not be connected to Tar L'rej. Nothing ever was; somehow, L'Rej knew how to keep his truths clean.

The remaining three guards looked around the smoke-filled room, taking in everything before settling on Santir. He felt anxious all at once.

The tall guard walked up to him and removed his fanged mask before he asked his question. "What is your name in full?"

"Detunae Santírek," his answer pulled by the child of Amina. The man wrote it down on his pad of shortleaf papers, nodding.

"What was your business here?" the guard asked as he directed Santir back through the door to the front bar room, his two men following. Daashana was talking to another city guard, her face indifferent as she answered questions. The drunks still played their rhythmic tune, and a drummer had joined them.

"I came to pay off a debt to Tar L'rej. I never met a Takircha named Maliot, never heard of one either."

"Right. Did you know the Takircha's number?"

"No. I do not usually keep track of a person's number."

"Of course you don't. Did you come alone?"

"No," Santir answered begrudgingly, the word straining against his lips. The child of Amina raised his brows, expecting him to continue. What choice was there now? It would be better to answer before another question. "I came with the Fair Person there."

"Who is he?" the city guard asked, using his chin to point to the blonde man seated at the corner table.

Santir thanked Three One that he had not paid attention to much of the Bilers' ramblings as words flew from his lips. "He is called Jaun-air something. I know little of him."

"What is the little you know of him?" A string of words almost spoken stopped at Santir's lips. *A smuggled foreigner, a Biler of Iceman steel and unholy upbringing, a nobleman.* Santir shirked, said nothing and fought retching. He knew it was a mistake to bring the Biler into Talosa. The guard asked, "Why is he here?"

"Coincidence. I think he is an idiot," he told the guard with a shrug, biting his tongue before he continued. "Half Fair, half something. Could be half rasush, no? He has that beak. The man does not speak a word of the Blessed tongue and glows a bit dim."

Quiet, Santir bit the inside of his cheek and waited. He looked at the child of Amina, at his judging silver eyes, fearful that the man might be as perceptive as Rae, who could always tell when truths were omitted. Always.

"Follow us," said the guard. "Bring the Fair man. We have more to ask both of you." The guard turned without watching to see if they would follow. Of course, they had no other choice.

I'm done, Santir thought over two years of crimes, no longer caring who heard. *My punishment will come soon enough, and then they shall send me to mine for years in the Confederation, and Yeroen will be locked away to confinement. Three-One, help us. Will Rae help us?*

"What is happening?" The rasush-faced Biler asked as a guard led him from his seat and out of the building. They walked behind the masked guards down city streets, and Santir avoided the prying stares of passersby; he tried to think of little when he saw the tapered ears.

"We are being apprehended for more questions."

The Biler whispered, "Apprehended?"

"Seized. Taken." Santir didn't know if he spoke worse than he thought, or if the Biler was too stupid to understand past an accent. "This is bad."

5. FATE OF BROTHERS

Mittrik feared becoming accustomed to waking with a headache. But he opened his eyes to find himself alone, and different fears became more immediate. He twisted out of his fur cloak, standing up in the warm room to assess his surroundings. A strong wind beat against the side of the mountain house, causing the walls to thrum. Eer combined with the unharmonious screeching from the world outside. Noise that cut through stone.

Jonn was nowhere to be seen, but his longsword and leather belt were set neatly atop one of the wooden chairs beside the table. Mittrik remembered that he left his own steel out in the small silver room of the flying stone, and he cursed his thoughtlessness.

He looked out the transparent wall and saw the western city folded neatly between two far off hills. It was more fantastic in the day, when the white walls were so crisp and bright against the green trees around it, clashing with the vibrant yellows and pinks freckled across the great distance. The tall tower Rae had called the 'sky eye' soared sharply above the low hanging puffs of white clouds, splendorous and shocking. Mist wove between the hills just beneath the mountain steep, rising from the trees like wisps of delicate lace. The sky was bluer than he had ever seen, not colorless or gray like the sky back home. He turned around the room again.

"Hello?" he called for anyone, peering down the corridor that led deep into the mountain, curving darkly into its depths like a tunnel.

He heard nothing in the house, only the constant vexing of the wilderness beyond the rock walls. A high-pitched cry twittered some obnoxious song, impossibly loud.

On the wooden table at the room's center, a slim goblet was

filled with water and set beside a large wooden platter filled with cut fruit— orange, red and yellow lined side by side. Mittrik drank the water in one loud gulp, and it was cold as a brisk rain. He ate quickly, greedily, his fingers dyed light pink by the red juices of the fruit.

"Jonn?" he called out. "Yero?"

There was still no answer.

He walked down the length of the narrow passage and turned left as it led him. He pushed open the first door on his left and looked into the room, which was small and empty, dust piled at its corners. He closed the door and called out once more to silence.

To the door's right a stairway led straight up to darkness. Down the tunnel further and to the right was another door, only this one was painted green and had watery flowers along its edge. He opened it slowly and was instantly surprised by the amount of light that flooded the room. Three large windows of transparent glass were angled at the room's ceiling, the sunlight beaming down into the mostly empty space.

There was a large bed at the right corner suspended by a yellow canopy. The only other thing to occupy the room were half a dozen large paintings stacked against the closest wall, and Mittrik immediately recognized many of the beautiful faces as Rae's. She looked like a captured memory, more life-like than any painting Mittrik had ever seen. Pale eyes ignited with joy in every scene, each something of wonder more confusing than the last.

His eyes fell to the largest of the paintings, where a man with eyes like moss had his arms wrapped around Rae's waist. They embraced between two cascades of blue water, both with toothy smiles on their tanned faces. The man's arms were marked, but not like the mage in those big blue curls; his arms and shoulders were covered in menacing thick angles of dark green and black. Even in the painting, his hold on Rae was tight. Mittrik realized the man must be the one that died in their war, the man Yero said Rae had loved.

In another painting, the marked arms wrapped around Rae's waist belonged to the copper skinned woman called Teia, her light curls and unmatched eyes giving her away. She was lifting Rae above her, sandaled feet kicking out in front of them, and Mittrik could see the delight painted on the women's faces so clearly, he could almost hear their laughter in the room. A woman with skin black as coal and short hair was to their side, dressed in elegant swirling colors, giving a half smile to the viewer; in her hands she held a bow and arrow. It appeared they were standing on wide branches high in a tree, surrounded by striped green leaves and long blossoms of orange.

In another, Rae was alone, seated on a black glistening rock in front of a shadowed waterfall, her back turned and bare to reveal her own strange marks running down the long length of her spine. The wine-colored lines were both sharp and smooth; jagged and curving, disappearing beneath the blue dress that crossed her lower back. She looked behind her shoulder to him, face half hidden in her dark brown curls, brows pinched over smiling eyes. He could even see the smallest droplets collected on her lashes.

Vulnerable, alone as he was with the images that seemed too real, he left the room quickly and headed to the front door of the home. He felt the need to piss and decided he would try and retrieve his sword from the air vessel while he was out there. He could try to place his hand on the glowing spot as he had seen the westerner do to lower the strange door of the stone.

The loud noises of the jungles quieted slightly as he walked out of the house and into the sunny day, and then picked up again just as quickly, as though the world had decided he was no threat at all. He could feel the thick dampness in the air settle on his skin as he walked down the even steps and onto the uneven earth.

A startling splotch of crimson against the light green leaves of the canopy caught his attention, and he jumped as his eyes met those of a magnificent and massive bird.

The bird was twice the size of a man, with ferocious black talons that glinted as it moved across the top of a drooping tree, shattering the brown skin of the branches with sharp serrated clenches; it stared at Mittrik all the while. Other, smaller birds flew off in fright.

The beast's bright head tilted back and forth, considering Mittrik. He moved to relieve himself in the bushes, keeping the menacing bird in the corner of his sight. As he finished, he turned to stare directly at the thing, taking in its viciously hooked beak and heaving yellow breast.

The great beast spread its imposing white wings and dove for him just as suddenly, its terrible *caw* slicing through him like a sword. Mittrik ran back toward the steps of the home as fast as his feet would carry him, jumping over the great roots that obstructed his path. He leapt over the steps leading up to the door, turning back to see the creature sat atop a tree directly across from him. The predator turned his head before releasing its dreadful shriek again. Mittrik spun into the door, shutting it tightly behind him as he made it inside the home.

He choked on his labored breaths, not quite believing how the bird had pursued him or how it had decided to stop just as abruptly. *Danger does lurk everywhere in the wes*t, he thought as he swallowed. *At least I managed to piss.* He ran his fingers through his hair and laughed to settle the nerves pooling in his gut.

He walked to the tapestry that hung on the far stone wall. Again, he saw the image of thirteen gods, just as the ruins, and just as he had seen from the sky when they crossed over that first western city. The gods were lined, shoulders touching, and the tight weaves of the drapery captured their harsh beauty and glittering crowns. The gods were surrounded by great curling waves and shattering mountains, fires exploding from the edges.

These are the Old gods, the gods of these people, Mittrik

discovered, amazed as he ran his finger over the detailed relief. *And these were the mystic people that once lived in the great spiraling towers of the Old Ruins.*

Boom.

Boom.

Pounding from the wooden door, and his hand instinctively went to his sword, but of course it was still in the air vessel.

Six men were suddenly before Mittrik in the front room, all armed and wearing black masks that looked similar to the beasts of the snarling wall sconces. They were all different creatures, some with dark straw manes and others with smooth pointed ears, and others even stranger. Their clothes were the same plated material that he'd seen on Rae, their arms and legs completely covered. The tallest, a tree of a man, had the fiercest mask of all, sharp white fangs covering his mouth and jaw and dark blue bristles like a mane.

"Are you Mittrik Hwaelin?" One of them asked, voice muffled by a bizarre beaked mask. He realized the person behind the mask was a large woman.

"Yes," he answered her. He had to. That familiar sensation of a witch stealing truth. He wondered how these wild people knew his name. When he asked his question, no one answered.

"Follow us," one of the masked people said.

"On whose command?"

The tree like man removed his mask, revealing dark skin, shining gray eyes, and a sour expression.

"Mine," he said. "I am one of the lead investigators of Talosa's city guard. You will please follow us, Lord Hwaelin. We have questions to ask you."

Mittrik looked at the company of masked westerners, each carrying a different weapon. One with a lizardshark's face, a thin and wiry man who had a two-sided spear tipped with a glossy red crystal; another had a short sword strapped to his hip and a quiver of feathered arrows at his back, but he had no kind of bow. The tall guard had two bastard blades strapped behind his shoulders. Even with his steel, Mittrik doubted he could take more than two before they killed him. Lacking a better option, he nodded and followed the wild party of guards.

He walked down the steps after them, looking to the mage's flying rock and wondering a last time about his sword. But there sat another strange stone-like creation, much larger and taller, that blew air into his ankles and lit up his eyes. This new flying stone was rounder, shaped like a smooth disk, the edges pulsing with a vibrant purple glow. It hovered a foot above the ground, releasing a warm gust of buzzing air that blew the tall grass apart. Mittrik's heart thundered in his chest as they approached.

The tall guard, with the steel colored eyes, placed one hand on the smooth side of the stone and covered his face with his lion mask. The stone let out a soft glow where his hand lay, and from nothing a large door released like a drawbridge, just as the other flying boulder.

Inside the larger stone, Mittrik was led to a narrow room lined with silver seats of rock. The masked woman placed a hand on Mittrik's shoulder to guide him into the middle seat, then took the place across the small space opposite him. The other guards filed into the room and sat on either side. They gave no more instruction.

Mittrik pulled the two restraints at his sides over his front just as he saw the woman do. None of the masked people acknowledged his presence again as he felt the stone ship slowly rise and jerk forward. His stomach fell into his groin as it had before. He itched to move but the journey lasted no time at all, and before Mittrik could calm his fears, they landed.

He was led out of the stone, straight into a damp corridor. It felt as though they were underground, and Mittrik fought the suffocating feeling that rose within him. *They will lock me up and do some magic on me now, sacrifice me to their gods. The thirteen. Where is Jonn?*

The one tall guard walked into a final room. It was cold and only contained a small table, two wooden chairs across from one another. Dips in the dark stone walls held colorful fires, setting off a steady prismic dance against the walls. The giant man shut the one door, motioned for Mittrik to take a seat, so he did. But the guard remained standing with unbent harshness.

"From where do you come?" he asked slowly, his western accent thick.

"Baeltaf." Mittrik felt the strain in his tongue as the word fought its way to be spoken. This guard was another child of Amina, as Rae had called herself.

"What is your full name and title?"

"Mittrik Hwaelin of Alluvel, second son of Tagnar Hwaelin, the High Lord of Kieln."

"Have you ever heard the name Shilera Badal?" the man asked, taking a seat across from him.

"No," he answered, watching as the man's face turned from suspicion to relief to suspicion again.

"Have you ever known or heard of a Skinchanger called Maliot?"

"No. A what?" Mittrik felt light headed.

"Have you ever known or heard of a Skinchanger with the given number four-nine-nine-seven-eight-three-three-eight?"

"No. A what?"

"A skinchanger, a Takircha. Morpher. Have you ever heard of a skinchanger?"

"No. What is that?"

"Your brother hadn't either. Why did you journey to Canyassor, Lord Hwaelin?"

"Adventure," flew up his throat. " My brother thought that there might be some danger in Kieln, so we left and found ourselves here."

"We have your brother," said the steel eyed questioner. "Do not worry yourself with what he thought. It is your time to answer. What danger is in Kieln?"

"I don't know. None," Mittrik said. *Jonn believes Father killed our Mother. That can't be true.*

"What kind of adventure did you seek when you came here?"

"More than I had," came his answer. "The kind that makes men more than they are."

They have Jonn somewhere, the thought distressed him. *What shall they do with us when the questions are done?*

"How did you get to Canyassor?"

"A man called Yero brought us over in the flying stone in exchange for gold."

"You made this deal?"

"Yes."

The man leaned back and rubbed his hands over his face. His fingers were thin and his palms covered with purple veinlike scars, raised skin shining gruesomely in the candlelight.

"The man who brought you to the Blessed Lands is one named Detunae Yeroen. When did you meet this man?"

"Two nights past, the very same night we left."

"Right. Had you ever met his brother Detunae Santírek before that night?"

"No."

"You didn't arrange to leave prior?"

"No."

"Who is the Other your mother wrote of in her letter to Rooj Talia?"

"I don't know."

"What do you know about the war of gold?"

"Nothing," he blurted. "War of gold?"

"Your mother wrote of it as well. Do you know anything about your mother's dealings with the west? Or do you have any thoughts, knowledgeable or otherwise, concerning her affairs beyond the Line?"

"No, no," Mittrik heard himself, but couldn't catch the questioner's meaning. *Could my mother have really dealt with the west, with this strange world? What is the Line?* "I do not know."

"Very well," the man said standing over him, "I am done with the questions. For now, Lord Hwaelin. I have heard much today from too many mouths. Please come with me this way."

Mittrik's fear grew as the imposing man led him down shifting tunnels and sharp turns, up a winding set of stairs and down a corridor that smelt of burnt honey. He remained quiet and followed the fast gait of the questioner. A narrow passageway opened into a cold white marble hall, lined on either side with wooden barred cells.

Inside the nearest cell, he saw Jonn seated beside the mage's brother and felt elated that he was safe, but Jonn looked in with rage.

Slim green windows filtered sunlight and cast the white room in a peculiar hue. There were three rectangular beds covered in the corner and a raised hole that looked like a privy. The questioner opened the wooden cage-like bars and shoved Mittrik inside. Mittrik heard the sound of a chain locking in place and the questioner left.

"You lied to me," Jonn said, standing at full height in front of him. His voice slapped the cold stone walls, louder than Mittrik ever heard his brother speak.

"I did," Mittrik answered as he stood back. "And I'm sorry."

"Sorry?" Jonn mocked. "You aligned yourself with the mage, dragged me to the Forsaken West, and now we may rot in this cell, and you say you're sorry with less conviction than when you broke my crossbow!" His voice had risen to shouting.

"You said we needed to leave Kieln," Mittrik matched his tone, "rambling as you were, that Mother did not end her own life. You wanted to go to Fair Isle, I haven't forgotten. Why? Tell me."

"I shouldn't have, I was wrong. Regardless we are both cowards for running. I was drunk on fear and delusion, but you were merely selfish, as you always are!"

"*Tufan*! Be silent!" came the accented voice of the westerner. "I would rather die than listen to you two. It is bad enough I am here with you, and my own brother is being hunted by city guard. Enough with this."

"What will they do with us now?" Jonn asked him.

The man laughed, but it was cruel. "How would I know what they plan to do with two Biler nobles? You should not fear. Blessed Men are not like Bilers. Likely the Tyano will decide due to your lank."

"Lank?" said Jonn.

"Your status. Lank or, or maybe rank— whatever."

"And the Tyano?" Mittrik inquired. "He's your king?"

"Tyano," the man replied, exaggerating the word. "But the great man is dying, so his children might be in charge of our fates. For me, Three-One willing. They have equal power."

Their king is dying, Mittrik's stomach lurched. The previous night, Rae told him that their Great Leader was known for compassion. He could only hope the same could be said for the sons. But he knew many sons unlike their fathers.

Jonn stared but said nothing, so the westerner continued, "But you do not care about me, so why does that matter? Just shut up and pray for mercies from your gods."

For the first time in two nights Mittrik thought of Leonara in Alluvel wondering where they could have gone. Sad and crying for them, perhaps she prayed in temple for their return. If she knew where they were she would be frantic, angry, inconsolable. She would believe them Doomed eternally for traveling to the Forsaken West, lost to prayer and salvation. She might be right. Mittrik wondered if he would die in this cold western cell before seeing her face again.

Night settled, half the city waking, half turning to rest. Fehatsi's fingers worked out tangles in Rae's long hair, twisting strands from her face with lightweight oil. Rae sat at Fehatsi's feet, her nose scrunched and stare intent, writing in the margins of a book written in a foreign script. Fehatsi watched as Rae scribbled furiously with her coal pencil, underlining and referring back to stained pages, all marked up similarly with her slanted writing of blended Biler and Blessed letters. Rae was not so great at languages, not naturally gifted for them like Fehatsi, but she was a persistent student. Her green eyes flicked above their heads every so often, distracted. Trying to stay on task.

Fehatsi might be jealous of wielders, but she never envied Rae's ability to see truelight. It seemed a horrid distraction.

To Rae's side, Ambos purred loudly in sleep, small paws curling and stretching to reveal his claws in sequence. The laijirei's bushy tail flicked contently in both directions as Rae scratched the thick tufts of fur behind his ears.

Teia was seated behind Fehatsi on the mattress, legs crossed, working Fehatsi's short hair into tight knots and covering them in the frothy cream from saso roots. The candles washed the room in a yellow that wavered on the walls like a flag, painting shadowed illusions on the draperies. Rae constantly changed the wall hangings, and the ones she had now were fish done in traditional geometric stitching, bright colors atop black cloth. Simple and beautiful.

The night sky was blocked from the three women, the windows long ago sealed with stone. Though it was not Rae's decision, she would say that she preferred her room this way; she would say it was calmer for her vision, but her eyes darted around them following something Fehatsi could never hope to see.

Fehatsi favored the room back in her family's home down the main road, where she had her own balcony on the fifth level that looked over shops along the flower vendors' circle, a shining curved window of stained sea glass. But this was Fehatsi's place, by Rae. She finished combing through her friend's hair and wrapping it back in soft Quo-Orinthian silks.

"I have been going over your letters. Will you write back to these people?" Fehatsi asked Rae, knowing the answer.

"No. You do that for me." Rae hated writing letters, and worse hated responding to admirers. Fehatsi wrote most that

Rae should have. "Won't you?"

"I will, but only if you have no more contact with the Bilers," Fehatsi finally said what she wanted, trying not to sound scolding. It wasn't Rae's fault that the Detunae brothers consistently worked to bring trouble to their lives. Respectable women of their names should never have met any of them, Detunae being so... ill-bred, and Mouwat being so *poor*. But Rae attracted any and all.

Rae stared at Fehatsi, lips pressed into a childish pout. "I don't see the harm in being kind to Bilers."

"The harm," Fehatsi scoffed. She watched as Rae stood to retrieve the Eastern tome from its secret place in her desk. Ambos growled at her loud shuffling and stood as well, slinking out and growing until he was the size of a large hound.

"The harm is that the Selection is in less than three passings of the moons," Fehatsi reminded her, "and you should be thinking of that. There are only eighty odd nights before you will be Selected and life changes absolutely. You will be a holy judge. Even this, us three as a unit like we always have been, that changes."

"That will never change." Rae scooped up the laijirei and tossed him onto the mattress, throwing herself beside him and opening the heavy book with a sigh. The black beast shrunk back to a cat's size,and curled in his spot on her pillow. The laijirei yawned, exposing his two rows of glinting white teeth.

Teia turned to smirk at both of them.

"Never. I am on your side," she said to Rae, "and I don't think the Bilers are a problem either. Even though one is obviously Fair, he doesn't look like a man with a scheme," Teia said as she wiggled her eyebrows suggestively. "Trust me, Feha, when I say these men are not the brightest stones."

Fehatsi scoffed again. "I don't think they would advertise their scheming. That man is not only half Fair, they are both half *Rooj*. Above all things you can count on the Rooj to be enacting plans in Biler country. Don't look at me like that, Rae.

We know nothing of these men. It is not safe. Teia is only supportive because she enjoys flirting with Detunae Yeroen, and he brought them here."

Fehatsi still couldn't comprehend why Teia was interested in the barred water-dueler. He was handsome, true, but Teia was beautiful enough to capture any handsome man's attentions. He was a gifted wielder but could not hold a tide against Teia's natural strength. Detunae's name held fame, but Teia's name held more, it was long established and did not yet carry any shame. Fehatsi could not understand why Teia risked her reputation for such a man, especially when the man was so much in love with Rae— not that he would ever admit it. Yeroen had more sense than that. Fehatsi was certain it was only sex between the Teia and Yeroen, but sex didn't seem like a good enough reason.

Though I suppose Teia has never much concerned herself with reputation, Fehatsi thought. *She's always known she can do anything, and in turn is contented with doing very little. It must be nice to be one of so many Leuanien, to come from a line of bold warrior women as Teia. There are more options for such people, well-to-do positions and high status could not be demanded from every person. She could have been a Select Child as well, if she had the foresight and will to do so.*

Teia shrugged to them both as she finished winding her fingers around Fehatsi's course curls and pinning them in place. "Yeroen understands me," she said softly.

"Because you are such a complicated person," Fehatsi replied, rolling her eyes. *He could not understand her as we do,* she thought. *Having commonalities is not the same as understanding. They're not the same. We understand her. She just likes attention.* Teia yanked hard on the last curl between her fingers, as if she heard Fehatsi's thinking, and she flinched in pain.

"Oh, sorry," Teia laughed.

Fehatsi glared. She would make her pay for it tomorrow at the Academy during training. Fehatsi could see Rae fighting a smile as she flipped through the pages. Teia might have strength over currents and great waters, but Fehatsi was skilled with a thin blade and faster than everyone, excluding Rae. No one was faster than truelight. Fehatsi worked twice as hard for twice as long, not having the advantage of being born a wielder. *Rae will get more practice at healing open wounds tomorrow*, Fehatsi laughed to herself.

She sighed before explaining to her lyaren, "I just don't think it's wise to rush into communicating with these noblemen. Their ways are strange, Rae, and we know so little about these people. I am on your side, no matter what. I want you to do what you need to do, but that starts with the Selection."

"Yes, it is not like we are unaware," Teia said without compassion. "In three passings of the moons, Rae resigns herself to congress every third day for the rest of her second planed life. Sitting there and sentencing criminals to their fate. And if you are going to start pretending that life is something less than abysmal, I don't think I am a good enough player to go along with the act."

Rae frowned at the pages in her lap and stretched her long fingers, letting them spark, so Fehatsi interjected. "I think your dramatics are fine, Teia. She is going to be the Select Daughter of Amina. That has already been decided. It is silly to keep on complaining, even though it is not such a happy thing. She will do her duty well."

This was decided the moment she was born, the words would only upset Rae. Unlike Fehatsi, Rae was not content with her place. To be one of the twenty-six Selected Children was a sure bliss, but Fehatsi knew that Rae never thought she would end up here. She truly believed that she would marry Mouwat Kloennian, a nobody menagerie boy. She thought they would go wherever the truelight took her, and they'd have a dozen empathic little children. Fehatsi had believed it, too, because Rae so often got her way, but deep down she wondered if they would have made it. She didn't think they would have, regardless of the war. *Rae's path always led here, and her path is mine*, Fehatsi thought.

Most of Rae's actions only gave credit to the stereotypes people believed of children of Amina. Her dreams were fickle and she put too much weight in them, her attention was often fleeting, and she was never where she was supposed to be, much to Fehatsi's annoyance. But Rae's power was something only written of in histories and holy scriptures. The residing Select Son and Daughter of Amina had been at her side since birth, encouraging and refining that power, closer to her than her own parents had been.

And Fehatsi was her second, her Korr in all but name, and that meant she would make sure Rae did her duty and behaved with honor.

"Is there anything in those old books that might help your father?" Teia asked after a yawn, her cheek resting on Rae's knee.

Rae's face changed into something between rage and disappointment, but her voice remained steady. "I haven't found anything yet, but I have only reviewed the one. Santir and Yeroen brought back five binded works. I am still holding hope, but all this self-called *healer* wrote of are atrocities Northmen inflicted upon Ku'dur during the Separation, and the experiments they did on their false eyes." Rae said the word 'healer' like she took personal offense. She shut her eyes tightly and shook her head. "The stuff of nightmares."

"Is that what causes you to thrash about in your sleep these past nights? Too many medical books?" Fehatsi wondered aloud, not expecting an answer.

"No," Rae said, but did not go on to explain. "I wouldn't call this a medical book."

"What is it made out of?" Teia asked, running a finger against the thin red cover. Rae looked up.

"I advise you not to ask."

Teia grinned. "Now I am more curious. What is it?"

"It is bound in Takircha skin."

Teia gasped and rubbed her hand roughly against the blankets. "Made of skin? How horrible."

"You shouldn't read it," Rae said. "All disgusting and cruel, and it might be I am reading it for nothing."

Fehatsi stretched her back before reclining on Rae's other side, sensing the conversation was over. Rae shook about in her sleep more nights than not; it was slowly getting worse, not better as Fehatsi's father had assured her—and her father was hardly ever mistaken. But the previous night Rae screamed so loudly that guards barged into the room, one with a sword and the other with his spear, ready for the fight. It was a dream about the Achkan woman, Rae had told them, but Fehatsi could tell it was more.

She did not understand why Rae was keeping secrets. They were her closest companions. Rae always told Fehatsi and Teia the truth in full, the horrible and disturbing truths.

And they had cried over everything together: the murder of Fehatsi's brother while he slept in his tent in CoБmak, and the death of Mouwat Kloennian in the collision of the battle, ambushed as they were. Both had suffered gruesome deaths —and Fehatsi shuddered but could not help and imagine it again—her brother choking with split throat, blood in his sleeping mat, looking up at the man who betrayed him. Fehatsi imagined the simple lands' wielder that had become her friend choking on the cursed chemical airs of a plague, fighting against Radicals to his last breath. Klo didn't deserve Rae, but he deserved better than that.

They had mourned together, and while killing those responsible salved some of Fehatsi's pain, Rae suffered more for it. Killing Sfar'Laki and his men changed her. Truelight was an effective, yet costly weapon.

Even after the deaths of Rajen and Kloennian, during those days and miserable nights after the fall of Sfar'Laki in the Wilder Tower, Rae had remained open with Teia and Fehatsi while she ostracized herself from her family. Rae told them of the torture she felt when the truelight took the lives of two

Takircha warriors and the Kud'dur warlord, described it to them in detail so vivid Fehatsi would vomit if she thought on it too long. Rae felt the pain of each life before extinguishing it; she felt it all in a mere second.

Now is not the time for secrets, Fehatsi thought. *Now is the time to stay close. What is she keeping from us? It must be terrible. Why not tell us if she must give it to the world? How can we help if we do not know?*

Fehatsi blew out the flames of the candles and returned to lay on Rae's right side.

"You should sleep," Fehatsi said.

"I will," she replied as she turned another page, her right hand positioned over the book, shining in the dark. Her fingertips caught sparks of soft lightning where they twitched. "Soon. But I feel like I am close to discovery."

'Soon'. A subjective truth for Rae, but Fehatsi nodded and rolled away from the torch of truelight. Fehatsi yawned when Teia did, and hoped she could convince Rae that Bilers were not worth time or care. She hoped Rae would turn all her focus to the coming Selection. The soft sound of Teia's snoring came, but Fehatsi was kept awake by the truelight at her back and a foul pressure building in her gut. It felt like a warning.

Jonn paced the length of the cell he shared with his brother and the westerner, trying to plan for anything. He knew that daylight was approaching by the lifting green light in the room, stretching sharp shadows on the floor. He got little sleep over the night, waking constantly with an anxious heart. Mittrik sat crosslegged with his head in his hands, occasionally raking them through his hair. He at least had the decency to look ashamed. Santir was asleep on the floor.

Jonn still did not understand how things had gone awry so quickly in the city. Wrong place and wrong time, that is what Santir told him, though it did not matter how or why once he was alone and the questioning started. He was powerless against the magic tongue of the dark westerner, just as he had been with the woman called Rae. It made him feel weak. He said too much to these foreigners, far too much. Jonn thought of what his father might say if he were put to this test, if he knew about such a people that could pull truth from a man's mind. Would his father forgive him?

He would have to, Jonn surmised. Could he forgive his father?

Would he have to?

He clutched his mother's letter in his hand, reading the words over and over again. It was the letter that set off a new flood of questions he was incapable of answering, leaving both he and the investigator confused and angry.

What danger did your mother fear in your home? Who is the Other, the Bringer? Do you think your mother took her life?

He did not know. He did not know. He could not know anymore.

Why did you want to go to Fair Isle?

"To avenge my mother," Jonn had confessed.

How? He didn't know. *You still want to avenge her?*

Again. He did not know. Jonn didn't think he could avenge his mother and also achieve that which he most wanted. He could not have his crown and vengeance both.

Jonn needed to get back to Kieln. There, he would decide a course of action. Think clearly without mages and daemons ruining his life. In Kieln, he would face his father.

The mage's brother woke, stretching his neck this way and that, the loud cracks startling Mittrik to look up. Mittrik and Jonn exchanged angry glances but said nothing. Jonn had never been so exhausted by his brother. Was he Doomed, now? Would Hetten really condemn him for traveling west when his brother made the decision? Would he be Doomed for his brother's mistake? *That's exactly what the gods would do,* Jonn thought, remembering the stories.

He heard the patter of footsteps approaching and turned to look down the shadowed corridor. The child of Amina, the cold man with hooking questions, came into the light, his mask in one hand. A chain of keys in the other.

"Lords," the questioner said as he came to the cage door, unlocking the chain that held the wooden frame in place. It swung open and for a while, he said nothing. But then, "The Tyanien wish to see you now."

"The what?" Jonn asked, squaring his shoulders.

"Tyanien," Santir said groggily from behind them. "Tyano's children. Good tufaned luck."

Jonn and Mittrik were led out of their cage, down wide corridors and up two levels of winding steps before a heavy steel door opened into sunlight. The left of the passing corridor was open and held up by round columns. From the gaps between them he could see the tall, multicolored towers of the city. The guard turned right at the end of the corridor and came before two wide wooden doors.

The high frieze above the double doors was elaborated with the designs of thirteen crowned people, their hollow eyes looking down in judgement. Four guards stood on either side of the entrance, faces covered in those awful animal masks. The inquirer pushed both doors open into a great hall, and they walked under an arch of purple flowers as they entered behind him.

The ceiling domed toward the heavens and large crystal chandeliers hung, suspended flames swaying prettily. Though there were no windows, the hall was warm with light. There were fiery torches along the walls, placed between vivid tapestries and delicate wooden carvings that stood taller than any of them.

The room was empty besides that and the dais, the throne at the center.

Two men stood above them on the high dais, a large white limestone throne behind them. They wore tunics of colorful stripes and the broader of the two men wore a dragging blue robe that was sheer over it all. Both men were deep brown in coloring, the larger with thick hair twisted with rich ribbons and chains of gold piled at the top of his head, a few locks falling over his brow. The other man's hair was closely shaven as his beard, making his thin face look sly.

"Lords of Baeltaf," the slender man said, his eyes the bright color of gold. He stepped down the steps of the dais. "You are welcome in Canyassor. I am sorry for any discomfort you have felt while in our great city. I am Tyanien Teviona Zyonhir, second child of our Tyano Iial. And this is Tyanien Teviona Bakéz, the first child of the Tyano."

"Lords," the barrel-chested man next to him said, nodding his head in greeting. His voice was higher than Jonn thought it would be. "My city guard told me the story of your arrival here. It is good luck we meet."

Mittrik was looking around the place excitedly, a hint of a smile showing. Jonn coughed out humidity before speaking to the dark princes.

"I apologize for your trouble. My brother and I only desire to return to Baeltaf, I assure you. It was a mistake that we came here, an accident. We had no desire to offend."

"And no offense was given, Lords, I assure you," the larger prince said. "I am told all. Be at peace, there is no danger for you here. I understand you find yourself in the Blessed Lands by chance, and what a chance that all of us will speak for once in nearly seven hundred turns. We have made arrangements for you to return to your Dominion on the morrow as the Great Fire, eh the Sun, that is, disappears. Does such a thing please you?"

"Yes," Jonn exclaimed. A weight lifted and he allowed himself to smile at the men. "That is great news. Thank you."

"Of course, Lord Hwaelin. But now, please rest. I shall have someone show you to rooms and see you are given fresh clothes after we break our fast. Are you hungry?"

"Ravenous," Mittrik said, beaming up the dais. "Thank you."

"No thanks are necessary, Lord Hwaelin. Men must be fed. We shall eat in the gardens. Please, this way."

They obeyed and together walked into a smooth white

corridor beyond the hall, trailed by the eight masked guardmen. They walked through a curtain of bright yellow leaves, into an outdoor space. It seemed Jonn was in the jungle again; sunlight trickled in through the breaks in the foliage. A flock of green flitting insects flew across the path and up into a tall broad-leafed tree.

From somewhere near, Jonn heard the trickling of a stream.

"This is incredible," Mittrik exclaimed as they turned right on the path past a sweet-smelling tree.

"Yes, the gardens are well maintained," the first son of the Tyano said, his light green eyes glinting fondly. "My mother planted many of the flowers. They were her joy."

The man spoke in the past tense of his mother and Jonn's own heart ached.

"My brothers and my sisters might be joining us this morn, lords," the thin prince said as they walked atop a wooden bridge that passed over the stream. "It is hard to keep secrets here, and some have heard that men of Baeltaf are in the palace. They are excited to meet you. Most Canyai have never seen a Biler."

Jonn still wore the scarlet and gold colored doublet from his mother's mourning day, and his brother was dressed in a boiled leather jerkin over a dirty tunic and rough-spun wool trousers. They were not suited to meet any western royals.

A dark wooden table came into view. It was in the middle of a ring of torches planted in the dirt.

A woman sat already, devouring a deep blue fruit. Half her head was shaved smooth and painted atop the hairless skin were designs of pinkish blossoms. The half of her black curling hair was let loose. She wore a blue dress, sheer over her midsection and arms. She might as well have been naked. Her skin was dark and appeared soft to touch, her face long and beautiful. The woman looked up and got a wild look in her eye.

She dropped the fruit to the plate in front of her with a plop.

"It is true," she said. "Bilers in Canyassor. I thought Pyaren lied through his teeth."

"Hanala," the older prince said to her. "This is Lord Jonnere Hwaelin and Lord Mittrik Hwaelin of Baeltaf. Lords, this is my sister Tyanien Teviona Hanala."

"Just Hanala, please," she said sweetly and offered her hand to Jonn with a smile. He took it and kissed the skin of her knuckles, soft like he suspected, as was his custom. He looked up into her keen brown eyes, hoping the gesture well received.

She smiled widely and passed her hand to Mittrik, who looked too eager.

"And the others?" the older prince asked his sister.

"Ammi is with Bapo. The rest are at the academy. This is better. I am less interesting compared to my siblings, and I have so many." She turned her back to them to take her seat around the table.

"Very good, it is just us, lords. We shall eat and then I will have you brought to your rooms, so you may rest and prepare for your journey home on the morrow night."

Jonn took a seat across from the princess, alongside his brother, while the dark princes sat at the head of the table. They began reaching for the high towered fruit placed before them. Mittrik wasted no time and joined the feasting. For the first time since his mother's death, Jonn felt something like hope.

6. FAMILY TEVIONA

Alone in the largest guest chamber Mittrik had ever seen, and nothing to occupy him. Jonn's rooms were just across the corridor. His rooms couldn't be *this* big. There couldn't be many rooms *this* big, Mittrik thought, perusing. He had slept for a long while, the plump mattress of the bed made it feel as if he floated on water, and now he was paced the dark floor. Mittrik wouldn't believe even the king in High Baeltaf had such rooms.

His stomach rumbled in nervous expectation; his hands sweat like the backs of his knees. He wasn't creative enough to anticipate whatever wild thing would happen next in this dangerous New World. He placed two fingers on the red glowing stone mounted into the wall, just as the servant girl had done when she left him here. The fires inside the glass walls died in an instant, and the rooms darkened except for the setting daylight shining in from the long, rectangular windows. He pressed his fingers on the scarlet stone again, and the warm glow behind the crystal roared alight in vibrant flames.

He let them clean him, dressed in their offering of clothes, and now he waited. He ran his hand over the shimmering, armored patch on his trousers, expecting the metal scales to clank. They did not feel smooth like metal. They felt stiff and solid as small pebbles, lined in uneven rows, but the breeches were weightless.

There came a soft tapping at the door soon enough.

The servant who showed him to the rooms and cleaned his bare arse was on the other side, looking nervously down the hall.

"Lord? Time for foods with family Teviona." The dark girl was buxom, timid. Mittrik liked girls like that. Her brown hair was short and wound into two rows of knots across her scalp.

Jonn stood in the hall behind her, looking as anxious as Mittrik felt. He also wore the foreign clothes, though his shirt seemed to be stitched together of blue woven strips.

The corridors of the palace were wide and winding, and Mittrik wondered if they would ever reach their destination. His hunger gnarled in his stomach. They followed the pretty girl down two stairwells, over a bridge,. She ignored Mittrik's flirting, and suddenly threw open a blue door.

A loud jungle appeared.

Tyanien Bakéz, first born, stood waiting with two women. He greeted them with a smile and open arms.

"I hope you have a strong hunger, Lords. Forgive my brother Zyonhir. He is too busy preparing for my brother's arrival from the Confederation to eat with us tonight. However, he sends his regards," the crowned prince said. "But this is the Onatae, or you would say Queen. The Tyano's wife, and Canyassor's Mother. And this is Kwalí, my wife, mother of my children, and a talented alchemist," he added with a kiss to the taller woman's cheek. Her shoulders were deeply colored and bare.

The Queen's cheeks dimpled when she grinned. She was considerably lighter in complexion than the rest, light as a southern lady left in the sun; brown freckles ran across her whole body—freckles the same color as her eyes. There was a graceful softness to her arms and wide flaring hips. She wore a blue shawl over her head.

"Your grace," Jonn said, bowing to the foreign queen. Mittrik bowed as well.

"Oh, no," she said, touching his shoulders and straightening him. "Dianis is just fine, Lords Hwaelin. I am not a fan of titles for myself. I never liked them, and I earned none." Her thick accent like a rythmic song. "Let us eat and you may meet my children."

They walked atop the mossy brown earth, and the westerner's sandals made no sound. A funny cuckooing came from above, and Mittrik looked up into the large shaded tree.

A hawk-like bird with a long gradient tail of rainbow colors opened its short beak to call again, and this time it sounded like a woman's laughter.

In another tree, a hoot came in response, and Mittrik saw a furry brown animal in the canopy. The creature swung with long arms from vine to vine and into another tree of bright pink and blue. As it got closer, Mittrik could see on its back a smaller dark mass that blinked at him. The leaves shook as the fuzzy mass screamed. He looked away, remembering the bird that attacked him at the mage's house.

He trusted western animals less than western people.

They passed beside a thick yellow plant, and he heard a buzz so loud it hurt his ears. Jonn looked to him, fear in his eyes.

"Those are the chipara," Bakéz said when he saw their glances. "They like to sing at night."

"Of course, they do." Mittrik looked around the life teaming parade of trees and plants. *And I thought my mother's garden was extravagant.*

They turned the corner around a cottony green bush and walked into the circular clearing with the long wooden table. Two dozen chairs placed for a large party.

The half bald princess, Hanala, and four men of her same dark complexion were standing in front of it; their loud foreign speech stopped when they saw Mittrik and Jonn. The men wore thin brown shirts with stitched details of bright color over long breeches. They all had the same dark hair. Two of the men had the very same face, the same long noses and hooded eyes, though one had a thick scar that swelled from brow to chin that left the right half of his face deformed and his beard sparse.

The shortest the men was without his left leg, cut off just above the knee. Either hand rested on the curled nodes of a glossy walking cane, leather bands wrapped around his forearms to secure them.

"Lords Hwaelin, these are my younger siblings, only five of the ten Tyanien, I am afraid. That is Malak," Bakéz pointed to the one with long hair and his mother's dimples. "And Pyaren." The man with one leg nodded.

"And the double born with the gruesome face is Janseyu, and the clean shaven one is Owéttan." Both men had the same vivid green eyes as Tyanien Bakéz, a green so light and barely existing that it was almost terrible.

"Ajísh!" the one with the scar said, coming closer to Jonn and Mittrik. "This is a crazy time for Bilers to find themselves in the Blessed Lands. Really extraordinary timing." And then his mouth rolled off in their native language.

"Will this be all of us?" the oldest prince asked his wife, his tone high and surprised.

The blue-eyed woman responded in their lilting way, cackle rising at the end and the others joined her; the princess Hanala snorted boorishly.

There was a rustling in the trees, and Mittrik turned to see the three women from vivid paintings come to life, walking around the cottony bush. Rae, the woman of bewitching questions, led the other two. She was dressed in a tight green gown, sleeves sheer. The bottom half was slit up the side to reveal the curve of her thigh; the thin hem just grazed the muscle of her calves. *Barefoot*, Mittrik realized and looked up to her face. Her hair was half pinned up. Braids wrapped around the loose waves that fell down to the small of her bare back. Her back covered in western tattoos. What a sight. Mittrik knew he stared stupidly.

Couldn't help it.

Prince Bakéz acknowledged her less so. "And my youngest sister, Tyanien Aadarae, who never fails to make an entrance."

"I have already met the Hwaelins," Rae said standing at his side. Teia and the darker woman disappeared into the garden.

"You have? When?" Bakéz questioned. Mittrik heard the tension of it.

"A night past." Rae smirked at the oldest prince before addressing them. "I didn't expect to see you again so soon, Lords of Hwaelin."

"Yes," Mittrik could only whisper the word, confused as he was. He'd thought the woman a commoner, a beautiful one, nothing more. A common western woman whose questions could never be refused, a witch who loved a dead man who died in war. A princess, he never guessed. Even looking at her now, bare legs and wild hair, he didn't know who would guess, Princess.

"Here, all! Let's eat," called the smooth faced twin from a chair, already eating. "I am near starved."

"Yes, fine," Bakéz said. He kept his eyes on Rae as she took her seat. "Let's eat."

Mittrik took a place to the left of Jonn, across from Rae and her twin brothers. Princess Hanala was at his right. As she sat, the cut in her dress moved to reveal her ribcage, the soft skin above her ribs were also marked with the designs of flowers. Prince Bakéz sat near the queen, their Onatae, who was prominently in the largest chair at the head of the table.

The food before them smelt of exotic, peppery spice, and pots of white, green, red, and orange let out trails of rising steam. Mountains stacked high with round flat bread, stacked in shallow baskets, their sides covered in colorful depictions of birds and flowers. Deeper baskets almost toppled with red oblong fruit, yellow round ones and pink berries, another fruit like lumpy brown apples. There was a blackish fare that looked slimy and less appealing. Between the steaming plates and mountains of color, clay jars and flagons held different drinks. Bowls of grain were being passed around, and Mittrik watched as the royals dipped their hands into the grains to scoop out their serving.

The queen called to one of the two servants attending, and shortly after, misshapen cutlery was placed before Mittrik and Jonn. She smiled to the men and said nothing.

Jonn thanked her and used his wonky fork to cut a piece of stiff green vegetable.

"How do you know these Bilers?" the dimpled one asked Rae, his round cheeks lifted in a kind smile. His chin dimpled as well when he grinned so widely. "You said you met them."

"I was at Klo's house when Detunae Santir and Yeroen came with them."

"Detunae brought them?" The twins spoke together, the unscarred asked, "They go beyond the Line?"

"That is very lucky for you, sister," the prince said and drank from his crystal goblet. "Very, very lucky that you keep such *batíseral* as friends. Unexpecting company brings unexpected treasure."

"Malak," the queen's voice was disapproving but reminded Mittrik of the man's name.

"Luck has nothing to do with it," said Rae. "I am blessed."

Mittrik dipped a piece of bread into the hot bowl of thick red in front of him. The moment it touched his tongue, there was burning. Delicious and salty the burning, but only for a second, then all Mittrik could feel was that growing pain at the back of his throat. He drank from the goblet in front of him, thankful for the cool water, and he tried not to cough.

He decided to be safe and pick at the different slices of colorful fruit. He ate at a yellow slice of sweet tanging flavor that made the back of his cheeks tighten painfully. What he would have given then for Roose's pork pie. Pork pie didn't try to hurt him.

Mittrik ran his fingers over the impressions along the table: those familiar thirteen gods lined side by side from one end to the other. The two visages before his seat looked angry somehow, two square-headed men with arms crossed.

"Your land is very green and beautiful, and the craftsmanship I have seen here is extraordinary," Mittrik said, trying to make conversation. "I have seen the great statues of the thirteen gods in the Old Ruins of Kieln. They still stand at great heights, even years since Old."

"The thirteen are not our gods." Princess Hanala looked at him oddly. "We have one god. The thirteen you see are our ancestors." She looked as though she didn't know how to speak to him, a face similar to Mittrik's father's when Leonara would ask a question, not yet old enough for the answer.

"The monuments of the First Children remain in Old Orinth?" Prince Scarface asked between one mouthful and the next. "But without wielders and stones, the Children cannot keep the tides back or control your winds, no? Just statues now. Pitiful, pointless."

"Pardon, I do not understand," Mittrik said.

"The First Children," said Queen Dianis with readily given, toothy smile. "They are not gods who get worshiped. The Canyassor was built on their blood, so we honor in their remember." Mittrik felt rather stupid, even though he wasn't the one butchering the language, but he nodded.

"I believe I heard something of the First Children when I arrived," Mittrik said, looking to Rae. She smiled.

"Shall I tell you the history of our people, Lords of Hwaelin? It is a fairly new one as far as histories go," the queen offered.

"Ugh, Ammi," Princess Hanala groaned and swallowed her mouth's fill. "They leave tomorrow across the Line."

"I have always enjoyed history," Mittrik told them, hoping to hear more of this world while he had the chance.

"See, Hanala?" The queen rebuked gently. "The polite noble knows when to speak and when to listen."

Mittrik ignored Jonn chuckling quietly into his fist, and the queen poured herself a glass of red wine. She spoke dramatically with her hands and took a drink in between the story.

"Forgive my speech, Eastern words are not natural on my tongue. Back two thousand turn-rounds of the Rock, in the time of Chained Men, when humans were bought and sold, the Ku'dur and Eerim— they controlled this world, and they were cruel. Three-One heard the cries of the people begging for freedom. First-One rose the ground of the Canyassor, the Blessed Lands, from the seas and placed upon its untouched ground two new humans— made in the Maker's hands. Their children were the First Children of Canyassor, blessed with the energies they wielded, thrice commanded to be stewards and protectors on the Rock.

'The first wielders of waters: Leu, Ashakai, Syornan, and Natinae. The first wielders of grounds: Emín, Hahnae and Byelro. The first wielders of airs: Jeyen, Fetín. The first wielders of flames: Yett, Rionae, and Tandilyen. And Amina, first wielder of truelight. Over the next two hundred turn-rounds, humans were freed of their bondage as the tribes grew and grew and warred against human and nonhuman slavers."

"Three thanks," Malak mumbled as he brought the food up to his mouth with his hand, licking his fingers. "That is the abridged version."

Jonn looked nervously at Mittrik before he said, "Thank you. Such histories are unknown to our people, your grace—pardon, Dianis."

"You should not leave tomorrow, you have only just arrived," Rae abruptly said, eyes brimming with excitement. "You should remain here for the union, the wedding of my brother Tyonar."

"When is that?" Mittrik asked, ignoring Jonn's shifting gaze. He could practically feel the dread take root in his brother.

"Only seven days and nights away," Hanala answered from his side, standing to pour more wine into the mismatched cups. "Fast approaching."

Mittrik glanced at his brother sitting back in his chair and drinking deeply from his golden goblet, then he turned to ask Rae another question.

Jonn cut him off. "The offer is generous, thank you, but I am afraid we must get back to our home, Alluvel, as soon as we can."

"Yes, of course, Lord Hwaelin," the first son of the Tyano said loudly.

Then Mittrik saw a daemon.

Without announcement, a man came into the garden space, strutting with a beautiful daemon on his arm. She wore a thick hood of silver, lined with black feathers, over a shifting blue gown that clung to her lean figure.

But Mittrik only saw her eyes. Whiteless and too large. All black. Elven eyes, tar pits to doom as the songs and legends said.

"Yasháno!" Prince Bakéz shouted.

"Tyon!" the twins and Rae yelled in unison, looking up in the same instant. They rose and rushed to the dark man and the elf.

"Teviona!" the man yelled back, and then whistled like a bird as five of the royals knocked him back with their hug.

The brother with one leg, whose name Mittrik could not remember, stayed in his place and continued eating. Mittrik looked curiously at Hanala, who also remained seated. She caught his stare.

"Because I have both legs you judge me for sitting," she said, reading his expression too easily. "He judges me, but not you, Pyaren. Judge me, Hwaelin, but I visited them in Sharann six weeks back." She shrugged, piling more small grain onto her plate with her hands. Jonn caught his brother's eye, clearly uncomfortable. Fatigued with Forsaken strangers.

At what point do we collapse from it all? Mittrik wondered.

"And these are the Bilers not coming to your union," Prince Scarface said as he led his brother to the table, and the older man took a seat across Prince Bakéz, his soulless lady beside him. "Lords Jonnere and Mittrik Hwaelin, this is Tyonar and his future wife Suni."

Jonn couldn't even swallow the food in his mouth. Both he and Mittrik were speechless and wide eyed when the woman lowered the plume-lined hood she wore, revealing long, tapered ears. Her lobes drooped low and were pierced with rings of gold and twining wood. *A true elf,* Mittrik clenched his hands on the sides of his wooden chair. *Everything is true.*

He and Jonn stared at one another. Not at the daemon. *What should we do?* Mittrik was drawn back to the elf, looking at her black nails, not her fathomless eyes. *A path to Doom if you stare too long,* Mittrik looked to the floor.

"You aren't trained in guarding your thoughts against

Eerim, Biler?" The twin with the gruesome scar asked as he sat down in his seat. "Do not worry, Suni does not speak Eastern. I do not think."

"And I cursed Zyonhir for lying to me, but who would believe such things?" The newly arrived brother laughed. He bent his head toward his future bride, then the elf giggled and said something in a choppy, clacking tongue, black teeth like chips of even coal in her mouth.

"Where is Zyon now?" Bakéz asked.

"Oh, you know. Shit to bury, gold to find. Busiest Tyanien." Prince Tyonar smiled at Mittrik, gold eyes shining like fresh coin. "But tell me, how do two noblemen from Baeltaf end up invited to a union between an Eerim and a Canyai?"

"Oh, I have heard one like that," Prince Scarface said with half a mouthful, pointing to the brother that shared his face. "How it goes, Owé? What was the joke? Something something... it went... a Biler merchant, an Eerim, and a Canyai go to a Fair Island wedding... not that, no it was about Takircha, yes? Yes, I remember now. No matter, Rae is the cause of this." He finally swallowed.

Rae's laugh was musical as the finest melody Mittrik ever heard. He wanted to make a song from it.

"Are you guilty, lyosháno?" Prince Tyonar asked.

"Yes." She sipped from her amber drink, batting long lashes at them all. "I am guilty of being unconvincing. They say they will not come."

"Please, attend my celebration!" Tyonar bellowed. "It will be a joyous event. And who can say that Biler lords attended their union? Not even Nelina, with her nenchai. The reporters will have quite a time." He added the last bit more quietly to Rae.

"Tyonar," Bakéz barked, "the lords have already declined. They want to return. Do not guilt them."

Tynoar did not stop his smiling, nor did his elf lady with her distracting black teeth. "Forgive me, lords," he said, "if I have put any guilt at your feet. As my brother said, the guilt most certainly belongs to Aadarae. This invitation is open to you, and you may stay in the palace as our honored guests until you desire to leave. But, I do tell you, the day will be quite the occasion."

"Talosa is the most desired ticket this season," said Rae. Aadarae. Mittrik felt like she was only speaking to him. "There's more people here than..." She stopped when she realized he wouldn't know the place she was about to compare, but they stayed smiling at each other. She asked him how many people were in the king's city, High Baeltaf, and Mittrik answered that there were too many. Eighty thousand perhaps.

She told him to add twenty more High Baeltafs onto itself, and he would have the number of people in Talosa during a royal wedding.

Jonn coughed, the family chatted around him, but Mittrik was lost to it. He wanted more of her magic questions, he wanted to ask his own. But it was late, and he was quite full of the sweet and burning foods, his head rippling back in Eberle. Wondering for his family. What was left of it.

The youngest princess noticed, because she called for a servant and then turned back to him.

"If you're tired, someone will show you back to your rooms. I imagine this day has been very tiring."

Jonn interjected in his place again. "Yes, thank you."

"Aya!" She called down the table. It quieted. "The Bilers are tired and are going to sleep."

"Yes, of course. Good Night, Lords Hwaelin, I hope your dreams are pleasant," Prince Bakéz called out in his loud, tinny voice.

"Good Night," both Hwaelins said in unison, like when they were boys blessing their modaire and parents. Jonn continued, "And thank you so much for your hospitality, Tyanien."

"Lords Hwaelin," the queen addressed them from her seat, "you are most welcome in the Canyassor. I pray you are of happiness, and that your travels be safe."

The brothers bowed, earning strange looks from the elf.

"Thank you." Jonn nodded stiffly, avoiding looking back to

the elf woman non-too subtly.

Jonn and Mittrik walked in silence behind the servant as he led them in reverse through the winding corridors and to their rooms.

The servant bowed and departed quickly when they got there, looking fearfully behind him as he turned a corner.

"Good Night," Jonn said as he opened his door with a click and much creaking.

"Good Night," Mittrik sighed, hesitating before his chamber.

"You want to accept their offer and stay for that wedding," Jonn said it like an accusation, turning back to stare harshly at him from the doorframe.

"Well, would that be such a horrible thing? We're in the west this once. I imagine we will never get such an opportunity. I am the sort of man that would regret not knowing what some of this is all about. The wedding is only seven days away, and then back to Kieln. What harm can a little adventure do before we go back to our lives forever?"

"I've had enough adventure for five lifetimes. This is almost over, Mittrik." And with that Jonn closed the door.

"Hwaelin!" a voice called and Mittrik turned around to see the scarred prince running toward him in long strides. "My brother says you are leaving tomorrow in the night, yes?"

"Yes." *Unfortunately.*

"Before Great Fire rises, I shall be here to collect you and your brother. You cannot leave Talosa without seeing the Academy. It is the sight of Talosa. Over five hundred battle halls. I show it to you, very rare opportunity."

"Very well," Mittrik answered tiredly, but the thought did excite him.

The twin's ruined cheek crooked into a smile.

"You, Lord's son, rest tonight. Tomorrow, I wish to fight you. Bring your sword, yes? I heard it has firestones! Crazy Biler."

The strange man left running down the hall, the muffled clanking of his shortsword at his back, and Mittrik was alone.

Rae freed Santir early that morning, just after the Bilers were taken away, yelling angry orders at the guards that questioned her right to do so ("I am as much Tyanien as either Bakéz or Zyonhir. You will release him!"). No one denied the Araeboril twice. Santir spent the day, sore from sleeping on the cell bed, walking up the road from the city.

The welcoming sight of Kloennian's mountain greeted his exhaustion, and he looked around to see if the nenchai was near in the trees. It was too dark to see anything but the outline of his home, so he made his way up the steps, wanting to run into his bed but too tired to attempt anything more than a snail's pace. He stopped just before the last step.

The door was ajar, the bolt broken. Santir pushed into the house with a loud metal whinging. In the dark on a pillow, rum in hand, Yeroen sat smiling.

"Second-One fail you," Santir exclaimed, trying to slam the door behind him. As it was broken, it didn't have the desired effect. "Where have you been?"

"Different places. Hiding from the city guard. Where do you think?" Yeroen replied and stood. "Rae released you quickly. I was worried they'd make you stand a trial before I could think up a plan. I can't stand a trial, I—"

"No trials for either of us. The Great Leader has blotted out our crimes," Santir sighed and sat down at the table, throwing his sack on it and resting his head in his hands.

"All of our crimes?" Yeroen threw back his drink. "Just so, he does that for *us*?"

"Because we have the Araeboril's pity." Santir looked up and felt he could hit his brother. He wouldn't win but he might get one good punch. "That doesn't mean you are free to go out and bring more shame on the name Detunae. If not for Tyanien Aadarae, we would both stand a trial for smuggling. All your secrets would be exposed, and I know you have many. The Tyanien does us enough kindnesses, and now the *Great Leader* himself had to get involved in our sad plight."

"*Tyanien Aadarae.*" Yeroen laughed abruptly, pretended to wipe a tear from his eye. "You have a sour mood."

"Maybe because I spent the night sleeping next to filthy Bilers. Where were you hiding anyway? They brought me in twice to question where you might be. I gave them the names I knew among your lenders, but they doubted you fled to Achka. I thought you might have."

"And get there how? Your ship won't fly. I went along the falls, into the trees. Damn luck, maybe Third-One, that I wasn't here when the guards came. I heard you leave this morning with that Biler, and I needed to get away and think. When I returned the door's lock was broken and the sleeping Biler was gone. I knew something happened."

"Perceptive."

"Be like that," Yeroen growled. "Why would you take the tufan Biler into Talosa?"

Why did you bring them here at all? Santir wheeled. "We didn't know what those Bilers were thinking, now at least the palace knows."

"And the entire Confederation by tomorrow, I bet."

"This is your fault. I beg First-One for a different name, so that you may not share in it and destroy it again and again."

Yeroen smiled. "I beg Third-One in you agree with that aim, bless you and guide you into a good marriage. Gain an old name not your own, some words maybe. Are those citron peels?"

They had fallen out of Santir's sack. "They are mine."

"Did you buy the stone of Yett for the air vessel before you were apprehended? If you managed to buy citron peels."

Santir stood, his chair scuffling and almost tipping backwards, and he stalked out of the room, up the stairs. Yeroen's laughs faded below him.

In his room he collapsed on his mattress. He'd clean the smell off himself later. He was far too exhausted to consider it now. Santir would be glad to be born senseless if he could have been nameless, too.

Anything but Detunae.

In that quiet, he missed Kloennian; he felt his absence too strongly. Klo would have made peace between him and Yeroen already. Talent of empaths.

This business with the foreigners was out of hand. Klo wouldn't have allowed any of it to happen, and he never would have introduced random Bilers to Rae. *They could be taskmen. They could be anyone.*

Klo would have stopped it.

You should have done so without him here, Santir told himself in the dark. *Third-One told you right, but instead you found yourself caught in your misdeeds, in a cell underneath the palace. Fehatsi was right. You are not Klo. You are not enough.*

Happy to feel so exhausted, sleep came quicker than tears.

Before dawn the next morning, Rae and her lyaren met the Biler nobles in the throne hall.

The three women were dressed in their training clothes, carrying their chosen weapons. Teia pulled her hair back into a ribbon as they approached the foreign men on the dais steps, her long blade neatly sheathed in the soft binding at her hip, and a new dagger tipped with stone of Leu strapped to the band on her arm. She could feel the stone of Leu like she could feel water thrum in her sense.

The doubleborn Tyanien were also there upon the dais, engaging in an awkward looking conversation with the foreigners. The Bilers had their swords, and the Fair-faced Biler's pommel was gilded with ancient, unrefined, pure firestones. *Do they not know how dangerous that could be if those firestones turned to life and warmed? A child of Yett could light those stones from a pane's length.* Teia could not help but chuckle at the thought. Rae had said that the Bilers knew nothing of science or nature's power.

But Teia sympathized with the noblemen after what Rae told her last night. The Bilers recently lost their mother, the Rooj lady, and Teia knew that kind of loss.

She thought quickly over the good memories she had of her mother to make that faint sting in her chest disappear. She thought of a snorting laugh, of strong marked arms that swung people in hugs, of times her mother would puppeteer water into the creature Teia wanted to see. Her mother would scold her for dragging mud into their home in Léurai; her mother would run off her full name without stopping to breathe: Léuanien Anjalá Mazo Teiabél.

To others, it did not matter what came after her first family name—*Léuanien* people noticed and admired. A weighty name. Teia knew she could not complain. She was ninth in a long line of captains who had left their mark on Blessed history, descended directly from the first Seawoman. It was a proud name. A humorously long name, but a good one.

Canyai no longer rode ships on open waters, not since the Decree of 8903. The future was in the skies— new models of air vessels made every turn, and the newest models could fly for great distances. Tyanien Bakéz would not change the law after his cloaking, no. He was of the mind of his father. Teia felt the unfairness of her place in time. *And now with so many waterways closed… is there a sea left for me?*

"Good Morn, lords," Rae said to foreigners in the eastern tongue. "That is your daily blessing, yes? I prayed for you before sunrise, Hwaelins."

The shorter Biler stared reverentially at her. He was at height with Teia, though if she stood straight she might be taller. "Yes, Good Morn, princess."

"She is a Tyanien," Teia corrected the man. "Daughter of Tyano, not a princess. The daughters of Tyanien is a princess, Lord. Teviona Aadarae is a leader. She is Tyanien."

Fehatsi stepped forward, folding her small hands behind her back. "Little differences in the govern's naming that have been forgotten in the far East, no matter. I hope you are ready to see the academy, Lords of Hwaelin. I do not know what Tyanien Owéttan and Janseyu have told you, but it is the finest academy in Canyassor. Only the Katar of Iri compares to its store of knowledge."

"Please lead the way, my lady," the Fair looking Biler said.

Rae turned first, and they made the walk into the private tunnels under the city that led to the academy, which was ridiculously packed with visitors and foreign merchants excited to see the union of Tyanien Tyonar. Tyanien Bakéz had been clear that now was not a good time for the three younger siblings to be walking the streets unassisted, and though they had resisted the idea of traveling underground indefinitely, eventually Rae yielded to her brother.

Teia and Fehatsi traipsed a little behind the Biler lords and Rae, who was speaking enthusiastically about the libraries of the academy, the fine craftsmanship and detailing of each stone. Rae must feel some sense of pride for the great Academy, which was only rebuilt as beautifully as it was under her father's commands. The Jarey, who had ruled two hundred turns past, had put turns of labor, thousands of hands and skilled wielders, and more gold than they possessed into the city's royal palace. Teviona Iial believed if so much greatness adorns his home, more should be done for the city's school. Of course, Teia knew beyond anything Rae felt guilt as well. The Academy was only rebuilt after the walls had crumbled on that terrible day. Sixty-eight people had died, and Rae, a child, felt one severely. It was the first time she killed with truelight.

Rae answered the Biler's questions and asked none, as Fehatsi had recommended. Riambo did not want to offend the foreigners with their Tyanien's gifts. Jan flipped a small dagger in his hand and looked over one of Rae's shoulders as she conversed, and her other shoulder was flanked by Owé, who kept a careful eye on the half Rooj men.

"I would like to know why we are allowing them to see her truelight," Fehatsi whispered to her in the blessed tongue as they walked. "All so they can fly home tonight and plan for war?"

"If they had that intention, we would know. It was Jan's idea," Teia responded. "That is all Rae said."

Fehatsi made a judicious noise from her throat.

"It should be her decision. It may be good for them to fear her power. Jan is not be thinking of consequence, and I don't know what *she* is thinking anymore."

"Rae is amused by them."

"Obviously. She has dreamed of something like this her whole life."

Teia saw her lyaren's calculating look. *So have you. Ambitions gold as Riam rum, gold as the Riambo eye. Unsettling when those old expressions contain undeniable truth. When wide meaning is made individual. Fehatsi inherited all the family traits, every ambition, just not the eyes.*

"You are not yet a diplomat, Feha," Teia said. "What does worrying solve?"

The shorter woman shook her head as they marched the rest of the way through the tunnels in silence. It was another Riambo trait she inherited from her father, that scathing fault-finding look, that inane ability to say everything she needed without saying a word.

It is unwise not to worry, came an unwanted mimic of Fehatsi's voice in Teia's head. It was often there to chide her. *If Rae is worried, we should all be worried. To think about your worries is not the same as worrying.*

But to Teia, it was.

Up the steps they walked into the first of seven private halls in the Academy, where the Select Daughter and Son of Amina, two of the twenty-six Select, were caught in a heated discussion. Teia could not hear them, but she saw the Select Daughter look fiercely over her eyeglasses, which had fallen down her slight nose. The Select Daughter raised her hands above her head in perceived defeat. At the sound of approaching company, the couple stopped, and the Select Daughter retreated up her spiraling stairs without saying a word.

"You are late. Dawn ended," the Select Son grumbled to Rae. "You missed prayer. I know your look, child. You think you have a good excuse."

Rae inclined her head toward the Bilers. He would feel her joy as she beamed and shrugged. Children of Amina only felt each other, unlike children of Hahnae, who felt all.

Fehatsi tried to explain for them, mentioned that they indeed prayed before arriving, but the elder raised his hand and she was silent.

"Léuanien," Daijirek acknowledged Teia with a nod, asked his single question,"did you pray?"

"No." But Teia never did.

Daijirek nodded again before turning to look at the Bilers and addressing them in their eastern tongue. "So, the rumors are true— Bilers in the Blessed Lands. What an occasion for it, too." He clicked his tongue on the roof of his mouth before walking away.

"Come, Aadarae," he called without looking back. "You are late."

The woman called Riambo Fehatsi courteously suggested that *perhaps* they might like to rest before their journey home tonight, and while Mittrik refused so that he could stay and watch more magical dueling, jesting with the marred-faced Tyanien like they were well-acquainted, Jonn had seen too much for one day. Fire and wind held in a woman's hand, lightning cracking between another woman's fingertips. Man after man falling at her feet.

Mittrik dared fight against the witch princess, and had lasted not a minute before her blade pressed against his throat. Mittrik who beat Jonn at swords every time.

They needed to get home, away from these witches beyond the Bitter who still possessed every legendary magic. Once home, Jonn didn't know what he would do.

At least he did not feel so vulnerable with his longsword strapped to him. The foreigners had preferred Mittrik's simple broadsword to Jonn's 'ornanment'. They laughed at the gilded hilt and encrusted rubies that ran down the blade's length. Their taunts would have sent poor Sterke into an uproar. The blacksmith had spent the better half of a month in design to make it perfect.

Riambo Fehatsi led Jonn back through the tunnels to the palace, taking a torch from the wall and holding it in front of them as they strolled together. She was skinny, with a flat chest and thin arms, but she walked so confidently you would not think her small. The torchlight set a stunning glow across her brown skin. Jonn could tell that she was thinking very seriously, still she seemed aware and met his stare. Eyes the color of liquid bronze bewildered in her round face.

"Your people have been surprisingly kind to my brother and me," Jonn said, trying to fill the silence between them.

"Why are you surprised, Lord Hwaelin? Blessed People are commanded to be kind to travelers and truth seekers."

"Forgive me, my lady, but little is known in Baeltaf of the west. It is very strange, this new world. Many believe the people beyond the Dominions are daemons and heartless savages that practice magic." *And these people call their sorcery something stranger and more powerful than magic,* he thought in dismay. And then he thought of how agile and spritely the woman before him had been, as she balanced atop a stone beam and shot blazing arrows, how she had dropped from that height and landed in an effortless tumble. She did not need magic to impress.

"Yes, and here we know little of Baeltaf. That is what happens when a kingdom isolates itself from the rest of the world. But ours is not new. Humankind is not the oldest but it is the best documented race on the Rock." She spoke as if she was born to the language, with the smooth accent of the upper class. If she did not look so different to him, he would think her a highborn southern lady.

"Yes, I imagine you are right, my lady," he said as they turned down another fork in the tunnel. "May I ask, how do you speak my language so well? You sound as though you were born in High Baeltaf."

"I speak nine languages fluently, Lord Hwaelin, and in three languages, I fear I am more glib than eloquent. I am a student of diplomacy and foreign law at Talosa's Academy. As daughter of the Korr, I am afforded many options, but I thought that course of study would be the best way to help Tyanien Aadarae achieve her mission."

"And what is her mission?" he asked, thinking of the bursts of pure light the witch produced. She said she could heal with it, but he had only seen her use it to bring down men.

"If you ask her, she wouldn't be able to give a coherent answer," Fehatsi said. "But her mission is peace between us. There has not been true peace between Canyassor and Baeltaf since the Separation, you see."

"The First Great War of Baeltaf," Jonn supplemented, and she looked at him strangely.

"It was neither a true war, nor the first of wars on your continent, Lord Hwaelin," her soft voice bounced along the stone walls. "But the Separation was great. The humans from the north, the Iceman from whom you descend, feared both the known and the unknown of other kind, and the humans in those lands rose up, still embittered from the days of the Chained Men. It started as a mass poisoning of the Canyai protectors and rulers of the Midkingdom's city states and the burning of the Rising Wood, which was connected in spirit with the Wilder Wood, though no more. Most of the humans in the Midkingdom rallied behind the Northmen as they came with their steel against other kinds. Only the cities of Orinth were evacuated in time. War usually involves battles, Lord Hwaelin, and there were none as we know during the Separation. Only genocide of innocents and clandestine slaughter, murder made in the night."

Jonn could not believe the western woman's words. He had grown up reading the accounts of the First War, the Battle of Highpartif, the sacking of the Bones, when Redbone cut through the last mages with his greatsword. But he had seen the kind of power these mages possessed over nature, and suddenly the thought that one man could take on the strongest three mages with just a sword seemed absurd. No battle could be won against these people, not any kind of battle Jonn knew.

"You believe what you say?" he asked her softly.

"Oh, yes, almost always. Though you will have to take me at my word, I am no truthspeaker. There are accounts of those times in the Academy—I can find them for you along with the appropriate translations. But many things have changed since then, for your people and mine, and I am happy that things could change for the better with respect to both our lands. I am sorry if my boldness offends, my lord, but I think it would be a wise choice to stay and see the celebration for the wedding of our Tyanien Tyonar. Nothing will be like it in history, I believe, and that will be doubly true if you attend."

"I must return to Kieln," he answered stiffly.

"And you shall," she chuckled, though it did not feel like she mocked him. Her laughter was pleasant and begged to be joined. "Of course, you will return home. I only ask you consider the offer Tyanien Aadarae has presented to you. Since she was a young girl, she has spoken to me of reuniting Baeltaf with the rest of the Rock."

"My family needs me."

"Yes, I know something of family and duty, and you know better than I what your family needs, Lord Hwaelin. If it is urgent, I understand. But if it is not, it remains your choice," she continued as they approached the door to his rooms. "You could leave here and not look back, but I hope you make the decision that could bring a newfound peace to our people."

"There is peace now."

"Do you think so? There is indifference. There is much your

countrymen have forgotten, and so much more they have never had the chance to know. Perhaps my people have lost something in this arrangement as well." Jonn found himself drifting to the soft cadence of her speech.

"I can see that there is much I do not know, my lady. Perhaps you are right," he said reluctantly.

"I am right, Lord Hwaelin, but regardless of your choice, know that the Teviona family has welcomed you and that you leave as friends. I shall see you before you depart, but someone will bring you food and drink. Rest and please, think on your decision."

Jonn bowed to her and she curtsied back, her stare never leaving him; and she was turning, striding gracefully away, leaving him alone in the dark corridor with too much on his mind. The space between them grew.

Bakéz' hand clenched before the door of his father's room, hovered... and did not knock on the wood. A moment just to breathe, to prepare himself. He stared at the fine carvings on the door, tall trees and needle-beaked buzzers jousting for a flower with folded leaves, a treeclimber staring at him with blank, brown eyes.

With one final breath he pushed the heavy door, and it swung open into dim and damp. Soft candles lit the floor, herbal scented. Bakéz pressed two fingers against the stone embedded in the wall at his right, and the corresponding stones of Yett set aflame in the large crystal heaters along the length of the room. The warmth giving light revealed the Tyano, once so lively and strong, laying feebly on his side and staring out the windows to the city towers. Daijirek Wanúm knelt at the Tyano's side with a concentrated face, one skilled hand placed over his liege's heart and another placed on his back letting off a very faint, wavering shimmer. Bakéz saw his father flinch from the touch of truelight, but knew Daijirek took most of the pain. The Select Son of Amina noticed Bakéz and rose, dulled hands dropped to his sides.

"Tyanien Bakéz," he said and the Tyano's eyes flickered open.

"Select Son of Amina," Bakéz replied reverentially in quiet voice, his right fist thudding over heart thrice. "Bapo," he said, looking at his father, "how do you feel?"

"Like a dying man, I suppose," he laughed softly as he sat straight to look at him.

Daijirek backed away from them as he spoke. "I shall give you and Great Leader Iial your privacy, Tyanien Bakéz, but he must rest soon. His heart is particularly frail today."

"Thank you, Wanúm," his father said smiling.

"Rest soon, my Great Leader," and with that the Select Son exited the grand room.

Bakéz turned back to his father in his light patchwork blankets. His arms and neck already turned that foul blue of prolonged plague. Half-moons of sunken shadow sat beneath green eyes. The Tyano wore a light top of soft fuzz from the muted pink pa bu flower, and Bakéz imagined he could count the ribs underneath.

After Bakéz made apologies for his absence, after pleasantries about Tyonar's union with the Eerim girl, his father demanded, "Why have you come to see me now?"

"I met with the Biler noblemen," Bakéz told him. "Zyon arranged for them to go back to Baeltaf at the setting of the Great Fire tonight. They were gracious." His father's expression remained steady as Bakéz spoke, and he did not try to interject. In sickness, that did not change. "My leader, I have come to find Aadarae knew about their presence in Talosa and did not tell me. She might have known of a smuggler's deal happening beyond the Line of Separation."

"She knew," before a cough. "And she told me."

"She told you?"

The Tyano sighed and pinched the bridge of his nose. "Yes, some time ago that Detunaes were trading of sweetleaf in the

Biler Dominion, which I have blotted out and pardoned. Moons ago. It is only sweetleaf, after all. She told me just the morning past about the noblemen's adventure here. What a strange happenstance."

Bakéz rose to stare out the window, unable to bear his father's piercing look.

This felt like betrayal. His sister, a truthspeaker, hid *this* from Bakéz. *I have been acting as Great Leader in all but title for eight passings of the moons, all but the Inquirer's Table I attend, and she did not tell me foreign nobles were on Blessed soil.* His sister, by holy design, could not consciously betray anyone, was unable to deceive. Though sometimes, Bakéz wondered.

He knew Aadarae kept secrets. She always had.

"Why not tell me?" he turned and asked, because he knew his father waited for it. "She should have told me."

"You are not her Great Leader yet, son. And even then, she is the Araeboril."

"Did Amina have absolute power in her time?"

His father stared, quiet, too long, and Bakéz felt himself shrinking. "Amina was equal in power with all the First Children, as you know. All judges and prophets, and there were no Great Leaders to muddle with Three-One's commands back then. I was little younger than you when my time to lead came, and like you I was not ready."

There. Someone said it to his face, Bakéz wasn't ready. Though true, and he'd known this truth a while, the words stung. *Truth is usually pain.* His sister taught him that lesson. A favorite lesson of truth speakers.

Too many doubts. Questioning the faith, questioning at all— unfathomable when his doubt led to Blessed People doubting God— or worse, doubting him. All Teviona were devout believers, because their lives depended on belief not their own. But his time was approaching, and they would cloak Bakéz as Great Leader before the steamwaters of Yettirai, submerge him beneath the Blessed ground and sea. Zyonhir would lift him and drag him to the coming winds, where they would stand together, or fall together. And he could not fall.

Though he wasn't ready.

"Enough vague criticism, please. What do you see lacking in me, Bapo? What did you lack when they cloaked you?"

"I wasn't prepared for my own weakness when making those difficult decisions. You rely too much on your siblings."

Nonsense. He hadn't made real decisions since the war. Make decisions when others decide, rely on no one, not even a brother, but trust the system to uphold them. Vaguest nonsense. Bakéz couldn't even blame the plague, his father always spoke like this.

"I don't make the difficult decisions, do I? I trust someone, a thousand other someone's to do it for me. And everyone else trusts me to do that and live well."

"And that choice of faith," his father said, "is the most vital you make."

"It's not a choice. Bapo, please... haven't I proven myself? I won your battles—"

"You lost CoБmak."

"I—"

"You were careless. Your victories bought with the sacrifice of others, the knowledge of others. Your brother is forever lame. Had Sfar'Laki been what he claimed, your sister would be dead, and you'd be in a war you couldn't win. And what concerns me most: you sent Aadarae to that blasted tower knowing she would either die or use truelight to kill Laki and win it all for you."

"Our intelligence insisted Sfar'Laki wasn't the Hasyal. My whole life, I've been told not to think on prophecies. I'm not supposed to believe the Hasyal *exists.*"

His father smiled that wretched, placid smile. "Yes, that is plain."

Iial could believe in the damn prophecy. The Tyano lay dying in seclusion, allowed whatever thoughts he desired. Bakéz' mind remained public domain.

"Why do you think Fair Bilers come now?" He needed to

speak of anything else, he couldn't think about prophecies and the end of the world.

"A sure way to know is to let them stay."

"You have no problem with Bilers in your palace?"

"No," his father said, repositioning the pillow at his back. "From what I am told, they are young men mourning a mother, brought here by accident and experiencing many shocks. Furthermore, your sister is delighted by them. I will give her delight where she can find it. I do not fear these men. Do you?"

"No," he answered back, but the words were not quite true. Bakéz did not fear the two peculiar Easterners, but their people's history of bloodlust made him wary. Suspicious. "But their mother, the Rooj... she wrote about 'the Other.' Hasyal. We have her letter."

"Imposters will rise until the true Hasyal reveals their face. Like last time, this means war, of course. One I won't live to see. I don't leave you in a pleasant world, my son. You will uncover truths of the matter, and then act accordingly. And keep your faith."

The day's light faded into streaks of soft blues and violets. Distant pinpoint lights of great fires cast high into the setting night, past the edge of their sky. He remembered the hour and the small council gathering. Most people would be in third prayers.

"I must get to the Council Table. It doesn't get easier, either." Bakéz stood. "It gets more complicated. My thoughts are... less, somehow."

His father's smile grew, wrinkling brown skin around his eyes like sun beams. "Listening to the spate of complaints never ceases to feel like duty. Your thoughts impact the world, and they always have."

Duty, compassion, blood. He kissed both his father's cheeks and squeezed his hand as tightly as he dared, not wanting to bruise the thin skin. "I shall let you rest, Bapo."

Feeling better and worse for his visit, he walked out of his father's rooms. There, he found Aadarae walking in his direction, head down in an old tome.

She noticed him and snapped the book shut. “Did you just see Bapo?” she asked, smiling a smile that didn’t reach her eyes.

“Yes, I did. He is resting now.”

“Oh,” she sounded defeated. In her hands the weathered book was clutched so tightly her knuckles turned white. “Was Master Daijirek with him?”

“He left when I arrived.”

“May I go with you to the small council meeting, then?”

He stopped short.

How could he deny her? Bakéz indulged his little sister when she was a child, as did all their siblings. Youngest of ten, who denied the child who lived locked up in her room? Zyon read to her for as long as she remained still enough to listen; Nelina and Hanala dressed Aadarae in bright masks and paints and forced her into elaborate shows of light for their mother; Tyonar let her practice healing on him when she was still so young Master Daijirek would not teach her, letting her untrained little hands leave jagged scars on his skin that remained today (they were the most impulsive, and together did the most damage); Malak and Pyaren trailed behind her when she found ways to escape her room. The doubleborn helped her escape. For as long as Bakéz could remember, all the Tyanien spoilt Aadarae rotten.

But at CoБmak, sending her and Pyaren to the Southern Wilder Tower so quickly, his guilt led him to avoid her as much as she had avoided him that first Rock turn after the war’s end. Bakéz had known what they were doing, what they were asking of her when they sent her for Laki— or at least they suspected. She hadn’t told him what she felt during the explosion of the Academy, but he saw how death affected her. Bakéz knew he was asking her to make a great sacrifice. And she did not question him then.

He nodded to her in answer now, and Aadarae walked by his side on the way to the small council room in the shortest eastern tower, humming as her fingers cast a shimmer. She swung her arms at her sides.

"I have these old writings from the Biler lands," she was saying, her feet skipping beneath her; the loose fabrics of her pants billowed. "Two were written in the years right after Old Orinth fell. I was hoping there would be something to help Bapo. But I have read nothing of plagues, not even the one that the Eerim children conjured during the Separation in 8188— can you believe it?— there are only things of torture. But I found a discrepancy, well much more than that really, but it was something in one of the writings that makes me think color deficiency in the fourth receptor of false eyes can be corrected using truelight in congruence with a powder made from a seed that was grown in the Rising Wood. We have these seeds, too, I could not believe it at first. I was hoping to show Daijirek to see what he thought. Did he say anything about Bapo?"

He strained to remain silent but could not. Sighing he told her, "Yes, it is bad. His heart is struggling today." None lived with the plague longer than three turns. Their father wouldn't be an exception.

"And it will get worse," Rae said miserably. "He has, at most, two years because we prolong his pain. There is still much to read, but I am looking everywhere I can think. I am trying my hardest to find something."

"You will," Bakéz encouraged her. "If it can be done, you will. You are the cleverest of us, sister."

"Suni is as sweet as Tyon described in his letters," Rae changed the subject, shifting uncomfortably from the praise. "I love union ceremonies. I remember Nelina's like it was yesterday. And yours, of course."

His union had marked the first day she was allowed out of her room, but that day they did not let her join the procession.

"The Selection will be upon us soon, and then you will enter a union with someone as well."

It was the wrong thing to say. Her face fell, and she slowed her pace to match his; the fingers at her side twitched and sparked, and her jaw clenched. Her eyes mapped around them quickly, never met his.

The union between Aadarae and the next Select Son of Amina would be a different kind of union, as their astral souls bound in a covenant with all of Three-One, a holy and ancient ritual of spirit. It was *close* to magic, Bakéz thought, but it was not called magic. Not by Canyai.

Bakéz wondered if Aadarae was thinking of her dead lover, the lands wielder that died in the attack of CoБmak. *How must she resent me? What I am not allowed to see?*

She looked at him, and she had their father's striking look, the one that stripped him of courage and left him feeling defenseless.

"Yes," she said, "the Selection Day is coming for me."

"Are you ready for it?" he asked quietly, thinking what he shouldn't.

"I am," she said. "Daijirek has been preparing me for Selection since before I could understand what it was, all the congress ritual and dealings of judgement, the sacrifice. I am also full of fear and dread for it."

Bakéz tripped on his right foot. "Fear and dread? You do not want the honor?"

"No. I never did, but wants mean nothing for children of Amina."

He felt stupid for asking. He had not wanted to know, not truly. It was the first lesson the Son of Amina had taught the Tyanien siblings when they were told of Aadarae's gifts: never ask a question if you don't want the truthful answer.

That first lesson came when the Tyano summoned his children to the throne— Bakéz had sixteen turns to his name — and told them that their newborn sister was more than a helpless screaming babe, but also the realization of a prophecy two thousand turns old. She was the Araeboril.

His younger siblings rejoiced, but Bakéz was older, knew the Scriptures, and had asked, "Does this mean the Rock will end soon?" He was told, No. Never think that. He was told to doubt the long-held interpretation of Scripture, but to never doubt God.

"I am so sorry," he said as they turned down the corridor, not knowing for which of his mistakes he was apologizing. *For sending you to certain torture with such little consideration… for killing your greatest love through my negligence.*

"Yes, I know," Aadarae said and rewarded him a gentle smile, placing her hand on his arm. "For too many things, Kez. I hold nothing against you. I cannot blame you."

He sighed. *No, I didn't kill Mouwat Kloennian. But my naivety and arrogance led to the waste of CoБmak, his death, and the people mistrust me before my rule begins.*

Her smile did not waver when she said, "There was nothing you could have done for him, for any of them, not without foresight or magic. And we learn who we can be in war. You led well, and you are leading well."

He smiled back at her. He did not feel it.

"I am not ready to be Tyano," he told her, faint voiced.

"But you will be one of the best," she said fiercely, and he knew she must believe her words true. Her words could give him courage just as her eyes could steal courage away. "I think there are some things for which we are not supposed to be ready, and we face them. Duty, blood."

Compassion, the word she left out.

They walked up the tower steps slowly together, his large arm placed over her muscled shoulders. She was still small compared to many warrior women, but her size concealed impossible strength and power. At last they came to the small council door, and Bakéz looked tenderly at Aadarae before entering.

The small council was already assembled, and his father's Korr, the golden eyed Riambo Rehonan, was already peering at him with an agitated expression. His uncle was a man of strict discipline, and he held everyone to his own esteem, judged everyone based on his standards.

"Blessings," Bakéz said as he walked to the largest seat at

the round table. His sister sat at her mother's side. "I have just come from visiting my father."

"How is the Great Leader's health today?" His uncle tried to hide the misery from his voice and failed.

"Poor," Bakéz answered shortly, not wanting to discuss it.

"Kez, now that you have met Suni, tell me: is she not extraordinary?" Dianis asked. "Have you gone to greet her family? They are lively. I'm not used to unspoken thoughts being answered."

Rae nodded a yes, while Bakéz looked faultily away.

"She is charming," *—like most with better hearing—*"I will greet them tomorrow. Let's begin, shall we?"

Talks of thousands of visitors of all kinds, of the camps settling in the flower gardens to make room for all the people. Talk that passed over Bakéz. Of food supplies and merchant complaints.

Tiredness made camp in his bones. He knew the city would teem with eager Eerim, open ears— they would also have an influx of Takircha and Ku'dur from the Confederation wishing to join in on the great revelry of the union.

Azún Kanila, the Tyano's warrior, stood by the Korr's side. The old General's beard and dark hair were flecked with white and gray, but his look was still lean and strong with those deterring patterned burns crawling up his forearms and neck, splotched red against his light flesh.

"Five hundred wielders have been brought into the city to add to what is already here, and the recent graduates are prepared to keep Talosa's peace, Tyanien. We are ready as we shall be," he said and sat down, pithy as ever.

"And what of the Eastern lords?" the Korr asked, yellow eyes blinking in that dark and dismal face.

"They will be boarding an air vessel to leave tonight," Zyon told them, but Rae was shaking her head.

"I convinced them to stay until Tyon's union celebration," she said. "Fehatsi was probably more persuasive than I, but they decided to stay. They are in their rooms for the night."

"Why did you convince the Bilers to stay for the celebration?" Zyon asked slowly, voice tinted in the ire of his nescience. Bakéz glared with a look that warned him of tone.

"Because I want to open the Line of Separation, and I thought it would be a good start at developing friendly connections with the Baeltaf lords. The process to peace will take a lot of time and communication. And you would not guess how powerful their leader of faith is, it sounds to me he will be hardest to convince of peace. That is strange, I think! Anyway these men seem kind, and completely overwhelmed, and frightened. I think they will enjoy a short vacation here."

"*Vacation*? Foolish girl," Riambo said. "These are descendants of the Icemen that poisoned Canyai by the thousands."

Rae couldn't just be silent. "Bilers are not our enemies now, uncle. The Line of Separation were a Jarey creation. The Teviona rule now. What compassion has come from Jarey laws? The lands of the Bilers have been isolated for so long they have confused fact with legend and are ignorant of the Rock's advances. These are not the same men that set the Rising Wood on fire, and we are not the same leading family that allowed them. It is a new time."

"But these men are cut from the same cloth as their kind, I am sure," Riambo said as his head shook.

"These lords coming to the Blessed Lands cannot be coincidence. It is First-One's design, a chance at fresh peace."

"I think we should discuss the letter," someone said loudly, and Bakéz sighed.

"After Tyonar's union. After the Selection. Now is not the time," Zyon answered.

"The letter?" Rae addressed the room, not directing the question at any one person.

"Yes." Zyon cast his golden look at her. "As Pyaren revealed to you yesterday, Lady Rooj Tisinda was found hanging in her chambers. Her elder son found a letter she wrote on the night she died, and it could be something treacherous."

"Treacherous... that is a vague description, son," Dianis said, her face concerned.

"Should we write to the Fair Isle? Send our sorrows to the Rooj?" Fajak Seirmona , a diplomat asked.

"No," Rehonan said firmly. "The Fair Isle has not yet sent word of her death, it would be unwise to write prematurely. The contents of the letter are what concerns us."

"And we shall discuss it after the Selection, when the city has calmed, and things are back to their normal pattern," Bakéz interjected. "We do not know what the letter means."

"I would appreciate if someone would explain why this letter is so sinister." Rae's brows were knitted over a sad expression. The room remained silent for an intake of breath.

"It mentions the shadow times. And you," Zyon said handing her the copy Rejadora had made for them. "And one she called 'Other'."

"She wrote about the Hasyal?" Rae asked. The name disturbed her, that epithet which Sfar'Laki claimed before she killed him. Bakéz watched her eyes roamed down the shortleaf, her hands trembled when she set it down.

"She killed herself?" Rae asked, looking to him, but Bakéz did not get the chance to answer.

"It appeared a suicide, but we are not inclined to believe that. Her sons don't. It may be that she knew something she was not supposed to know," Zyon answered again. "The Rooj have spies everywhere."

"This Other she mentions," the General said, "you think it is a true wielder of void? How could the Rooj know the Hasyal before any, even Eerim?"

"There is no second coming," the Korr interrupted Azun's next question.

"Xonieren was thrice cursed, Kanila," Fajak Seirmona said. "His power left the Rock. The prophecy of the next Hasyal is metaphorical."

"As much as the Araeboril sitting across from you."

"Nonsense," Fajak sneered. "I've read the ancient texts. Her power is a holy blessing. Our Rock isn't dying."

"Come now, Seirmona, even Daijirek believes though he won't admit it," Kanila cut in. "If the Select Son of Amina believes the Books of the first Araeboril are literal, who are we to disagree? Hasyal is coming, and she will be prepared."

"What do you think of this, Aadarae?" Dianis asked, placing a hand on her youngest child's arm.

"I agree with my brothers," she said standing from the table. "We can discuss it after the Selection. Forgive me, I am going to try to sleep. I am very tired. Goodnight, Ammi." She kissed her mother's cheeks.

"Goodnight, blessed one," the Onatae hushed as she smoothed Rae's frizzing hair.

Rae vanished beyond the door, down the steps.

"She is worried," the Korr said.

Bakéz thought, *If the Hasyal is real and wielding void—*

Stop, but he couldn't, *he would have Radical tasks running and buried already. If he is a pretender, like Sfar'Laki, the same is true. We should all be worried.*

7. THE ARAEBORIL

The witch princess stood in Jonn's doorway, shadows beneath her wild eyes, asking if she could come in. She wore knives strapped to her waist like a soldier. Flirtatious smile on her face like a whore.

"At this hour? Is that appropriate?" Jonn, dead tired, only wore his long tunic.

"Why not?" she asked.

Instead of proffering the awkward truth, Jonn bit his lip and turned his body to let her into the dark room. He was very aware of his bare calves. Of her own.

"I know it is late. But before you slept, I had to come speak with you," she said, sitting on his bed, lighting the space around them with a violent orb in her hand.

"Why?" Jonn asked.

"I need answers, Lord Hwaelin. Why did you leave your home? Only because your mother died? Or was there another reason?"

"There was, for, for my fear. For the pain, I..." He hated losing control of his tongue. He hated this witch and her power, coming in, demanding answers when he just wanted to sleep. And forget for a while.

"Only for your fear and pain?"

"I... I don't like my truth. I'd rather not say."

As if hearing his thoughts (and if elves could, why not this witch?) she whispered,"I wish I didn't have this power. I know why people hate it, almost as much as I do. I wish it was someone else, anyone else."

Jonn yawned, and switched his stance to his other foot. "It must be difficult, being unable to lie. Though I imagine the reward of never being lied to is greater."

"People can deceive me. Clever people can. I can't lie, but I can be wrong. It's not often. Were you close with your mother?"

"Yes," Jonn answered. "Yes, she and I walked together. She would advise me." He couldn't have courted Ritra without her wisdom.

The witch nodded. "My father is dying," she admitted. "I don't know how to live without his council. Who councils you now?"

"My father... I suppose." And how Jonn hated that.

"Do you think he knows you're here?"

"No. Gods, I hope not. He'll kill us both if he learns we're forsaken."

"If you believe that, why did you both come here?"

"Mittrik, he, well..." Jonn sighed and took a seat beside her on his bed, disregarding all propriety. "Mittrik did what he does, which is wander into dangerous situations that require someone saving him. Only this time, I led him to the danger. Planted him directly in it. I wanted to leave because the pain of staying was so great, because somehow everything and nothing changed in one night, but now we're forsaken, and I feel even worse."

"My power isn't only a curse, Lord Hwaelin. I can use truelight to take your pain. For a time. If you allow me. You'll sleep better tonight." The witch held out a bright, magic-warped palm. Silent storm grasped in her calm like it wasn't terrifying.

Jonn reeled and stood abruptly from the bed. "You want to take my pain? I don't know what pain I feel. That of a forsaken soul? Is it the pain of a son abandoned by his mother? Or the pain of believing my father might have killed her?" *And beyond pain, self-hatred because either way, I covet the crown. More than anything. More than her life.* "You don't want any of this, my lady. Forgive me, but if your questions are done, I'll ask you to leave. I'm very tired."

Mittrik couldn't sleep. How could he, after everything? He

couldn't wait to dream, yet denied rest. Denied the empty pitch in his heart in favor of climbing excitement.

Every last legend was half true: elves, mages, and groles roamed the west freely as any man, but the world did not seem fraught with evil and devastation for it. No, this world was wildly glorious because of such freedoms. Magic and men came together here.

He loved Old legends as a child, read them more fervently than anything put before him. They were filled with songs and tales of heroes that lived before the First War— descended of Hetten, gifted with power over seas and skies to overcome inner weakness and defeat monstrous evils. Better than the classic romances, like Gerdwill and Rosette, these Old stories. Filled with demigods, and demigods lived *here*.

Jonn agreed to stay for the royal wedding, to Mittrik's shameful delight. He knew Jonn agreed for fear of these westerners and their offense, though their disposition was anything but threatening.

Except perhaps the princess, Rae. A fighter more formidable than even Sir Arne with two blades, and Mittrik imagined Alluvel's High knight and master of arms swinging his swords up against hers. He imagined Arne's face at her conjure of lightning. She was a more dangerous opponent than all the knights he knew because she moved faster and more unpredictably than any human should. Inhuman. Beyond man — that's what she was. It was horrifying and wonderful. Mittrik wished more than anything to see Rae fight Sir Arne in the courtyard of Alluvel, to see her win. He imagined the Bear's beaten face.

Will I be Doomed for coming here? Or am I condemned for loving it? Do I care? He tried to remember the verse his sister always quoted at him from the Good Thyne's Gospel. *The gods are cruel, but they are just. They have your life mapped ahead of you.*

If gods were real, and Mittrik was not inclined to believe they were, his fate was already planned in the stars, and he merely followed the divine trail. If gods were real, if Hetten and the Sisters did look down at him from their heavenly perch, then they worked to guide him to his adventure. The Sisters, cruel as they could be, provided the tragedy that pushed him here; perhaps it was only a necessary step toward his own great triumph. Maybe it wasn't his mother's fault.

Mittrik thought it might be worth condemnation in his next life if this one truly mattered. It was worth never being reborn if in this singular life he was great, heroic, and lived freely.

If the gods weren't real, none of that mattered, and he was here anyhow. More had crossed his eyes in days than his whole life combined. He was here, in the Forsaken place and did not feel forsaken at all. How jarring, that only seven nights past, he sat at supper with his father, sister, and mother in Alluvel.

Only seven days? Mittrik could scarcely believe it. So much had changed for him. Seven days since he found his mother's corpse, too thin, ashen face staring at him from the rafters. Seven days and he was resting on a fluffed mattress in a western palace, welcomed by foreign royals, stomach full of sweet and strange foods and drink, heart anxious for more. His whole body thrummed with heat, and he felt he was at the beginning of a quest like Caeth and other demigods.

He could no longer stare at the gossamer canopy. Mittrik rose from the bed and walked to the great window along the room. Below, three roads lined by colorful, pointed roofs converged around the circular center, quiet now, though it had been bustling before. The small folk here were louder than those in Kieln, and it seemed even the lowest of them lived in high towers. A sweet smell held above the circle and drifted to Mittrik's nose, like honey and bread and something exotic he hadn't ever smelt.

A bird landed on the window's ledge. One small, delicate creature with a blue crown and a long yellow beak, black masked, beady eyes looking expectant. Its tail, long feathered, fell off the side of the wall like a bright green ribbon. The bird hopped twice to get nearer and Mittrik backed away. He'd learnt caution regarding western birds.

"Hello," Mittrik whispered, and it responded with a falling six-note warble. "You're right, I think. It'd be a waste not to take in all I can while I'm here. You never know, Jonn might change his mind tomorrow, and I'll have miss chance. I shouldn't just sit and do nothing."

The bird tweeted its pleasant song again. Flew off to it's own venture.

"Indeed," Mittrik agreed and clasped his sword around him, put on his now cleaned socks and boots, and was out the door of his chambers.

At the same time, the magic princess he first knew as Rae emerged from Jonn's room, her hand glowing like a torch to lead her. Her eyes on her feet.

"Rae!" He called out, and her head popped up, eyes curious and smile heavenly. Her hair was twisted into a solitary plait that hung at her back, and a small wooden bird hung from a cord around her neck, resting on the beaded armor of her breast. Similar to the bird who just visited him. The bird's eye was a droplet of pale emerald; but Mittrik's eyes lingered on the two sheathed wideblades strapped to her hipbones.

"Lord Hwaelin," she whispered. Mittrik felt at once very loud and discourteous.

"You were in Jonn's room?" he whispered, but even his question was wrong, and he felt his face redden.

Here he was, walking about her family's dwellings surreptitiously in the black hours of night, questioning *her*. Jealous of whatever she was doing in his brother's room. *But what was she doing in there?* She didn't notice his embarrassment, rather ignored it if she did.

"I had questions for him, but he didn't answer me well enough. I'm sneaking out," Rae told him.

"Sneaking out," Mittrik parroted. "Of the palace? Why? Where?"

She eyed him with pouted lower lip, measuring if he was

worth the answers. "Somewhere special in the jungle because I cannot sleep. Would you like to come with me, Lord Hwaelin?"

"Yes," the word came before he thought to think or try to stop it. No matter, he would not have said anything else given the choice.

A mewling came from a circling shadow at Rae's feet.

"*Doom*! That's a spiritcub!" Mittrik blurted, leaping yards back. Is this how he would die?

"No," the princess sighed carelessly. She actually picked up the black creature. "Ambos is full grown. He just likes to be carried as a babe."

It clung to the fabric of her sleeves with hooked claws and looked at Mittrik with slit eyes. Mittrik dared not look, lest his soul be stolen.

"We have legends of these beasts," he said. "They steal souls and bring nightmares to life."

"I don't think he can do that. Most laijireis, spiritlions as you call them, lived in your Rising Wood but went nearly extinct when it burned. Ambos was rescued from smugglers turns ago and gifted to me by a Council Master of Ku'du that wished to earn favor." She stroked the sleek black fur along its back, and it let out a deep cry. "It worked, obviously. For a time."

"It is your pet?"

"No, you cannot own a living thing, Mittrik Hwaelin. He is a friend, and he might be offended if he understood your question. But, luckily for you, Ambos doesn't get much practice with the Eastern tongue, so maybe he didn't. These creatures are intelligent. Some stories say they are wiser than humans, second only to Eerim. But let's go now, before the guards come around on their watch." And she tossed the spiritlion over her shoulder, draping him around her neck like an ermine scarf.

They walked through a glass-floored corridor overlooking the gardens, around a brown partition and into a small atrium with hundreds of triangular windows. She led him through slim cracks between the walls that would open into quiet places with upside down fountains, hanging statues and colorful tapestries. She led him down a winding stairwell, past the sound of men laughing together, and then through another maze of blue crystal walls. All the while Mittrik tried to ignore the spiritlion, who continued to gawk awkwardly from the princess's neck.

Asudden the princess stopped in front of a carving in the wall, a man as tall as she was etched into the stone slab, armored heavily, feathers at his back, and with tears falling from his eyes, dropping into his open mouth. She turned back to Mittrik, whispered, "This tunnel will take us out of the city walls by the back of Ashakai's gate, and then we'll head west to the trees. It is a great walk, I warn you."

Already it had been. Rae placed her palm on the carved relief of a looped vine, and something that looked like swirling dust and shine grew beneath her hand. The crying man moved, and the wall opened before them to pitch black.

Mittrik heard a cough behind him. He turned with his hand by the hilt of his sword, breathing in. Rae's scarfaced brother leaned against a rock pillar, his arms crossed. He, too, carried his weapons, and Mittrik knew he was skilled with them. At the Academy, he and his twin fought as efficiently as three good men, so Mittrik supposed Tyanien Janseyu was man and a half.

Rae raised a finger to her lips, smiled like a fiend while the spiritcub purred. Her brother grinned at her before heaving himself off the wall dramatically and walking away, mimicking perfectly the airy six-noted whistle of the blue crowned bird. Mittrik blew out his breath.

Rae grabbed an unlit torch of sharp metal from the now open wall. She rubbed a finger against the red gem at the torch's center, pulling back just before it roared into bright flames. Countless steps lit up soft gold as she held the torch in front. The stairs led down forever.

"Are you ready?" she asked.

"No," his feeble answer, despite strong desire.

"Good, but I am going."

Mittrik followed her into the dark, smiling.

The Select Son of Amina had a restless night.

Aadarae was a child.

Himself, a younger man, not yet gray and not as tired as he was in his waking hours, stood straight. He wore his white and blue garments and the thin silver ringlet about his head gilded with a solitary stone of his ancestor's design.

Stones of Amina were rare. The last of them had been mined out of the mountains of Mítarr in the years following Amina's death. There had been no others formed from seeds of the patagua since those days, since no one but Amina could wield truelight, and after so long, many stones were no longer as stable to contain the erratic power. Now with Aadarae, this would change with some practice in their make. Wanúm anticipated, in time more refined stone could be made through wielded force. It was a tedious process, and Aadarae was impatient. *When she is older*, his head hurt with the thought. He ignored it.

The remaining stones of Amina were not often used for adornment or decoration, their practicality as tools of healing and their power of conduction outweighing their beauty, but still Daijirek appreciated the amaranthine gem above his brow. It set him apart from other men.

He was a good Council-member, the most sagacious of the twenty-six Select, he believed. He sent more missionary healers to the Confederation and beyond the Wilder Wood than the men in his position before him, and he had fought to open the Line of Separation for covert healers so that people of Baeltaf may receive true medicine. He had developed the newest and most widely taught combative technique of using truelight to stun, of course that was when he was a much younger man, and he could recite the ancient texts backwards if it was asked of him. Daijirek Wanúm preached compassion, toil, diligence, and steadfast love to Three-One and nothing less.

Of course, Three-One would choose him of all men to teach the second Araeboril.

First-One designed all things, and energies were of balanced nature. For this, family Teviona was ordained to bring to life the second Araeboril, the leading family whose words were *Duty, Compassion, Blood.* Amina preached compassion above all things, just as Iial. Three-One blessed the Great Leader for it.

Wanúm stood in a compact training hall of dark shale, an obstacle course of ropes and ladders behind him, listening to his student's chirping voice. She was young, a girl of only five Rock turns, prattling on about the changing colors of some obscure plant she found near the river of Ashakai, eyes moving in every direction, to the bookshelves, to the firestone globes above them, darting. Her eyes were two green balls passed between invisible, capricious jugglers. Wanúm was patient as he listened to the child speak at length about nothing in particular, but she was already beginning to exacerbate his serene disposition. She had a talent for it.

She was a typical child, though she was the only child he knew so well. He never had one of his own, never wanted to. For so long his relationship with the Select Daughter was only that which was expected of them: a divine bond of spirit but nothing more. Little more than politics, beyond that supernatural energy, held their lives together. There had not been love or real communion between them during those first decades as Selected Children, for she was inflexible and he apparently could not understand anything. But somehow this chosen child changed much of that.

Aadarae would be Selected on her twentieth turn, the youngest to rise to Select Council in history. Wanúm had been older and more learned when he was Selected on his thirty-eighth, but even he was considered young for the position. The holy ceremony came every thirty-five Rock turns, and while

Aadarae was just a child, he felt as though her time was fast approaching. *She has so much time to learn*, he told himself. *I have much to teach her*.

She talked and bounced around the room, opening and shutting books before moving on and looking out the window and poking the snapping flowers. She was perhaps the most insolent girl to ever be Selected, and he told her as much.

"But I don't want to be a Select," she eyes bobbing over everywhere, her head rolling on her shoulders. Her hair curled wild around her face. She had a bad habit of cutting the strands that fell in her way, so her curls were uneven and disheveled, frizzing around her ears. "I won't be a Select."

"You will." They had this same fight many times.

"Can't someone else be Selected, Master? I want to go east and be a covert healer like Cyenae was, only it was illegal when she did it. But then she was Selected and knew which laws she wanted to change. I could heal Bilers that don't have access to medicine, and I could mend broken bones! Or I could go west, to Achka or maybe to the Confederation, to heal and I wouldn't have to hide being a child of Amina. My father would think that was safer, don't you agree? Will you let me? Owé and Jan would want to come, too, probably. Can't we all go? You could convince Bapo, I know it. He listens to you. I want to travel and heal people, Master, not sit in stuffy congresses and force people to suffer for their mistakes."

"Wants are not for the likes of us, Aadarae." He straightened his robes, trying not to chuckle. "We must train ourselves to only want to serve and sacrifice our selfishness. Children of Amina must be selfless in our desires so that we may best help others, forgetting the self is essential to channeling truelight. You should not speak of the Select Council in such a way, young Tyanien. It is one of the highest honors a descendant may achieve. But since you're so anxious to learn healing, I have good news for you."

Her eyes met his and she smiled crookedly; one of her front teeth had still not grown in, had been punched out by her older sister. Wanúm extended his arms and pulled back the blue sleeves of his robes so that he may have free use of his hands.

"Today you are going to learn how to properly channel truelight through your fingers."

She gasped and rocked on the balls of her feet. He instructed her to be still and hold her hands in front of her. She shot them straight out, fingertips pointing at the ceiling.

"I can already grab it," she told him, her left hand reaching to prove her point. Sharp daggers of lightning stretched from her skin, cracking with sound and brilliance. She stuck out her tongue in concentration and pushed it away from herself. Wanúm watched the truelight move. "And I can guide it, and I don't need to forget myself. I told you that it was easy." The truelight spun and bounced off her hands until it disappeared above her head.

Wanúm had managed to *feel* truelight when he was only ten, and he was considered a prodigy of his descendance. Catching truelight at only five turns was an astonishing feat that spoke of her innate power. The girl was born with faint radiance dancing between her fingers, and for that her mother had named her Aadarae, an old Blessed name that means 'dance with truelight'. The name of Amina's youngest daughter. The Rock knew what Teviona Aadarae was since that day.

"Grabbing something is not the same as using it, and guiding is not channeling. Now are you going to pay attention and stop interrupting me, child? Or will you go back to the ropes until your mind is calm?"

"It is calm, and I am calm-like." Her chin sprang up and down, her pale eyes never leaving him.

"Now, the truelight moves in a constant wave," he told her, but the girl crossed her skinny arms in front of her chest and scrunched her features at him.

"But that isn't true," she blurted, her head shaking dramatically. Had she been any other student, she would have faced real discipline for discordance with a master, more severe since her master was a Select Son, but as she was the youngest Tyanien and his very special undertaking, Wanúm merely narrowed his eyes at her.

"Oh, it isn't?" He tried to stay patient, folding his own arms in front of himself and matching her stance. "Am I not a truthspeaker? Tell me then, what is truelight, child? Since you, in your extensive wisdom and study, know more than a Select Son."

"It is like..." He watched her eyes flit around the room, blinking, trailing out the window to the row of towers and back up to the dangling fireglobes. She spun her head to look at something, and suddenly she was spinning in tight little circles, her arms drifting out to her sides and humming, ignorant of the harsh look on her instructor's face. He sighed loudly, realizing she was lost to him.

"Aadarae," snapping his fingers to call her back to attention.

"Oh," she giggled. "Sorry. It isn't a wave, Master. I mean, it kind of is. Partly, sometimes. But more than that it isn't. Does that make sense? It is... difficult to explain."

More difficult to understand, he thought tiredly, *and this child thinks she sees it all so clearly. I wonder if Amina suffered this pride.*

"Very well," he said, deciding that science was beyond this child. His best chance at getting her to listen might be the poetic descriptions from the ancient writings, from the first Araeboril herself. "Truelight is everywhere, and it goes where it may. It is one and many, pulsing veins and searching vines that reach out to touch. They look but they do not see, mindless but with a mind acting."

She was focused now, her gap-toothed smile never leaving his face.

"It is pure and good, my child, and it resonates with all life. It is countless, and countable. As a healer, you must allow all that you can to consume you before you are able to manipulate it effectively. You forget your wants, your desires, and you can connect."

Somewhere else Wanúm barely woke, he heard shouting, *Stop!*

"Let it consume me?" Aadarae looked up to him with bug's eyes. So innocent. "I don't like how that sounds."

"Then I will rephrase: you must reach out and allow the truelight to enter every living cell in your being, let it capture every smallest part and then expel it back with a willful push in the physical. In the spiritual, pray for peace. You must have faith to do so and you must imagine it happening as you go. Have faith in the truelight and in our God, and you will channel. I believe it."

The child kicked her left foot up and back behind her, and Wanúm feared he was losing her attention again.

"Trust me, Aadarae. Feel the pinpricks of the energy and let that go through every bit of you, like a wave from your hands to your spine and to your hands again. It is subtle at first. It will feel as though you are waking from a dream, but you must remain. Lose control to gain it back tenfold." It was the same advice his own master had given him when he was a boy. It had taken him a half moons' wane to successfully channel the unstable force, but Daijirek expected the Tyanien would manage it by the day's end.

Arrogant fool! came a voice again, and he shook his head, looked down to his pupil, who no longer smiled.

"Will it hurt?" Her voice, smaller than it had been in life.

"No," Daijirek answered honestly, but felt as though he had swallowed a living firestone. "This has been done by countless children of Amina for thousands of turns. You are a child of the energy, more than any since Amina, and when you allow it to enter you in its totality, it will be painless."

"Do you promise?" Her eyes shifted again until they settled on her sandals, and her toes wiggled in little curls. He didn't imagine the shimmer there, her toes caught truelight, too.

"Tyanien Aadarae, what is the third rule of mastering descendance?" he asked, throat burning, patience wearing thin.

Stop!

"Trust your master who is older and wiser in sense," she gave back, not missing a beat.

"Would you like me to demonstrate this thing?"

"No. I have seen truelight channeled. It won't be difficult… only…" and when she looked up at him, he swore tears were collecting in the pinks of her eyes. "What do I do once it consumes me? What will you do? And if it does hurt, how do I stop it?"

Wanúm kissed the top of her head. "Once it consumes you, push it out of your hands. You will not need to stop anything, little Tyanien. When I first allowed truelight in completely, it felt warm. Like diving into sun-soaked water, breaking through a surface, and over as soon as it happened. As I said, from hands to spine and push back. And from there we will begin channeling in its form to heal."

"I worry about pushing truelight out of my hands. When you say, 'allow it in completely—" she tried but Daijirek cut off her question.

"Enough diverting, child. Stop finding distractions. You said it yourself, it is not difficult to do."

You, stupid man! Stop!

She held her hands out in front of her, her eyes finally settling on her twitching fingertips, her top knuckles bent. It was blinding at first, the surge of power that set off in her hands; he blinked and shadowed his face under the sleeve of his robe. The truelight flashed as blistered air in a storm, jagged and winding around her hands and feet, obstructing her face and quickly raising her from the floor. Daijirek blinked and stared, and he might have screamed as he saw her eyes turn to moons of white. Her head rolled back, her body soared higher, and her scream pierced his very spirit. Truelight exploded off the child like a flare.

It knocked him to his knees, so hard the bones broke.

In life, the Academy walls shattered, and the room had been filled with rubble, fire and smoke. In life, Daijirek Wanúm, like hundreds, had been rendered unconscious by the wave of energy, and did not wake until days later with many broken bones. In life, he slept while over sixty died from the walls caving. While one Achkan woman was consumed by the Araeboril's power. In this dream, he watched as the globes above them fell onto the carpets and book piles and dipped the room in flame, and he watched as the child fell nearly three levels with a resounding crack; and though he ran as fast he could, his feet did not allow him close enough to get to her.

Aadarae shook violently and blood wept from her eyes, her ears, her nose, her lips, and though she stared at him, Daijirek did not think she could see past the blinding white light in her eyes. He ran but did not move, he shouted but there came no sound. Aadarae's leg and arm bent sharply, terribly beneath her, and more blood puddled from the ripped wound of her shin, pierced by white splintered bone. Her fingertips, singed black, were the only part of her that did not rattle atop the stone. Her once-jittery hands lay still, dead. She screamed as the fire reached her, and it was the most horrifying sound.

Stop!

He woke, finally, in his bed, drenched in sweat and guilt. The sheets clung to him. His eyes focused on the muted candles in the room.

"You were fighting something," Cyenae, Select Daughter of Amina, said from her seat by the window, one of Aadarae's "secret" Eastern tomes positioned in her lap. Of course, Aadarae meant to keep all of the smuggled writings secret from her masters but could not. Though nothing of plagues, the girl uncovered disturbing and complexing experiments, riddled with magic and ancient medicine, and cruelty most of all.

"I was dreaming of the explosion," Wanúm said as he righted himself against the pillows, his muscles sore and stiff around old bones. "I was reliving my infamy."

"My sorrows for you," Cyenae said without looking at him. She didn't feel sorry at all. She thought he deserved all this pain and more. "Your night terrors are increasing as hers are. These are only dreams. Aren't they?"

No, Daijirek thought, lucky to be the only man in Canyassor who didn't have to answer her. *Worst dreams are memories.*

At the crossroad, where the path met the treeline, the western princess tossed the spiritcub onto the ground with little care, and it darted beneath the leaves, disappeared in a blink. The beast moved even quicker than the princess.

They had seen no one but a handful of herders and dogs on the thin road from the city to the treeline, and Mittrik thought that was rather lucky, but it was still dark. This beginning of day WAS much *too* warm for the winter; he felt pulled out of time entirely. The sun had yet to rise behind them and the whole of life was set to a faded blue color: the dripping wet leaves above, the busy undergrowth, the leaves beneath his boots, the princess's skin, his own. It made him feel not yet awake, and not sleeping, like the moment between where nothing could be remembered.

But he'd remember it all.

"Will he come back?" Mittrik asked of her vanished spiritcub.

"He always appears where he needs to be."

The road ended at a great line of trees, dense and dark against their faded blue world. The great grass shifted in the trees beyond. Something walked just out of sight, just under the grass. Mittrik could not see it but he heard the rustling, he saw the way the vegetation dipped as if being tread on, and he heard a thunderous roar come from the distant west. Birds flew off at the sound.

"What was that?" he asked Rae, who did not seem bothered. She walked into the brush with her wide blade drawn.

"A cunju," she answered. "They are like spotted tree-wolves, only bigger."

Mittrik never heard of a tree-wolf, but it didn't sound like a pleasant creature despite its spots. She made him laugh when she promised to protect him from cunjus and other evils, but truthfully he was relieved. He drew his sword and entered the wilderness with her.

Now they had been walking for long hours in the trees, and the sunlight loomed well above them, orange peaking through gaps in the leaves and decorating the space in speckled shadow. Mittrik had known only clear, wide spaces, which in their vastness called out to be roamed. Skies open that would not dissuade anyone. Fields and sparse forests lacking pine or wolves. He had ridden across those expansive marshes and hills his whole life and had loved looking out and seeing the world splayed provocatively before him. All for him.

These jungles were dense— smothering—and he could not imagine what hid behind the trees. This place was not inviting and open, it was barricading and teaming with living danger, woven tightly with green-colored mystery. It reminded him of those stories miners told of the golden caves, suffocating and monochrome and glamorous.

He noted that Rae, the princess, walked akin to a knight: with a proud chin, squared shoulders, and a long, steady gait that resembled a march, though there was a lively vigor in the bounce of her feet, a loveliness in the swing of her hips that was unique to her. She had to wait for him at the top of each hill, much to his chagrin, but she never said a word regarding his slower pace. He wondered how she didn't lose her footing, her steps so quick, light and effortless. Her stare constantly shifted around them and scrutinized every twitching branch and howling thing, but in those brief moments when their eyes would meet, she smiled at Mittrik, and they talked. Of anything she wanted.

"You give over your lifewater just so?" she asked when he reached her at a canopied peak. The chittering of distant birds grew louder, mingling with other bizarre sounds

"Yes. Every Crestday the lowlords gather, you give the gods what is their due, so they may bless your dwellings and underlords in the following year," Mittrik said, trying not to pant as a dog. The air was hot in his chest. "It is not much blood, just a cut really on Hetten's shrine, and only the family of the Dominion's High Lord bleeds. The houses of the lowlords watch and sing."

"You make a blood oath every harvest, with your own blood." Her eyes were wide at him, and he noticed the dark circles that sunk above her freckled cheekbones. *She is exhausted, too,* he realized.

"Sure," he gave, smiling at her. "But it is not as serious as you think, just ceremony."

"There is power in ceremony, and power in blood. It is interesting that you see magic in wielding, but not in yourself or your lands."

And she walked ahead of him again, so agile and quick that it made Mittrik huff and stalk faster against the pushing wind, despite the sore stinging in his calves and backside.

"Explain to me something, Lord Hwaelin. I do not understand why your people ask forgiveness through a holy man, to your gods who you claim hardly care, rather than ask forgiveness from the person you offended in the first."

Mittrik laughed and clenched his clamming fists. "I suppose it is because gods determine your fate, and not men."

She stopped at the base of the hill and looked back to him. "Do you believe that?"

"No, I don't," he sighed against the pull on his tongue, growing accustomed to the pleasant sensation and feeling freedom in it. She nodded at him and went on down the path. She asked a lot of pleasant questions, though at times he believed she would ask something too invasive, too searching, and he would want to fight it. She did not, however, and kept on questioning about holy vows and knighthoods, asking questions that amused him endlessly. They talked of all the things Mittrik liked.

"What is this '*torreny*', you say?" she asked him as the day got hotter and stickier, and he liked the way her tongue rolled the word.

"Tourney, a tournament." Mittrik had been describing the jousting on his last birthday, when he unseated Patrik Osmond, broke the lance right against his helm to win his prized courser. "Like a great competition and sport for all the highborns when they gather, but the commoners watch as well. There is a central melee, jousting, archery, tree tossing, juggling and the like. And ladies sit in shaded pavilions to sip wine and watch."

"Tournament, yes I am understanding that word. A demonstration of skill." She nodded. "There will be plenty of those at my brother's wedding, though our people demonstrate a different variety of skills. If you would like, I can find a man on a horse for you to hit, and he, of course, could hit you if that would add to your enjoyment. I have only ever seen jousts in Biler paintings, but I think I could make it happen."

Mittrik laughed. "No, no that is alright. Thank you for the thought, but I am sure I will enjoy the celebration without. I am excited to see more of your people."

At the top of the next hill, he took in a quick breath of cool damp air. A soft mist was rising from trees above them, and he watched as the white drifted into the sky and slowly grew thicker, and the winds rushed the soft clouds toward them. It sprinkled their faces and clothes, but Rae did not seem to notice.

"Would you like to see a joust?" he asked.

"Oh, yes. It sounds like a wonderful thing. One day, maybe I will see a Biler tourney. Have you seen many?"

"Yes. Many more than most, I would say. I havc competed in just under ten, and attended a few more besides. You would be most welcome to come see them in Baeltaf, but compared to this place, I do not think there is much besides that you could consider wonderful."

"Maybe not."

As they hiked through that pure, white mist. the day grew warm. Never was there silence in the trees. They walked beneath a tree of strange string leaves, each bundled thin and pale as Leonara's fine hair. Rae raised a hand to them, and the bundle flicked like a horse's tail, as if guarding itself from her touch. *Stupid plants,* Mittrik thought.

The variety of life was constantly surprising him. Flowers of strangest shapes: some pink and yellow ones that hung and twung in wind like the large bells of a temple, others that would open, close, or buzz as they walked by them, ones that looked like purple heathers upside down, and more that changed color as they passed. The land surrounding him never stopped living, bleating, and chittering. It was all he could hear, and while it was wonderful it was also unsettling. Past the green cover, he could not see as much as the hidden saw, but he felt the hidden look deeply into him. He wanted to hear Rae's bright voice again above the rest, to hear her laughter rise against that hectic clatter of things unknown.

"What do you call that magic you do?"

"Not magic," she said with a throaty chuckle, and just as she laughed, rain came down on them. "I wield truelight."

The rain was not bitter and cold as Mittrik knew rain to be. It was warm, and the ground welcomed it with sweet petrichor. The princess did not seem to notice the rain, even as the sky darkened, and the water fell in heavy sheets. Her pace never changed, and Mittrik panted and dragged his wet boots as he trailed behind her.

"What is truelight?"

"An energy beyond nature," she said as though it were plain. He looked at her dumbly, rubbing the back of his neck. He felt a stinging there, as though something had bit him.

"I do not understand you."

"I wield one unnatural energy as opposed to natural energies, Lord Mittrik."

"Forgive me. What do you mean by natural or unnatural energy, princess?"

"There are four natural energies flowing through life. In canyaéo we say ya du, ya sor, ya shiar, and ya hak—the energies of the waters, the lands, the winds, and the flames. Those that only wielders sense."

"You speak very strangely," he said, dropping his head as he remembered her proper title, "er... Tyanien, but I have never heard of such powers as I have seen these past days. Not like yours. Not even in legends."

She turned back to look at him curiously, eyes cutting him as deeply as her smile. Mittrik thought, *My family sigil is made of sharp swords, and so, too, her smile.*

"But the legends are true, as well," he added, closing most of the distance between them. "Spiritlions and elves walk the earth."

"Eerim," she corrected gently, walking ahead of him again. "Elf is a crude and racist Fair Island term."

"And groles?" Mittrik wondered.

"Now I am not understanding you."

"My brother said while he was in your city he saw creatures covered in eyes all over, those that have extra fingers on each hand. Groles."

"Oh! You mean Ku'dur." She spoke the word like a sharp snap in her throat. "I have never heard of groles—that is new. But yes, Ku'dur people have nine fingers on either hand, and they are all covered in their false eyes."

"Their many eyes are not real? What of their sorcery?"

"That's just what we call their eyes, they are not really false in the way you might be thinking. False eyes are Ku'dur eyes, but it is a distinction we say. As for their sorcery, magic is true and the Ku'dur credit themselves with its creation but most forms are outlawed."

"Then why call their eyes false?" He wondered if he would ever understand this world where words he knew hd new meaning. Mittrik walked and focused on his moving feet to keep his head from spinning. *Is it possible to learn too much?*

"We call them false because... well, that is what they told humans to call them thousands of Rock turns ago, before Canyassor even existed. If you stare too long into false eyes, and you let your guard down, if you are not aware of yourself, you can become entranced. When our eyes look into false eyes, it can be like a dream. Now it is illegal for Ku'dur to try to affect someone by this, so it is not so terrifying as when humans were enslaved. Most are cautious to not look into them regardless. What do the false eyes of the Ku'dur see if not us? That question inspired much terror in the turns before humans broke their chains and still many after. And then Amina was born and asked the question, and their eyes are much like ours. Their eyes see like ours— what is right before them, all around them. They see the same with more color, we know. Just like us but a bit more."

"Perhaps that is more terrifying." *It is possible to learn too much at once.*

"I think you have the right of it," she said and laughed as they climbed higher into rain and mist.

They walked through warm air under trees wrapped in thin purple vines, birds with golden crowns and red tarsus flew into brown nests hanging and oddly shaped like twig teardrops from arching branches. As they stepped, the ground released a grassy sweet fragrance; Mittrik stepped on an orange flower and it released a soft yellow pollen that tickled his nose. A bug the size of his palm landed on his shoulder and startled him, and its shell-like wings reflected the soft sunlight like the sheen of a sword. He knocked it off quickly and picked up his pace.

Mittrik was trying hard not to wheeze as they came atop a craggy peak. The path split in two at the top, one way leading north seemed heavily trafficked; another more treacherous path went south, vines crossing overhead, large rocks and thick roots obstructing the way.

Rae pointed north, to the well tread road, as she said, "If you follow this path for two days, you come across my grandfather's arácuy grove."

"Your family are farmers?"

"Yes, but we are going this way," she said, her feet skipping her down the hill south, over the large black roots of a drooping tree.

"Your father is a king and your uncle a poor farmer?"

"Well, not poor like Biler farmers. My mother's family work the lands in the village called Papetí," she said to him, looking up at the cradling intertwine of canopies. "She grew up in these mountains. My father met her while he was exploring. She helped him down from a cunju trap."

He stared at her back, the defined muscles of her arms that swung carelessly at her sides. Her tight breeches allowed him to see the rocking and swaying of her hips as she walked. The hill descended steeply for some time. Mittrik's bones were weary, and his chest was unaccustomed to the heavy, wet air.

When it stopped raining, they were deep in a valley of tall palms and soft yellow bushes covered in sparkling black bulbs. Rae warned him not to touch the sparkling bulbs unless he wanted his hands dyed for a month. The path had long ago disappeared, the bent grass allowing him a hint at the destination. But he could only see so far.

"I am hungry," she said, stopping abruptly before him. "Shall we break for a meal? It is very late for first foods. Forgive me for not thinking of it sooner."

And then she was hacking away at thin vines that looped around red branches, grabbing the ropelike bundle she collected and returning her wide blade back to its binding sheath. Hers did not look like any scabbard Mittrik had seen; it looked light and flexible, but solid somehow, a deep blue fabric woven taut.

The princess walked beneath a tall palm, thin with all its leaves clustered at the top, and then she positioned the cut strips of vines around the soles of her feet. She hooked them in a loop around her heels and positioned herself at the base of the tree. She was climbing straight up at once, leaving Mittrik staring at her rear as it shimmied up the palm. She moved so quickly, she could have flown into the leaves, and Mittrik stared at the place where she disappeared. Large round fruit fell in deep resounding *thuds* atop the soft earth near Mittrik's feet, and once the fifth striped green fruit had fallen, she was sliding down the thin trunk of the tree, the vines wrapped around her hands.

She took one of the striped fruits, and hacked the top off with one of her wideblades. The shell of the fruit was hard like tree bark. Mittrik enjoyed watching her work— she held the wideblade like an extension of herself, no matter which hand held it. Either suited her. In Baeltaf, women were not interested in swords. Perhaps some were, but none that Mittrik had ever met.

Of course, Leonara proclaimed that she wished to fight him with a sword, but she feigned interest in whatever Jonn and Mittrik favored just to be like them. He thought he might teach her how to fight with a sword after seeing what was possible in the New World. She would like that.

The princess finished cutting the striped fruit.

"Drink this," she said, handing one to him. It was heavier than he thought it would be.

The liquid inside was clear like water. He hesitantly lifted the whole thing to his lips as she did the same. It was indeed water, but slightly sweet. Little white chunks floated in the liquid but they were soft and sweeter.

She gathered smaller, darker green fruits into her arms. "These are called guiba, and they are very good. They will also help us finish the trek, give us a little more strength," she told him, sitting atop a thick, exposed root. He went to sit on a rock beside her.

"No, not there!" she barked, and he stopped. "Look, there are daggertails there. Has no one told you about the daggertails?"

Mittrik shook his head and looked. There were four lobster-like bugs on the rock that he had not seen before. They blended so well to the rough gray color and texture. He only saw them now because one had its dagger tail raised and ready to pierce him, hovering above its shelled body waiting, claws held high.

"Oh," Rae said, "well just always make sure to shake out your boots before putting them on your feet, because daggertails are everywhere." She moved so that he could sit beside her on the great wide root. It was as tall as a chair, but damp and not nearly as comfortable.

She unsheathed a shining dirk that had been hidden at the stone padding on her calf, and he simply stared. Mittrik wondered if she had more hidden weapons, and couldn't imagine where. She sliced the violet crystal edge against the tough skin of the darker green fruit, cutting it into thick wedges. Where her thumb grazed against the blade's colored sharpness, sparks lit up as though someone had struck chert against firesteel. Oddly enough, that did not worry him. She handed him half of the fare as she cut, and each piece was an odd dripping thing, marbled with red and white; the red looked like the jelly of a tart, and the white soft like fur.

The red part of the fruit tasted sweet as a berry, while the white juice came out sour, but wonderfully so, and the softness did not feel like fur to his tongue. Together they mingled and turned into something truly fine, and it woke him up. Suddenly he was not so tired, or so sore. The amount she picked were gone too quickly, and then she was bringing her wide blade out again to cut palm sized, round bark-like pieces off of the water fruit. After splitting the fruit in halfs, she used the round piece to spoon out more of the soft white flesh for them to eat.

Mittrik clenched his left hand, feeling an ache and stiffness, and he felt how hungry he really was.

"Your swords," he said, "what is the crystal along the edge that lights to your skin?" He wanted to hold either of her swords in his hands, to see if they were very heavy or very light. The look of them did not give much away.

"Refined stone of Amina blended into Bavarian edimus, metal good for weapons. The stone of Amina stores truelight that I can manipulate. I saw that your brother's sword is decorated in degenerated firestones, though he's no wielder of fire. Why is this?"

"I don't...the rubies?" he asked, and she nodded hesitantly. "It is a greatsword suitable for a High Lord, decorated with rubies and gold for our house. The Hwaelins have been mining gold and rubies in Kieln for centuries, and iron too though it's not so good as the iron in Brimtone."

"If they are pure stones, and they look it to me, that could be dangerous. It is good your sword is without these adornments. Is your hand hurting?" she asked, pointing with her red stained lips to his flexing fingers.

"Yes," he said, wishing he had not, but he could not take it back. "Only very little. An old pain, I broke it as a child falling from a tree. I was lucky it wasn't my sword hand."

She looked at his hand intently, and all the while Mittrik looked into her eyes. He thought he could see a soft orb of light build beneath the pale irises, like a growing ring moving toward the rim of dark lashes. She finally looked up at him, just as he was sure of the light, and it was gone. *Am I imagining things now?*

She ate another piece of fruit. "If you would like, I could fix it for you. I can heal a badly mended bone."

"You can heal it?" Mittrik asked.

"Yes. I have studied healing my whole life, among many things, but healing is my favorite. I am very good at it, actually. It would be quick, and then the pain would be gone."

He nodded and tried not to laugh at her, for it sounded too insane to be true, but then again—he had seen the kinds of things she could do. The Tyanien smiled, drawing closer to him and wiping her hands against her breeches. She told him to take off his golden ring, and he pocketed it still trying not to laugh. She extended her muscled arms out before her body, hovering her palms over Mittrik's left hand, and then all the tips of her long fingers bent strangely. Her hands were rough and brown. Dirt under her nails.

The blood beneath her hands was blue beneath brown, at once shining. Veins glowed beneath her skin, and then Mittrik saw something like a hundred thin, fractured lightning bolts extend from her hands to his. Warmth touched him, like gentle sunlight at Eberle, as he saw her lightning jolt into him though her hands never touched him. Soon the blood of his hands and arms echoed hers in that brilliance and shining. Mittrik could make out the segmented bones of his hand and fingers, and he wiggled them slowly to see how they moved.

"Stay very still," Rae told him, but then it felt like he didn't have a choice.

His hand felt trapped by her power; he could not move if he tried, suspended in the beginning twines of light as they parted from her hands and clung to his. The bolts grew thick, appearing like ropes braiding around his fingers and wrists. Mittrik looked to her face, now sure of the orbs of light in her eyes.

He looked back to his hand and watched as the bones set alight, his knuckle and the small bones near his wrist. He could see all beneath his flesh, roads of veins leading up his hand and disappearing again as the light faded at his shoulder. The bones moved and jerked beneath the flesh, one way then the other before settling back neatly where it should be on his hand. Mittrik watched aghast, but there was no pain. And when she pulled away and the light faded, there was only a soft tingling in his hand as if he had laid on it in sleep.

"What did you do?" Mittrik asked, flexing. There was no pain. "How did you do it? How did that not hurt?"

"I aligned the bones and took the pain using truelight."

"You took it?" he asked and laughed because he couldn't understand. He looked down at his hand, free of stiffness and any ache.

"You could say I filtered nervous activity that translates your pain within myself using truelight, so it was not a thing you felt, but I did due to the connection…" She sounded unsure, and Mittrik had no clue what she was meaning. "Somehow. The science of truelight's nature is more speculative than natural energy, and your tongue does not have words enough to discuss it. Unlike the other energies, truelight was not something so... definable. There's an entire field of study dedicated to theory. I hate talking to theorists."

"You felt my pain," he realized, "that I should have felt."

She nodded. "Yes, healers absorb pain in such matters. In an ideal situation, a healer can use natural medicine and truelight, and healers that cannot wield truelight must use stones of Amina. This thing with your bone is not so difficult for me. Your pain is nothing to me at this point in my training."

"You should not have," he said. *What else can I say?* "But thank you."

She smiled and stood from her place. "Yes, I should have, Lord Hwaelin. I am a healer, it is what I do. Do you feel better?"

"Yes, much," he answered, standing, too. "Please, call me Mittrik, Tyanien."

"Call me Rae. Titles will be nothing. I prefer it. Your hand should not hurt you anymore."

He nodded, still flexing his new hand. They continued walking and the breezes became jumbled, the trees thinned if only a little.

After more than half a dozen ups and downs and covered hills, Mittrik could feel sluggishness again.

The Forsaken heat.

Rae looked back to him, then walked to a sagging tree with yellow leaves, wrapped in black vines dotted in orange bumps. Rae jumped up and stripped a vine of those orange bumps. She rolled them in her hands, and Mittrik watched as round petals turned to a vibrant powder.

"Your skin drinks too much light," she said. She smeared her stained fingers across his cheeks and forehead. "Now you will not burn."

"Thank you," he said, a staying thrill where her calloused skin touched him. Her hands were hard, not like a lady's hands. There was skill and strength in them. Purpose.

"We should get to the cavern by the Great Fire's highpoint," Rae said, nearly bouncing as she marched. "Come on. Good thing it did not rain on this side of the mountain, or we would be sliding down. But that can be fun."

Mittrik followed without hesitation. He didn't think of himself as a follower (though he never considered himself much of a leader either), but he realized he could follow her off the world's farthest edge and likely still be smiling, forgetting the rest.

Fehatsi woke to the sound of Teia humming. Blinking crusty eyes, candles lit the floor, illuminating what the blocked Great Fire couldn't. There was no way to tell the time— Fehatsi never acclimated to Rae's windowless room.

Teia sat in front of the mirror, braiding back amber ringlets in four rows close to her scalp, the curls all coming together at the base of her neck. She was already dressed in training clothes.

"What is the time?" Fehatsi asked, dragging a hand across her face. "Where is Rae?"

"Don't worry, you have plenty of time to get ready. I wouldn't let you sleep late."

"And Rae?" Fehatsi repeated the more important question.

Teia sighed. "I don't know. She and Ambos were gone before I woke."

"Gone?" *Of course, she is. Of course, she can't stay still for a day.* "What could be going on in her head? With the Bilers here, and the union coming," Fehatsi said, rolling off the bed and cracking her knuckles.

Teia would always defend Rae. "She needs a distraction from the union planning."

"She is addicted to distraction."

Fehatsi did not mean to sound harsh. She loved Rae as a sister, and like a sister, Rae wasn't shielded from anger despite being the Araeboril. Fehatsi was two turns younger than the youngest Tyanien, three turns younger than Teia, and still she was the most mature and reasonable of the three women. She was certainly the only one to consider the repercussions of her actions. *Rae should know better, she does know better.*

Fehatsi huffed, deciding on a long blue dress. Teia helped her tie it behind her neck and lent her a green sash to tie around her middle.

"I am starving," Teia said when she was finished laying down the edges of their hair neatly.

"You could eat with me and my father, if you want," Fehatsi offered. "There will be oat pudding, your favorite."

"I will steal some sweetsop from the kitchens before I go to the Academy."

"You should not train in the Academy today, on this Moima of all days, too. People will talk of your lack of faith, and there are more ears than ever in the city. There are other ways to spend your time."

"For me, training is like resting and prayer, which makes everyday Moima."

Fehatsi rolled her eyes. "Nadya would understand if you decided to take the holy day for once. You are always welcome to join my father and me for first foods, you know," Fehatsi told her. Teia did not look tempted.

"Thank you. I should train. Give my best to the Korr."

Fehatsi watched Teia leave to the Academy, and then jogged the rest of the way to the Korr's tower. Fehatsi hoped she would be alone with her father today. Most of their shared meals were also shared with village representatives or council members, foreign noble-bloods and the like. Her father loved to introduce her to powerful people. It had been Rajen before that had to deal with the primary politics of being a Riambo; he'd had the talent and taste for such a life, a fluency in charisma. Fehatsi was a Riambo, so she had the talent to impress diplomats and perform political strategy underhand, but the taste was still unsavory and bitter for her. Rajen had wanted to be a member of the Honorary Council, and he would have been, too. Fehatsi was sure of it.

Her father had the highest of hopes for her, she knew. But she had not been alone with him in nearing four moons' wax and wane, and she had much on her mind. Nothing she wanted to share. She felt like there was much she had to say, only she didn't know yet how to say it. She should have thought of all the words by now; she had enough time, more than enough.

She did not bother knocking, since she was invited and already late. When she opened the door, she noticed that all the fires were lit and warming, despite the brightness of the day. The decorative plants looked as though they had not been watered for a while. Her father was writing, like he usually was. His bald head was glaring at her. His beard, was dark and shaved close to his skin, though she was beginning to see the light dusting of gray on his chin.

"Fehatsi," her father said without looking up from his rushing pen. His pen was a beautiful gift from her mother, with a carved and painted long-tongued lizard wrapped around its length, the green scales still shining despite the years. "I am glad you have finally arrived. My stomach was beginning to speak to me in your absence, and it lacks your eloquence. Take a seat and I will join you in a moment."

She did and waited for him to finish. Finally, he sat with her at the round table.

"Where is our Araeboril today?"

Fehatsi swallowed. "She woke before I did. I don't know where she is."

"You... don't know?"

Instead of chastising her, he asked, "You have met with the Bilers?" as he cut and peeled back the skin of a mangae.

"Yes, though not much," she answered. "Have you?"

"No, I have not been blessed with the opportunity."

"Will you meet with them before they leave?"

"I have yet to decide," he said, wiping the strings of fruit off the corner of his lip with the cloth. "You must be careful with these lords of Baeltaf. Their ways are not our ways, though I have been told that Tyanien Aadarae has taken great interest in them."

"Aadarae cannot help but be enthralled by their arrival,"

Fehatsi said as she sipped on her juice. "You know she has always wanted to go beyond the Line. She wants to open borders and end the barricades, start trade again."

"Mm, I know. And erasing the Line of Separation is a noble pursuit, to be sure. Noble, hmph." He leaned back in his chair. "There have been over four hundred Great Leaders since the judges of the first days died and the regency was created, not all noble, but some have been. In all of our time, since the Blessed Lands rose there has only ever been one Araeboril before now. Amina didn't have a second, but if she did, we would remember their name. You are Aadarae's Korr, Fehatsi, her second."

"I know. I know I am."

"Yes, then as her second, you must encourage those plans of peace that she has, and the influence she has in her wisdom, but you must reign in those foolish desires she will also have."

"It is very difficult to change Rae's mind once it is made up on a subject." *Much like every single Teviona in this palace,* Fehatsi thought. *And like you, Father.*

"You must be braver than you think you are capable. You must, if you hope to stand at her side. You are named for your aunt Fehana," her father said, but Fehatsi knew that. "My sister was the bravest person I knew, the greatest Onatae there could have been."

It takes more than bravery to stand against Rae's fortressed will, and Onatae Teviona Fehana was known for little more than her golden eyes and pretty face, Fehatsi thought with some bitterness, but held herself from worse thought (because it was not really her dead aunt she resented in that moment). *And of course, Onatae Fehana is remembered for disappearing without trace on the westernmost seas and leading thousands after her. And me? I will be known for so much more.*

Her father stared at his plate for a long time, finally deciding to dunk his sweet bread into the jellied mix. "Do you wish to serve on the day of the union, or would you prefer to run off and enjoy the sights?"

She knew what she was supposed to say. "To serve, of course. I am to be a public servant one day, Three-One will it. What can I do?" She also knew that Riambo Rehonan asked questions when he already knew the answer, and of course her father knew she was lying.

"You will assist me in hosting and entertaining the Eerim Council as they travel behind the procession. Of the forty, all will be present and thirty-two have the better ear, so it will not be a day of idle thought in the least."

And there goes all diversion for me. It is all for Rae and Teia, and some damned Bilers. "I can watch my mind when I need to," Fehatsi assured her father, smiling pleasantly. *But I'll think what I want to now, while my thoughts are still my own. Still nothing is ever private, nothing is solely mine. My path is Aadarae's and my truths belong to whoever has the will to hear or extract them. How is that just?*

"Thank you, it will be a great help for me. Your mother is not coming for the celebration. Your uncle's plague is progressing, and she wishes to remain in Riam with him before he passes."

"When she comes back will she be staying in the tower house? Or might she stay in Riam even after Uncle Asalir dies?"

"Why do you think your mother might stay in Riam?"

"I just doubted that she would stay in the palace with us. I know that your union is ending." She might as well be honest with him, direct and without more delay, even if he could not afford her the same courtesy. It was not such a rare thing, for people to separate, though public figures were certainly scrutinized more for it.

"You listen to Academy rumors now?"

He meant to tease her, but she did not think it was funny. Rumors were rarely that in a world where thoughts were currency and truths were token, and Fehatsi had good sources in her cousins that lived on the greater island, and greater sources in the Eerim embassy director who was sweet for her. Rumors were, at very least, influence.

Fehatsi said, "Only when they're true. I understand that my mother needs to be away from this place. It is a store of memories. It has been difficult since Rajen died." Her father flinched at her brother's name, and her throat tightened. She continued, "I am done not speaking of him, even if it pains you. I think Rajen would be angry if he knew how little his name was spoken between us all." *We cannot forget him,* Fehatsi thought, skin beginning to crawl. To itch.

Her father nodded sadly, then turned his face from her to breathe, to drink water from his cup, to ponder all while nodding and eyes glistening. It was his way— he never spoke outright in reaction, a trait of a politician. Fehatsi thought it was meant to show her he really listened to what she had to say, and that he tried to understand it. Whether he succeeded in doing so, however, she hadn't decided.

"Perhaps he would be angry. It is still so fresh, and we get so little time together these days. I find that I would rather it be filled with cheerful conversation than anything else. But if you wish to speak of Rajen, and honor him in this way, we can."

Fehatsi was suddenly less sure; her stomach flipped and all she could picture was Rajen laying on his mat in sleep, waking to the face of a friend, dying in the chaos, dying on his back. She tried to bring up her memories of him smiling, and fighting, and arguing with her. All her brain gave was blood on sand, betrayal and dark red. Why were the images she conjured more vivid than the memories, the real things her eyes had seen? She didn't know what to say, but she could not be silent now with her father's golden look on her.

"I miss him. He would have enjoyed this commotion, and he would have thought Bilers in the Blessed Lands was a wonderful thing." There. She spoke of him and didn't vomit.

"You think so? Hm, maybe he would. We all miss him. But he is in the first plane living a life we cannot fathom. And here we must remain missing him until our time comes."

Fehatsi nodded, her father took a large bite of his bread and somehow that was that. *How does he always manage to silence me so deftly?* It seemed second nature to him, and that bothersome feeling in her gut persisted. *I am only silencing myself, really. I am deciding to shut up now,* she told herself, because it was what Rae might do. Rae would take responsibility in every choice. Rae never put blame on anyone other than herself. And while the blame for most anything often belonged to Tyanien Aadarae, she took credit for the bad in everybody else, too. Her self-inflicted martyrdom was at best annoying.

Fehatsi's father asked, "Are you angry with me?"

"No," she lied, which Rae could never do.

"Your mother and my business is just that, our own. It has been difficult dealing with all this grief, and know I do love her."

She wasn't sure. "Yes, I know."

"Your mother and I will not separate publicly or end our relationship legally, and we will come to a happy conclusion after her return, I am sure. I understand the apprehensions you might have on how this would affect your position in finding a good partner. You don't need to worry in that regard, we will do whatever we can to secure your place."

Fehatsi had never worried on that. Being first lyaren to the Araeboril outweighed any scandal her family could bring upon itself, and she had no interest in finding a partner just yet. "You are right," she said, "I would prefer more cheerful conversation."

"Ah, yes," her father chuckled, content that she was agreeing with him. "Tell me what you think of an Eerim entering the royal family."

"I have told you before, I think it is a wise choice despite her not being a noble woman, better even for that, and I am glad Tyanien Tyonar gets to marry for love."

"But now in regard to these Bilers?"

"I don't understand what these Bilers have to do with anything. They came for no reason and will leave much the same. Do you think the Eerim's Council will be opposed to opening the Line? Or do you think that they are offended by the Bilers here attending the celebration?"

"I don't think the Eerim are offended, but it is always wise to have the better ears on your side. Though it is impossible to be sure when they are. The Council likes to cloak themselves in mystery and ancient legacy, but it merits some respect. Their kind lives hundreds of turns, from birth to death they hear millions upon millions of thoughts in their periphery. Never underestimate their importance, not when they are consistently overestimating it. The nature of their powers seems to have been forgotten in Baeltaf, from what I have been told."

"Truth turned to legend, as it goes. The Bilers will be unskilled at watching their thoughts. Do you want better ears in Baeltaf, listening for the Blessed Lands?"

"That would be illegal, Fehatsi, on more than one account. No, having ears in Baeltaf is not my meaning. My meaning is you can never have any ears that aren't the one's on either side of your head, but the Eerim are the most valuable of allies and the most dangerous enemies. They know their worth, and more than that, these Bilers do not."

"This is your style of cheerful conversation?"

"Don't disrespect your father, child. Another topic, then? I have one. It is a great gift that Tyanien Bakéz allows you to tutor his daughter on the mornings of Moima," he said when he was finishing all the food on his plate, drinking the tepid tea beside him. "A sure kind of bliss, a seed planted that you will sow in time. I know it will only help in your life when Princess Janila rises to be cloaked Tyano on her day." He leaned back in his chair and smiled, and she could see herself reflected in the twinkling of his eyes.

"I am sure," Fehatsi agreed, thinking of the little brat being Great Leader of the Blessed Lands. "Master Paserin says the best way to learn is to teach properly. She has harshly criticized my lesson plans more than once, but I am ready now, so I suppose that is a bliss, too."

"Very good," her father said. "Well, I must be heading to a meeting with General Azún Kanila. Every street taken into account and all, every guard questioned, and their backgrounds thoroughly researched. It is time for me to listen and agree with a more knowledgeable man."

"I will see you on the union day." Fehatsi stood on the points of her toes and still her father had to lean so that she may kiss either of his cheeks.

If he was tired, he couldn't feel it. Mittrik wished time would stay still for him. For hours Rae had pointed out things he would not have seen otherwise, animals that hung from trees, ones that climbed and swung in them, rodents the size of bears, snakes mimicking the countless green vines. She knew much about everything, and he was realizing he knew so, so little.

He heard the water before he saw it, but he could not imagine what the next rise and fall of one hill would show him. Dozens of loud waterfalls tumbled over the stacked array of green mountains below them, rushing south and lowering at each level into pools and intertwined rivers. Louder than whatever life teamed in the canopies, the water's sound. There were taller mountains and wider falls beyond these that disappeared past his sight, sparse colorful trees along the edge of the great collision of rivers, waters that gleamed as glass. Rae stopped to let him stare at the view, and then quietly asked a question not so pleasant that caught him off guard.

"Why did you leave your home?"

"Because I always wanted to leave it," he answered, "and then my mother died and Jonnere gave me a reason, or an excuse."

"I am sorrowful for your loss," she said. "Why did you always want to leave your home?"

Mittrik felt it hard to swallow. He had never asked himself that question, but he had the answer now. He did not like it.

"I wanted greatness for myself different than the greatness for which I was fated. I did not like the idea of doing what I should have, fighting in a war I did not believe in or marrying some woman I did not love more than life. And I always admired the heroes in the songs that faced true magical adversaries more than I admired the men I know. It was a boyish silliness before. Now... Well, I felt a kind of call from the unknown to come and know it. The desert-call, my mother would say." His rambling sounded stupid to him, but she did not laugh. She looked pensive.

"The desert-call. But were you born on Fair Isle?"

"No, I was born in Alluvel. You have heard of the desert-call?"

"Yes, it is a known thing this side of the Line. I did not realize it was known to your people as well, since Fair triewthblood is kept secret from Bilers. Though I imagine, not to you, with a Fair mother."

"Triewthblood?"

"Had you heard of it?"

"No."

"That surprises me. You are Rooj, even though you look nothing like a Fairman. Aya, so, I am a truthspeaker because I am a child of Amina, but Fair People are truthspeakers for being born on Fair Isle."

"People born on Fair Isle cannot lie?" asked Mittrik. "That cannot be. My mother was born in Waterhaven, and my sister, too."

"Then your sister is a truthspeaker, too, and cannot speak her lies. And unlike you, she can feel the real desert-call."

"My mother told me, all Islanders feel constant desire to be on the Fair Isle, that it's where they're safest. I was a boy when I told her I wanted to travel to the Forsaken West and find true magic, and she told me that it was the desert-call, and if I ever decided to leave Kieln, I should listen and go straight to the Isle. To the Isle, not the West. She said there was more adventure in Waterhaven than any forsaken place."

"That is a nice sentiment, but the desert-call is more than that for Fair People. It is a warning sense they possess, an instinct. It moves in their triewthblood heavy when their life is in deadly peril. The Fair have always said the desert-call lures them to Waterhaven to find refuge when they are in the worst kinds of danger. Did you leave your home for a feeling like that, for feeling your life threatened?"

"No," Mittrik admitted. "I left because I wanted to know whatever was here. I felt already a tiredness began to settle in my life, one I feared I would sleep in forever, and I wanted to feel born again as something else."

"Born as what else?"

"A hero." He laughed at himself. She did not.

"I hope, if such a thing is good, you can have that. Only one more hill and we will get there," Rae said, grinning, half-shouting over the roar of water. He could not help but smile back at her.

"Your brothers won't notice our long absence?" He asked her, short of breath, sprays of river froth wetting his face. The river moved so fast here it was muddled brown and vicious white, and he saw whole trees being carried downcurrent.

"My brothers have many things to take care of in the Blessed Lands, and I am not one of them. They have been very preoccupied since my father was cut with a plague, and they had to take over the war effort. Even now that the war is won, Bakéz worries every day. Only one steep hill more. Come on."

"I've heard mention of this war. When did it happen?" She was jogging ahead of him now, impossibly agile.

"The War of Radicals. It ended two years ago, lasted little more than a year before that in our knowledge, but my brothers and I stopped the Ku'dur warmonger and the onslaught of magicked plagues he sent across the westerlands. Sfar'Laki, the Pretender, thought he was chosen. But, he was not. He was destroyed in the Southern Wilder Tower." Her voice was angry, but her face set in sadness. "I killed him."

"You did? You fought in the war?" Mittrik asked astonished,

legs burning.

"Yes," she answered, slowing down at the top of the peak for him. She leaned against a knotted tree.

"But you are a woman."

"I am." Her voice, a challenge.

He remembered the look of her fighting her brothers, her effortless speed, her steel against theirs, braid flying behind her. She moved around them as if her violence was a taunting dance, like she knew how they would move before they acted, and it was nothing like Mittrik had ever seen. He longed to fight like that, but he could never be so quick. That beautiful light she created with her hands had blinded him more than her blades reflecting. Blinded now, he could not look away. He stared at her though she was like the sun.

"Right, you are," Mittrik managed when he reached the top of the peak and stood close at her side.

He saw her standing precariously close to an ominous hole in the rock that led straight down into darkness, as if a god had taken his finger and poked to the center of the world. Rae kicked a few rocks into its black depth.

"I hope you trust me, Mittrik Hwaelin," she said, smile bright and eyes wicked like the Sister moons. "Enough to jump."

He was about to ask: What do you mean? But already she dived head first, down the dark hole. He closed his eyes and cursed, then he fell after her.

Yeroen strolled around the spice vendors' circle, keeping an easy smile on his face in the hopes of not looking as despondent as he felt. His brother's speech the previous day had bothered him. Santir thought that Yeroen had given up on their name, but he still had a dream to change his brand of fame.

Detunae was a small family of little to no history, though two hundred and fifty turns past some ancestor had come about with Ashakai's sense, which indicated an unresolved marital scandal. As children, Yeroen and Santir had spoken of leaving their name on history's pages, for it to be as known as the great old families', and unfortunately, Yeroen had done just that. His little brother wanted a new name, for Detunae now connected him to Yeroen's shame. His stomach twisted, not only from the commotion in the city.

People churned, shopkeepers calling out their wares from their shaded stores, others with their goods displayed on makeshift tables aligned around the crowded way. Yeroen used to love crowds, the feel of everyone echoed within him. He felt connected. Their excitement was his own, his heart replied to theirs. War ruined that communion.

"Fine pata'gua seeds!" a vendor yelled.

"Sweet pana, sweet pana here!" yelled another.

Above him, on the third level balcony of a sunburnt yellow building, a Ku'dur and her child hung nectar jars from peasnap branches for the swordbeaks and green bellies. Yeroen watched as they rushed in and fought each other for a taste of the sweet, lifewater buzzing within.

A Takircha in form of a handsome woman bumped into him. She winked a red eye at him, and then continued down the market. He admired the way her form moved as it turned around a cart of dried fruits.

Talosa filled with more people of different kinds, all to see this unprecedented royal union. An Eerim entering the royal family, one with the better ear. Who could've predicted that?

Not Yeroen. *Maybe those bastards in Ach—*

No.

His thoughts were loose, passed the point of weary long ago; the chaotic swings and disruptions in his strongest sense took a deeper toll than they would otherwise. He tried to focus on his other senses (loud conversations of the crowd or the sweet smells of fresh baked bread, his shoes scuffing on the pavement). Not distracting enough.

Presently all he could smell, taste and feel was every

discordant rush of lifewater beneath the flesh of every living kind around him: the steady flow within humans, the viscous sludge that coursed through Eerim's double hearts, the rolling spasms from the thin muscle of Takircha's projected forms, the stand-still blue blood of Ku'dur. Yeroen felt all of that and he struggled to find his own breath amidst the chaos. His own heartbeat lost. There were so many people, and it was all pounding in him as a thousand war drums, making his own blood feel as though it was spinning down every veins.

He wanted to run. To swing his arms and flex the du around him. He needed a drink.

Rum.

Just breathe. You don't need *a drink. You need air.*

And peace.

Yeroen jogged his way down narrower streets to avoid anyone who might recognize him, and he was able to steer clear of the potters' circle entirely, much to his contentment. He turned down the last road onto Sweetwater Pass, hearing pretty singing and seeing the welcoming yellow door stark against those black walls.

He opened the carved door of the Oolingo Trap, the quaint and pleasant tavern that always smelled faintly of dried blood, rum and sweetsmoke. Takula Daashana, the barmaid, saw him when he entered, and he gave her a flirtatious smile. She returned it with a vulgar gesture of her hands. Yeroen supposed he deserved it.

Music was being played, as lively as anything else of the Blessed Lands. Two men banged loudly on different height drums, a small woman blew breath into a hollowed reed flute, and a woman with a deep voice bellowed as she ran her fingers across her standing vertrona. She sang a song with which Yeroen was familiar, a quick drum-reliant beat called "The Eerim and the Captain's Wife" and the other drinkers called back her song in time. *Now this is something to drink to*, Yeroen thought as he took a seat, looking at the two couples that were dancing and spinning on the other end of the bar, laughing amidst themselves.

"Water, please," he asked Daashana, who quickly delivered.

"Only water?"

No. For now.

"Yes," Yeroen said.

Yes. Only water.

"Good for you," said Daashana. "It will be easier to watch your thoughts if you're not drunk like always."

Watch my thoughts. They own my fucking future, what's a thought now?

A thin woman behind Yereon spoke loudly, "What joy that the Great Leader may see another of his children married before he passes to the first plane. A great gift, this union."

"Too many Eerim in one place, I say. Talosa has never seen so many. I like to keep my thoughts to myself, thank you very much," said the loud-mouthed tavern owner, a barrel-chested man. He'd owned the tavern since Yeroen first found it at fifteen, and in all that time Yeroen learned that the man liked only two things: Achkan whores and the sound of his own voice.

Yeroen took a long drink and then another, another till his glass was emptied. Daashana poured him another glass of water without being asked, and Olirian continued talking, and the topic was turning quickly to something near sedition.

"If you ask me, Tyanien Aadarae is the only one fit to be our Great Leader. She was the one of all Iial's children to put an end to Sfar'Laki. Her sacrifice won the war."

"By that logic," said a man Yeroen did not recognize, "Crazy Pyaren should lead the armies. He gave up a leg, Tyanien Aadarae gave up part of her soul. Way I hear, they both lost their mind to Laki's magic in that tower. Neither are fit to rule."

"They're both of sound mind, don't let the false papers trick you. What were Tyanien Bakéz and Zyonhir sacrificing in CoБmak? Our people! Half the wielders died, but our Tyanien fled without plague! And Teviona expects us to be happy for Bakéz' cloaking?" Olirian usually drank more rum than his patrons. "I want warriors to lead during wartime."

Yeroen agreed with him, but his loyalty to Rae made him say, "Good that the war ended, then. I heard you liked to keep your thoughts to yourself, Olirian. Those are best kept, no?"

"I'll say what I want in my bar, *Detunae*. Thought you'd see things my way."

"Detunae?" the thin woman asked, leaning over the table to get a better look. "*That* Detunae?"

That should be Yeroen's cue to leave. But he answered, "Can't a cursed man enjoy a drink in peace?" *Even if it is just water.*

And they stopped speaking to him.

No one had to tell Yeroen that Rae should lead the Blessed Lands, that her brother was a fool. He knew what kind of ruler Rae was: compassionate, brave, honest. She led him and three hundred men to The Southern Wilder Tower, and killed the Pretender herself. Among her siblings she was best for the position. She was above all things loving to every damned person and living creature, to the point of aggravation.

Rae loves too fiercely, Yeroen thought. *How long did she chase for Klo? How long did it take for such a virtuous lands' wielder to break at a Tyanien's decrees of love? It might have been just over a Rock turn, her saying it without his response... A longer time than any sane man could endure. Though she could tell the truth by his eyes, as we all could.*

Rae loved Mouwat fiercely from the moment their green, kindly eyes met.

"Are you really running tasks for Achkan gangmen?" Daashana whispered to Yeroen, face so close he could kiss her.

"You could be arrested for reading illegal papers," he whispered back.

"No. Buying and selling gets you arrested. For someone who studied Holy Law in the Academy, you sound uneducated on the subject."

Yeroen smiled. "I'm sure you remember I was thrown out of the Academy almost as soon as I arrived."

Daashana matched his smirk, but hers looked cruel. "For

gambling on Holy ground, yes. Everyone knows."

Everyone knows everything by now. At present, Yeroen ignored the political arguments around him. He drank, and when the water sloshed in his stomach, he stood to enter into the gamblers' room. He couldn't be entirely perfect, after all. And his bag was just so heavy.

In the gambling room, a delightful mingle of Erabian sweetsmoke and peppery Achkan clouds dimmed the fireglobes' light. There was an Eerim playing cards at the corner table, so Yeroen checked his own thoughts. Started singing an annoying song in his head and made for the exit

"You! I know you," a man called from the corner table in broken Blessed speech.

"I think not," Yeroen replied without looking, disappointed that he wouldn't get a chance to play a round of moz'daur. But it would be worse to be recognized. *Damn it thrice,* Yeroen cursed, and prayed directly to First One: *Do you not want me to have any fun at all? Too many eyes, and ears here. Damn whoever listens beside God.*

"Yeroen," The man said, which caused his head to spin and look. "It is me, Garald."

"Ivrahen!" Yeroen barked, grinning and then pulling the man into a warrior's embrace, their foreheads touching and their right hands at the back of each others' necks. "Where have you been these three turns, coz?"

Yeroen met Ivrahen, a half Zepeyan wielder of waters distantly descended of Ashakai, when both were stationed at the garrison of the river village Sharann in the early months of the Radical's War. Garald had stayed in Sharann when Yeroen was sent to the sea beneath the Southern Wilder Tower, and Yeroen doubted he would ever see the man again. Garald also doubted. Though the two had little in common, they were easy friends in those days of watching and waiting for attacks along the river.

"I have been living in Kizar, well first I went to Quo'Orinth and married."

Yeroen laughed. "Pity. No, I'm joking. Blisses upon you both. Are you here for the celebration?"

"Why else? My wife threatened to strangle me if I did not let her come frolic with her friends. She hates my family, and the Zepeyan living. They hate her, too, so it's all even. She's in the flower circle watching a play."

"There are too many players and stories to see. And many singers in the flower circle set on the day. No one has time to hear it all."

"Well, I care little for singers. I am spoiling myself in steam at your bath houses, and fattening fast on your foods. We are in the Blessed Lands until the Selection, and I am excited to see the sacrifice to your god and the hypnotic force that appears from the first plane."

"Ah! Only hypnotic to those Selected, Garald, and to the rest they will look like pretty lights."

"Even so, I am excited to see such a thing. Would you join us, Yeroen? We are about to start another round and my pockets are burning from the last time we played. I wish to win back my small fortune."

"I have it now. If you would have asked me three nights ago I would have had to decline."

Garald laughed and patted Yeroen on the back. His easy expression was practiced like most merchant's sons, but Yeroen knew Garald's truths were as clean as his face (most Zepeyan men did not grow hair on their cheeks or chins, but grew it all on their heads and arms in thick bushes).

"That is Mado of Kizar Zepey, and the Eerim is Kai Delmi of some town in Iri, of course. They both work for my father's sentinel. Sit, coz."

"My ears lack better hearing, do not worry," said the Eerim man, Delmi, flicking his long pierced lobes. "I am not a cheating man, no fun in that. Unfortunately, these are just for eminence. But I shall take your money, wielder of waters, if you are eager." He dealt the four of them six hand-painted moz'daur cards each, and then passed out the tallied twigs and silver ringlets.

Yeroen looked at his cards: the swallowing mountain, the Onatae's chalice, the third moon, the barking dog, the altar of the sacred trees, and the First of the Four. A lucky hand. A lucky day.

Maybe he'd order that rum.

One drink wouldn't hurt.

The men went around leftwise and placed ranging bets of coin on their hand, setting up for other ways to gamble as they spoke. They bet on the twenty six new members of the Select Council, on the music and food of the day.

The men continued betting on their cards as well, and Yeroen thought of how in a different life, his name might have been among the chosen. At fourteen turns, he was sent from the academy at Leurai to the grand rebuilt structure of Talosa's Academy, with its towering walls that rivaled the palace built during Jarey reign. His childhood master at Leurai told him that if he went to the capital and proved his greatness to the masters, she believed he could be Selected as Son of Ashakai when the time came. *What must the woman think of me now?*

Yeroen ordered that coveted drink, the sweet rum burned, and he placed his last bet on the table. He flipped over his final card, the queen's chalice. The rest of the men groaned. Yeroen, smiling, pulled in the rings and counted how many Standard Silver he was owed. Only the card of the barking dog did not pull in coins.

"Another round, Yeroen," Garald said, laughing.

Yeroen, already reacquainted with gold in his bag, liked the sound of that. He also appreciated that Garald had not yet mentioned what happened in Achka, or anything of Yeroen's ban, and he doubted he would now.

And there it was, peace within him that should not exist. Life wasn't as good as he felt it. It was the rum, it was the money. It wasn't within him.

Yeroen thought of the upcoming Selection, of Rae marching the steps of the House of Three-One, next to some strange son of Amina, a new Select Son, bonding her spirit to his in the light of the Great Fire for all Talosa to see. For Yeroen to mourn.

Do better.

Yeroen agreed to a second game, a second drink, feeling his sense of peace trail away. He wanted to get up and chase it out of the tavern. He wanted all the gold in Garald's purse.

But he lost the second round, and ten gold Standard, which made this third round imperative. His cards were worse this time. His options limited.

"You were in Achka recently, right, coz?" Garald asked. And Yeroen's mind conjured memories of his blood on a magician's blade by the River of Swans. Of the task they gave him.

Bring me Mittrik Hwaelin, the taskmen demanded Yeroen.

But he brought the Biler to the Blessed Lands instead.

"Yes, just visiting," he answered, tossing away a bad card. "I like the snow this time of year."

My blood's in their hands— Don't think of it.

"You're getting predictable, Detunae," said the Eerim man.

Predictable. Am I? Did they know I wouldn't deliver Hwaelin to them? They have my blood, they must've known. Why do they want a Biler noble here? This Biler that found me… Poor Delmi is going to get bit by that spider on his arm.

The Eerim flinched, and his eyes flickered to his arms. Yeroen shot up from the table, reaching out and throwing the Eerim across the room. The Eerim staggered, but before he could get to his feet, Yeroen had him pinned against the wall.

"Like what you hear, you cheat?" Yeroen smiled at the fear in Delmi's pure black eyes.

"I don't know what you mean, boy."

"Yeroen, please," Garald said, putting a hand on Yeroen's shoulder, "I've known Delmi my whole life. He doesn't have the better ear."

He does. You do. What are you looking for in my head, huh? Did you find it?

Delmi didn't react at all, so Yeroen slammed his back against the wall again. *Why lie?*

Olirian, the tavern's owner, walked into the commotion. Perfect timing. And he'd seen enough to make a verdict.

"Get out, Detunae," he demanded. "Violent son of a whore. And don't come back until after the Selection Day. Add this to your list of bans, boy."

Tufan.

Tufan. He *would* have to find a new bar.

Mittrik and Rae sat near that frigid water, his hands sliding across stone slick as wet glass. She was crouched in a bowing position, her forehead against the rock, murmuring something he could not hear, praying to — not the Thirteen— but whatever god.

He rested his head back, enjoying the cold of the stone and the bright light that came in through the hole above them. So high above them, and they simply *jumped.*

They were in a deep cave of black rock and crystal, the expansive walls around them looking so like the night sky, it was eerie. Awed by this chalcedony night, more awed than when Mittrik first saw the great city's lights against the earth. He thought, *What a glory it would be to hail from a world that resembles heavenly lights, to live in a world made of stars and darker mystery.*

This was the very cave from the large painting in the mage's home, from those that were so detailed and real. Mittrik had not noticed it at first, for all he had thought as he dropped from above was, *This is mad*, then, *and bloody cold*, as his body hit the water.

The painting had captured the cave just as it was, with the tumbling of the waterfall blanketed in shadows that blurred its shape, the circle of sunlight that gently wavered at the center of the pond, like a lonely moon on the water. But what the painting left out had Mittrik entranced. He looked at the cave's sloped ceiling and two great faces looked back at him.

They were molded out of the opaque, dark crystal. The larger: the visage of a boy with a smiling face that bulged his cheeks big and round, and the second, on the other side of the hole, was a girl's angry glare. The deep pits below their protruding brows seemed to glow a deep black.

Can darkness glow? Mittrik wondered, and then looked at Rae's wet hair splayed atop the rock. *It can shine.*

He looked at the tips of swirling wine-colored scars that peaked above her armored top, looping in jagged ends around the base of her neck. Rae rose from her bowed position as if noticing his stare and looked at him with a tired smile.

She asked, "I would like to hear of your truthspeaker sister. What is she like?"

"She is wonderful and trusting and good," he answered without thought. "So honest, I should have guessed she couldn't lie. Her name is Leonara, she's youngest. I had a brother, too, that died as a babe."

"My sorrows with you. Your sister must miss you."

Mittrik nodded, but he did not want to think of Keelan or his little sister now. "Your marks, on your neck," he began, but changed direction. "Why do your people mark themselves?"

"Different reasons for different people, but some for recognition in their descendance or prestige, others for tradition."

"Why did you mark yourself?"

"For fun," she answered with a laugh that smacked the walls and bounced back to them. She reached behind to lower the cloth of her top down her shoulders, revealing more of the strange design. "Teia wanted to be marked with patterns of her mother's heritage, Yeroen wanted marks so he could be recognized easily in the wateryards as a child of Ashakai, and I didn't want to be left without. My mother wanted me to wait, but we snuck into the city to receive our marks. We were less than sixteen."

"Is it most permanent?" Mittrik asked, now intent on those raised and channeled lines that looked like the thinnest and most intricate of scars.

She covered herself again. "No. All marks remain with the body, and decay with the flesh."

A contradiction he didn't contradict. "Did it hurt?"

"Much. Traditionally, children of Amina are marked on their palms and that hurts less than on the spine, but that didn't suit me."

"Why do it if it pains you?"

She seemed to consider his question, eyes drifting around as fluid and dark as the water. "Bilers don't live avoiding pain, neither do we. I think you'd avoid just as much fun trying. You hit each other with sticks while riding horses, we mark ourselves. It's not so different. What peculiar questions you ask."

"You have peculiar answers. Those marks are extraordinary," he said to her above the sound of crashing water. "You seem different here. More at peace."

"I am different here," she answered just above a whisper, positioning herself so she laid on her back by the water's edge. He had to look at her lips to discern her words precisely, though Mittrik would not complain. "Or rather, truelight is different here, and I am able to be at peace. Only I can see the truelight for what it is, and it is so *distracting* up there. But here, not at all. Truelight is refracted and scattered here, soft like a shimmer. It can't penetrate the black stone. Up there it can be terrifying, but never here."

"Only you can see it? I see it in your hands. Other children of Amina do not see truelight?"

"You see truelight because I am giving it purpose. Children of Amina don't see it, but they have another sense for it. Enough to use it in forms of healing."

"Describe to me what you see."

She closed her eyes. Her smile didn't waver. "Countless veins, frayed, stretching everywhere and pulsing power, or something more than power. Truelight is delicate and rough like a storm's crashing and smooth and soft in other places, gentle to the touch. It has a sound, if I strain to listen. Like," –a moment passed, and her smile grew wolfish and wide— "very distant singing, millions of voices singing a million songs. It is beautiful and terrifying."

"Why do you see it, and not others?"

Rae opened her eyes and worried her lower lip. "Other children of Amina aren't born with the ability to wield truelight— that's only me. Amina's children can learn to channel truelight after much study, heal with their skill, but that's all. I-I am something else." Her voice faded to just above a whisper as she finished explaining.

"Araeboril?" Mittrik asked, using that curious word he heard others direct at her so many times at the Academy. The name she introduced herself with. *I am called Araeboril by many. By few, Rae.*

She laughed without joy. "Yes, they say I am."

"What does it mean?"

She turned her eyes to the two looming faces above them, tilting her head this way and that. "Roughly? Truelight-bringer. Most easterners just say Lightbringer. There is not a word in the eastern tongue that implies the truelight which extends into the sky and beyond our Rock. There is a part of our history that my mother left out in her telling," she said. "The saddest part of Canyassor's beginnings. Amina, the youngest child of the First Children, was the first Araeboril. She wielded truelight as I do, or I do as she did. The truelight, *ya rae*. Her brother that was doubleborn with her, Xonieren, wielded power opposite to truelight: the truedark, *ya muiove*, hollow energy with matching strength.

'Scriptures say evil spirits gave Xonieren a cursed blade from another Rock, and he tried to kill his sister here in this cave, in their twentieth turn, but in the struggle, she managed to disarm him. Xonieren repented and claimed the spirit overtook his body, but he was exiled beyond the Wilder Wood, and Three-One cursed him, cursed his descendants so that none of his children would share his power. They would live just as other humans. But there must be balance—it is natural law—so all of Amina's children are also born without her power. Until myself, only Amina was born with the ability to wield truelight."

"So, you are not a child of Amina, truly," Mittrik observed, the tale spinning like a fantasy in his head. She scrunched her face at him, confused and large eyes blinking. "You are not descended from her as the others," he told her. "You wield it the same as the first Truelight Bringer. You are not a child of Amina, you are like Amina reborn."

"My people do not believe in rebirths," she said, but something in her eyes looked fearful; he saw a soft spark at a twitch of her thumb. "We believe you are given one life on this plane of constant time, and when you die you move beyond time in one direction or the other into eternal existence."

Mittrik's mind was racing. "If you have the powers you possess, could a second... Xon-erm, one with those dark powers you described, be alive in the world as well?"

Her teeth caught the soft flesh of her lower lip again. She looked at him with the blue glow of the sky, eyes reflecting every crystal in the cave.

"That is the question. Some hold that view, yes. Prophecy... there will be a wielder of truelight and a wielder of truedark to announce the end days, is the prophecy. The end begins when they meet. It is hard to know where legends and truth diverge, for all of us, not just Bilers."

"What do you believe?" he asked her.

She closed her eyes. "Yes, there is one living with opposing power. I can feel it. I dream of him sometimes. I've seen him, killing me here with that cursed blade."

Mittrik shuddered, cold and frightened. His eyes saw clearer than ever before as he looked at her wet face, dark hair that lay flat on her temples, and her dripping clothes which clung to her tightly. It felt as though his whole life had been something of a tedious dream, and he was only waking from that drear. His new reality was fearsome and astonishing, and so, so magical. She woke him, he knew she did.

"What does that mean?" Mittrik asked. "What does that mean for you if someone is out there plotting against you?"

Her eyes opened, and her fingers twitched. "I am just a person. I tell myself the one Hasyal with Xonierien's power is probably just a person, too. Hopefully not plotting against me. I want to kill him, but I don't know if I should. My dreams aren't prophecy."

The Other that Mother wrote of before she died, he thought. *Could she have known?*

Mittrik did not think the woman before him was just a person. Rae was a creature of power beyond his imagination, obviously destined for some kind of greatness. She was the Truelight Bringer, and somehow, Mittrik was destined to meet her. She was the hero of her people, he realized, and if gods were real then by fate's design they were here together. If gods were not real, he found her himself.

He moved closer, asked, "The faces up there, they are of Amina and her cursed brother? She has the same flat nose and wide set eyes as the other statues I have seen of the thirteen, like in the ruins in Kieln."

She nodded. "Yes, that is Amina, though this is the only place I have seen her likeness angered. In every other carving, Amina smiles."

"I used to make up names for the statues of them at the Old ruins. I called the last one the Daughter often, since she's the shortest of them." *Always a goddess of virtue or forgiveness, fertility or springtime,* he did not say.

"I like that."

Mittrik had no more words to occupy, so the silence stretched between them until the light from the hole above turned darker blue.

"I saw the most immaculate paintings of this place in Yero's home," Mittrik finally said. "They looked so real, it feels as though this is my second time here."

She moved away from him and dipped her feet in the water.

"Yes, those pieces are masterfully painted. Beautiful."

"Who painted them?"

She took a breath and kicked her feet back and forth, sending ripples toward the cascade of falling shadows. Mittrik watched her clutch the necklace at her throat before answering. "A man named Mouwat Kloennian. He is gone from this plane, moved on to the first. He was a descendant of Hahnae, and that means he was an empath and wielder of lands. He was a great artist and builder. He carved that home into the face of the mountain with his own two hands. A man of perfection."

The man she loved, Mittrik could tell by her soft and ever-distant-growing tone. He did not question her further, the sadness in her eyes was straightforward and silencing. She stood very suddenly, looking down at him as she sighed. "We should be leaving back to Talosa, Mittrik Hwaelin. This should be enough running away. Today didn't go as I planned."

She leapt off the oily black rock and into the deep water. She smoothed her hair back when she emerged to look at him.

"The only way to leave is to swim," she said, her voice echoing back from the stone. "How long can you hold your breath?"

"A minute, perhaps more. I don't know." He jumped in after her, waded beside her, struggling with his boots. "But I won't drown, do not worry for me."

She laughed and swam away, toward the harsh tumbling of loud water. "The way out is through the fall. The tunnel opens into a pond between the hills."

He nodded but she was not looking at him. She went into the crashing water, and he took in a long breath before submerging beneath the cold pool.

He opened his eyes and saw she was guiding him in that murky water with the soft pulsing glow from her hands, lighting the way to a large gap in the stone underneath the swirling froth from the waterfall. He swam after her and could not help but notice the elegant way her muscled legs propelled her forward.

The crystal and pure black stone of the cave faded, turned into tunneling brown and fractured rock. It looked less like he was swimming amid stars and more like he was trapped within a narrow barrel, with no surface in sight. A song came to mind, one of the few that his father had liked. He tried to distract himself with it, since the burning in his lungs spread through his chest.

Hetten, guide me in my victories
Sisters, guard me 'gainst my whims
I'm the least worst of many, many.
Gods, you know what lies within.

He kept kicking forward and kept following Rae's moving light. He noticed her sandals had changed, and on either side of the soles, little fins had extended and helped her glide like a fish through the water. With her light he could see the strange veined fins of her sandals, thin and much liked the webbed fingers of the unfortunate lot of House Borner.

His lungs burned and burned and the pressure behind his eyes started to pain him.

Air.

No, he was fine, more than fine, he assured himself and stared at Rae ahead of him. He struggled against his chest pain and the pressure behind his eyes, swimming forward, keeping the song.

Hetten, shine where you mind to
Sisters, keep me from tempting harm
I am the blood of cold dirt and gold
Gods, keep me ice and keep me warm.

Mittrik needed air.

He forced down a panic, because he saw the end of the tunnel before them, another large crack in the stone that opened to light blue water.

The water around Rae's body lit up in luminous blue and gold specks as she swam on and exited the tunnel, and he was stunned to see that as his hands pushed the water out in front of him. There, it lit up as well. He was swimming amid stars again, but a different kind. Thankfully she was swimming upward, and he kicked out his legs to speed after her. His head broke the water, his lips sucked in a shaky breath. And another, and again.

Night had fallen quickly. The trail of water behind them looked like a reflection of the sky as they stirred up the dazzling pond stars.

Mittrik stopped swimming.

Near the edge of the lake a fully grown spiritlion was lapping up glowing ripples of water. It was twice Mittrik's height, and its huge paws clawed at the soft earth with a crunching sound. The creature looked up at them with large pitless eyes, and Mittrik's stomach dropped. He closed his eyes and prayed for Hetten to keep his soul for whatever good it did.

"Ambos," Rae said softly. "Are you ready to go home? See, I told you he always shows up when I need him."

Mittrik opened his eyes. "Do you mean that is the *same* spiritlion from before? But it's huge! How is that possible?"

"Your legends speak of spiritlions, but you do not know they can alter their size... I am wondering how that is possible." She answered, her laughter ringing beautifully. "I find it interesting what fragments of the past your people forgot and which they kept. Do you know of projected forms?"

"No. Of what?"

"But it is how skinchangers put forth themselves. I am sure that there are still skinchangers in the Biler lands, there must be. All could not have died. You do not know of them?"

"I do not." Mittrik could not pay attention to her or her questions. All his focus centered on the large spiritlion near the edge of the water. The creature bent lowly as Rae rose from the lake, the specks of blue light fading from her clothing as the cool air hit them. It looked as if the creature bowed to her. She went up to it, and the beast's hulking head rested against hers.

"But it was so small before, and now it is fully grown."

Mittrik said and climbed out of the water. "How can it become something else so quickly?"

"He is not something else, he is the same Ambos. They change their molecular density, from what we can tell, but it is also something a bit more complicated than we can understand. But everything is more than one thing, laijirei especially, and they are any size they want to be."

Mittrik did not understand a word but reached out a shaking hand.

The spiritlion closed the gap and nudged his large snout into Mittrik's palm, mewling and whiskers twitching. Mittrik exhaled his hanging breath, looked back and smiled at the western princess.

"Are you ready?" She asked him, smirking a half smile that went straight to his heart.

"No, I—Ready for what, Rae?"

"To ride back to the palace."

"You mean atop this beast," he quavered. "You cannot be serious."

The growl of the spiritlion resounded, and to their right birds fluttered; crawling things swarmed into the dark layered gully, shaking the night.

"I am, usually."

The beast crouched low enough that she could pull herself onto its back. She reached out a hand to him, to help him up. Mittrik didn't hesitate to grab her hand, and the princess hoisted him so he could swing his leg over the spiritlion, like he was mounting Ilder, and then he sat behind her. *I'm sitting on a spirit lion. What in Doom…*

There was no saddle, but the beast's back was wide and strong enough to carry them both.

"Hold on tightly to me," Rae said. "Laijirei do not move like other four-legged ones."

His arms tightened around her waist as the spiritlion shook its haunches like a cat about to pounce for prey.

The spiritlion did not run as Mittrik expected. It jumped

and climbed the closest trees, and did not hesitate before jumping again onto trunks, onto branches and vines, landing with a crashing sound like thunder. One place to the next and never going where was predicted. Where the beast landed, the place where it's paws touched set alight, like Rae's hands, like her eyes. And sometimes, though it happened so fast Mittrik could not be sure, the beast seemed to land atop nothing but truelight. The wind was harsh in his eyes, and the leaves and branches beat him, and he was sure he screamed at first.

Despite all this, Rae was solid and moved like she was part of the animal, never shocked by its change of direction or moved by the branches that hit her bare skin. It seemed her eyes knew where the spiritlion went before he jumped there. Mittrik gripped her a bit tighter to stay mounted and held the beast between his legs, fearful of falling from the great heights. Riding a horse would never feel as great as this; and even as he enjoyed this feeling, he mourned for the moment it would end.

How long Mittrik rode the spiritlion atop thinnest branches of trees, ducking beneath vines, did not matter. He didn't even mind the slicing of his skin when leaf or tree bark touched him. He hollered and watched Rae's skin shine and heal. *Will she heal me again?* He was sure she would. Her waist firm in his arms, when they reached the gate by the river, the river that fed into the city and came out the statue's mouth, it could have been minutes or hours. It wasn't enough.

8. THE GRAND WEDDING

Jonn was livid to say the least. Not one day passed since he reluctantly agreed to stay for the foreign wedding, and Mittrik managed to disappear. Early that day, after Jonn realized his brother was missing, there came the call of a knocking servant who led him to breakfast with Tyanein Malak and Hanala in the gardens. Both of the Tyanien seemed perturbed yet unsurprised that Mittrik was missing. The conversations were more awkward, stiff and difficult without his brother, and they continued for much of the day.

Tyanien Malak showed Jonn "a small portion" of the palace, far too much if Jonn was honest. The winding halls never ended; walls opened from the touch of his hand, and there was always another stairwell to climb, a new plot of garden or a new statue of great import to see. At their midday meal, there was a procession of musicians. Tyanien Malak said they were auditioning for their spot on the procession line, the late-comers from the farthest places.

After dark Mittrik finally turned up, and Jonnere resolved not to speak to him, not even to scold him. That resolve didn't last long. There was no little argument between them.

For the next six days and nights, as they were shown more forsaken marvels, Jonn did not leave his brother's side. He feared Mittrik would wander off again and do something so stupid that he could not be saved. They even slept side by side on the same bed, and if Mittrik was gone for more than some minutes, Jonn would feel anxious until he would come around a corner and see him. It was a tiresome sort of duty.

They shared a great chamber in Alluvel when they were small boys, with a bed so large that Jonn could stretch out both arms and not know Mittrik was there. When they became men, Mittrik started bringing girls to bed sooner than Jonn had, and the painted whores couldn't be ignored. So, he would end up sleeping outside in the corridor until the whore would leave, until the very last time. Jonn had been fourteen and his father had caught him sleeping on the floor. He got a good smack across the face to wake him, and Tagnar told him great lords didn't sleep on cold threshes in their own castle. The High Lord only smiled when Jonn explained why he was out in the hall. Mittrik didn't get slapped for bringing such women into Alluvel. Mittrik never got slapped. The next night Jonn was given one of Alluvel's eight guest rooms as his own. It was smaller than the room he had shared with his brother.

When it became clear to Mittrik that Jonn would not leave his side until they left for Baeltaf, only long enough to piss, he acted overtly offended.

"Will you keep on like a worried modaire, fretting over me?" Mittrik asked on the third day of roaming the palace gardens, out of earshot of Tyanien Malak who was talking and talking without stop with one of the twin brothers, the one with the unscarred face. "I'm not a child."

"You were a better child," Jonn said. "You're a more difficult man. If you insist on being an arse, I'll tie you to a post until we're back in Kieln. You cannot act with carelessness here."

Mittrik scoffed. "I'd like to watch you try to tie me to a post."

Jonn wouldn't continue the argument. His brother was an arse, and dramatic. *He would make a better mummer than a knight or lord.*

At this point, Jonn didn't remember if he'd said that aloud or not. They had not spoken since that day.

But neither had they seen the witch princess since, so there was that.

The two moons were both at their fullest now, opposite and low in the sky, representing the time of equal harmony and chaos in the heavens: the Sisters' Greeting. In a life unForsaken, Jonnere was riding to Brimtone to end Lady Ritra Gilgar's Courtings, riding alongside his father and the dwelling guard. He should be wooing a woman, leading the men, honoring his father's name. Jonnere was supposed to be doing many things in Kieln right now, but he was in the Forsaken to attend a wedding between a prince and an elf.

Mittrik had spent the last hours looking over the scrolls and translations that Riambo Fehatsi had sent to them. In the scrolls were detailed accounts of the First War of Man, what westerners called the Separation. No battles were documented, just thousands of small attacks of terror, city states surrendering after the poisonings of kings and queens and rulers, and mass revolt among the race of humans toward the daemons. Jonn thought it was too clean and easy to say there was no large scale of fighting, no men at arms on the ground. In every war, innocent blood was spilled on both sides, but of all wars, most righteous blood was spilled in the First. *The heathens and daemons tortured our kind,* these were lessons Jonn had only ever thought of as Old stories.

"You're regretting your decision to stay," Mittrik said, still perusing over the pages. "Why did you decide to stay? I've wondered, when you're so fearful of everything here."

"I decided to stay because I feared what this royal family might do if I offended. Mages are extending kindness to us, and it would be foolish to refuse it." *And because upon returning, I have to decide if he killed her, if avenging Mother is worth a throne.*

Mittrik turned a frayed page without looking up at him. "You're making a lot of decisions out of fear as of late. What might Father say? Not very becoming of a High Lord."

"It is not." Jonn hated that what Mittrik said was true and that he had the spite to say so. "You're right."

But he was a man of his word, so he would attend this western wedding, and he would make sure Mittrik did not get himself killed. Then he would get back to Alluvel. Then he would…

No, he wasn't ready to face his father, to face that decision. Crown or vengeance.

"It's unreal, isn't it?" Mittrik finally looked up after so long. "None of the histories we learned of the First War are true. Humans fighting mages with swords? All that aidares taught us growing up, what Doctor Petrard and our modaire taught us of Redbone, Hwaelin the Hammer—all the stories of Old and the conquest are lies. How could humans vanquish magic and mind-readers? Unreal."

"Unreal, exactly. But notice there are no monsters in Baeltaf. Not all we learned was a lie, Mittrik," Jonn reasoned, because that had to be right. No history contrived of lies, or entirely of truths. "I don't like this place, but we're already Doomed. After this wedding and celebration, we are free to go home and put it all behind us, and I don't want to hear another word of it after that."

Mittrik nodded, did not say another word.

Jonn looked out the window to the full moons. *One more night, one more day.* He leaned his head against the pillar, cheerless, tired. *One more night, one more day then all this western nonsense, all its dangers will be behind us. And I have to decide. Could I be a kin-slayer? Crown or creed… Father or self.*

Jonn turned back to Mittrik's furrowed brow, his hunched shoulders in study of the foreign scrolls. He looked so much like the boy he once was, studying Hetten's demigods. Mittrik wanted to be a demigod. He nearly convinced himself of it as a child. Vivid the memory, Mittrik screaming, wooden sword in hand, "Jonn, be the monster! I'm Caeth! I'm best! I'm chosen!"

His concentrated look worried Jonn, and he thought, *Him or me.*

Santir woke up angry, shivering though the night was warm, and his window was closed to wind. His were horrible dreams, sad and haunted, and those feelings persisted from the time he opened his eyes to the time he slept again. On it went, in sticking feelings of shame, loss, and rage. It had gotten worse since the Bilers arrived. *Dreams are not life,* he told himself.

He stood and wiped the crust from his eyelids with balled

fists, and then he heard a loud *clang* from downstairs. Another clutterful *clunk-clang* as he opened the door to his room, grabbing for his bag.

Yeroen was in the main room, cutting slices of mangaes, yapayas and imported Quo'Orinthian sourplums, tossing them into a bowl. He whistled as he went.

"Look at you, up before dawn," Yereon said as Santir sat. He stopped whistling and served them both. "Early for you. Have first food."

"And a drink, too?" Santir said, watching as his brother poured two short cups of rum.

"Yes, a drink. It's union day." Yeroen lifted the cup in salute before shooting down his rum. "To Tyanien Tyonar and whatever in the tides his bride's true name is."

"She calls herself Suni," Santir reminded his brother before drinking, but Yeroen didn't seem to care. Santir ate a few slices of mangae to chase the burn in his throat.

"Yes, to the Eerim Suni, to whatever Three-One and her parents call her. Are you wanting to go already?" Yeroen asked, pouring out another round and pointing to Santir's bag with his lips. "I don't want to walk before first light. Remember that cunju turns ago that tried to kill you? It has been some time since Klo has been able to keep us safe from cunju on the road. I will be ready at first light, though."

"I am not going to the city," Santir told him, declining the second drink his brother held, grimacing at the tingling in his throat, though it was sweeter now. "I don't care to go and dance and swallow rum all day."

"You are not going to see the procession at all?"

"I have seen a royal union before, I know what to expect. I am going to the falls instead."

"Because that sight is more unexpected? You know what the falls look like, little brother, not what an Eerim girl looks like in union paint, blessed by a Tyanien crown of flowers. I bet it's specially designed to go around her long ears." Yeroen gasped. "What if each of her ears has their own little crown? Do you think they thought of such a thing? And watch it become the next craze in the Tearstairs, all Eerim and otherwise. Today is history tomorrow."

Santir didn't answer, so his brother asked after another drink, "This is about Rae?"

"No," Santir lied, the angry instinct of his dreams not settled. "This has to do with me. If you can believe it, for once something in my life doesn't concern the Araeboril."

He moved to stalk out of the house, but heard Yeroen mumble, "I don't know why she still comes around with you being so sour... no longer fun."

Santir decided to drink down another glass of rum before leaving. As it burned, he wondered, *How is my life so strange? Why coudn't I have lived a simple life in Leurai and worked the ground beside my mother? Only now does that sound so great. Rae should have stopped hanging around us when Kloennian died. Three-One, lead her far away from me,* Santir prayed but did not know if he meant it. At least, in this moment, it felt like truth. He shut the door behind him and walked down the steps, onto the path.

Santir always hated working the field, and he knew from a young age he was meant for better, cleaner work. To his mother, there was nothing greater than picking and selling the Blessed fruit she grew. Santir's father had not liked farm work, either, and he'd held tides outside Leurai for some years before joining a captain's fleet. Santir could not remember him well, and if he tried too hard to remember his father's face, his mind would always confuse itself and morph the face into Yeroen's.

Being a mechanic was not cleaner than plucking mangacs from trees, and few Blessed men would say the work was better, but it was Santir's, all his, and he was good at it. He hadn't looked for work since the war ended, first hoping Yeroen would win enough in the wateryards to get them both out of debt. One fight, one bonus, and he could have done it. Instead, he was banned for killing that man, and they both had turned to smuggling. The job was quick, it was not so difficult, and it was still better than sweating in the field for a living. He told himself it was.

Santir needed some semblance of glory for his life. A name people respected. He wanted so much more than he had.

His life changed in countless ways when Tyanien Aadarae latched herself onto Klo seven turns past. They met by chance. Klo had been working with the palace's animals when he met the Araeboril. He invited her to one of Yeroen's duels in the wateryard. Because of chance, Santir was at once expected to be of good repute and moral character. Elevated thought. He was expected to be someone worthy of the talk they made —whatever that meant—still intimidated into understanding his lower place by men like Teviona Malak and Riambo Rajen. Santir was given a fine apprenticeship in the city for their *friendship*, and he had dined with Tyanien in the palace garden more than once. That was something most couldn't say.

His simple mind probably couldn't understand all the ways his life shifted in the instant Rae decided to love Klo more than any.

Santir hated her at first, when she met them with such grace and striking presence that he couldn't look at her face. As an ambitious boy, he hated her for bringing the realization that staring at the floor leveled him. Lowly born, he was. Then he hated her more because she acted as if it did not matter. But it always did. He only began reading the printed news when his name started appearing in them for his association with the Araeboril.

It was worse when he lived in the Tearstairs during those years while Yeroen toured fighting. Before the war. In the Confederate nations, the rumor mill was worse than in the Blessed Lands, as their news cycle lasted but a day. To stay noticed, Confederates were always doing the most outlandish things, thinking and plotting where they would be heard by scoundrel Eerim. It was illegal to sell another man's thoughts, but it happened. The Confederation couldn't maintain their short news cycle without invention and speculation permeating even that fallible truth. Many had been claiming that Rae was a prophet since before she could speak, that she was born with seer dreams. The reporters called her a murderer, a war criminal, a hero, an omen, a saint. They didn't call Santir much of anything, mostly speculating about his birth. Bastard or true born son? they wondered of the Senseless Detunae.

Santir wasn't a bastard.

He was a Detunae, even if he couldn't bend du.

And Rae told him long ago that her dreams were no different than any other person's. She promised, her dreams meant nothing of the future, that she was no different than any child of Amina. Santir's dreams, however— they were different from his usual dreams, and as he recalled their detail, his anger grew.

In no time at all, lost in the memory of dreams more real than life, his stomping got him to the falls. He stood on rocky river bank where the River of Ashakai met the mouth of the River of Many Sacoyes. The sound of the water was loud to the north, the dozens of falls looking like yarn strings hung to dry in the dark of morning.

There was sweet bubbling of water against the stony shallows before him. In front of Santir, the river deepened and opened at this converging point. From this view, he could see how each river split, their separate paths. Dots of simple houses in the jungle hills.

Santir sat on the smooth bank beside the water and packed his pipe with ground sweetleaf.

The pipe had belonged to Klo, crafted by his own hands. It was carved of dense bavo wood, light as caramel. Like Klo's skin. Santir stroked the tail of the pipe. It was long and shaped into the form of a coiled snake, and he had to kiss the serpent's fanged mouth to take in smoke. Mouwat Kloennian had been an artisan among many things; he had loved to create and make old creations new. Santir ran a finger against the small score of white and red gems that looked like scales, and the bowl lit softly, gently, to just light the herb. Santir inhaled and focused on the sound of rushing water and shaking trees. Birds and howling tree climbers.

It was still dark, but the houses were waking to begin their celebrations. The lifting sky blended into the blue hued city. There began the persistent twinkling of firelights in windows, and somewhere out there, a child cried and then quit, likely lulled by gentle arms. Santir turned away from the city, back to the falls and remembered better times.

This had been their favorite location to play and rest. In these waters, he laughed and cried with his yaren and brother, with Tyanien Aadarae, too. Here, Santir grew closer to Riambo Fehatsi when the War of the Radicals took their friends away. They sat together in silence and prayed for their friends who could fight, those with sense beyond them. All of them had spent many Moima here, Klo and Aadarae reading scriptures together atop the rocks; Yeroen and Teia would spar with the river water. They had lived in peace and been friends for turns. At a glance, they could have been simple children of the same village. But they weren't.

Never were. Only Mouwat and Detunae were simple names.

They played a game here, turns ago. A stupid game of names that Yeroen made up. Santir recalled the warmness of the dry season, dryer than it was now, the river a second home to them in the long days of heat.

"Will this be better than the last game you tried to teach us?" Riambo Fehatsi had asked.

"No, definitely not. If I had words," Yeroen said and stood on the wet rock, acting as if he would lose balance and fall in the water, "if my family was great and old and wrote the language, what would my words be?" Yeroen jumped and raised a carpet of water to catch him so he would not go under.

"Ignorant," Teia supplied, crashing his wave and smiling. "Undependable. Reckless. Ambitious as a Riambo, do those count? No, they must be your own...Pleasure would be one. You live for pleasure alone. What is another word for braggart?"

"None of those are good." Yeroen laughed, spouting water.

"Only good men get good words," said Fehatsi, "and if your family was famous, it would not be for good reasons, I think."

Yeroen only got louder. "That is easy to say when your words are those of Riambo, when your family has been royalty since before Blessed Lands were raised. As a child of Leu, your words are 'blood of free water', yes, Teia? Are those good enough for you?"

Teia had shown off her strength, lifting her right hand. From the river sprouted four swords of ice; they melted, froze, and melted again before she spun them into each other. "My words are coherent, not a string of attributes I would like to be, but who I am. My words mean something."

"All words mean something," said Tyanien Aadarae. "I understand the game. So, tell me what my words would be."

"That is not the game. You were born into great words, and they are yours," said Fehatsi. "Duty, compassion, blood. This is a game for simple children, Tyanien. It is not fun at all."

"My mother was simple, and born without words," Rae said in way of correction. "I like the game. Santir, what do you want your words to be?"

"I... don't know." Santir couldn't think of any, not one *exceptional* word he would want. A half-dozen words that might describe him enough, words that were just mediocre (apprentice, farmboy, senseless), words describing who he wanted to be (strong, brave, remembered), but that was not what Rae asked. She had asked what *words he wanted,* but truly Santir never wanted for words. Fame, glory, riches, respect, all the rest, of course. More than anything. But never the words. Great words were for great old families, and he knew he could never be part of all that. He had told her, "Damn the question, Tyanien, this is not the game. Families do not decide their own words anyway, they are given."

"Given by those who already have words, he's right," said Klo. "You must decide what his words would be."

The Tyanien looked Santir over with her eyes the same color as the river. "Stubborn," she said, and Santir felt his cheeks burn. Then, now. "Stubborn and honest. Loyal and ambitious, too, but not as a Riambo. Ambitious as a Detunae, the people might say if your family were old and known by everyone."

"I like all those," Yeroen said at the end. "We would have the same words, as brothers. One day we will get them!"

And they'd all laughed at him, but Santir knew he wasn't joking. He could imagine their joined laughter in the hills now, so common then.

Later, that same night by the water, when they thought everyone else asleep, Klo had asked her, "If I had words like a great, old family what would they be, my Tyanien?"

"Duty, compassion, blood," Santir heard Rae whisper, keeping his eyes closed.

"You do not understand the game still," Klo had laughed. The dearest sound. "It's to make fun of someone."

"Maybe you do not understand what I am telling you. I say that if you were part of a great, old family, you would be part of mine. If you want words, I will give them to you. I would give you anything. I love you, Klo."

Silence. Then, "I can't leave him. He'd never forgive me."

He did leave me. And haven't I?

It took Klo another two turns of the Rock to tell Rae he loved her, on the same day he asked for her hand. Three turns after, Klo was killed before he could marry Rae, and Yeroen had become the most infamous dueler of the age. In all that time, Santir did absolutely nothing, so no simple boys got words.

Santir had taken it all for granted back then. He and life in its new form were *sour* compared to how it had been. That was the word his brother used for him, sour like bad fruit. Like mangae plucked too soon.

Maybe that's what he was. Plucked too soon.

Santir had thought being the Araeboril's friend made him something more than other men, and that which defined him most was about to be taken again. Santir was Klo's yaren, and that had defined him, too. But now, without Klo, there was a great gap in the middle of their lives, and Rae was the only one trying to keep their friendship the same. She would be Selected soon, and then that would change. She would be great, and Santir would stay simple and be forgotten.

At least, his debt was paid, and for that he could feel some relief. Santir and Klo had only needed to come up with half the gold for a comfortable air vessel, and still they could not afford such a thing and had to seek out Tar L'rej and his riches. Klo had spent all his inheritance on his mountain when he had thirteen turns, and Santir had only the smallest of plots outside Leurai to his name. Tyanien Aadarae could have afforded the whole air vessel, and she would have paid for it all, but his yaren would not have it. Santir could only listen and begrudgingly go along with Klo's tiresome righteousness. *And still, I keep these secrets from her for you, yaren. But at least the debt is paid.*

At the time, they had reasoned seeking out the rich Ku'dur was worth their great intentions for the future. Boys playing at manhood, unready but sure. Santir truly believed their plan in certain moments, in the sweetest of times he more than hoped. He trusted that in time, they could all have their fantastic adventure. If the Araeboril believed, why shouldn't he? *How stupid was I?* he thought, sighing out to the trees.

Santir was heaving in the smoke more than breathing it.

The dreams of far west adventure had been first theirs, only his and Kloennian's, (more Santir's than Klo's truly) before Tyanien Aadare welcomed herself into their lives. She included herself in their planning, had put up half the money for an air vessel, and somehow that made it almost real. He wanted to believe her, but more often than not, Santir thought her hopelessly naïve.

Santir knew she would never actually join them, that in time she would be Selected, that the Great Leader and the Select Son of Amina would deny her wishes. He had often imagined the approaching Selection day, he used to picture his yaren by his side. Before the war, he envisioned a tearful Kloennian looking up to the First Children's circle, where the monuments loomed around the holy steps and sacrificing altar at Talosa's northern wall. Santir had always imagined the day as a tearful one, as Rae climbed three hundred steps and bound herself to another. Back then, he thought the day would feel like victory. He never imagined his own tears falling at the sight, his own jealousy.

If Santir knew she would be Selected, if he had predicted it, then she should have. She should have known in her holy given wisdom and not led Klo on in his affection. Her love for Kloennian had not been wise.

Rae was given wisdom at birth like Amina, but she was naïve, and she was fickle, and she was so caring it was careless. Santir hated her, and could almost hate Klo because he, too, had known all along and still loved her.

But Klo could not help loving her, just as Santir could not help himself now.

He loved her when he shouldn't. Even while he hated her. And he'd always hate her for taking Klo away.

The Araeboril was to love every living thing she knew, and the world couldn't help but respond in kind. *Is it possible not to love her? Is there free will in love and hate?* He didn't know. He didn't want to know, so that he could blame more than himself. It was easier to blame Rae and Three-One. The palace should have never let Rae run free. It wasn't right to let her loose on the Rock. They should have kept her locked up forever, away from him.

Santir's First ancestor, Ashakai the River Daughter, had written that every person's life was made of their own choices, moral or immoral, and that was the only freedom humans had that could not be taken. Choices were what defined any kind of spirit. Santir wasn't proud of his choices. Yeroen chose to fight in the war, as did Klo. As a Tyanien, Rae had no choice but to fight for Blessed Lands and defend the innocents.

And Santir chose?

To stay in the Blessed Lands and fix broken vessels; he watched them fly off time and time again carrying more people willing to die for him. He'd thought to join the forces, but he was no wielder or warrior, not like those Academy trained. If he had joined, perhaps he could have been there in CoБmak and fought with Klo like he should have, like a good yaren does. And then they both would have died for their people, and for the Confederates. *And maybe that would have been better after all. What am I?* he asked, not knowing the answer. *I was a hateful coward, and now I am a purposeless taskman.*

He was a simple man from Leurai, who once dreamed of uncovering far western secrets. Turns ago, one skinchanger crossed over from the Wilder Wood with the wildest stories. The first returner. And the last. The adventurer brought back inventions of electricity that forever changed the Rock, and Santir wanted to be remembered as someone like that. Both he and Klo were dreamers, that is what Mouwat's mother called them.

His dreams were different now, not of mechanical stars guiding him to treasure, but of dead faces and guilt. Klo asking him if he could feel an emotion besides jealousy. Klo declaring Santir's love as tainted, always tainted with hate and envy. His yaren staring with scorn. It made Santir feel like a stranger to himself in waking hours. Half a whole now, yaren without yaren.

Behind, he heard a rumbling and then something like a cat's meow, but deeper. The sound was not a cat. The laijrei named Ambos appeared at Santir's side, rubbing his soft fur against Santir's leg as he paced with sparking paws. Santir sighed and turned to look. If the laijirei was here, she would be. When he peered into the trees, he saw her at once, and she walked out of the jungle toward him.

"I came here to be alone," he said and batted away the laijirei before it tried to settle in his lap.

“As did I,” Rae said, sitting an arm’s length from him. “Do you want me to leave you?”

“No.” *Never.* How he wished he could tell her, “yes.”

“Good, because I have come all this way, and it is *my* favorite view.”

Santir handed her the pipe. The smell of her, like dirt and sweat and sweet oil only rich families afforded, against the smell of the garanha trees affected him. He loved that smell. Hated it. He rubbed his hands over his face and smelled the fading scent of sweetleaf and mangae on them, but she was still there.

“How is your mother?” she asked, holding the smoke in her lungs and returning Santir the pipe.

“I don’t know. I have not written to her in a long time. She keeps busy listening for gossip from neighbors like she always has done. That always takes up half of what she writes. Leurai is as varied as Talosa with its port. She loves that her gift of hospitality gifts back.”

“I know it. Leurai may be more varied, I think, except for times as these,” said Rae, coughing and blowing out sweetsmoke. “I have not been to the port since I had sixteen turns. It has been a long time since any of my family has been to the city. I would not mind a trip. Your mother would love it.”

Santir didn’t want to think of his simple mother or the hut of his childhood beside the Araeboril. Rae would pretend not to notice the dirt and the smell of manure. He would hate that. Santir remembered his good manners and asked concerning herself and her family, her mother and gravely ill father with utmost respect, and finally her brother the bridegroom.

“Do you think your brother will be happy with a better ear sharing his pillow?” he asked. "Never knowing her true name?"

“Of my siblings, only Tyonar has the mind good enough to attract such a person, I think. She adores him. I asked. Hanala told me it was rude to ask, but I didn’t care. I am very confident he will live all his years with her with more blisses than he should care to count.”

The Eerim will have all her many years after he is gone, Santir thought.

Another reason Eerim did not often marry humans: their lifespans were so different it was unseemly. Every person is given his allotted days, only Eerim were all given the same number. A healthy Blessed person could expect to live little past his one hundred and tenth year, few warriors made it there, while Eerim were born one day, and always died exactly 217,211 nights later. Santir believed all Eerim must have in their brilliant minds some sort of clock continuously running down the hours. He knew he would, if he were born Eerim. Some Eerim passed peacefully to another plane within a good night's sleep, others tried to live their last night wildly to the final breath, but all ended the same. A human life spanned only a fourth of what an Eerim expected.

Did Tyanien Tyonar feel like he was to be given a citizen's portion of his lover's life? Did he think it was just or was he contented with what he was given? *Great men always want more.*

Rae looked at Santir; her beauty struck him, unexpectedly as it did sometimes. *God...* He hated her. He remembered to breathe.

"Do you remember when we were younger," she asked, "when we were new friends, and Klo jumped from that rock there and broke his leg?"

Santir did remember, and he remembered how Rae screamed when Klo fell from the high place, and how she healed him in a worried haste.

"Yes," he said. "Do you remember how he tried not to limp in front of you after, so that you could think you did a better job in fixing the bone than you did?"

"Yes, I remember. He was very encouraging in that regard."

"In every regard. In ten days it will be two full turns since he died," said Santir, all nervousness to bring him up with her. "Two turns have passed since CoБmak. Does it feel like it for you?"

"I don't know. I have lifetimes within me, starting with the Achkan woman when the Academy fell. Sus'Laki, and his men. I feel how pain can fade, just not mine. Time passes. I am told it heals. Not as effectively as truelight but... Truelight cannot bring life to death, it cannot heal a piece of you that is missing. Kloennian is a missing piece of me. At moments, it feels like yesterday I had him, and other times it feels like a dreamish, distant memory that he was ever here. Those days feel the loneliest to me. Too many days like that."

Santir, holding in smoke, said, "Only seventy eight days and nights until the Selection, but I am sure you are counting them down."

"No, but Feha counts, so I can never forget. It seems you are counting, too, which surprises me."

"I can count to the hundreds, Tyanien."

"That is not what I meant. It was never on my mind before the war, it was not on my mind right after the war either. I never thought I would be Selected."

"Rae." Santir's tone conveyed all—that he didn't believe her, that he was angry and insulted that she could even say it. She shook her head, eyes flitting to the west. *Always west now,* he noticed. He inhaled from the pipe deeply and turned to look where she did, as a distant piece of rock flew into the sky from the farther spaces, burned down like a falling ember.

"I never thought it before," she said. "We bought an air vessel. We were going to go if the war hadn't started. We were going to go East and then the Wilder West, whether it was covert or illegal, and I wouldn't be Selected, and Klo was going to paint everything we saw."

"You were going to heal the whole damned Rock."

"And you were going to find ancient treasures beyond the Wilder Wood, like the Mechanic Scrolls."

"Ha! Yes, treasures and mysteries, scrolls, all of it. We imagined a great little adventure for ourselves. Klo and I knew that it would never come to pass. We both knew you would end up here, and if you were honest with yourself, you knew it, too."

"No," her voice broke, but she straightened her back. "I didn't think it until he died, and if he had lived I would not be here. You must know that. We would all be together and flying in that vessel east or far west, or wherever we wanted to go. If he— we wouldn't be here."

"You are more naïve than I thought," he said it with venom, wanting to hurt her as he hurt. "You lie to yourself so easily, it makes me wonder whether you are actually a truthspeaker at all."

"I think that is unfair of you. I never wanted this, Santir, but I am doing my duty now. Duty, compassion, blood," she repeated the words of Teviona. "I have a duty to my blood. My brothers are about to take over the Blessed Lands, and the People do not love them. I don't know what else to do. It is not what I want, but without Klo, I can't leave. So, I will be Selected. I will do what is good for my family."

There was once a time when Santir thought that their little group was like a family, back when they had all laughed together and swam in the pools and climbed in the trees. Rae had said as much to him once, that she thought of him as one of her own blood, that she loved him as much as any of her Tyanien brothers. The memory of all of them whole made him feel warm and peaceful, or maybe that was the sweetsmoke. Some of Santir's anger vanished, but he held onto that last bit and gave her the pipe. *She is not naive. She is a master of truthspeaking. Manipulating. She cannot speak her carefully thought words at me and make me forget. No matter how much I love you.*

Hate you.

Rae inhaled the leaf and closed her eyes. "You must go see Giana," she said when she breathed out the smoke. That helped him love her less. For bringing up Klo's mother, he hated her more. "She tells me you haven't been to see her in over six moons' wax and wane."

"Have you come here to make me feel worse about myself,

Tyanien?"

"No." She handed the pipe back to him but did not look at him. He wondered if his attempts to distance himself were finally working. And it scared him. She said, "I told you I came to be alone. Giana misses you, and it isn't fair for her to lose both sons while one still lives."

"I don't think she would miss me as much if she knew all I have done. She'll look at me and see a man walking where Klo should be," Santir spat, thinking, *Her real son,* and then he took a long breath of smoke. "She wouldn't want to see me."

"That is not true," Rae said. "I believe you know that is not true. I think you are too expert at making excuses."

"You and me, both. Why are you out in the jungle now anyway? Shouldn't your lyaren be styling your hair for the union ceremony and procession?"

"No one will see my hair under my crown. My mother won't notice my absence, and that's what matters. But she will ring my neck if I miss first foods with Suni's family and the Eerim Council, smack me whatever is near if I miss the whole thing. She is ecstatic, you know, that the whole family is together. We haven't been since Nelina's union. I came here to clear my mind before better ears hear and better minds judge me."

"Clear your mind of what?"

"Let's see, there's the Selection. I almost killed a helpless Biler. I am too tired to be around Eerim. I am bad at checking well rested thoughts. Thank Three-One for laws against Eerim reporting thoughts to the masses, little good they help, or the Rock would have too much of me. They have too much of me. I could be losing my mind, and today a small crowd will listen while I pretend to be mindful. And by tomorrow, the Confederate's illegal papers will all say, Araeboril Gone Mad."

"You didn't really answer my question."

"I did and I didn't."

"Right. Children of Amina lie by omission. Is evading truth something you had to be taught, like a Fair Person, or is it easy?"

"Please," she said in a strained, flat tone, and he remembered his place. She was the second Araeboril, a Tyanien, hero of the Radical's war. She Who Slayed the Pretender and all that. *And what am I?* Sitting next to her, Santir couldn't think of a good enough answer. *I must stop asking myself.*

Rae breathed deeply, and when she spoke again he could tell each word was intentional, maybe she had practiced them. "I can't sleep at night. I have these horrible dreams, and they keep coming. They get worse despite the sleeping draughts and... I cannot escape from anything."

"What do you dream?" Santir had never wanted to know something so badly, so he could share his own nightmares and grief. Maybe she dreamt of Klo, too.

"I cannot tell you."

"Then I might just read the illegal papers to find out. We are friends," he reminded her, but it felt wrong after treating her so unfriendly. "You don't keep truths from your friends. Or, you never did before."

"I cannot tell you, and I will not. It isn't enough to say what is true." Her voice picked up and he could tell she was becoming anxious, as her fingertips twitched, sparked and she blinked more rapidly. "I can only speak the truth, but that makes it worse because people think they know what that means. You have to say what is right at the appropriate time, at the right time. And the right people need to listen, or rather need to understand. They cannot when I cannot, and...and they think everything means something more, and they miss the heart. You cannot just say the truth, all of it, and let that be. I cannot, Santir, ever. People would go mad. I can't even think the whole truth. Or I will."

She pulled from the pipe and passed it back to him while the herbs still glowed, and he inhaled the sweet numbing smoke while she spoke.

"Amina was a person like any, and they took her dreams, her personal writing and correspondence, and made them prophecies. And she agreed and later disagreed, agreed again —and then who knows? Blessed People have promulgated her words as near divine, deconstructed every verse in every conceivable way. They held the First Books up and quoted them to me since before I could speak, especially Amina's writing. From my perspective— to imagine everything I say brandished in time after I am gone? —that sounds terrifying, absolutely *terrifying*. It makes me not want to say anything at all, and there I am paralyzed by fear of failing, so unlike what I need to be. I am just a person, too, and everything is permanent. Once I believe something, it is for the Rock, and everyone is so serious. I don't think I was made for seriousness, Santir. I wish I was made for lighter things."

God, she rambles when she smokes. "It is the end times. People are entitled to feel seriously."

"That is not funny."

"It is. A little." He shrugged. "People complain when I joke, they complain when I don't. Maybe I'm just not funny, since you say. Blessed People are only serious in their love for you, Tyanien. You could say nothing wrong in their ears. Amina predicted the end of the damn world, and the People embraced her."

"I have wondered if I could say anything, think anything, to turn them all against me. Singing my name in the streets, but I wonder why they do not curse me. Many think I have cursed the Rock by being born, and when I travel to the Confederation, I hear the hatred and fear. The Blessed People treat me like the first Araeboril, with undeserved praise founded on...hope. That their first prophet was wrong? I am mortified to feel their love. They can somehow think I was born as a sign of the end times, but call me a savior like Amina. Amina could not be great as everyone thinks. I find it impossible to believe she was everything they claimed. She was a woman like me. Or maybe, I am not great and she was everything people said."

Amina was not just a woman, and neither are you. And the end times are not real, those prophecies are not truth. You said it long ago, and I believed you.

"I must clear my mind of this before they hear it. The Eerim Council already considers me delusional. Can you see how worried I am?" she asked.

Santir let go of that last shred of anger. He wondered what was worse: being remembered in ways you cannot control, or not being remembered at all. He realized Rae cried. It was unnerving how still she remained, unmoving despite the strength of the wind and the volume of her tears, but her posture was from turns of rigid practice. Santir remembered a time when she could not stay still for anything.

"I know the difference between nightmares and prophecies," he said, lost for words to soothe her. He was never gifted at comforting, that had been Klo without effort, but Santir supposed it another duty he might inherit with Klo gone.

Santir placed one of his shaking hands atop hers. Her fingers would shake if she did not pay them mind, but now she held them firm as unwieldable stone. Santir felt a soft warmth and tingle where their skin met. That sensation, whether his feelings or the truelight beneath her skin, addicted him.

He hated it.

He said, "I am simply bred, but not entirely stupid. These are dreams, Rae. You told me that you are not a prophet, and that must be true if you say it. You would know if God spoke to you. We don't live in a time of prophets, and your dreams are not visions of the future. These are just dreams even if you are the second Araeboril."

"I don't know if I am, and I shouldn't lie to myself." Her words were colder than the night, more chilling. "I don't know anything of prophecies. All I know, I know so little, and that is how I am kept. I know nothing that gives peace, and I have killed such broken, desperate people. I don't want to be a killer. But… I could not save *Klo,* and I should have been able to. I left him in Coбmak, and I knew I shouldn't have. I am no savior. Sometimes I think Sfar'Laki was right. I already failed when I killed him."

Can she feel guilt for the Ku'dur bastard? Santir could not imagine; but he would never hope to imagine what she felt. When her rays of truelight killed, she absorbed the pain and memory of the dead, and it stayed with her in ways Santir could not know. She had said few words before the war about the Academy explosion and the Achkan woman. He never asked about it.

To despair over Laki's death? Santir couldn't fathom. Despite her curse to love all life she met, she could not love Sfar'Laki like that. His plagues killed Klo, cut her father for death, devastated thousands. Rae couldn't save Klo, but she avenged him. Santir often prayed for such a chance, though he knew there was no one left that he could find. All Sfar'Laki's closest men died with him in that tower, either killed by Tyanien Pyaren and his warriors, or killed by Rae's blast of truelight. The remaining followers of the Radical creed were sought out and put down, though rumors existed that hundreds fled beyond the Wilder trees.

Santir took his hand away from Rae's, gripped around the pipe though the hot bowl burned him. "You can speak freely with me of dreams. I won't put weight on them. Even if we did live in a time of prophets, I know what you are and are not."

"Klo used to tell me not to worry," she said, sniffling, "because everything that needed to be said has been said by someone wiser, probably said by an Eerim that heard it first. The world is old, most great thinkers spoke and died, and the pressure was only in my mind, he would say. Don't worry about being impressive, just say what you need to. They will hate you, love you. They are divided anyway. No one tells me that now."

"You make him eloquent in death. He was simple, remember, despite what you made him. Klo said many stupid things, too. But he..." Santir struggled to find the words, and he focused on the distant fires in the pitch of night instead of Rae's expectant stare. "He cared about you most of all, and he believed in you. Whatever it is you fear, Rae, you are not alone. He loved you so much."

"And you loved him," she whispered.

Santir froze. "As you did, Tyanien." He'd never confessed his love to her. Would she pity him like Klo did? Poor, stupid Santir, jealous of the Araeboril, in love with his yaren who could never love him the same... He certainly had a type.

Rae sighed. "All I want to do is fight. I don't know why I fight, or *who*, but I fight. If I let go for one breath... I feel like I am up against something impossible, like my will means nothing compared to some higher power of design. Damn Amina's *prophecies*. I can't believe in... anything, or the Rock believes it, too. And the truth that my will is all I have to defend myself is terrifying."

Santir wouldn't look at her. "I know the feeling."

The morn dawned blue and bright, divinely. Mittrik had never seen *such blue*, a color he thought he knew but never with such clarity and perfection. Clouds drifted above the city for the vision, like swelled woolen rovings pulled to wisp, and the temperature did not seem so oppressive and heavy as it had days prior.

Mittrik heard the knocking at his door as he peered out the window to the bustling and crowded streets, to the sight of fire shaped like dragons of legends, flying all the way near him and back down to the streets. Below, the natives crowded and danced together in big spinning circles that traded people (so far below they looked like ants), but he couldn't hear the music. The smells made his mouth water, which was so contrasting to the smells of cities in Kieln. The sun heated his face delightfully. Jonn was the one to open the door, because Mittrik could not pull himself away.

The tall, dark woman Teia was on the other side, dressed in a sort of gown that fanned in light sheets around her knees and wrapped tightly around her waist and chest. Her miscolored eyes were adorned with a shock of yellow paint that made her skin shine, and most of her hair was braided close to the roots, while the rest curled around her ears. Large beetle gems of gold hung heavy on her lobes and made her look somewhat elfin.

She told Jonn and Mittrik that she was to escort them into the city and stay with them for the duration of the wedding on orders from the Tyanien. She advised them to leave their swords, though Mittrik hadn't thought to bring it, and led them away from their apartments with great civility. She was not as talkative as Rae, and not as dignified as the darker Fehatsi, but not bad company. She held herself proudly, and Mittrik quite liked how deep her voice sounded and the confidence with which she spoke. She did not act familiar, keeping a bit of an exaggerated distance, but tried to make pleasant conversation.

"This union is special for many reasons," Teia said. "It is the first time a human of a ruling family becomes one with an Eerim, and Tyanien Tyonar and Suni unite for love. They were both working in the same orphanage during the War of the Radicals, and this is how they met. The singers have plenty of romantic inspiration."

"Watch your pockets," she later apprised in the tunnels, "and make sure your purse strings are knotted thrice. Skilled winds wielders can lift a coin from a purse without you feeling a thing. Just always be mindful, without too much thought. But enjoy yourselves, lords."

This tunnel was as long as the tunnel through which Rae guided him, and Mittrik's eyes tired of the dark.

"Please remember, lords," Teia said, "to always be careful about what you are thinking. You are never alone in your head, not really, and your thoughts are no secret. Do not think of secrets or of having them. There are many Eerim with the better ear who would wish to listen to some Biler contemplations. I believe most Eerim will leave you alone, knowing you might be overwhelmed, but there are many who are eager to listen. Think nothing you would not say to a thousand."

"These elves can really hear unspoken thoughts?" Jonn asked.

"Not elves, Jonn," said Mittrik, coolly. He liked knowing more than Jonn. "They're called Eerim. Elf is a rude thing Fair Islanders say. And not all Eerim have what they call the better ear, but they all have ears and eyes like that."

"Yes," Teia agreed with him, or she was answering his brother. Jonn's face seemed set in a permanent grimace.

"And how do you know which of them can hear your thoughts if they all look the same?" Jonn asked.

Teia responded, "You cannot, so always be careful even if you don't see the pointed ear."

The tunnel ended at a solid wall, but by now Mittrik knew it would open for them when Teia placed her hand atop the rock. He could not anticipate the rest, however.

The rectangular arch in the wall let them pass onto a busy street, and many faces turned to see them, but stood back a respectable distance. The space closed behind them once they were on the street, blending perfectly with the slabs of stone in the wall.

At once, the respectable distance was breached. The street was full of people, elbows piercing and heads edging for a view, and they all looked peculiar and shocking. Some were dressed as others he'd seen, with their thin clothing that revealed much painted skin, while others had brightly colored hair and more colorful gowns that resembled what ladies of Baeltaf might wear if they were insane. These ladies' skin was dyed to colors like magenta and green. Their gowns were heavy, surely too hot in the current weather, and layered to make their bottoms look like bells.

People seemed to recognize their escorting guide, called out her name in gladness, and she waved and smiled with the grace of a royal.

"Come this way, Bilers, before someone thinks to talk to us. I swear I might finally hit a Confederate reporter today if any try."

They followed her without a clue where they were going, but Mittrik craved to see every little sight he could.

A man confused cups in front of a little grole in child sized robes. The grole slammed his hand atop the farthest left cup, and it turned to powdered dust as he smashed it; he screamed. The man lifted the center cup to reveal the pretty rock and gave it to the little grole. Mittrik smiled and watched as the creature clutched the rock tightly to his chest, the eyes of his face closing tightly but the ones on his hands all staring at his prize with obvious affection.

Around the street Mittrik saw men mold pots and jars out of stone and colored clays, forming with their bare hands, and the clay seemed both soft and hard as they worked it. Others stretched bright liquid fire with unburning red hands, and Teia told him they were artisans of glass.

By hands that looked more like his own, baskets were being woven from thin strands of colored leaf, and the patterns on them were vivid: spiritlions with green eyes, spotted dogs with long snouts, flowers falling and birds in flight, and some were designed with the lettering of their language, a looping, intelligible kind of writing. Teia told him that all the baskets will be presented to the Tyanien and his bride. Most of the artisanal works were already aligned along the side of the street beside their vendors, who all spoke to one another and called out to the throng.

Near the back of a large crowd, Mittrik saw five tented pavilions of blue and white set in a tight circle on the side of the street and around the tents, wafted dense purple smoke that had a bitter, though not unpleasant aroma. People spoke in hushed voices around the tents. Mittrik was instantly curious.

"What is that?"

"Fortune tellers," answered Teia.

"Is their magic real?" Mittrik asked, intrigued. "Can they know the future?"

"Maybe. They are here in the morn, and they are usually gone before a guard can come and ask if their magic is real. This is the only time they can make money off the people. If they are asked and it is true magic, they will be sent away, but if it is false magic the people will know they are frauds, and no one would spend a taro."

"Why would they be sent away?" Jonn asked.

"To see someone's fortune true, it requires their blood. Blood magic is forbidden on the Rock under the Civil Accords, which dictate how the races live together. Practicing any form of magic work is forbidden in the Blessed Lands, though some get away with it. Forms of true magic still exist in the Confederation. Oh, there! I see children dancing down the street near the palace gate. Follow me. We call it the Beautiful Gate, *ya Meliat Sirta*. It is accurate naming, yes?"

They agreed and walked with her to the golden gate, standing the height of ten men. From the slats of the gate Mittrik could see a large courtyard and the bottom of the palace stairs, and above the walls he could see those steps lead to the large façade with its pale stone and dark doors.

The children dancing at the gate were all shaved bald as little eggs, painted in colliding colors of white, gray and yellow, dressed in brown grass skirts. They had masks like those Mittrik had seen before, faces of animals baring teeth, but theirs were more crudely made, brightly painted and covered only the lower halves of their faces. The children all stood in a circle, clasped each other's hands, and began running round and round. They were lifted off their bare racing feet, and Mittrik could feel the winds behind him rush to the center of their circle, drawing him in. All at once, they let go of one another and the children were thrown from the whirled wind that they had created. Some flipped backwards in the air, others soared high above the crowd, but each one landed on spry toes, and their spinning wind was sent toward onlookers. The gale came stronger than Mittrik expected, pushing both Jonn and him back a step.

"Children have such power," Jonn whispered. "Mounted knights are nothing to small mages. A thousand longbow-men could fire on them and they need only change the wind."

"I know," Mittrik laughed. "Is it not wonderful? Could you imagine all the poor children in Kielntown able to do that?"

Jonn stayed silent.

"The children are students of the Academy of Talosa," said Teia, "and all are children of Fetín there. They will perform the dance of seven windy nights again after the Great Fire's fall at the Mouth of Ashakai, and they shall also perform the dance of the flutterflyer with the children of Jeyen. That dance is very big and by the end, everyone joins. It is a union tradition. If you have luck, you may fly a little."

He stopped—too fast, Jonn ran into him. He might fly?

Mittrik felt every bit of excitement imaginable, and his cheeks hurt from smiling.

Then the whole crowd stopped churring as the men atop the palace walls trumpeted from huge brass tubes that hugged their middles, and on the ground, every man with a pipe began playing the same song only higher. A five note song, like a bird's. The drummers banged their instruments again, this time much louder, faster and it shook the whole city.

From behind, Mittrik heard Teia exclaim, "Ah! Here they are."

He turned as the great black doors of the palace opened.

"Talo*tha* *tho*va cha-cha tatin bogu yeba *tho*llim. Cha-cha koke."

Talosa is truly the greatest city I have visited. Truly koke, the last a word with no Canyameo equivalent. A word that meant, very human and animal in much the same way. Fehatsi listened to the Lord of Bogu Etka, an Eerim who possessed a cunning tongue, though it lisped. His name was Cairo of the clan Tayer. Not his real name of course. Eerim never gave their real name to anyone. Lord Cairo traded in furs with the Barons of the Tearstairs and of all the Masters on the Eerim Council, his lands in Iri were the flattest and yielded little besides livestock. That is all Fehatsi knew, but she didn't think of any of that. He had the better ear.

The Eerim man did know the blessed tongue, of course he did, but it was a courtesy to speak Liem, and Fehatsi loved to practice the duosyllabic and choppy dialect that the upperclass, such as Cairo spoke. Fehatsi loved languages and did translations in her free time, to relax and improve herself. The best way to learn about a people was to understand how they spoke, what they said and why they said it. The heart of any culture is the tongue.

"Asad nutu, Luxe Cairo." *Many thanks, Lord Cairo.* Fehatsi's accent was spectacular.

The Eerim continued to compliment the baskets and potter's work along the road, to the artisans and to Fehatsi, who could not keep thanking him after some time. She went to the back of the procession, hundreds marching down the main streets. Fehatsi found Teia and the cleanly dressed Bilers for a few moments of respite.

"How are you?" she asked Teia, as the procession commenced again under the greatest flowing aqueducts. Teia linked her arms with Fehatsi's, and they walked in step with one another.

"I am feeling well," Teia said. "The basket presentation was beautiful, but I am finding it just as entertaining to watch how the Bilers react. The Fair one's eyes turned lidless, and got stuck like that, I think. And the dark-haired one keeps touching everything, looking back as if I might scold him. How are you?"

"I am having fun," Fehatsi said, and she thought that was true. "I talked to Luxe Cairo about Achkan fashion trends, and how much money was lost by the investors of purple Waban dye."

"So exciting. Anyone I would care about?"

"No, but important people nonetheless. Cairo being one."

"A pity that fashion trends are all Achkans recycle. In a

season or two, interest in purple will come back and those investors will not be lacking food or coin in the meantime, unlike many."

"That is how the conversation with Luxe Cairo went, yes. And a promise of a prayer for the poor investors, the land owners and their workers."

"If I had prayers to spare, they wouldn't be for globalist investors."

"Teia," Fehatsi's voice whipped her friend to attention; an undeniable blush colored the water wielder's cheeks. *Is she drunk already? No, she isn't. Can't be. Wouldn't— isn't.*

Stop.

Teia knew not to speak that way in public, and Fehatsi should not think these thoughts with Eerim near. Fehatsi's mind sped past the mistake. Eerim were forbidden to make public reports on Blessed People's thoughts unless the thought was dangerous, but everything ended up in the illegal papers. And then some. Not that Fehatsi read them.

"All my prayers are going to Sharann and the villages still affected by the Radical attacks," Teia said, and Fehatsi could see that now her thoughts were more precise. Calculated.

Fehatsi turned to the Bilers who were only just keeping up with it all, constantly turning back to look and linger. Their necks would hurt tomorrow. She spoke to the taller, the older, the one who didn't run off into the jungle with Rae. "Lord Hwaelin, I hope you are enjoying the celebration of the city."

"Oh," he said, realizing she was there, "aye, it is extraordinary. I've never seen anything comparable." He seemed a perpetually tense sort of man to Fehatsi.

"And how long does this go on?" the other Biler asked her.

"We will rejoice for the next many days, but the union celebration lasts until the next sunrise officially. The procession goes until the moons are opposite above us, and everyone goes to the River's Mouth for the firelight show which lasts some hours. The city dances until sunrise and the royal family hold feasting in the palace for their visitors. The remaining food, which is always plentiful, will be given to the city for the morrow."

"How wonderful," mumbled Mittrik Hwaelin, who Fehatsi already disliked. "The whole city involved and celebrated, my eyes gifted to see it. There is an abundance of everything here, of life most of all. Thank you for convincing my brother to stay."

Teia, all manners, said, "It is the pleasure of the Teviona to have you attend, Lords Hwaelin. I am glad you are enjoying it."

Fehatsi sighed and looked up to see the black length of Ambos shoot like a cannon between the narrow alley of Underwater Street, bounding like a streak of night and lightning against sunlit roofs. Rae was on his back, leaving the procession and the crowded street. The people noticed, screamed, cheered and riled. "Araeboril!" they shouted.

"Did she just run down that in-between?" Teia asked in the Blessed tongue.

Fehatsi's jaw clenched. "Yes, she did." Her brain turned white to not think. She wouldn't think poorly of Tyanien Aadarae. She wouldn't ever.

Teia smiled. "Well, the celebration has begun," she said. "I will take the Bilers up to the flower circle. Better shops, better food. I am sure Rae will end up there before the Great Fire sets."

"I should go now, too," Fehatsi said and then leaned in, hoping the crowd was loud enough, that the procession was far enough ahead. "Remember to watch your mind when you interact with the Bilers, wherever you go. Did you make certain they understood that their thoughts were being heard?"

"Everyone told me to."

"Teia, please. They understood you?"

"I may not be a student of foreign tongues like you, but I am an educated woman. I can speak well enough to tell Bilers not to think stupidly. Please stop underestimating me, my friend. I am entertaining our noble guests, speaking and thinking in all good manners about how great the Blessed Lands are. What else can I do?"

"Forgive me," Fehatsi said and straightened. She walked away toward the rolling wheelhouses. She didn't think of Teia's record of missteps, or that she was smelling like strong drink.

Fehatsi saw her father ahead, riding a striped horse beside the Onatae's white and green painted wheelhouse, the dried sweza leaves of the roof shading her as she waved with both hands. Dianis never learned how to appear before the People.

Tyanien Tyonar and Suni had stopped the procession to dance with the children and spin them around, complimenting their little flower chains and grass skirts. Suni loved children, Rae told Fehatsi twice. Though Suni and Tyonar were of different kinds and could not have children of their own, they planned to take in children who were orphaned from the War of Radicals. Tyonar was kind and generous, perhaps the most generous of all the Tyanien. He would give the cloak off his back to a common without any prompt or any people near to watch him do the good deed.

A Ku'dur in thin white robes and little adornment headed in Fehatsi's direction. His private eyes, below his brow, and antlers were wrapped in golden cloth, his chest bare. Peering in all directions, but most of his eyes locked on Fehatsi. She recognized him at once. Master Sus'Laki, the old magician. The Pretender, Sfar'Laki's father. He'd done nothing in the war, to help or stop his son.

Fehatsi bowed her head when the Ku'dur stood beside her. She was not thinking about it, but he had a reputation of a loon. She wondered, briefly, if Sus'Laki hated Rae for killing his only son and heir, and if that hatred extended to Fehatsi. Couldn't help but wonder, really. Unrefined as the thought was.

"Master Sus'Laki, I hope you are well."

"Yes, Iyaren Riambo of Teviona," the Ku'dur said, and bowed his head. "Rich in joy today. I see Tyanien Aadarae vanished into the air, somehow. She is very fast, that girl. She moves like the laijirei she rides. Caged animals set free, the two tof them."

Fehatsi lowered her head as well before replying. "Yes, I apologize if her absence displeases you, Master Laki. I hope you know Tyanien Aadarae would never intend to offend anyone." *Further.*

Rae never meant for any of this.

"Oh, I understand completely. Nothing soils a party like a council of mind hearing politicians, I fear. I imagine it makes it hard to enjoy yourself, and what a shame as young as you are, lyaren Riambo of Teviona. You should be having a good time in the masses as well."

"I prefer to stay close to the procession. And if a young person cannot watch their mind and have a good time, then they aren't a very intelligent person."

The Ku'dur chuckled hoarsely, from deep down in his speckled belly. "Yes, yes, you have your father's wit, Riambo."

Not even my wit is my own. Everything attributed to the Riambo name. Fehatsi did not think all that she wished to. She was skilled and did not let the thought of wishes form.

"It is said," Sus'Laki drawled on, "that Amina, daughter of Iial, was so wise, so beguiling that every prince in Zepey gave her one hundred ships and every man she met asked for union with her. How many ships has our Araeboril acquired? How many princes and how many hearts, I wonder the number."

In the turns of the First Children, there had been near one hundred princes of Zepey, all warring with each other for dominance over the continent. Each of them had given the first Araeboril ships, gold, and pledges of fealty to her cause of freeing humans from slavery. It was the first time the warring Zepeyans agreed on anything. Amina united many kingdoms and healed most of the warring in the southeastern plains.

Aadarae had only caused division.

In these times, there were only thirty Zepeyan princes, but each had given Aadarae two hundred ships for her fifteenth nameday, and Prince Abdulan of Mennu Zepey had given her too many verses of poetry; he kneeled before her on her nameday, after only one meeting, asking to be sworn to her service for life after she refused his hand. He would have given up ruling the largest Zepeyan province to be sworn as her shield.

While she gave out her love freely to any she met, Aadarae had only ever wanted to marry Mouwat Kloennian. That sort of love had been reserved for the simple, distant descendant of Hahnae with little land and no title.

Amina had used her ships to break the chains that bound human kind; she and her siblings, their descendants, ended human slavery on the Rock thousands of turns ago. Rae now kept her ships docked by Yettirai, near the steam waters, where they collected barnacles like metal collects rust. The Great Leader forbade Blessed People from traveling by sea, affected by the loss of his first wife. Fehatsi did not think of her aunt or of the Great Leader, would not in front of Eerim. She only thought of Rae's many, many ships and their sad uselessness.

"Almost as many ships and just as many hearts, I assure you," she said to Sus'Laki. "It might be she has more admirers than Amina with all of the Rock watching and knowing, and reporters making it so unlike how it used to be. Tyanien Aadarae must be at least as beguiling as the first Araeboril."

"But not as wise?"

Fehatsi face heated, her throat scratched when she swallowed. "I could not say for certain, good Master. People compare the two much too often. I never met Amina, but by her writing people assume she was wise. Tyanien Aadarae is certainly wise for her turns, but as Eerim say, wisdom is attained with enough aging, so she will only become wiser."

"The first Araeboril was a seer, pardon, a *prophet*, but she was only assumed wise. Is that your meaning, Riambo?"

"No. My meaning is that it is easy to assign attributes to people long dead, for the romance of history. I may be cynical, for Amina appears the wisest of her time. Her character seems wise and compassionate to us after so much a separation from the past, a rarity. Amina wrote some great proverbs, just as the other First Children. My favorite writings are those of Emín, not Amina."

Fehatsi had studied Amina's writings more than any of

other First Children's, and in truth, the Books of Amina were mostly made of strange dreams and ramblings that she did not comprehend, letters to different people across her time. The Second Book of Amina was half scribblings, clearly meant to be kept personal and private.

Still, she had to be ever polite, politic, now. Careful. Ku'dur listened to what you did not say as closely as Eerim listened to thoughts. Rae was wise as any educated Canyai could be, but she was still just a young woman of only twenty turns who let impulse rule her. She had much to learn. As did Fehatsi. It was wisdom to acknowledge that. She explained her feelings to Sus'Laki eloquently enough to earn a smile of satisfaction.

He responded, "Wisdom comes by living long or by living much, and Tyanien Aadarae has lived many lives in her own and would find herself in the latter group. Forgive me for upbringing such unpleasant talk, but the youngest Tyanien has lived with more than her own life's pain, starting at six turns. That is what they say. Life increased by death, and death by life it could be theorized, a sad and remarkable thing. I imagine that creates a kind of wisdom," Sus'Laki blabbed airily and then changed the topic with a waving hand. "I saw the royal laijirei went with her when she left. Before it expressed itself in smallness, with much shyness, I remember. It has gained comfort with greater size, I see."

Sus'Laki was the one who gifted Ambos to Rae when she had thirteen Rock turns.

"He has, and Tyanien Aadarae has him well-trained. They go most places together."

"A wonderous thing they found each other, perhaps the only two creatures living with the ability to see truelight. I have not heard of anyone else with a living laijirei in the past two hundred turns. I am glad that the Araeboril has such a companion that can share in the brightness of her vision."

"She is thankful to you, Master Laki. I am sure Ambos is thankful as well— that is what the Tyanien calls him."

"A respectable name, but I am the thankful one. I have

not stopped being thankful since the day my ship intercepted the smugglers. It gave me the opportunity to unite two like spirits."

"It is difficult to imagine them apart after all these turns."

"Only nearing eight, my dear. That is not long at all to a Ku'dur."

He was right. Fehatsi misspoke. "Forgive me, good Master. For a human of eighteen Rock turns, eight does seem many."

"It certainly does, lyaren of Teviona. But I will tell you a secret, if you ask for it."

"What is the secret?"

He huffed through the slits of his nose. "Oh, I thought you were a clever girl, Riambo. Not now, of course, with mind hearing politicians."

"If you mean to elate my interest, you will be disappointed to hear that I am not intrigued, good Master. I would need much more for that." The procession was beginning to pick up and move, and Fehatsi wished that she had been given a striped horse to ride.

The Ku'dur's eyes all blinked at different times, the eyes on his arms and hands a pretty shade of blue, while the eyes on his cheeks and neck were brown, like her own eyes.

"It concerns the end times, Shadow Times my people call it," he said, "and the stories about farther floating Rocks with their own life."

Tufan, what? Old fool. Awful slip, but still Fehatsi fought the urge to roll her eyes. "Oh," she said quickly, and she reminded herself that she could not laugh at a Great Ku'dur Master. "You mean to tell me a secret about ancient aliens and the end of the Rock. Here I was thinking you had an actual secret, good Master."

"A few, if you find that you are intrigued."

"I regret to tell you that I am not."

"You may believe in Amina's prophecies about the end, or you don't. Every culture has stories of a beginning, and I've found most have a story for the end. Most are in agreement within our realm in saying that in the end, existence will be at its most depraved. Are we there, lyaren of Teviona? Are we so detached from good?"

"Existence has been worse." *Who could say the world was more depraved now than when humans were enslaved and oppressed by Eerim and Ku'dur and Takircha all?* Fehatsi checked herself. She couldn't afford a flippant thought. "I believe we can always do better."

"Your people seem as distressed as they are divided by this belief in the end. But you must believe Second-One saves us from evils that might try to come and harm us from beyond, the enemies outside our sky. If not aliens, what do the Books of the First Children mean when they say 'the enemies of outer spaces, darkness waiting beyond this Rock'? And to think, only three gods to help you against the rest of the expanding universe and its destruction."

"Just one God, and yes, that is Second-One's task. As you said, these are all beliefs, good Master. Every religion makes claims about the end in order to strike fear into followers' hearts. We Canyai believe First-One created us, Second-One protects us, and Third-One guides us within. One whole, three faces, like a moz'daur card." Fehatsi placed a hand on her heart. "Is that not sufficient?"

"Do you think creatures like me recognize a word like 'sufficient'?" His inflection didn't translate well on Blessed tongue, his joke awkward.

Fehatsi laughed, for politeness, but she didn't feel well with it. " I might ask you about your secret another time, Master. Consider me intrigued." She was not. The man was at best an odd kind of person, and at worst— well, a human girl of only eighteen turns could not imagine the worst of a Ku'dur of four hundred. Fehatsi would not imagine the worst of him now, but when her thoughts were her own… "Excuse me, Master Laki. I was on my way to speak with my father. Enjoy the celebration."

"Yes, of course, lyaren of Teviona. Forgive me for taking so much of your time. I do hope you seek me out, child. Secrets such as these don't keep long, and I would hate for Tyanien Aadarae to be the last to know."

Fehatsi bowed and walked away. That terrible rumbling in her stomach, which she now thought of as a warning sense better than Teia's, made her sick.

Yeroen loved rum. His reasons for quitting the drink might be at the bottom of his next cup.

Rum warmed him, reminded him of his father often and his mother on special occasions. His favorite taste came from Riam, and he had rolled over laughing when he met Riambo Fehatsi and she told him she didn't take strong drink despite her family owning most of the lands that grew the sugar cane. Rum had been Yeroen's favorite since he started drinking — too young, but he was born Blessed. It blurred the water beyond him. It made him laugh louder, and it numbed that extra nerve he gained across the Sweet Sea; dulled that new, anxious pace his lifewater picked up in Sharann. He felt that even now, with so much joy and celebration around him. Crowds would always be unsettling in his best sense. Crowds which he'd fed on, drained him now.

He tilted the flask and drank. He really loved rum.

The little, round flask had been his father's, and the metal was heated, curved, and set by a friend of his father's, some son of Tandilyen that Yeroen could not remember. His father once told him, while slightly drunk during some village celebration, that if their family had words, he would have them engraved onto the flask. When his father gave it to him before leaving, Yeroen thought that one day he would gain fame and fortune, claim some words as his own and put them there. The flask was still bare, no design or inscription marked, and Yeroen preferred it that way. He didn't need words to live by; he lived well enough without.

As he took a deep drink, he felt a terrible shudder, a halting pain, every heart of water in him held still. He was not stronger than whoever held him. He could not move. The rum would not go down his throat, stinging where it stuck. It was over just as it came, and Yeroen coughed and shook out the vulnerable feeling, taking possession of his own lifewater.

"Teia," Yeroen said, turning around. "You are an evil from the third plane."

She laughed. "Sent specifically to torment you, Detunae."

"I will take you to the Select Council next time you stall my lifewater." Though his threat was emptier than his flask, it was illegal to manipulate a living creature's lifewater, but Teia could get away with such things and knew it. In public though, in such crowds, she was especially careless today.

"No one believes the rumor that I've done that. And with your record? Go ahead, son of Ashakai, I am confident that I will be pardoned. It would be your truths against mine. I stalled the rum."

"I thought you must follow the procession," Yeroen said and groaned as he looked behind her. "And you brought the Biler men with you. Leuanien, why do this to me? I am trying to be good and kind, servant's heart and all that shit."

The Bilers looked different. Now both men wore loose, plain brown and green cloth spun from wool and plant fibers from the Blessed Lands, but they still did not fit in with the rest of the crowd. Pale cheeks burnt red, their necks constantly rolling on their shoulders, and their slack jaws were what set them most apart. Even the Achkans, with their dyed skin and puffy dress, didn't look so out of place.

Teia made a face. "Watch your thoughts. I have been charged with them by Tyanien Zyonhir for the day. Why he chose me, not even the better ears can guess, but I serve all my Tyanien. And I follow Rae not the procession, but I thought to intercept her here. She is coming to see the dancing, I am sure of it."

The crowd started clapping and a group of dancers was exited the stage place.

"They have already started with the dance of rising flames," said Yeroen. "You missed a good fire show."

"What are fire shows today? This," Teia said, nodding with pouted lips towards the newest dancers who were taking their place, all dressed in thin blue pa bu strands, all marked as wielders of water. "I have been looking forward to this all moons' wane and return. Now I get to see it twice!"

Yeroen was curious about Teia's childish anticipation as all the dancers lifted their arms, and from the aqueduct above them, snakes of water exploded and reached to the calling wielders, and each swirled about ten Standard pounds of water over their heads, passing and juggling between themselves. As the water passed, colorful dyes were added discretely as they traded hands so that the swirling worked rainbows above them.

The two dancers on either end were children of Ashakai as Yeroen. Their skin was marked like his. The remaining nine were children of Syornan—the thick blue marks around their whole middles were the darkest color of blue, almost black.

"They spin pretty torrents with their arms and shoot colored water good as fountains, why are you so excited?" he asked Teia.

"And more than that."

"What is the *thwah'kahum*?" An Achkan word that meant what a performer presented that was unique to them, what made them so special amongst a sea of people with the same hopes and aspirations.

"Just watch and feel, son of Ashakai. Watch, feel, be silent."

All eleven dancers spun the water in tight circles above them, he didn't need to watch to know it. He could feel it like a constant symphony in his left side, in his skin and brain and that place within his blood. Yeroen joked with Teia about the juggling, but gave up, realizing she would not speak to him for the rest of the dance. He wiggled his toes and played his fingers against his flask and allowed his sense to tune into the performance.

The song picked up with the deep banging of drums, and Yeroen recognized it as the Song of the Lost Tevi Bird, very old and traditional, depressing. With every deep smacking sound of the hundred drums, the chasing water would stop motionless before continuing on its path, and Yeroen felt it resound in his gut. His breath changed pace.

And he understood what must've entranced Teia: the story the dancers told with their movements. Water bent into a large ship, into the sea splashing against it. One dancers stood on the ship, pointing west. A captain that searched for the Tyano's first wife. The Lost Onatae, Teviona Fehana.

The captain vanished with her ship, turned to mist, and gone.

Gone like Teia's mother, and Yeroen's father.

The water swept into the crowd. Wet wind above him made Yeroen suck in an involuntary breath, and the music stopped. The water fell, and though everyone was soaked, they received the loudest applause of the day thus far.

The dance left Yeroen feeling very alone despite such a crowd, with a flurry of emotions that would not settle. It was their thwa-kahum, and it was beautiful and sad.

In his heart he was alone, in his sense he felt everyone. He reminded himself, *I am not alone.* The crowd would not settle. He felt cold without and warm within; he thought he could see the same thing in many of the other blue-marked people; he felt more eyes wetting beside his own. Of one thing Yeroen was certain: these dancers had lost someone to the seas of the westernmost, as had Yeroen, and Teia, and so many others.

Too many had gone to search for the lost Onatae, Teviona Fehana, born of the great family Riambo, the mother of the first four Tyanien. Onatae Fehana had been sailing to the Confederation, and the crewless ship washed ashore in a Takircha village shore a moons' pass after she was expected to arrive in Iri. She disappeared in the turn 8882, six turns before Yeroen was born, and since then more than five thousand ships had disappeared in their attempts to find her. Teia's mother, the great Captain Léuanien Anira had taken three hundred ships with her to the westernmost seas, and she was one of many great captains to leave. By the time his own father had boarded a ship to find the lost Onatae, Yeroen knew he would never come back. No one did.

"What kind of dancer thinks it is a good idea to make people cry on a celebration day?" Yeroen asked as the woman bowed and the dancers rejoined her in the center. The crowds applauded and cheered.

"Oh, shut up, you know it was beautiful." Teia clapped loudest of them all, whistling and howling. "She cannot see, did I mention that? The woman who acted as captain. She was born without sight, and she dances with her best sense. She is so beautiful, her talent. I wish I could wield like that."

Yeroen nodded. "Do you think they'll perform that dance in front of Onatae Dianis and the Tyanien?"

"We will know later, won't we? I wanted to be a dancer when I was small, before my mother went," Teia said, wiping the last tear from her eyes. Yeroen felt the droplet even as it became the moisture of her skin. He shook his head and grinned down at her.

"You are flexible enough for it."

She shoved him, smiling with her full, soft lips. "I am. But Three-One knows where we are most needed, I suppose."

"Yes," Yeroen said, drinking. "I suppose. You said Rae was allowed to leave the procession?"

"I don't know if she was allowed, I said she did leave, and I assumed she might come here. And where is your brother?"

"The ugly one?"

"You have the one brother."

Yeroen shrugged. "I like to make the distinction, especially since his face has been a plague to me since we left Achka. He weeps in the mountains. I doubt you will see more of him until that day of Selection."

"Is he weeping over old aches or has he found a new pain?"

"Knowing Santir, the safest bet is both."

It was Teia's turn to shrug uncaringly. "I'm glad for his absence. More people should find something to weep for in the mountains, and then maybe we could walk a step without bumping shoulders. I have never seen Talosa like this."

There is time for weeping, time for celebration. Yeroen decided to lean into a polite inclination and asked the Biler nobles in their own tongue, "Biler lords, you are feeling in good way, yes?"

The shorter one answered, "In the best way. This is unlike anything I have seen. How many of your people are gifted with their abilities for natural energies?"

"More than half, as of last census," said Teia. "Over six million Canyai wielders, maybe two and half, three million wielders of other lands since the diaspora."

"Does such a number frighten you?" Yeroen asked, no longer wanting to try at politeness. Their shocked looks were too funny.

After laughing at them, Yeroen did try his best to be kind to the foreign men, because Rae had commanded it of him, but also because anything other than kindness felt wrong after being struck by Rae's truelight. He used to be able to be rude, or uncaring, and not always was that voice of righteousness there to bother him into repentance. Now, however, the voice was there before he could wrong, before he could choose to be rude, and the voice was always Rae's. *Do better,* it would tell him, and he didn't need to ask what better was.

Yeroen still did not care for the Bilers, but both seemed stunned to utter silence as they looked around the flower circle, so at least there was a little bliss.

Another dance began of winds and flames, but Yeroen did not feel it deep in any sense like he had with the water-dancers' performance. He wondered how the wielders of winds and flames felt at this dance, which to him was just a bunch of swirling red and orange, a man riding a great fire beast above the ground as the drum matched the sparks of blue that erupted from its snout, and the crowd echoing his song. It was traditional, and a bit boring, nothing like the silencing storytelling he witnessed.

Yeroen felt a cold, then hot thrill in his blood, a feeling in his gut that told him Teia felt it too, and a tension down his neck and spine that indicated it was moving in his direction. Near lifewater so quick and sporadic, it did not feel quite human, but Yeroen was familiar with it. He knew it well.

"My friends!" came the clear and effulgent voice of his Araeboril. "I found you." And she was hugging her lyaren before he could turn to see her. She was veiled, most of her hair tucked beneath a pretty patterned yellow wrap, but if anyone looked too long they might recognize her by her high cheekbones, her pointed chin, and the distinct tevi green color of her eyes, the trait the old family was named for long ago. The tevi bird that Klo carved from pagalug seed was hung around her neck, her only jewelry for this day. Since Klo died she had not taken it off, shunning expensive gems and gold chains for her simple cord and bird.

Teia asked, "Did you see that dance I was telling you about?"

"No, just the last splash," said Rae. "Ambos took the long way around the city. We went all the way back to Ashakai's Mouth before he smalled. And then I had to run all the way here to keep up with him. How is my hair and appearance?"

"Beautiful," Yeroen and Teia had to say. Teia leaned in to tuck curly getaway strands into Rae's veil.

"Thank you. Where are the Bilers?"

"They—I don't know. They were here, I promise you. Tufan," Teia said, standing on her toes to look around. "There! I see them by the fried pana cart."

"And where is Ambos?" Yeroen asked, looking around for the laijirei.

Rae shook her head. "I don't know. Bakéz told me to not attract attention, so I asked Ambos to go back to the palace. But he didn't go that way, and he didn't seem happy with me for it. I think he wanted to see the dancing, so you might find him somewhere. And what is that?" she asked, pointing to Yeroen's flask, wiggling her eyebrows at him.

It was freeing to love her when she was like this, playful and light. Loving her felt like being unchained from dead weight.

"Rum." He gave it to her. She smiled and drank.

"Thank you, thank you, thank you," she said. "You should not have left the Hwaelins alone, Teia. Imagine if they had caught on fire, how distressed that would make them. I doubt our guests would want the Line erased if they caught on fire. Come on, I want to dance." Rae headed that way, shuffling through the people.

There were not many Eerim in the flower circle, but Yeroen could tell who the few were by their turning heads. They did not stare long. Eerim were too proud for that, as proud as Bilers but with much more refinement.

Both Bilers were watching an animated competition of shiardau, a game for wielders of winds that entailed balancing on a turbulent cloud over which your opponent held dominion. They could do whatever they wanted to the other man's wind, and the first whose feet touched the ground was the loser.

Experienced wielders usually added the element of flame, to liven the game and make the audience more excited. A flames wielder on either side heated the spinning winds beneath the feet of two men with shaved heads. Yeroen wondered what kind of games lords played in the Biler lands.

A group of men across the flower circle lined up for the turnabout to a drum band's wordless song, and Rae started hopping excitedly when she saw it.

"Dance with me, Mittrik," she said to the shorter Biler, and both Teia and the Fair looking man raised their awkward faces. Yeroen scowled as the one called Mittrik nodded and held a polite hand to Rae, which she grabbed and yanked toward the center of the crowd, spinning him round, round with the deep drums' sound. "You all, come join!" she shouted back to their group.

The blonde noble stood apart and only watched as his

brother and the Tyanien danced with a group of Canyai. Yeroen found more to drink, and Teia floated between them all.

"Your staring is pitiful," said Teia. "It is very reminiscent of when she first came into society at fifteen and every rich man on the Rock came to wait on her, and all you simple men could do was glare and make her feel worse."

Yeroen looked into his flask. "I don't like how the little Biler looks at her."

"You mean with lust? Or do you think he's already in love with her?"

"No."

"No?" Teia asked. "He is."

"He is?" asked Yeroen, not surprised but resentful.

"They shared some private conversations. She cannot help but love him, and he will perceive it, and think he knows what it means. They say Biler men fall in love easily. It would take little, if any, persuasion."

"Bilers scare easily, too. She must love the Fair-faced Biler for her nature, and he fears her as he should. The little one is just the same but with more drink in him and bigger balls."

"You lie whenever you can, like everyone," Teia laughed at him; it was her drunk laugh, which ended in a little snort. "Fear and excitement are near emotions, though, and the little Biler is excited. Undeniable to anyone who senses lifewater. Focus on him. No, better than that. Feel how fast his heart beats when she gets near, where his lifewater centers, low. What were you saying of his balls? Oh, I have yet to tell you!" Teia shouted. "What excitement! You will hate this. They disappeared together, and she took him to the cave of Xonieren's stone. Did she tell you of that? They walked through the mountains and returned on Ambos' back. The strike of Teviona combined with the Onatae's mountain hips against the self-restraint of one Biler… Oh, *Detunae*, the poor man can't help himself. Poor, blameless, Biler!"

"You speak too loudly and too much. You don't know who listens."

"Yes, I do. Everyone listens. Put yourself in a better mood, Detunae, or I will have no use for you. Don't bore me. Just tell her what you need to say, whatever it is, and stop being passive aggressive. Santir owns that trait, and it suits him better. Rae sees you struggling. She will never ask, you can trust me."

"Aya, how about you don't preach to me today, Teia?" Yeroen handed her his flask. She held his stare a moment, then took it and tilted her head back, wincing.

"Very well," she said. "I understand you."

She did. They were the same. She took another heavy-handed drink.

She handed the flask back to him (he felt it empty) and said, "You should put some juice in that, like yuaba or something. And then your breath wouldn't smell so bad."

Yeroen continued to stare at Rae dancing. She was not graceful. She moved to the rhythm of the truelight, not of music, Yeroen was sure. Her name said as much. The little Biler clearly did not mind her funny movements, while the Fair looking Biler did well to keep a straight face and rock to the drums. The fast beating of his lifewater through his heart proved his anxiety.

At the end of the song, Yeroen looked back to Teia, having almost forgotten her quiet presence there. She hadn't been looking at him either.

"You speak the truth," he said. "We both know that silence is not for me. I will tell her what I need to say before she starts asking questions."

Teia nodded. "I said she wouldn't ask questions, but I'm glad you are not a coward."

"I'm starting to think you were right. I felt it all along."

"Yes, but don't forget— it is two different things, when the truelight touches you, and when her hands do. Confusing them will only hurt you. I am going to find some food, but you will seek me out later, Detunae," she said as her form slid away from him and into the crowd.

"Will you dance for me tonight?" he called.

She puckered her lips and threw a kiss. “And you can show me your thwa’kahum.”

Yeroen laughed and enjoyed the sight of her leaving, then turned his attention back to Rae. He went to take a drink, but remembered his flask was dry. He might get more rum and then talk to Rae.

Do better.

He should just do it. *Now, Yeroen. Soon, the whole Rock will know, except for her.* He pushed calmness into his quaking nerves and approached her and the Biler lords. He had to do this, even if it meant losing her. *Just say, I’m sorry. I gave up my blood, and someone holds my future.*

“Rae, may I speak with you alone?”

She stopped dancing, looked about her. “Of course, but I do not know where you think we can be alone. If you want it to be between us, we should wait for another time.” Her breath was also hot and smelled sweet like rum.

“No, too many people know already. This day is perfect. Follow me.” He didn’t wait for her to excuse herself from the red faced noblemen before he grabbed her hand and pulled her aside, behind the fried pana cart where no one stood. The sizzle of oil felt like static in his sixth sense. *We are not alone, really, but damn anyone listening. Damn everyone who already knows. I mean it, damn you. I need this. She should know.*

“Where did Teia go?” Rae asked him.

“I am not exactly sure. She went searching for something to eat.”

“Aya, I want to eat. I ate little first foods because I had to spend the whole morning talking to strangers, and you know how nervous I get around people I don’t know. I always say the wrong thing, or worse, *think* the wrong thing today. Eerim lined the walls. What did you want to talk about?”

Yeroen tightened his throat, bit his tongue and inhaled. *Oh, Three-One, help me.* “My future, and what I have needed to say for some time.”

Her eyes barely narrowed, but her muscles turned to stone.

He could tell she would not ask him any more questions now. Her wall of defense was positioned and reinforced by her weariness. It was always unsettling to see Rae afraid; it reminded him she was only human.

"My brother is a good man. Klo was a great man," Yeroen said, not knowing how else to begin. "That is why they never —well, I never thought of myself as such, and that is why I must make a confession. Because you have some right to know, I believe. And it makes me selfish, not a good man, or just another distraction for you, but I need to say this."

He was rambling, but Rae didn't say a word, only kept looking at him, motionless.

"I love you. Before your truelight hit me in the Half Sea, I..." Yeroen realized he could not say everything. He was not so brave, not so selfish. What if she condemned his sins right here and left him? *What happens when the palace finds out?* He'd traded his blood for a little bit of time, and by law should lose all right to know her. Men with compromised futures couldn't be friend with the Araeboril.

Yeroen couldn't lose her.

He straightened his back and breathed again. "I was changed after, and you know how. You do. Now I wish to follow you anywhere you may go, in seriousness. That's all I want to do with my life if you let me. I would lay my life down to protect you, and not because you would do that for anybody. I wouldn't do it for anybody, you know that, too, but on your command I would. I only ask that when you decide to go across Line with these Bilers, as you know you will—

"I will not—"

"Ay, let me finish." Yeroen held a finger up to her face. "When you go east and cross the Line, I want to come with you that I may serve and fight by your side. Araeboril, please do not leave me here wondering when I can just as easily be there fighting for you. I will kneel, if you wish, and make the oath how it should be done." He moved to lower himself on his knees before her.

She stopped him with strong hands. “None of that. You have knelt before. Remember?”

He laughed, remembering. “Yes. You were a child, and I was… different then.” Joking, always. He hadn't been serious .

Or maybe he had been.

“There is always a place for you by my side, Yeroen. I will never let you be without a livelihood, if that is your concern. But I am not planning to go to the Biler lands.”

“Perhaps not yet, but I know you. I have known you for many turns, so I know that you won’t be idle and wait for this Selection to swallow you and make you something you are not. You are no judge.”

Rae moved away from him, looking toward the setting of the Great Fire. She blinked so fast, Yeroen thought she might be trying to hold back tears, but he could not feel them.

“I don’t judge you, but that doesn’t mean I am incapable of the position. I am going to be Selected,” she said, but he could tell she was speaking to herself at the end, so he didn’t argue.

He said, “No matter what you decide, I follow you. I am no longer a dueler or a good enough gambler to live by those means. If you do not go east, Select Children need personal guards. Tyanien always need guards. Do we have an agreement, Tyanien Aadarae? Or must I kneel?”

She sighed and smiled at him, a sad, beautiful smile. “Never for me. We have an agreement, Lieutenant Detunae. Do not worry.”

Yeroen didn’t, even as he met the crude, knowing eyes of Eerim.

Always shouting, always a new kind of strangeness jarred Jonn and clipped his breath short. Drums pounded different songs, and the skirling of laughter mixed with the thin whinging of flutes to sound like animals fighting. On one alley street, animals did fight between a crowd of men exchanging money. Crowds of monsters, of people that looked like beasts, embraced.

Was there anything Jonn had not seen? He had almost been scorched by a cannon of fire, one these forsaken mages could toss at one another in their unburning hands. Dancers juggled swords, women skipped in the open with bare breasts, other women were dressed in stiff dresses that moved the crowd apart before them, and children were literally flying. Groles, elves, little red beasts with tusks and long fur huddled together, and Jonn made effort not to stare, not to think for the listeners. He couldn't make sense of his thoughts and thought elves would have a difficult time of it, too.

He was often knocked over by men larger than he (a sight still new to him), and he'd regain his balance, look up and see a group of young girls laughing at him.

This happened more than once, the first group of girls with large braided hair pieces and colorful gowns fanned themselves and hid their faces as they jeered together, and the second group of girls were all shaved bald, legs bare under short skirts. They stayed near him to giggle and point. Some aspects of human nature were transcultural, like the shared love of young girls of mocking men. Jonn tried not to let it bother him.

He did not know the dances or the music, did not know the faces, did not know a Doomed thing. Though the same could be said of his brother, that didn't stop Mittrik from joining in on the wildness and song. By nighttime, Mittrik was very drunk and when he spoke with his hands, he spilled all his drink on the witch princess, Rae.

"Pardon!" he exclaimed. The front of her green dress soaked, transparent. "Oh, forgive me, Rae."

She only laughed, said, "Always, Mittrik Hwaelin, but today forgiving is unnecessary. Forgiving is second greatest command for Blessed People, but only drunks anger over spilt rum."

"Or poor men," said the mage, pouring more liquid fire into Mittrik's wooden cup.

Warm rain poured soon after that, and when Jonn tasted it on his lips, he realized it was very sweet. It could have been a fruit's nectar falling from the clouds, and at this point Jonn would believe it if someone said so.

"Sweet rain from the northwest, it comes rarely," said the witch princess, suddenly beside him, looking to the clouds. "The winds wielders in Byelirai sent it along. It does not often reach the capital, but they get sweet rains every dry season. A blessing for this day. A good omen."

Jonn nodded, jumping back as a bald man beside him let out a hollering, vibrating shout like a beast before flying into the sky.

"Hewandam gaai to'o!" hollered every wild person as they jumped up and down, some touching clouds, others unable.

"Hewandam gaai to'o!" Mittrik called, too, accent appalling.

The festivities went until late night and Jonnere was alarmed by the number of people that gathered by the river. There were so many people, he felt quite alone. His brother was lost somewhere in the crowd, or perhaps swimming in the river like so many. Jonn watched humans dance with elves and sing with groles, watched mages practice their magic over earth, fire, water, and air. He was sure nothing else could shock him. Then, something sharp pierced the palm of his left hand.

When he felt the pain of it, he whirled around to see an ugly horned grole holding a blade in one looming hand, a thorned flower in the other. Jonn's left hand stung, his blood wet on her knife.

"You stabbed me," Jonn said stupidly, wishing he was not unarmed. He would give his whole left hand for his sword, looking at how the grole eyed him with disdain and simultaneously eyed his blood with hunger.

"A mistake, an accident, please forgive my carelessness, good man. I should not walk through crowds with my stem cutting blade," said the grole, eying bloody knife with much intrigue.

"You should not," Jonn said, holding his hand away from the

grole. "You can do real magic with blood, I know."

"I can, especially with ruler's blood, so much you control, and it would be a waste not to use it."

Panic spread through his whole body. "You would use it for what?"

"As you say, magic. I will tell you your fortune with it, young man, if you pay me a compliment."

"A compliment?"

"Small price. Would you not agree? I can tell you how your future will be, and the only thing I ask in return is a compliment from a comely Fair man, to stroke my vanity."

Trepidation for that, but Jonn was most tempted to know his fate. "You—I—I mean, you are… quite handsome."

The grole hissed like a cat at him, and one thousand eyes turned to cruel slits. Her forked, blue tongue licked her lips slowly before she spoke again. Her voice was unpleasant to Jonn, like the braying of an animal forming words. "A true compliment, nothing false. Tell me a false compliment and I will repay you with a false fortune, Biler. Sometimes false fortunes come true, and you would not want that. How terrible that could be."

"You desire a true compliment of your appearance?"

"Is it difficult for you to see beauty past another kind's make? Imagine how difficult, to see truth past time. I might not even try, I might jumble it up. You cannot compliment my mind, you do not understand it. You cannot compliment my kindness, I just stabbed you. So, go on. Compliment what you can see of me."

He looked at her pale gray skin, gray like the skies back home, foul looking like the texture of oatmeal. Each twitch of an ungodly eye caught his attention. Each eyelid, and there were so, so many, wrinkled and partnered with crows' feet, and the eyelashes sparse.

Dizziness spilled into Jonn's skull like lazy honey drizzled into water, and one part of him became tired and sluggish: his bones, his skin, his breath; another part of him felt too much alive. He was aroused and his heart beat too quickly. He could feel it painfully in his breeches and his chest but could not manage movement. *Run, run.* He stood there and gazed.

Eventually he heard himself say, "Your eyes are a very pretty color, madam. They are quite captivating." Then it felt as though someone splashed ice water on him, and the sluggish arousal vanished with his dignity.

"And all the same, too," the grole said. "Thank you for a true compliment."

He remembered, *Groles can take your mind if you look too long in their eyes. Daemons want your soul and will trick it away from you.* Jonn felt ill, violated.

"You took my blood," he said, "so your magic is true. Isn't it?"

"You get one question from beyond, lordly man, and I will give you the absolute truthful answer that I am shown. Think hard on it."

One question. He dared not give over the question he desired to ask. A question that had been haunting him for a year now. The grole smiled, and Jonn realized that he already thought his question, so he might as well say it aloud. He hated this place of mind hearers and wondered why anyone would willingly live in such a self-exposing world. He leaned in close to the fortune teller.

"Will I ever be king?" Jonn asked in a whisper and looked not into her many eyes, but at her blue lips, though he knew nothing could conceal his heart. He had just laid it bare.

The grole wiped the red flat of the blade on her large palm in a quick motion, then used that hand to smear some blood against the eyes on her chest and neck and chin, spreading it thinly. She licked the blood that remained on the knife. Every eyelid fluttered rapidly, then opened dazing and wild. The grole laughed, and it was a beastly sound.

"Good man," she whispered and got closer. "You wear a crown like your ancestors, and you sit on a throne of liquid silver, copper and blood. Gold beside you, but gold hidden. The throne is not yours, nor will it ever be, still there you sit. Your people will call you Most High for a night, then the valleys will get lower than you can see. You will get all you want in the beginning, and hate it. In the end when we all melt into our destruction, you will be first of men to know."

Anger, swift, overcame other feeling. "You speak of destruction. What does the rest mean, 'of silver, copper? Blood and gold?' Did you promise me a fortune or a riddle, witch?"

"You were promised one answer to one question. What could you know of witches, Biler man?"

"That they are evil," Jonn said, regretting having asked her anything.

"I've heard the same about Biler men, but I am not afraid. And I am not evil, instead I am generous. For your brother, I will give you a telling free."

A riddle free. "You do not have his blood."

Her laughter, incessant like the wet rattling of a wheel, wobbled. Loose. "Sometimes you only need look into a man's eyes, and there find ruin. In your brother I see insecurity and arrogance. Two opposing forces cannot live long together. He wants more than he will get."

She could barely finish speaking between her cruel fits of laughter. She was still laughing as Jonn turned to find his brother in the multitude.

He could see Mittrik now, stuck out among the Forsaken. Mittrik had his arms around the shoulders of two dark westerners, dancing with them, being lifted by them, turning to drink with others. Smiling like he did on his birthday when he won the joust. It was unsurprising that the people embraced him— most people did at first. The witch princess stayed near Mittrik, dancing with her veil and skipping with the drums. When she was not looking for Mittrik, Mittrik looked for her, and whenever their eyes met, they smiled.

He is enamored with that woman, Jonn saw, fretted, *with this whole Forsaken world. He feels like a demigod on a quest. Why would he want to go home?*

Two opposing forces. My brother's will.

Mine.

Jonn held on to the smallest hope that his brother would return to Kieln; that Mittrik would sacrifice this kind of magic to fight with him, for glory in victory, and for the legacy of every Hwaelin. These mattered most to Jonn, but to his brother? Much had always mattered more.

Smallest of all hopes.

"And what's your fortune for him?" Jonn asked, feeling that sluggishness again, but when he looked back the grole was gone.

In Jonn's open palm was her dagger, clean of his blood. He held the blade up, eyeing his distorted reflection in the silver. Eyes too pale, face too long, expression too dour for the joy around him.

And how the joy blurred around the sharp edges.

He slid back into the crowd, not knowing where he needed to go, but pulled towards the center. Like he would trip on his own feet if they did not carry on.

And then his heart sped when he saw another grole, dressed in white finery, with the eyes of his forehead covered in gold cloth. Jonn had no thought, no desire or awareness as he drew near the daemon, so close that every eye on the grole's right side widened, in what Jonn would later call recognition.

But the grole said not a word, not even when he plunged the dagger into into the beast's chest did it scream.

But someone else screamed, then many others, and Jonn felt that wash of cold across his body and spirit, the release of compulsion. The flood of repulsion and ignominy. He faltered, wiping blue blood off his hands and onto his strange clothes. *Why, I just—*

Killed a grole in cold blood, he did. In front of thousands. The daemon lay unmoving at his feet.

The witch princess held Jonn's face in her hands. "I asked you a question?!" *Has she?* "Why did you kill Sus'Laki?" Beseeched, he had no answers. "Who made you kill the

Pretender's father?"

Who? Awareness jerked into Jonn's dizzy mind, fully conscious as the city guards descended and grabbed him.

Part 3
Baeltaf II

From the Gospel of Good Thyne Angus II, who spoke for the gods in the years 668 to 699 AC

'Pray to Hetten for light, to the Sisters for quiet.

Pray to Hetten for good life, joy, favored fortune. He gives to those worthy who take for themselves and do what is right.

Pray to the Sisters that they may not set free their whims and works. They take your gain out of their jealousy and love of provocation.

Pray to Hetten for your sons in battle, for victory and justice. He grants what you require.

Pray to the Sisters that they may close their eyes to you and love the sound of your name.

9. A LESS GRAND AFFAIR

Maisie was for her fifth year serving Dwellings Hwaelin, but she had served the High Lady of Kieln for over seven. It was out of loyalty, and out of habit after all the years, that Maisie found herself at the rocky beach while the sun failed to stretch through a gray sheeted sky. She huddled her seal skin cloak around her, hugging herself, fisting stiff hands and watching her breath color white…fade.

She waited for forsaken daemons. If a priest or lord, or anyone found out what took place on this beach, Maisie would hang. She wondered who protected her now with Tisinda Hwaelin dead.

Hetten, help.

White… to nothing.

She waited.

Maisie had never seen a beach or a sea before coming to Kieln. She'd seen streams and the wide Distress River that rushed very fast from south to north of Eiselver, the banks of Burry Lake, but that was all. Her father, and grandfathers before him, had been brewers in Eiselver, in a quaint town called Rour, which was eight miles from the dwellings of Lord Amory Redneck, an underlord with the attitude of a man with Higher status.

Before Rour was a town, it was pure magic trees, and like most children raised by the two middle forests, Maisie heard the strangest tales of the magic that still dwelled there. The land of Rour had once been part of the great magical forest of Old, the forest that was whole and stood long before Baeltaf formed. The dwellings of Lord Redneck, that awful castle Bluddnell with its gargoyles and sharp pinnacles, was like many Eiselvan castles— made of what could be salvaged from the cursed forest. The doors of the Sisters' temple in Rour, too, boasted the dark spectacle of black and brown striped wood, carved so that the goddess Sara's face looked out of the right, and Neva's peered from the left. The likenesses of the Sisters were forced to always stare at one another in their contempt.

Maisie often wondered if the cursed wood is what brought the Sisters' chaos upon Rour, for it was one of the first villages to be affected by the whooping flu that spread through the north when she was a child, right at the end of the Fourth. It had killed two of her older brothers while they marched with King's men, and her youngest sister while she waited for their return. Maisie, too, had been struck with the illness, but was able to come back from the worst. Still, her lungs were weak for her age of twenty and nine.

Every man, woman, and child of Baeltaf knew that there was a profound, terrifying difference between the two forests in the middle of their land. Daemons, like fae, still roamed the Dreadwood. But they didn't touch the western half.

For reasons unknown, perhaps curses left unbroken, though every tree burned in the First War, one half grew back lovely though trees were thin and few, while the other was crowded by hulking trees with spiked roots and snarling branches. Nettles and thick bush of wild. The forest beneath

Rour was of the new and beautiful, with game and fresh streams abounding.

Maisie did not know why the two sides of the Old trees grew back differently, and why one half of their world was still cursed by the magic of heathens long dead. *Magic*, she reasoned and let be. She was alright with not knowing these things, because what she did know was more valuable to her. Each piece of knowledge hard earned.

Maisie fell in love with a man named Hoop in her seventeenth year while she still lived in Rour. He was a dyer's apprentice with hands and arms stained blue past his elbows, but his face was comely and smooth, and his disposition gentle. His kindness was welcome after her father, a different kind of man.

After Hoop promoted to journeyman, they married and came south together, seeking opportunity in the golden country, but they traveled before a harsh winter, and bandits met them early on the Coast Road. Their pig, small possessions and small purse of coin were stolen, but they left with their lives. They trekked down the way, without food or coin, but the sweeping chill took Hoop before they could even reach the Sidgen River.

And Maisie lost their child, a girl with cherry hair, in a blood bed beside a fire, in a brothel outside Sharp Point, without her Hoop or her family. The painted women knew much about birthing and had been kind to take her in and help, but surprisingly they knew little in the ways of comforting a sad woman. Perhaps it was just Maisie they didn't like. They took her stillborn girl from her shaking grasp and left her to cry alone for one full week, until her throat was stripped raw by her wailing. One woman held her, but then that same woman told Maisie she must go if she wouldn't whore. They kicked her out in a dead winter.

She tried to find work in the town just outside Sharpspear's Motte, in the inn called Hower's Tarnish, and she was just about to make the dreaded walk back to the brothel. She offered every person she saw her help, to clean, to cook, to take care of the children, to do anything for a place to sleep, perhaps for some food. Safety at night. The innkeep, the grim man Hower himself, told her to get gone and lost, he had enough help, enough mouths to feed.

Despairingly she sat a table and hung her head, no more tears left to cry after all. She was good as dead and could not travel back to Rour now. Many young girls died traveling alone, and many more girls suffered worse from the road. On the road or on a den-mother's bed, Maisie knew which one was better.

Someone came to sit beside her and asked, very quietly and simply, "Are you good at listening, at keeping to yourself with your eyes and ears open?"

"Yes," she whispered back to the hooded man, seeing his yellow teeth and clouded eyes, then she whispered, "Or maybe no. Why?"

And by the end of the night the innkeep had a change of heart and offered her a small bed beside his daughter. The hooded man with yellow teeth came back every third day for the next five Sisters' passes, and he taught Maisie how to read and write, and *he* paid *her* to do it. He said his name was Woolringer, but she hadn't believed him then. When she asked him why he did it, for whom he worked, he smacked her across the face and said: "I work for lady love. Don't ask questions you shouldn't suppose. Wrong questions kill in our world, dolly. That's lesson two."

And when he left that very night, that was that. She'd never seen Woolringer again, thankfully, or heard of him in all these years. She never asked what the first lesson had been, but of course it was probably literacy.

Nights after, though, Maisie received the first of many letters penned by High Lady Hwaelin herself, stamped with the desert palm of Rooj.

For five years Maisie listened diligently in that inn and in others; she traveled much in those days. She heard knights that went looking to spew drunk tales, about the lords that buggered them and the better whores, the bastards and beat-down. She was sure she knew every scandal and rumor in gold country and farther, and then she was called to work in the highcastle of Kieln. She had never even dared hope for such a thing.

Maisie was important under High Lady Hwaelin; not just a brewer's daughter or a dyer's wife, or a peasant, or a woman. She was also top ear, one of the highest, and that meant that Maisie knew things that few in the realm did. She knew more than some lords, especially underlords like Doomed Amory Redneck. She might know more than King Ornund.

Maisie certainly knew more about the Forsaken West than most any Mainlander. The fact she was alone at the beach on this day proved it.

Every lowlord of Kieln had traveled to Alluvel for the mourning day of High Lady Tisinda, and some brought their sons, but no ladies came. Maisie at first found it odd that none of them brought their ladies, but then she realized why the highborn wives stayed in their castles. The lowlords would leave with High Lord Tagnar to Brimtone, and then beyond Daggerlone to meet with Northmen at the highcastle in Midhold. High Lady Tisinda had known of this gathering at the Midrock and told Maisie little of it. War plans.

War plans, she had written her sister, Maisie thought of the letter she found beneath the High Lady's mattress. The letter Maisie had lost, meant for Talia Rooj. She'd stuffed it in a crack in the wall, and it didn't just walk away… *I've never lost a message before.*

Another reason for the absence of the Kielnish ladies'— the High Lady did not keep any friends, so none felt tempted. High Lady Hwaelin only had her Fair sister for friendship.

Poor, shy Lady Leonara did not have sisters. And few friends among her father's court, but fewer among the lowlords' daughters. It was a pity for her that none of them arrived, but she received many letters. Maisie had read the letters first and concealed them as she was taught, and while she would like to say it had been her habit of reading everything for Tisinda Hwaelin, it was really because she was downright snoopy. This job had done that to her.

Every fourth week for the past four years, she would come to the beach between Sharp Point and Kielntown and the forsaken daemons would meet her. From the sea, their forsaken ship would rise, made of glossy metal, and an evil looking creature would bring her a message from the West. Her lady had called it the Deep. This was only one of the informants that brought whispers directly to Maisie. There were plenty others.

The water sloshed beside her and she started, but it was only a fish. The days were getting colder, and her cloak, though finer than anything she ever had before her work, did not protect her from soul snatching. She wouldn't have to wait much longer. These monsters were at very least punctual.

She heard the faint humming beneath the water and saw the ripples touch and circle along the sea as though it rained. The ship rose from the shallows and a scaled beast crawled out at once, standing on its hind legs when it hit the beach. He had the snout of a fabled dragon, the scaly skin of a sculpin, eyes like some dead thing. Sometimes these clawed, green creatures came to the sand, and other times she had to wade knee-deep into the frigid water to collect a letter for her Lady. Today, the beast would have to come to her, she decided. Maisie stayed perfectly still as the daemon came to her with waddling steps.

In his slimy hand there was a letter made of purple paper: a splotchy, thick kind of paper with which Maisie was now very familiar, so she wasn't surprised when her fingers touched the unctuous thing. Paper like seaweed.

"Bad news, fear," the beast said, sharp teeth and thin tongue affecting his words. Years ago she could not quite understand them, but now she could. "Tell her that we will have the little bastard found within two moons come and go. Lost him in Canyassor. We sends apologies."

She wouldn't tell the daemon that the High Lady was dead.

Tisinda Rooj had been Maisie's protection. Now, without her, Maisie was not important. She was just a loose end to someone else's plot. She shouldn't have come today.

She nodded, though his words were meaningless to her, and she struggled to whisper a small, "Very well." She would not look into the yellow, unblinking eyes of the beast.

My High Lady is dead, Maisie thought, counting back the days in her head. *She's been dead twenty days and still I rode here in the night like a stubborn eejit. Why come here at all, just to ride back through the cold with this? A forsaken letter for no one.* She tried not to look at the paper too closely, and then decided to stuff it away in the pocket of her apron.

She watched in silence as the boat dipped under the water again, out of sight and gone, bubbles of foam frothing and popping at the surface. Watching the daemons leave always felt like waking from a nightmare, and she had to bend over to catch her breath.

On her way back over the hills of northern Kieln, she thought of Hoop and her High Lady, both in some next life doing something other than thinking of her. She was forgotten by them. Hoop was likely born as some great man, an aidaire she hoped, for he was smart when she had him. Her High Lady was surely Doomed. Maisie could do little else but think of them, for she was a loyal woman in this life and could not easily move on. *It would be easier to move on if I had somewhere to go.*

Maisie left her horse with a man in Little Lake as always, for chambermaids didn't have beautiful mares to ride, and she walked the remaining hours to Kielntown. The curtain wall of Alluvel came into sight after dark and she sped up, sighing heavy puffs of white and letting the cold come over her. She was already resting in the candlelight she could see by the windows of Bell Tower. Soon, she would be by a warming fire and the cold would be forgot, and she would eat whatever was left in the kitchens, and she would dry her stockings and socks and stretch her aching toes.

The man on top the wall leaned against the merlon, and another shorter boy peered down at her. She heard the knight mumble something.

"Who are you?" a voice came out of the air. It belonged to the bigger squire, the young Torner Osmonde, and Sir Artur Kensgood was beside him.

"Maisie, chambermaid," she called back. *Bloody know who I am. I've been here longer than that wee freckled shite, and we both sleep in Bell Tower.* But the knights, men-at-arms and squires slept at the top levels, and Maisie was at the bottom.

They called for Alluvel's gates to be opened, first the knight and then his stupid squire, and the call was repeated down to whoever it was that actually opened it for her. She didn't care to look, she kept her head high and straight.

Maisie walked into the busy lower bailey and head for the kitchens. In the corridor just outside, she could hear men gossiping. She stopped, stooped, and listened.

"Thank gracious Lord Hwaelin for these extra pigs to feed us and the visitors," she heard the thunderous voice of the cooker, Potbelly Roose. "His High Order are good for killing men, not game. They went out again yesterday and came back with only less than ten pheasants. What can I do with pheasants for a hundred men?"

"High Lord's sons were good at hunting." A voice like a changing boy's, cracking and unreliable. "Eh, I remember the day they both shot a buck each, Lord Jonnere's went through the buck's eye, eh, and Mittrik's arrow through the neck. There was plenty of meat when they were here. All summer grand."

"Lordlings got more time to hunt than the dwelling's knights. Hunting is all our Mittrik Hwaelin does in summer."

"Do you think they could be dead? Right queer to go off in the night, eh, when the Rooj was here. I say, it's really not right."

"They'll turn up in some whore house in Hailspring, take my word for it," Potbelly said. "That Mittrik is always fondling some other man's woman, getting into trouble, and Lord

Jonnere follows as always to get him out of trouble. They'll turn up as always. Jonnere is getting it out of him before marrying the Gilgar girl."

"Why would they leave, without telling a soul? Eh, no, I don't think— not even High Lord knew of it!" cried the boy. "Rooj was right upset, too, until the telling turned for foul and people were fearing. They couldn't act offended after that."

"Yesterday you heard those Sharp Point fishers, Vinnie," the softer sound of the pantler, Homar. "War is coming fast. The banners of black foxes are rising, and they've started training the small folk for footers. Most like, the lowlords of Hailspring, Gold Harbour, and Blue Valley are doing the same. Soon it's us. Well, not *us* us, but Kielntown. All marching."

Maisie knew that every smith in Kieln was working on making weapons of Brimmen steel, the kind that took hundreds of years to rust and wouldn't break against anything but the same. Maisie knew, and she knew that it was still meant to be something of a secret. But once a secret got to the kitchens, it was not.

"So, Jonnere and Mittrik left for Sharp Point?" Vinnie asked.

"Dundy loaf, they rode south dinne they?" Roose said. "Sharp Point's north."

"So, what's south?" the page boy asked, but then answered his own question. "The Fair Isle."

"They're south alright— south of Doom, I tell you. Both dead as these pucker-fish," said Homar. "Like High Lady. Unlike Jonn Hwaelin to run, and if High Lord don't know where they are, they aren't to be found."

Vinnie said, "I bet High Lady would have known were she alive. Her ears would've sussed out the truth right by now, whether they're dead or not."

Dead or not? That was Maisie's question, too.

"Maisie?" came the loud and high voice of a child from behind.

"Oh!" Maisie turned, clutched her bosom, inhaling. It was little Lady Leonara. She looked just as scared. Maisie was surprised that she hadn't heard her walking close. *The silent little mouse,* she thought. *If she weren't a lady, she'd be a fine spy.*

"Oh, m'lady, beg your pardon. You gave me a real fright, but I didn't mean to screech out like that."

"I am sorry," the girl said. "I didn't mean to frighten you, but I've been looking for you all morn."

"For me, Lady Leonara? Why, what for?"

"You were my mother's chamber maid."

Maisie nodded. "Yes, m'lady, for near five years." She heard the kitchen quiet, heard the men scuffling to get back to work.

Quieter, Leonara asked, "What else did you do for her?"

"M-M'lady?" Maisie stammered. *Tell all I did for the High Lady? I couldn't! All she had me do? No, of course not all, for she has a child's ears: open and wanting. And a highborn lady's ears as well: critical and desperate. They always are. How much does she know already?* This was a trial, but Maisie passed all others prior.

"Did as any maid. Cleaned after, dressed the High Lady, did as she bid, ran her errands in Kielntown. I don't know what you're meaning."

The lady child grabbed Maisie by the arm and pulled her away from the kitchen. "Do not lie to me, Maisie. I have little patience for lies. What you did for my mother, you will now do for me, starting at once. All of it. Understand? My uncle instructed me to take you on, and you will serve me now as you did my mother."

"Of course. Well, yes, here you go, m'lady." Maisie fished out the purple letter in the pocket of her frock. She should have expected the High Lady's brother to have a plan. He had always been in close correspondence with High Lady Tisinda, and Maisie always assumed that most reports went directly to Rhion Rooj. She whispered, "It came from the docks today, from one of them underwater ships."

"You're one of my mother's ears," the little lady said as she took the letter, nodding and looking at the seal of green wax. *How little does she know?* Leonara made a face at the slimed texture of the paper and then looked up again. "Did you say underwater ship?"

"Aye, m'lady. I collected many whispers for your mother. Me and others, though she only trusted me with these ones coming from the Forsaken. She had me collect the messages from the west, since I don't scare easy, and I would deal with some of the petty voices in town, in the taverns."

"My mother had ears in the west? The *Forsaken West*?" Lady Leonara's eyes bulged palely in their sockets, but she had the good sense to whisper. Maisie wondered what good it did now, looking around to make sure they were really alone in the corridor. The High Lady had always said that if there was one spy in a castle, you could count on a hundred.

Maisie drew closer to the little lady. "She did. She let me risk Forsaking, and every day after the Sister's Greeting some report comes from the scaled men. And every three Sister's passes, a northern ship called *Lubell* comes and a little deck boy that listens for her gives me messages. The ship hails from Old Galligray, but she goes to the Forsaken West as well, and neither lord nor crown knows it. Just your mother, me and her crew, and now you, m'lady."

"And her other ears, you know of them all?"

"I know of many, most that are in Kieln, but I doubt I know all. I might not know as many as I think. High Lady Hwaelin kept much to herself, m'lady."

"I know she did. All the ears you do know, I want them listening for me now. Do you understand?"

Maisie nodded. "Yes, m'lady."

"Good, now I would like a bath. And some cherry tarts, if there are any."

"It'd be lucky with all these lords about to find tarts leftover. If I do find, I will sneak them for you."

Maisie found and was able to sneak one tart for the lady, and one for herself, nibbling on it hungrily as she filled pales with hot water. Maisie had Rose, the young girl who cleaned after the High Lord's daughter, light the candles and help her change the threshes by the door of Lady Leonara's chambers. Together they made the trips to the bath with the pales of steaming hot water. Maisie welcomed the comfortable scalding of her hands.

Rose left them after, and Maisie was left alone with High Lady's Tisinda's shy daughter.

She was so unlike her loud Islander mother, though she had the same pale hair and eyes, both almost white. The girl tucked a fallen strand behind her right ear. She had mousy ears that poked out just a bit, but still she was a pretty child.

"Thank you," she said to Maisie, staring at the bath and at the curls of steam that faded atop the water.

Maisie wanted to be helpful. "Shall I wash your hair, m'lady?"

"Oh, please do. That sounds lovely."

So, Maisie did, and she was happy to see the look of contentment that finally fit on the little lady's face. Leonara had cried many times a day since her mother died, more since her brothers had gone, and she often looked gaunt and red-eyed. Now, she had her eyes closed, her breath was steady.

"How long have you listened for my mother?" the little lady asked.

"Almost half my life, the nicer half."

"I did not even suspect you of being one of her ears before my uncle gave me reason. I knew you listened for her, like all her servants, like all maids listen. I knew not to speak around you unless I wanted it to get back to my mother, but I didn't realize in full what you were. I am most oblivious."

"High Lady valued people that could be underestimated, m'lady. She employed many of the kind."

"And of my brothers, has there been any whispers about where they might be?"

"Not ones worth listenin', by any means, m'lady" Maisie said. "Cookers' gossip, nothin' more. They talk as much as fishers' wives when they sort in town, or as painted broads like, not havin' much good to say. I wouldn't trust Roose with anything but pork or lamb."

"I know they talk, and I know the difference between gossip and truth." The little lady crossed her arms over her flat chest, causing water to pour over the sides of the tub. "At least I know it as well as any other person, but I know between gossip and real talk of merit."

"I've heard nothing of your lord brothers, m'lady. Gone into the night, south. They found one of your brother's horses near the village of Bitterfarthing. Just that."

"Bitterfarthing is all the way near Hailspring. They took my mare, you know. It's still lost. The cookers say they're dead, I heard them earlier," said Lady Leonara.

"Just cookers' talk, nothing more. Goss in the pan," Maisie soothed, pouring water over her head to rinse out the suds. She wrung the girl's thin hair over the bowl and then began drying it with a clean cloth.

The little lady cried into the tub but Maisie didn't say a word; she just kept working, that is what High Lady Tisinda had preferred.

When the tears stopped, Lady Leonara let Maisie dress her into her underclothes and night dress. Maisie was still very hungry and was counting down the seconds until she could leave back to the kitchens.

Leonara asked, "Will you comb out my hair?" She held out a golden comb with tiny sapphires and rubies. It was beautiful and worth more than anything Maisie had ever owned. "My mother used to do it when I was very small, and she'd sing as she did. Will you sing?"

"I'm no singer, m'lady."

"That's alright, neither am I. The gods still ask for song."

As do stubborn little ladies. Maisie took the comb and did as she was bid. The lady's hair was soft to brush, and the tangles easily split, though there were many. Maisie didn't know songs good enough for a highborn, she remembered few from youth, but her voice wasn't a lovely thing, so she didn't truly sing for the girl. Maisie hummed but that seemed to please her.

She finished quickly and the girl got into her bed. "Shall I blow out them candles for you, Lady Leonara?"

"No, leave them, please. I don't like the dark, and I plan to read for a time."

Maisie nodded, curtsied, and made for the chamber door.

"Maisie," Lady Leonara called out before she could leave, "do you get nightmares?"

She sighed, tucked back her red hair and paused before turning around. "Everyone does, m'lady."

"Do you have recurrent ones? Has the same dream come to haunt you night after night?"

"I used to have, when I was a girl. I would dream of a grole eatin' my bones, or of mages sackin' my town like they did to Twil and Norch in the Old tales."

"I wish I could dream of mages and groles." The little lady set a little black book down beside her. Her voice had shaken. "What does it mean when you have the same dreams again and again? Do you know? It feels like a very bad thing."

"I'm not so knowledged a woman, m'lady, forgive me. I don't know of interpretin' dreams and such, but it could be a message from the gods. My guess would be your head's just stuck on somethin', is all."

"I think my dreams mean to scare me."

"Dreams don't mean to do nothin', m'lady. Just imaginins made up in the mind."

"Why would my mind make up such terrible things?"

"Because terrible things have happened. It's not so strange. Eventually bad dreams turn into other, sweeter ones again."

"Are you sure?"

"At least in my livin', m'lady, dreams have gotten better as life has." Maisie used to dream of that bloody bed; of her daughter's crying, of her daughter's silence, of Hoop and crossing the Pass. Maisie thought, as she left the chamber, that she could not remember the last time she dreamed at all.

Leonara read her book that night until her eyes no longer

discerned one word from the next, and they all bled together in black ink and white paper, dizzying gray shadow.

Her eyes couldn't cry more. They could blink, tire to see, blink.

And she wouldn't sleep for the nightmares. Not for a long time.

The shadows came off the page and attached to her walls, watched her as she tried to sleep. She watched back. This was becoming something like a tradition for her, and she was as dedicated to this new tradition as she had been to going to temple. She already read the black book once all the way through. Still, she knew that she would understand more the second time she read it, and more the third time.

All the Rooj gave her something before departing, though not all of equal value. At the dock, her uncle leaned down and enveloped her, uttering, "Find the ginger maid and employ her," rushedly in a quiet tone.

That she had done, and it brought on more questions than answers. Now she had a letter covered in chicken scratch shapes of smudging ink, with no hopes of deciphering it. She did not know if it was a foreign western language or a secret code, and all she could do was wonder. *But you have mother's ears now,* Leonara told herself. *At least some of them, and that is something.*

"Don't trust the sparrows," her grandfather whispered against her temple during his farewell, so soft that only she might hear; then the older man dipped to hug her. He smelled of lemon and saltwater. Leonara did not understand what he meant but had resigned herself to the fact that Rhinere Rooj liked it better that way.

On the docks her aunt told her, "You are your mother's child in face and virtue," but her gift came the night before the Islanders left Kieln. Lady Talia knocked ever so quietly on Leonara's chamber door, and when she had opened it, her aunt held the small black book in her hand. The binding was cord and old leather, with the faint gold script of the cover thinning, though Leonara could just make out what was spelt: *Subtleties by A. Aatii.*

It seemed her father was almost right about Island children learning to scheme. But it wasn't quite scheming; Fair children learned how to keep their secrets while still being truthful, or close to truthful anyhow. They learned how to speak and live fairly in an unfair world, when everyone else could lie so easily. A. Aatii wrote, that above all else, truth was fair. Fair children learned to turn words into puzzles so entangling, it was hard for anyone to tell their truth at all. There was much in the book to keep her awake.

All these things I would have learned and could have known long before now. How much easier would life have been if I knew how to misdirect and answer in half-truths? Leonara would never know how her life could have been; she had what was. Her brothers missing, her mother—dead.

She read until her eyes burned, and when she finally closed them, her lids felt like fuzzy blankets. She dreamt of some lovely woman singing some sad song, and she watched herself dance with a man she didn't know. He was handsome and regal looking though she could not rightly see his face. A tender dream among the mangling others, and she twirled her skirts and hummed to the tune that played. It was the first sweet dream in so long, and she was tearful when she woke. She was also bloody.

Leonara lifted her fur blankets and shrieked out, then cupped her hand over her mouth. They were stained red in a circle around her middle, wet and sticky between her legs. Her first blood had come by the Sisters' grace; she was a woman now. She scrambled out of the bed and made a face at the sight.

Maisie rushed in, saying, "M'lady, are you well? Oh!" She gasped, taking in the bloody night gown and sheets. "I'll change the linens and serve you warm water, Lady Leonara."

Leonara watched as Maisie tore the sheets from the bed, and at that very moment her priestess came into the open door, hands clasped in front of her.

"I heard shouting." Modaire Nexitha bristled, straightening the sleeves of her simple gray gown. "I see what it must have been about. When you bleed again, be mindful not to shout and cause a scene when there are guests in the highcastle. In this instance, it is good you slept in, as most of the men are all awake anyway."

Her featherbed still stained with that ugly light brown spot once the thick linens were removed, a dark mark commemorating this auspicious moment. Maisie left the room with the soiled sheets, and never once looked back to Leonara or her modaire.

The priestess turned and looked at her with her crone-ish, wrinkled face. "Well, you are a woman now, my lady."

"I don't feel any different. I just have a headache."

"A side effect of womanhood, regretfully. It is a hint of intuition, I say. Get used to headaches, for they will become as close to you as your children." She walked to the bed, made to fluff the pillows.

Leonara's stomach had time to sink to her bum right before *Subtleties* fell from the pillowcase and onto the floor.

"And this? You keep hidden literature under your pillow now, my lady? And written by a *woman*?" The modaire careened her head, and the sagging skin of her neck rose above her wimple. "Leonara Hwaelin, a scandal you may turn out!"

"It was written in Fair Isle," Leonara said quickly. "By an Island woman, a true educated lady. Highborn women are allowed to write books and do many other things there. They have schools for women."

The priestess huffed. "And vile *temptations* abound with such women. Fair ladies get away with too much. Island women may steal a brother's birthright, divorce their husbands, leave religion, remarry. Ugh! With such freedoms come lascivious sins and moral qualms not suited for highborn daughters."

"It belonged to my mother once." And at this, Modaire Nexitha's shrewd eyes softened, if only a little. "There's nothing in here that I think Hetten might condemn in all his right," Leonara said, heartened by the old woman's silence.

"I see you are in the very early pages, still. That may be the reason."

"My father, in all his right, might condemn a little more," and though Leonara had meant to tease, the priestess didn't laugh.

"Oh?" Nexitha picked up the little black book and began reading the page Leonara had folded. "'It is better for a woman of Eastern society to not voice her complaints, in any way, for the listeners should not know such inner contemplations. These thoughts may stay hidden yet, an otherworldly advantage. It is best to give a noncommittal sound, a soothing note, and perhaps smile if the desire is to persuade love, but one must never divulge any notion of opinion before thinking long and plainly. Alone."

"Is that such awful advice?" Leonara questioned, and the modaire raised a scandalized bushy brow. "Not the bit about persuading love, of course. Just that it is wiser to think about something long and intently before expressing any opinion. Everyone should think before speaking."

"There may be as much meat in here as salt," the priestess said and placed the book back down on the table. "But books written by a woman's hand are forbidden on the Mainland."

As are many other things that men still do, Leonara thought of Mittrik's many paid indulgences at temple for whores and ale, how the priests and priestesses were grateful for his bountiful sins. She thought of the knight's cursing when they thought no lady was around to hear.

"It belonged to my mother," Leonara said again, looking at the lace of her dress and the blood. The book was one of the few physical remembrances left of Tisinda Hwaelin, and the girl she was before that, Tisinda Rooj.

Leonara would lose it, too, wouldn't she? She decided suddenly there was no point of attachment, especially where it involved physical things. Priestesses tossed out books. Mothers died, brothers disappeared. Favorite horses are lost. Anything could be gone overnight, and what did gods care of books and smaller things? Still, she clutched *Subtleties* tighter to her chest.

Modaire Nexitha sighed. "Perhaps, then... we shall go twice this week to the temple and ask for clemency, and I will wear a chain for you whenever you wish to read such a thing."

Leonara looked up. "Truly, Modaire? You will let me keep it?"

"Let it be our secret. As you said, my lady, the book belonged to High Lady Tisinda, and I have served her dwellings and children long. You are a woman now and must make your own decisions without a priestess hovering over a shoulder. Keep the book but be wary of it for my sake."

"For yours and the Sisters'! Thank you, Modaire!" Leonara, for the first time she could remember, hugged the priestess. The embrace was short; Nexitha pushed her away, commenting on her soiled clothes.

The priestess brought sticky medicine after she cleaned and dressed. Leonara wore a bright red gown that she had never before seen, simple goldstitched collar, still demonstrably mourning.

Nexitha was old, with a curving, humped spine and a puck-marked face that made her fat nose stand out more than it should, but Leonara loved looking at her. She always had new wrinkles, new spots, and her lips twitched funnily when she spoke of certain things. Her dressing was long and black, and her hair was always covered, as were her hands. Modaires might be bald under their shawls, Leonara didn't know. Aidares shaved the top of their heads, to feel the blessing of sunlight. Women must be shielded.

There was not much need for the aidaire to lead their family in daily prayer as so many other house Doctors did, since Alluvel was the only highcastle in Baeltaf to not boast an ajoined temple. In other Dominions, high families prayed to the gods apart from the peasantry, only nobility and their servants could enter Dwelling temples. But the public temples in Kielntown were both nearly the size of the Glittering, both constructed before the Glittering, and they had always been magnificent enough for the Hwaelins. Though her father never spoke much of the gods, and he didn't go to temple daily, he had told Leonara that the temple was a reason why the people would always choose to love them. Faith to the gods was faith to your liege. *Its best to pray with one's own people,* Leonara reflected as Modaire Nexitha finished reviewing her.

"Whence do dreams come, Modaire?"

"Dreams?" the old woman asked as she handed Leonara another cup of medicine. She drank it without pausing to think and it tasted bitter, making her want to gag. It was a similar feeling to when she tried to push a lie out, but it was over quickly and then there was only a sticky layer of the green stuff on her tongue, growing sweeter as it faded.

"That will help with your headache and most other discomforts, my girl. What is this about dreams you ask?"

"Yes, dreams," she said with another dry swallow. "Why do we dream? Do the gods give dreams to people or is it just nonsense? Does Hetten or do the Sisters care enough about us down here to cause us dreams?"

"Are your dreams troubling you? I have something for that."

"I don't want more medicine," Leonara said, still feeling the sticky film on her tongue. "I just wanted to know if the gods cared about dreams and wishes."

By every aidares' words, they do not care at all for the wishes of a highborn girl like me, she thought. *Gods are busy with other things, whatever the Doom they are…* but still she remembered something from the tale of Caeth the Blessed. He was a demigod, but his wife was recognized by the gods and given dreams.

"There are stories about Hetten coming to people in dreams to guide them," she said.

"Stories always change after an age, and those are stories of demigods from ages long gone. His own children Hetten may have spoken to and still not often, my lady. Normal men dare not wish for Hetten or the Sisters to look upon them so closely that they could receive a message. The gods intervening on a level so personal is not a blessing and can only bring chaos for their amusement. If the gods wish to send our kind a message, they do it through the Good Thyne and it gets spread to the whole."

"But how do they tell *him* what they mean? With dreams?"

"It is not for us to know how the gods speak to their messenger. Dreams are unlike wishes and wishes are unlike prayers. Could be each holds a little power of their own, but all are surely unlike what our gods do with their chosen. Aidares are taught that heathens of Old believed in the prophetic power of dreams. They believed their gods could communicate with them only in sleep, when we are at our most susceptible to magic. The gods now, however, care for our dreams as High Lords and Ladies care for the dreams of insects. Dreams come from within ourselves, from our heart's own miseries and desires."

Leonara did wonder what an insect dreamed. "I heard that before. I don't believe I'm imaginative enough for it. I've never dreamt like this. I've dreamt awful things every night since my mother died, and I just want it to stop."

"Would you tell me of your dreams, my lady? It might allow you some peace to tell an old man like me of such things. I've heard quite a number of dreams in my time and I might know what lies underneath."

Leonara wanted to tell it all, to tell someone. But her brothers were gone, and confessionals were for recounting sin. "I see an army of brides in silver gowns, in armor, too, eyes burning like hot coals, red and ghastly. Some look like my mother, some look like me and I can't recognize the rest—faces I've never seen before. They all wear crowns of gold, melting from the heat of their eyes, and the crowns drip onto their toes. Not burning, though, not their skin or their hair, just their eyes. They march together to the sound of drums but without feet touching the ground. I always think one of them is about to reach me and speak and tell me something I must know, something of great importance, but they never do. They do not talk at all, but they look on forever with wide mouths and scare me so. That's what they want to do, Modaire. They want me to be frightened, that I know for certain."

"Who wants that, my lady?"

"The dreams!" she exclaimed. "Or I don't know. I thought perhaps the gods were warning me of something, but you say gods don't communicate with anyone but the Good Thyne."

"He is our gate to the words of the gods, their chosen holy mouthpiece. When he declares a message has been sent from all high, it is like the gods are writing with his quill. We are not so lucky."

Then why even pray to gods if they are insistent on not answering, if they only think one man among us all is worthy of their words? Who could benefit from gods like that but the one man? Leonara shocked herself. The Good Thyne was Hetten's representative on earth, to doubt him was to doubt the gods. She had always been such a strong believer.

She still was. She believed, she was only a bit confused. She didn't understand how in a world of truthspeakers, one man who could lie like any other was given authority by the gods to speak for them. *And what could gods have said to the Good Thyne that concerns my plight? They would not say anything, because they are gods and they are not here for anyone's benefit, for no man at all. They do not care. I would care if I was a god.*

"My lady, these dreams seem like a dreadful memory of your mother's condition and end. In the day, try your best and not think of it, and perhaps by night the dreams will fade. Are you certain you do not desire medicine, dear?" Nexitha asked, and her bushy brows drooped in worry. Leonara appreciated it. "The brides would leave you alone completely if you drank of it."

And if they're not meant to leave me alone? If they do have something to say? The thought alone filled her with terrible dread. She shook her head. "No, thank you, Modaire. I think these dreams will—" *fade,* but she could not say it. The taste of bitter medicine was in her mouth again and she swallowed, keeping mindful control of the reflex that made her want to retch. "The dreams will serve me in nothing, nor will my dwelling on them, and I must not fear them. They are just—" *dreams,* brought up more bile.

They weren't just dreams.

She thanked the priestess for the medicine and for her kindness, but not for her advice.

At high noon, a servant came to Leonara with a message. Her father had called to meet with her before they dined together in the great hall at night.

How shocking that her father could spare her any time at all with his lowlords and underlords staying in the castle. They all came for the second mourning day of her mother, to watch her pyre burn by the Bitter Sea at dawn. But none of their daughters or wives came; all the lords brought their sons and nephews. Though she killed herself, and though she was a reclusive High Lady, Tisinda Hwaelin was still theirs. Leonara tried not to let it bother.

Many of the guests slept in the great hall on makeshift bedding while her father had rooms prepared for all his lowlords. When she walked by the great hall, she heard the loud raucous of men.

Leonara walked up the serpentine and down the corridors of Alluvel with an anxious belly. Could her father know about the book? Could he know that Maisie now worked for her? Should she tell him about Maisie and her network of listeners? She shook her head slowly and thought, *No, those are mine now. Mine, like they were my mother's.*

When she reached the entrance to her father's solar she knocked tentatively.

"Who is there?"

"Leonara."

"Yes, enter, my girl," she heard, so she leaned her body's

entire weight against the heavy door, and it groaned as it opened.

High Lord Tagnar was at his writing desk, pouring gold wax onto a letter and giving it the impression of their family's sigil.

"How do you feel?" he asked, putting the quill and inkpots away.

"I feel well," she said, thinking: *well enough.*

"I hear you have received an unwelcome gift," Tagnar said as he looked up.

She told him, Leonara seethed as she walked closer to the hearth, not meeting her father's stare. *Doomed harridan told him about* Subtleties. *Aunt Talia was right, they're all liars, even priestesses.*

"It was mother's first," she blurted.

Her father laughed. "I know very well whence you get it. I am thankful you have your modaire in such close affections without a mother to guide you. I called you here because now that you are a woman, it is time that I speak to you as one, that meaning frankly and in the open."

He doesn't know about Subtleties. *He means my first blood,* Leonara realized squeamishly, and she practiced that noncommittal noise.

Her father smiled, and it wrinkled his cheeks. An odd expression on his face. "Where to begin? Let's see. A test to see how well goes your lessons, perhaps? I hear from Nexitha that you have improved."

Her modaire did lie. Leonara had been doing worse in her studies since her brothers vanished and her mother passed, dozing off in lessons because the bride dreams exhausted her.

"I've been reading more," she said.

"So, I shall test you. Tell me what happened in the two hundredth year after the Cleansing," her father demanded.

"The Battling of Brother Houses," she chimed, but then remembered. That was what the peasants called it, for they came up with the more memorable names, but her modaire had been sure to teach her the proper term for the war. "The

Kielnish Union, I mean."

"Hmph. And what can you tell me of the Kielnish Union?"

"All that I know," she nodded. The accounts of great battles were the only interesting bits of history to Leonara, the rest was just long lines of lineages and marriages and repeating names. *But the Battling of Brother Houses is not boring.* "Hammish the Hammer took Kieln from the heathens, drove them all out. He gave the land to his two sons, but their sons and their sons battled over territory for generations. Havlant and Hwaelin."

Her father nodded but looked at her like she was meant to continue. She did, sighing, "Lord Havlant allied with the three other Dominion lords, and the other Dominion of the south did not stand on either side... the, uhm," but Leonara could not remember the names of the other houses or Dominions that fought. They were dead now, wiped out by her own house, why should she remember? She decided on another direction. "Even still, with the odds against him, Keelan Hwaelin and his men won the battle on Smallstab Hill, and then he killed the members of the coward houses that joined Havlant. He united Kieln. Since then, all of the mining lands and the southern coast is ours. After, every knee south of the Sidgen knelt for the H of swords."

Leonara thought she was finished, hoped she was. She walked by her father's desk and stood before the ornate golden fox paperweight with red eyes that seemed to follow her, inanimate as they were. Her father coughed, and she looked up to his critical stare.

"There is no such thing as brother houses," he said. "There is only one house, and your house is Hwaelin. To be part of a family is to sacrifice for it. Do you understand me?"

"I think so."

"Good... good. Now I fear that the disappearance of your brothers has come at the worst of times."

Are there better times for disappearing brothers? Leonara thought but would not dare interrupt. She ran her fingers along the back of the golden fox, stopped and let her pointing finger rest on one of his ruby eyes. *So that the little fox can't see me, can't judge me in that false red way. Glowing like dangling brides.* She then removed the finger from the ruby and corrected herself. *No, let the beast see. I'm not a child anymore, and he's only an ornament. They're only dreams, aren't they?*

"It is a pretty thing, isn't it?" her father asked, stern face raised at her. The sleek, golden hindlegs of the fox bent the light of the hearth, its orange licks of flame.

"Yes, it is."

"It was made in the time of your great grandfather. He had it made for his own daughter's dowr, though it never went with her to High Baeltaf. He had her name etched beneath the front paw there."

Leonara picked up the heavy weight and turned it over, seeing the curved letters spell out her own name. "Does that mean it's mine now, since it's my name, as well?" *Only my name now, since Father's aunt died as Leonara Osbur. Though I suppose I will die with another name, too, and I doubt it will be as good a name as either Osbur or Hwaelin. And I won't ever be a queen, fated a lady.*

Her father leaned back in his chair. "It will be part of your dowr, yes. I think that is precisely where it is meant to go. You know that I had plans to have Jonn wed Ritra Gilgar, and now that he has gone, these plans have fallen through on my end. I planned to ride to Brimtone nights past on the Sister's Greeting to end Lady Ritra's Courtings, and in that union Kieln's gold would have Brimtone's rustless steel. I need a strong alliance with Brimtone before winter comes in full force."

Has Jonn run away from this wedding? Leonara entertained the thought but dismissed it. Jonn was far too noble to run away. But what was the other possibility? *They aren't dead.*

"Leonara." Her father's voice was strong and deep. *The gods knew that Higher Lords needed the sternest voices.* "You will have to carry the burden now, and wed High Lord Gilgar to secure our ties with the Eighth Dominion."

Her mind reeled, but all thoughts vanished, and the only tangible emotion Leonara could recognize was fear. She had met the High Lord at Mittrik's birthday tourney, and she remembered him as fat, old, and sour smelling. She also remembered High Lady Gilgar, an older, full-figured woman, face imprinted with laugh lines.

"He's already married," she protested, "and he's old."

"No, he's not a young man unfortunately. But the gods permit men two wives since the earliest, and this alliance is necessary, my dear girl. It may be easier, having a sister wife to help you in running a dwelling. Even Hetten has two wives."

"But the Sisters are jealous of each other for Hetten's love and filled with horrible wrath. And he's a coward. They call him Craven behind his back because he didn't fight in the Fourth. I want a man brave like you."

Her father nodded at her solemnly, dark eyes apologetic. "He didn't go through the Dreadwood, but not every man can fight daemons. Gilgar did fight men, flesh and blood, during the Fourth. He won battles, and he can protect you."

"He's fat."

"*Ha*, yes," her father quickly stifled his chuckle because Leoanara breathed too deep and too loud, too much air and not enough relief. He placed a steadying hand on her shoulder. "Cragin Gilgar is a large man, but that means he has the wealth to keep you and your children as well fed. And it is just as likely, I'm afraid, that your relationship with your sister wife could be as the Sisters'. The first High Lady Gilgar may be jealous and wrathful, for you present her husband an opportunity for heirs and she has birthed one daughter, and only stillborn babes for years. But you are young, smart and caring, and few womanly hearts cannot melt to such earnest goodness."

Leonara breathed through her nose, made that noncommittal sound though she wished to cry. She wouldn't yet. Her eyes were so sore.

"If Jonnere and Mittrik come back, then one of them would marry Ritra Gilgar for the alliance? Couldn't you?"

"It is custom for a man to grieve his wife one year, you know it is, and I grieve for your mother deeply. I need this alliance now, before summer, and Gilgar wants our houses united sooner than that. For your brothers, we can't raise our hopes before reaching a vein, dear girl. No word of them has come. I have sent men all over the marshlands, north as well, all the way to the Dreadwood and Blacktree Hold. The owls carry messages that say nothing. Nothing good."

"You won't make me marry him, will you?" His eyes told her he would, so she pleaded. "But if Jonn or Mittrik come back, please say I will not marry High Lord Gilgar." *For even if Jonn has fled his wedding, Mittrik would wed Lady Ritra to save me from such a man, such a fate. He will come back.*

An old aidare's voice echoed from somewhere in her mind. A rough voice like the Archoverseer's, one she heard in Hetten's temple for so many years. *Your fate is mapped before you already in the starry heavens, the gods have decided before your conception.*

Another voice, her aunt's: *gods are false.*

Her father's uncommonly soft tone brought her back to the present. "If your brothers return in time, you will not have to marry him, no. I am not signing a wedding contract, my girl, not yet. Only an intent of betrothal, an arrangement of your dowr, so that you may be housed in Daggerlone to settle while I make arrangements in Midhold. I ride for Midhold then Eiselver next."

"If they return in time for what? Why travel to Midhold during a time as this? Can't I stay here? Or I could visit Deardrea while you go," she kept pleading with him, but he gave her a severe look to make her face drop to the floor.

"You will know everything that concerns you, Leonara. On the morrow or the day after, lords from the Pearls arrive, and they will ride with us to Brimtone in three days. Do not worry, for as long as I live, I will make sure that you are safe."

But Leonara did not feel safe and could do little more than worry.

Maisie always worked hard; this week with so many lords and knights at Alluvel, she worked five times harder than usual and felt like such events aged her fifteen years. There was a great, big feast that very night in the great hall of Alluvel for the arrival of the Pearl Islands lowlords; highest of them Lord Egan Norr, who was Lord of Limper Island and Lord Chamberlain to King Ornund. Maisie had heard of the man who sat at the right hand of the Osbur king, but what she heard varied.

He was a man too old for fighting, and they said he did not fight much as a young man, though he had once been knighted. Tagnar Hwaelin seemed to trust him, though, and he was no stupid man. Maisie liked Norr better than some other Pearlmen, who did not hesitate to swat her when she walked by. Norr was at least better mannered as a man of the Table, and she imagined it was harder for him to swat at girls since he always carried his Chamberlain staff.

Two days after the Pearl lords arrived, High Lord Hwaelin and his lords, all the Pearlmen, and some castlemen were prepared to leave Alluvel. Leonara told her the night before that she would be going with them, so Maisie cleaned out everything from where she slept, burned some of it to keep secrets, and packed away few things for herself: a small blade concealed under cloak, a wooden bowl and fork as well so she wouldn't need ask anyone for anything, a burlap bag with her one change of underclothes and dress and a pocket full of eighteen golden suns. Lastly, the piece of blanket that her daughter had been wrapped in. She kept it these many years. Maisie had to pack much more for the little lady.

The lady decided on taking Rose as well, bless her. Rose was the sort of girl who needed to work or else she'd find herself in trouble, and it was an odd sort of relief to Maisie that she would get to watch over her in Daggerlone. Rose's uncle was the horsing master at Alluvel, a loyal man (and unbeknownst to him a Kensgood bastard), and it was through him that Rose had gotten the position of scullery and maid in the highcastle. She was not the hardest worker, but she was young and would surely grow into her place.

Rose, all of sixteen, thought she knew more than she did, but Maisie liked to talk with her. It was a more pleasant kind of pastime than scrubbing chamber pots, or walking in silence with open ears.

They had left, three hundred men and two dozen wagons, and now Maisie sat by a fire that was all but lit ember, barely giving off any warmth in the beginning of winter's hard chill. Her and Rose's rolled up aprons were their pillows, and they made sure to set apart from all the men, less someone mistake them for a painted follower. Those women slept closer to the tents, a lucky few inside them.

Maisie pulled her cloak tightly around her and stoked at the fire with a long, fallen branch. They had traveled three days on the Kielnish Arm until it threw them onto the Nineway Road. The Nineway wound them north about for another twelve days to reach the highcastle of Brimtone.

From their place on the hill, they could barely see the tall curtain wall of Daggerlone past the tall pine trees. It was a day's ride away, but she could see the five sharp pinnacles peeking above the two hills. It was funny to Maisie that Alluvel was such a pretty castle in a hideous part of country, while Daggerlone was such a hideous castle in such beautiful river land; it seemed right somehow in its balance. Her stomach growled, and the noise was unsettling, like the growl of an animal. She didn't feel hungry, but for some reason, she was nervous.

"Did you hear about the red daemon the knights found before we left? In the Goldwood?" Rose asked, too loud in the dark.

"I did." Of course, she did.

"Sir Skinny Legs was shivering off his horse when they

returned. I've never heard of a daemon this far south. I wish I'd seen it."

"No," said Maisie with a patient sigh, "you don't. Don't wish such a thing at night near the wood, dear. Not near me."

"I'm more scared of those Pearlmen than daemons. Have you seen how they stare at my arse? Oh, come on, Maise, laugh. It's only a joke if you laugh."

"You can't always be funny."

"I hear there's ghosts where we go," Rose said.

"Who said it?" Maisie asked, and the girl's cheeks flushed.

"Everyone knows about the ghosts, but Snaggletooth Tarner told me once. He says all Old castles have ghosts and Old netherspirits of daemons, and that a daemon's magic can never be cleansed away, no matter how many aidares or modaires go to bless the ground in Hetten's light. Places that are dark as that just can't go back to being right and normal, can't happen. Like faes in the Dreadwood, you can't get rid of it."

"Snaggletooth is a townie butcher 'prentice who can't read, mind, I wonder what he knows about Higher Lords' castles and netherspirits."

"I heard of Daggerlone there are so many towers, and they look so sharp as that, like a row of black needles against the sky. I heard that the walls can cut you."

"Walls can't do that. If people are being cut, it's by something else. I've only ever seen two highcastles, and Alluvel was by far the prettier. I imagine close up Daggerlone will not be able to rival its beauty."

"I'm glad to be gone from Alluvel, even its beauty. I needed something different, and perhaps that means something ugly but be it so. Ugly does not mean worse necessarily. Sara, bless me please, is the better wife after all and despite her face, Hetten prefers her. In Kieln, I was far too comfortable in my ways."

"Same ways in a different castle, same soup on a different fire. You'll keep your head down and do your work if you know what's good, and be better for Daggerlone. But, do you really believe in them heathen ghosts?" Maisie wasn't sure if she believed in them.

"Completely!" Rose almost shouted. "Don't you? Ghosts, spiritlions, and shadow-crawlers, and well, you know, evil things. They're all over where heathen magic was strong. Daggerlone is so great and lasting because it was built by mages, you know. They say there ruled a heathen king who still haunts it. The king's name is a curse that kept his spirit there. He was a wicked mage that kidnapped young virgins with a magical song. Some say maidens can still hear it in the towns by Daggerlone—that wicked song calling for pretty girl's maidenheads."

It sounded rather stupid to Maisie. "And how do you know all that?"

"Everyone knows it, Maise. I heard it from someone, I'm sure. I think I've heard it at least three—no, *four* times."

"I've never seen a ghost." A twig snapped behind Maisie's back, she fought the urge to spin around. *Just an animal. A hare.*

"I have," Rose said, looking into the trees. "Everyone who grew up south of the Dreadwood has heard and seen strange things. This was all heathen country, before the First War, and it's not all forgot, not here. We're more superstitious than northerners."

"I'm Eiselvan, not northern."

"Eiselver is north of the two great woods, love. Am not shaming you, just saying us truest southerners know about left over magic is all."

Humans knew nothing of daemon magic. Unless they were Forsaken or Rooj. Maisie sighed. "Well, do you want to know what I've heard from learned men such as Doctor Petrard concerning ghosts?"

The girl nodded.

"Ghosts aren't real, dappers and netherspirits aren't real. Daemons, mages and witches, sure, but they're all west now. When we die, our soul moves on to our next life or we are

Doomed. There is nothing in the middle, no lingering for those departed from their bodies. I heard the southern doctor tell that to Lady Leonara when she was a little girl and asked such questions. And Petrard went to study at the Glittering Temple as a boy. Folk like us couldn't even count all the books he's read, and we're betwixt them and worser poor."

"That old man knows lots about everything, right. He's an aidaire that follows Good Thynes to the verse and a doctor beyond, so he's read lots about all manner of things. But trust me, Maise. There are ghosts in a castle like Daggerlone. There has to be, and it's not poor to believe it, either. It's just smarts. Lots of rich are stupider than us, but I bet if Doctor Petrard saw that castle he'd believe it, too, and might even give me a gold chip for warning him. He stills got his sort of maidenhead if he's such a good aidare. Someone ought to warn poor Lady Leo of them ghosts before they come for her. Should be you!"

Maisie thought that Rose was a good listener but she would make an awful ear. Ears didn't have mouths, that's what High Lady Hwaelin had said, and Rose could talk nonsense forever if allowed. Maisie yawned into her hands and listened to Rose's nonsense until she slept.

Sharp as needles, Leonara heard of Daggerlone's row of thin, evenly spaced towers called the Fangs. It was no lie. They did not look like fangs, but exactly like the needles of a giant. The five towers were indeed sharp, straight, thin and piercing the belly of a dark gray cloud. *Stitching it together to hold off the rain.*

She sat in the wheelhouse as it rolled under the curtain wall after her father's horse, his guards', the row of twenty Kielnish lords behind her. Through the window slats, she saw the bright colors of ladies' dresses standing there waiting, and she pulled herself back from view. Leonara was not ready to look at the Gilgar ladies, to be looked at, and she would never be ready to be one of them.

Since passing over the Petty Hills into Brimtone, she'd seen the townspeople that would soon become her people to protect and rule over as a High Lady, and she imagined the kind of life she would have. *I will be a second High Lady, though, so I will always be second heard and second thought of, and no one will treat me as great as the first High Lady of Brimtone.* Her own mother always pitied second taken wives.

Brimtone itself, the country, its rivers and forests, was beautiful as her brother described. The journey almost distracted her from the thought of arriving, and so she found herself ill prepared to meet with any of House Gilgar. It all came too soon. It was all so rushed.

Leonara saw her father dismount his horse and took it as cue that it was time to exit the wheelhouse. Sir Baynard was the one to pull open the door for her, and she took his hand as she stepped out onto the compact dirt. She thanked him, and then finally looked to see the waiting party, the whole highcastle and more.

Gilgar was standing very set apart, stepping forward at once with much perceived dignity and clasping her father's arm. He wore a greatly detailed surcoat of brocaded fabric, and his cloak was lined with thick black fur. Her father looked very slight and plain compared to such a grandiose man. Her father, stark in red, looked more severe than anyone else in the yard.

"You are most welcome here, High Lord Hwaelin, Lady Hwaelin," Gilgar said at once. "Lord Chamberlain,"—his fat chest was held in front of him like a bird's proud crest, his boar sigil quartered on his surcoat— "you have made quite the journey from High Baeltaf to join us. Sir Redcastle, why, it has been a long time, indeed. I am eager to speak with you and hear of your family. Lord Norr, a grand set of rooms have been prepared for you and your underlords in the Fanged Towers, and for the rest of the Pearlmen as well. I have many rooms here, I'm sure you know. And for you, High Lord Hwaelin, in the Grand Keep with my own family there is a place."

"We were very grieved to hear of your High Lady's passing,

my High Lord of Hwaelin," said the High Lady of Brimtone, Aurel Gilgar, stepping up to them. She turned to Leonara and smiled sweetly. They had exchanged pleasantries once at Mittrik's birthday tourney the previous year, but Leonara had forgotten how pretty the High Lady of Brimtone was. She had dark auburn hair and brown eyes. She wore a brown and blue gown of samite and satin. Leonara had remembered her as old, but she was not so old as that. Her wrinkling face did not seem to age her, but gave her more character and history; crow's feet for her happy days, deeper lines between her brows imprinted by anger.

"Thank you, High Lady Gilgar," Tagnar said.

When Aurel Gilgar spoke, Leonara was reminded of her mother by that self-sure and dignified manner with which all High Lady's possessed themselves. "And for you, Lady Leonara, for your sorrow, I have prayed every morn to Hetten for his light. I know how difficult it is to lose a mother so young."

Leonara curtsied and smiled. "Thank you, High Lady Gilgar. And thank you for receiving us into your dwellings so warmly. I am astonished by Brimtone's beauty, truly. My brother boasted of it."

"You'll find more trees up here, that is certain," said the young woman to High Lady Gilgar's side, Ritra.

Ritra had her father's face. Some said that Jonnere ran away because she was ugly, and he was Fair and vain. Leonara didn't believe it, of course, and besides—Lady Ritra was not really a terrible thing to look at. One's eyes could rest comfortably on her face for a long time and be perfectly fine. Leonara admired her thick brown hair, braided back to the nape of her neck and buttoned with pearled pins. There was fine lace atop the bodice of her black gown; the dark bronze cuffs of her sleeves resembled a knight's armor and matched the sunlight reflecting on her hair.

Metal cuffs on a lady's sleeves were a new trend and something too modern for Leonara's father's approval, but she thought true gold would look nice on her own dress and would represent her house very well. Maybe the dressmaker of Dwellings Gilgar would make something for her. It was all she could hope to enjoy at Daggerlone.

"I am sorry to hear of your brothers, Lady Leonara," Ritra said. "Jonnere is so very missed. I pray to the gods that both your brothers be returned to us soon."

"Thank you very much, Lady Ritra. I pray the same." She had prayed the same weeks ago, often and desperately, but her prayers had been more self-concerned since she was told of her imminent betrothal.

"I am pleased we are finally introduced well and properly," said Ritra. "Introductions are so difficult to do well at tourneys, and not nearly as memorable as the sports. At last year's tourney at Alluvel, I did not have the good luck of speaking much to you. I was in the Wellsoul's pavilion for much of it. Joanne Wellsoul is my mother's cousin. I have so desired to know you, though, and I am quite sure that we will grow to feel very warmly for each other. We are destined to be like sisters, I know it. I have known it since I heard your brother speak so well of you."

Leonara did her best to respond in the affirmative. *She is kind enough. Verbose, gods help her, but Jonn likes kindness. He would not have cared about her looks if her heart was good. If he were alive, he would be here to marry her as father wished.*

No, it couldn't be true. *But what if both of them are already living their next life? Then I'm all but Doomed in this one to be with Gilgar.*

"Our hospitality and dwellings are honored to host you and your company, High Lord," said High Lady Aurel. "I am sure you are very tired after your journey up the road. I shall take you to your rooms. You may wish to rest before the feasting tonight. We have prepared something very great for you."

Her husband huffed and interrupted her. "We should sign the papers before the feast, at once, so the announcement is backed by ink and gods."

"Whatever you desire, dear High Lord," Aurel Gilgar said,

and curtsied to him stiffly.

"Do you not agree, High Lord Hwaelin?"

Her father nodded. "I follow your direction in this instance, in your great dwelling, High Lord Gilgar."

"This way, High Lord, my lady," said Gilgar. "We will sign the intent in my personal rooms."

Her father led her away with a hand on her shoulder. Leonara stopped to look back into the courtyard at High Lady Aurel and Lady Ritra, and her father stopped with her. He squeezed her, but she did not move, staring into the center yard. The High Lady and Ritra were watching, too, and their eyes met Leonara's. There was nothing of kindness in those brown eyes anymore.

Aurel's perfect posture reminded Leonara of Modaire Nexitha. It also reminded her to lift up her chin. Another pinch from her father, and she turned to walk into the highcastle after Gilgar.

Leonara caught onto the rumors about the highcastle and decidedly did not want to live in a place built by magic heathens of Old or be trapped in such a place as a ghost. If she lived and died here, that was her fate. She did not want to see a ghost in the corridors either, like some claimed. She wondered if she would. *This castle will make the bride dreams much worse.*

Leonara already missed Alluvel terribly. She missed the pretty light corridors, the wide windows, and the smooth construction of perfectly placed stone, never an edge or crack in sight. She missed the servants who smiled at her kindly. Brimtone was dark and filled with cracks that must whistle when the hard winds came, and none of the servants smiled.

Leonara missed Doctor Petrard, their weathered aidaire, who had been placed as castellan. She missed Modaire Nexitha, who had hugged her too tightly at their farewell. She knew that soon she would even miss the gossiping cookers, but she supposed Daggerlone had their fair share of those. She missed her brothers most, and her mother, but they weren't in Alluvel.

What she truly missed was that nurturing Alluvel she

knew as a small girl. She must be braver than a girl, and besides, the Alluvel she left behind would never again be *her* Alluvel. It could never be her Alluvel without Mittrik, Jonnere, her mother. The highcastle of her childhood died and was no longer a home, just another place filled with ghosts like Daggerlone.

All this distracted her as she was led by her father and Gilgar to his private solar on the second level of the castle.

From the solitary window she could see the yard where she had just met the Gilgars only minutes earlier, and she felt the horrid rushedness of it all again.

The signing of the betrothal agreement was a simple, dull affair that sounded of crinkling paper and quill scratch, her silence, and just like that her Courtings were over before they began. Leonara did not even have to sign, only watch as her father did. She was glad for it. She didn't want to be the one to sign over her life. Better it be her father and her father alone, so that she could blame it all on him, hate him. She was angry above all else, but she knew how to hide it. Anger was the ugliest emotion on a lady, her modaire had been in the habit of telling her after one of her mother's outbursts. Leonara's fate was dressed in blue ink, her ire hidden in golden honor; none of it was her choice, and that did not matter. *I must do my duty,* she told herself, thinking of her brothers. *I must make this sacrifice and do what needs to be done for my house, no matter what that means.*

Her father smiled at her guiltily. He sighed, placed a hand on her shoulder, and expressed with no little sincerity his praise, how exceedingly happy he was with her, how much glory she brought to their house, how great a child she was to him. Gilgar praised her beauty, he told her he was happy to have her. Gilgar said he was in no hurry to see their wedding day so that she may become comfortable here. She nodded and listened and fought tears. She already hated Gilgar. She could not hate her father no matter how hard she tried, but try she did.

At the feast that night, Leonara made herself appear calm

while Gilgar spoke of prosperity and new hope for Brimtone. She saw she was not the only one troubled by her marriage, but the troubled faces vanished in less than the breath it took to announce the engagement. Older ladies raised brows but clapped their gloved hands beside their lordly husbands, who cheered for their High Lord of Gilgar. She saw some younger ladies look at her with pity, and it was a small wonder that they could do that while smiling. Ladies always smiled in Baeltaf, regardless of what they felt.

Leonara did not feel like smiling. She saw all the variations of a smile looking at her now: the pitying ones, the sorrowful ones, the envious ones, the truly happy ones (and to her those were strangest). They all looked wretched to her, painted faces on paper people that she did not know. They might as well be the dolls she set up for make-believe feasts as a child. They were lies, they were her future truth. Nameless characters she wished didn't matter.

The highborn wore smiles to protect themselves, and a smile was the worst kind of armour. Her father told her so when she asked him why he never looked happy, even when he was. He told her that the best kind of armour was armour, and the second best was gold.

What was that in Subtleties *I read? Your face can tell a thousand lies when words cannot tell one, and you should never express any emotion outright. Let your face be a liar while you think for words.* Leonara smoothed her face, tried to seem the High Lady she would become, elegant and refined. But she did not smile back at them.

She would abide by every other necessary convention. She would marry Gilgar if she must, because it was not a choice to refuse her father's match for her. The sole duty of highborn daughters was to marry as your house needed and birth sons. When she thought she would marry a handsome knight or rich young lord, Leonara did not mind that she had so little to do. Now she hated her status. As she watched serving women set food on the tables, getting groped by drunk men, she thought that it was very awful that she should wish to be a maid over a lady. But she did. They could marry whoever they pleased, as long as they were pleased with lowborn men same as them. Leonara would rather be groped by Gilgar while serving his wine than be his wife and share his bed. At least as a maid she could take some refuge in the kitchens.

Food kept pouring out from said kitchen and each course was meant to show off Gilgar's wealth and lavishness. Leonara's father brought salt fish, prawns, crabs, and lampreys from Kieln to Daggerlone, and the cooks had prepared those as well. Leonara never much liked seafood; she preferred almost anything else, but she wasn't feeling hungry at all this night. She pushed the prawn around the thin butter sauce, imagining that it could have been swimming in it, eating the little flecks of tomato and parsley that she did not want.

A silver bowl of course salt was placed on the table of the high dais, though no one touched it and the rest of the tables went without for the first many courses. Her mother had told her that in the Fair Isle, no man was beneath the salt. All men and women were of the salt there, even the poorest. It was their right.

Wheels of cheese sat on every table, different kinds with different ages and spicing, some holey and others not. They all had an undesirable scent, though, and the closest wheel next to her had green splotches. Mittrik once told her that the older and smellier the cheese, the better and richer it was considered. Leonara dared a look at her future husband, and High Lord Gilgar tore some poultry off the bone with fingers like greased sausages, chewing loudly with prickly cheeks full. She decided a man like Gilgar made such rules.

Being old and smelly doesn't make anything better, cheese or men. It just makes them old and smelly.

Gilgar might have seen her looking, because he decided to talk to her. "Your father tells me you turn four and ten in the next Sisters' pass. I shall throw a feast for you here if you desire it, and you may send for every young lady in Kieln to see it, or a tourney like your brother's last year. Do you enjoy the sports?"

"I do," she said.

"Then it is decided. What is the day and what is the pass?"

"I was born on the thirteenth day of the thirteenth Sisters' pass, my High Lord."

He snapped— a pageboy jumped to attention and poured more wine. "I will remember to have someone remind me. The Fair People name their Sisters' passes do they not? Strange custom. I have heard Fair call them by something other than a number, and their calendars are different."

"Yes, they call months by their names, given by the ancient saltmen after depictions in the stars. The thirteenth is called the month Underguard, named for the constellation called The Guardian. We are just Underhelm now, out from Underheel."

"Does that mean something to Islanders?"

"Islanders believe children born Underguard will have long lives."

"Let us hope they are right, my dear. Fair Islanders have strange ways, indeed. They are different from the rest of us dominions, and queer. That day is fast approaching. Tell me what you wish to have for your birthday, and it will be yours, my lady. Of diamonds, rubies, fine gowns, what you desire or whatever you lack—though I doubt you've ever lacked for finery. For who is finer than a Hwaelin? After that day we shall marry, before the springtime ends." His hand reached for hers on the table.

On reflex her hand moved out from under his just in time, and she folded both in her lap. The High Lord chuckled drunkenly.

"Oh, you already scared of me, now?" He spilled dark wine on the table as he sat his cup down. "Can't bear my touch? Or are you a shy one? Don't worry, you won't be in my bed for some time after that, especially with you looking like a beggar boy in lady's clothes, you skinny bird. I could pick my teeth with your little arm." He laughed and drank and laughed some more.

Leonara felt anger like a red-hot poker in her heart. *I am not any kind of bird or a beggar boy. I am a Hwaelin, you stupid, ugly man*! If her father was sitting here and not chatting up Lord Norr and the lowlords, he could tell Gilgar so, but she was alone.

He will be my husband, and if I said all I thought, he'd hate me. I hate him already, and I cannot tell what he's thinking. I can imagine, though, and still resigned to be with him. Being a woman is too difficult, and Modaire Nexitha was right about the headaches.

Of course, that could have been the wine. Leonara found a strong thirst this night and the Mardielan red tasted sour and good. She was on her fourth cup when usually she was only permitted one. Her modaire wasn't here to scold her now.

Many lowlords and underlords of Brimtone came up to the dais to congratulate Leonara and the drunk High Lord Gilgar, people that she would have to know and remember if she was to be their High Lady: Houthers, Terrents and Smallkins, Sharpsons, Snurers, Thedges and more. *Ugh.*

It was common to hear Kielnish men speak of Brimmen as proud, self-important people, but Leonara found they were as proud as any highborn. They came with big personalities hoping to be remembered, courtesies of empty words, and some lords introduced her to their wives and children, and some of the children were older than she. The lower ladies stretched their long goose necks from their pleated collars, searching Leonara's position as the night hobbled along. Their eyes seemed unsatisfied with only seeing, and she knew they could never get their full. Much like her future husband.

The only time Leonara gave a truthful smile was when Gilgar's soft-cheeked nephews told her she was very beautiful and an honorable addition to their family. One of the nephews came closer and complimented her necklace and her eyes. Her aunt Talia had warned her about young lords with a talent for flattering. All flatterers are liars, and all men lie, or something the like, but the way the boy spoke made her blush. And though her mind rang, *Liar*, her heart thumped, proud.

She wondered if she'd ever dance here in this grand Hall of Hearths, as they called it, but now that she was a woman promised, her betrothed must first ask before others were permitted, and High Lord Gilgar was too drunk for dancing. She thought of what dancing with him would look like, his clumsy thick hands trying to move her around the floor. *Gods, no. I would never want to dance in front of these nameless characters with such a man, it would humiliate me to tears. I'll never dance again if it means a dance with him. There are greater losses, though, and I was never the most graceful partner.*

High Lady Aurel was silent through the whole night, and her smile looked like it was carved from white stone. Also a lie, Leonara knew. Surely High Lady Aurel hated her for coming to Daggerlone. She would prefer her daughter to have Jonn, of course.

Aurel was the perfect southern High Lady, elegant and soft spoken with soft, warm eyes that thanked everyone silently, all the time, just for being in her presence. She was what High Ladies of the realm should be, and so unlike what Leonara's mother had been.

Tisinda was discourteous and short with serving people and lesser lords. She was a private, often inhospitable woman who hated to entertain and refused to sit and do needlework or recite poems with the lowladies of Kieln despite expectations. She loved hawking, riding, and sometimes dancing after a glass of Mardielan red—and the dances of the Fair Isle were as peculiar as their songs. Leonara had wanted to do those things, but her father had not allowed it.

She didn't think she would be a High Lady like Aurel Gilgar, and she was not the kind of woman her mother was. Leonara did not see herself as a perfect southern lady or as an Islander, despite her triewthblood. She didn't know what she was in this world, only beginning to realize she didn't quite fit anywhere.

Singers sang of demigods, and of her father's triumph in the Dreadwood, and pipers went along with them. Leonara had to leave the feast momentarily to relieve herself of all the wine. On her way back to the dais from the privy, Lord Uther Osmond of Mirkwik and Hailspring stopped to speak with her.

"Lady Hwaelin, you do look quite lovely and fair for the occasion," said he, his portly belly held in front of him proudly, demonstrating the red bear sigil of his house. Leonara often had trouble determining whether people meant to call her fair, lovely, or Fair, vain. She gave Osmond the benefit of her doubt. His hat was eskew, his hair beneath it stringy with sweat, and his breath was strong of wine, but Leonara imagined her breath was much the same.

"Thank you, my lord." She bowed her head graciously, liking how he still called her by her father's name. *It will not last. Soon they'll all call me Gilgar.*

"How do you like the looks of Brimtone, my lady?"

"I like its looks more than anything. It is greener than Kieln, more trees, and the weather is considerably warmer than by the sea, even so close to winter."

"Fine weather is good for your health, and flash flooding does not harm the eighth Dominion like the coasts. But do tell me, how are you feeling tonight, my lady? Deardrea did beg to join me, you know. She said she would send a letter by owl."

"I received it today, yes. I feel how one does in a hall full of strangers, but I thank Hetten for the familiar faces of you and the other lords. I don't think Brimtone has seen so many Kielnish men since the Fourth War."

"Daggerlone will be a great home for you, I am sure of it. A High and deserving position for our High Lord's daughter. All your fathers lowlords and underlords are sad to know you leave Alluvel, myself especially, but all are as equally proud."

"I do not know if am deserving of such praise, but I give you my thanks."

"All Hwaelins face their battles in bravery. I was there in the Fourth with your father, you do know. I saw him in the Dreadwood slaughter daemons. He faced harrowing evils with confidence, and you are no different," he said. "Your father is a man of Hetten, and you are his child. Though Gilgar is not quite so threatening to old men as an army of fae, to you, I am sure he seems worse."

"You believe I am brave as my father, my lord?"

"I do, indeed. If my Deardrea was given to such a fate, she would have cried enough tears to fill Eberle twice. I should have known not to expect a tear from Tagnar's daughter, though. You wear your duty most honorably, my lady. I should never have expected otherwise."

Deardrea Osmond would drown herself in tears and look a sad mess if her fate was mine. Respectable ladies do not cry at feasts, High Ladies never. But Leonara did want to cry so badly. *I thought I hid it with my face, but my face isn't a good enough liar. If Uther Osmond can see the truth, everyone else can.*

"Excuse me, dear Uncle, my lady," she heard, and turned her head to see Sir Arne in his fancy surcoat and oiled boots.

"Sir Arne," Lord Osmond said. "How are you, good man? Are you having as much fun as I am?"

"Never as much fun as you, uncle. I hope you have had a pleasant night, my lady," he said, and Leonara nodded and said nothing.

The men spoke back and forth of the Pearlmen and how they drank more than the Kielnish, how they were truly fish, how Lord Chamberlain Norr drank nothing, and how the music at Daggerlone was fit for a wedding.

People were dancing across the floor, the ladies on one side, the lords on the other. Every sixth or such song was a couple's song, and the sides would mingle, then go back to their respective walls and gossip about the exchange. Leonara almost swayed to the lutes, and she felt the drink make her sleepy. She blinked and noticed that either she was indeed swaying, or the whole hall was.

Arne asked her, "Are you feeling very tired, my lady?"

"Sir? Oh,"— his words pieced together to make sense— "oh, yes. I am feeling a bit tired. It has been quite a day, indeed, and such a long ride we had this morn. I am not accustomed to much travel."

"Uncle, I believe Lady Leonara has had enough feast and song. Her father has asked me to help her escape back to her chambers without much a scene."

"Oh, of course!" cried Lord Osmond, with a low bow and a cordial smile. "Good Night, my dear, young Hwaelin. Nephew."

She thanked Osmond and said her blessing, curtsied and watched him leave to a table of his men, who welcomed him with drink and open conversation. Relieved to be done speaking with him, she sighed, but for some reason, that tired her more.

"You are welcome," said Sir Arne, and she realized he teased her.

"Thank you, sir. I am not feeling very gracious for talking. My father sent you to fetch me?" she asked, searching the crowd for his face. Her father continued in his own company with Lord Norr and the Pearlmen. "Did I do something meriting disapproval to be sent to my chamber?"

"No," the knight replied, "but I saw you standing there so helplessly and thought you might need saving from my uncle. He has ten words where other men would have one. You do not have to sleep now, my lady, but I did tell your father I would escort you, and Uther might be offended if you do not exit the Hall after taking your leave."

He was absolutely right, and she wanted to be done with the feast anyway. She wanted to be alone while she could be. Leonara nodded to Arne when he spoke, but that made her feel dizzier. She had to slow down to balance her head.

"I should bid Good Night to High Lord Gilgar and his wife," she said.

He agreed that she should, but when she met his eyes, there was something mischievous in them, like when Mittrik let her in on a lie. Leonara looked back at the dais; Gilgar was uproariously drunk speaking to one of his lowerlords, his High Lady was whispering to a servant; Ritra was no longer there. Leonara did not want to say her blessings to them, and it was clear Sir Arne would not make her. It was the smallest rebellion, such a small thing not to do, but it somehow made the whole night better as she felt the exquisite fires of defiance in her heart. The wine had dampened her fires a little but no longer.

"Will you lead the way, Sir?" she asked, and Arne nodded, and he led her out of the Hall of Hearths into a cool early winter night.

She thought she heard Sir Arne ask something and looked up at him rather stupidly.

"Did you quite enjoy the wine?" he asked, louder.

"Oh, yes, Sir." She felt the heat in her face and knew she was beaming red. Sir Arne chuckled, and she felt all the more embarrassed for herself. Her belly turned sick, though it was a different kind of sick feeling than when she tried to lie. She would not be sick now. She couldn't be shamed in front of Arne Osmond. He was her father's closest man, a true knight, and here she was drunk before him. *I am drunk!* she realized a little late. *Oh Sisters, I am really drunk. Why does Mittrik like feeling this way, all confused and swarmed in dizziness?*

"I might have had more than usual," she tried to add courteously. "When I close my eyes, I feel like there are angry marbles swimming in my head."

"Angry marbles," Arne laughed again. "How peculiar, I would think marbles to sink, not swim. An unfortunate feeling but some water might float them. Lying to sleep will make you feel better anyway. You can take my arm if you need it, my lady."

She thought she did, since slowing down did not help the dizziness as much as she had hoped. "I am grateful, Sir. Thank you and Good Night to you."

"You are always quick with your blessings."

"Not always."

"No. Your father's daughter could never bless her enemies. Good Night, Lady Hwaelin."

He did not congratulate her once as he walked her to the

chamber she shared with Ritra, and she was all the more grateful.

Alone, Leonara poured herself water, and however exhausted, she couldn't sleep for the noise of the feasting downstairs that traveled through the cracked stones and floorboards. Late into the night, Ritra came in giggling. Snoring as soon as her head hit the pillow. Leonara kept turning onto either side, trying to find some comfort.

The next day, she kissed her father goodbye in the upper bailey of Daggerlone before he left with his lowlords and Lord Norr's great host of Pearlmen. Leonara's father, who looked murderers and fae in the eyes, could not look into hers.

Good, that he be ashamed. She watched from behind a narrow grated window until she could not see the trail of horses and carts, the rotten fish banners, or the golden H of swords anymore.

10. NOTHING OF REPENTANCE OR DREADWOODS

Hwaelins had always been kingmakers, but never had they been kings.

After the First War of Men, Hammish the Hammer placed the iron crown atop Redbone's ginger head, and Ashard Hwaelin crowned Alrik Turner with the new crown made of Kielnish gold and rubies and garnets seventy years after that. Ormon Hwaelin crowned Ruthar Redhorn after the Watermelon Rebellions, and Jonnithar Hwaelin crowned the first Osbur king, Ornund I, on the steps of the Glittering Temple before gods and men. The Good Thyne handed the new king his scepter. Hwaelins were among the victors (the usurpers) every time. These days it was only the Good Thyne who placed a crown atop a new king's head in coronation.

Tagnar Hwaelin, third and youngest son of his father, planned to place the crown atop his own head, Doom a Good Thyne. It was past time for the kingmakers to make themselves.

Cold autumn solidified in Kieln, turning to storms of wretched hail, but not in Brimtone yet. Rain came and drenched the men's clothes and morale the first nights on the Nineway Road, but at least it was not hail. Egan Norr talked even when it rained, always looking over a shoulder, like any conspirous man.

Tagnar rode silently up the Nineway near the front of the column, listening to Norr talk about the walls of High Baeltaf and what would be done. They would attack from north and south and besiege the city, it should not take longer than two years, he kept saying… They would burn the crops across the Bones just as this winter arrived. They would surrender, Norr kept saying. The eastern seas were of the Pearls and the lords of the Pearls would barricade Tunure's ships. If Aze agreed, his

Northmen would hold them off by land, drawing them back to protect their homes, and getting rid of the Dawnbursts would only be added blessing, Norr said.

All well, but Tagnar could not think too hard on any of it right now.

He was remembering his youth, his young love for a Fair woman who was loud and unapologetic. She'd always been something desirable to look at, as beautiful in her middle age as she had been when they wed. She'd been promised to both his older brothers before him, but he had not envied them. Like most men of Kieln, Tagnar distrusted the Islanders, but then she became his. On their wedding night she had made him fall in love with her, before he even took her.

"If you strike me or hurt me or leave a bruise on my body, it is as Dooming as striking a queen," she had told him, not yet undressing from her silver wedding gown. He was already half naked. "My ancestors were kings and queens long ago. Gods from another world before that. My blood is powerful, and my house as much as yours. If you strike me, or hurt me, or leave a mark on me ever, I will go back to my home with however many children we have and leave you with nothing before you can stop me."

"You're threatening me on our wedding night?" Tagnar had laughed, half appalled and half amazed.

"I will not do it often. I hope you will not often threaten me. In this way, we will be better than the rest of them." Then her dress came undone, and any resolve for anger.

Tagnar loved her then, and for years after, until she turned bitter and manipulative like the sea. Even when he hated her at the end, he never struck her or left a bruise on her body while she lived. He made sure of that, and while he had hurt her there was no regret. He did not even think there was sin.

Tagnar thought of how Tisinda would have hated this eighth Dominion as much as Kieln. She would have hated this weather, this green land, this betrothal, this new plan if she knew of it. But she was dead and could do nothing to stop him now. She tried, he suspected, and he had killed her for it.

With poison. When he was young, he'd judged men who couldn't hold the blade. They were cowards, but he thought differently now.

Tagnar had long ago recognized his fading ability with a sword, and like most old men going to war, he'd known it was unlikely to see the end of what he would start. He would always fight, because he was a man who knew no other option. But now, he must fight and live or none of it mattered. None of this had been his first plan, not his second. His third may as well have been torched, so a fourth must do. Nothing could have prepared him for the loss of both his sons.

His sons were likely dead, and the Rooj were to blame. The Rooj couldn't know for certain the true manner of Tisinda's death, only the doctor and Arne knew, but they must suspect him. The Rooj knew of Tagnar's plans to take the throne, Tisinda's ears told her and she would have told her family as soon as that, and they were not going to help him. Rooj decided to be enemies first.

The Fair Isle always chose the side of the crown, and up until now it was what kept them safe. Tagnar was a good man, and he'd protected his wife's legacy and their children by turning treason against her own husband into mere suicide. In this way, only the remembrance of her would be affected, and Doom whatever that was worth. Their wealth afforded a handful of blights, Hwaelin was a good enough name. It would be the finest name, indisputably, when Osbur was gone.

The Rooj knew, though. They were not fooled, but neither was Tagnar. They'd done something to Jonnere and Mittrik, he was sure. His sons must be dead or held as captive for information or future ransom. It would be better if they were dead. Better for his plans.

They would not run away from their duty, and as much as Tagnar wanted to believe that they were safe, it was easier to just mourn for them now and not withhold hope. He had believed in Jonnere entirely; he knew he would be a great king, and Mittrik a great High Lord of Kieln.

Jonnere would have been of the greatest kings, Tagnar thought, *just and good, but now I must be different. Everything must be changed, and I must live to see the change. I must live to the end or my daughter will be truly lost.*

Tagnar had too many concerns: his daughter, building his numbers, northmen, missing sons, missing journals. Tisinda.

Three days north of Brimtone, they came upon a village with a small temple for Hetten. Tagnar could not remember the last time he confessed a sin, but if there was any reason to seek out the gods' forgiveness, this was it. He felt tremendous guilt. This was the sin by which he knew Hetten would condemn him, if the gods existed.

His men were surprised he wished to stop in the temple, but Lord Norr joined him inside. It was a quaint building of four walls and a sloped slate ceiling. At the front of the temple, a statue of the sun god, muscled and glorious with his wives on either side looking up to him.

The confessional was a black wooden box on the right side of the front wall, smaller than the confessional in Kielntown's great temple. It was for skinny peasants who lived nearby the fields, not for fattened lords and aidaires. Tagnar took off all his jewels before he entered the confessional, an aidaire stood with a bowl ready at the small door.

Tagnar was a modest man, only wearing his signet ring and a fine necklace of thin gold vines. The oily aidare craned his neck to see the sigil on the ring, coughed as if he hadn't. Tagnar entered the box and made himself comfortable on the wooden bench, all while thinking of Cragin Gilgar stuffing himself therein, too. Tagnar waited a moment before speaking.

"Please, Overseer, seek out Hetten's forgiveness for my sake. Seek out the Sisters' if they would amuse to grant it."

A reedy voice came from behind the slatted partition, "What is your fault, son of man? Speak it aloud to show contrition, and I will beseech the heavens."

He swallowed, nervousness and shame rolling around

together in his soul.

"I have sinned against mine own blood," Tagnar finally whispered, folding his hands and wringing them red, red, almost red as his coat. "It is the worst thing I have done in my life and I've done… much influenced by evil, Overseer. I have wronged my own heart now, and I'm ashamed. I betrayed my blood."

"What is this betrayal?" the Overseer asked.

"I signed my daughter's life over to a man that is undeserving. It was a treason against her, but it needed to be done for my assurance, but it will bring my daughter no happiness. Her betrothed is wealthy and old. She is young and cherished and soft of heart. She will never find love with him, she will cry and be miserable, and I have done it all." *And with the little joy she already has, I wonder if she would follow her mother's example, the example I made of her,* the thought came to him, and he tried to shut his mind to it, but already rooted fear. *No, she is strong, perhaps the strongest of my children. She must be now. Leonara is as Hwaelin as purest gold and tempered iron. When I am king, I will make it up to her. She will be called Princess, and all will be well. She will forgive me.*

The Overseer nodded his head behind the thin slats, but not too dramatically lest his hat fall, and Tagnar could hear his dry lips smack together. Finally, the old priest said, "The only sin is what your heart feels, that compassion a father feels for his daughter. Not a treason, my lord, by Hetten but by the Sisters. If you did it for her good, there is no Dooming sin. Still, to cure your guilt, wear your copper chain for one week, and be on your knees in prayer to Hetten for your daughter before the sun rises for the next three morns and all your sins will be absolved, my son. Pray to the Sisters that they may not bring her sorrow or destruction as you fear, pray to Hetten that she may have sons of good health."

"Thank you, Overseer."

When he walked out of the confessional, the waiting adaire gave him his ring and golden chain, and then with shifting eyes, gave him the copper chain of penance and situated it well on Tagnar's wide shoulders. It was heavy, but it was meant to be so heavy one could never forget it's weight, forget your sin. It did not seem enough.

He walked back to the center of the temple and up the two steps to the offering bowl. Tagnar paid the indulgence, a small amount really. Too small. He added a few more silvers to quell the aching in his chest, but it did not work, and a modaire came to take the copper off his neck and hang it around her own. The weight was gone, but also it was not. He told the modaire his penance lasted for three weeks instead of one, and she nodded, never raising her eyes to his.

He gave one last look to the colored glass windows at the front of the temple, where yellow sun shone on a castle, where stained red roses grew along every edge. Brimtone fashion. These were prettier images than the stained glass in Kielntown's temple, which not only immortalized the gods but also Kielnish battles for gold and glory. *Leonara will prefer flowers to the blood.*

He walked out of the temple, to where his men waited alongside their mounts.

"Are you alright, High Lord?" Sir Arne asked, holding the Hwaelin banner of crossed swords, looking concerned.

"Better now. We'll ride until nightfall."

11. THE GOLDEN FOX

At almost four and ten, Leonara had seen three men die in her life. Few compared to other ladies. Nothing compared to lords. She once spoke of it at length with Deardrea Osmond, her only friend. They had been together at Mittrik's birthday tourney, where she'd seen the third man die. Deardrea boasted her superiority because she'd seen six men die including the day's, and that attitude made Leonara very confused, why seeing death would make people proud. It didn't make Deardrea brave.

The first dead man had been when Leonara was five, and their old doctor had a sudden painful spasm of the heart that took him into his next life right before her eyes. Her brothers had been in the yard practicing with their swords, but she was left inside the castle with Modaire Nexitha. She could not remember Nexitha leaving her alone, or why she was with Doctor Stefen, but she remembered that awful look in his eyes when his knees hit the floor. He coughed and sputtered and clutched the air, but it was over so quickly. It all happened so very fast that she did not realize what happened. She shook him and shook him and convinced herself he was probably just tired, and then her mother walked into the room. She had been so calm and unbothered that Leonara thought then that her mother must have seen many men collapse from tiredness. She picked Leonara off the floor and Doctor Petrard arrived from the Glittering Temple in less than a Sister's Pass.

The second man was one who had raped a scullion and her father had him hung before everyone in the highcastle. She had almost enjoyed it for just punishment, as her mother and father told her she would, if not for the sounds the man made when he choked.

The third man was he who died at Mittrik's birthday tourney, a Mardielan knight who ran the joust just before

Mittrik. Sir Willam Thedge's spike had pierced through his opponent's eye; the visor of his helm was made wider in the outlandish northern tradition, and he was dead before he fell off his horse. She could not remember the dead knight's name, but there had been a black lion on his breastplate, so he had been a Rainfroy. She could remember her father saying that it would make the day more interesting and make it sweeter for her brother when he won.

She had thought of the dead knight perhaps once since that day, but now she thought of him whenever she saw Sir Willam, who was guest at Daggerlone's court. He spoke very loudly of conquests of blood, maidenheads and battle spoils but always bowed when he saw her.

She did not know if Sir Willam's presence made her think of every other death she'd seen in her short life, but now she thought of Doctor Stefen every morn and night, the very first thing in her mind and the last; she thought often of being alone with him and feeling so helpless and small and weak when he fell, and she remembered that awful look he gave her most of all when he died. She could not do anything then, and she could do nothing now. Little had changed.

You have not changed, Leonara told herself. *You still act like that helpless child waiting for someone to come pick you up from the floor. Hetten help me! Be a High Lady, not a child!*

She tried not to think of distressing things when she was in anyone else's presence. Her face was still a terrible liar.

At present, she thought of nothing and watched as High Lady Gilgar took the light chain of thin keys that hung from her waist and used the iron one to unlock the small redwood spice box. When she lifted the hinged top, a confusing jumble of smells hit Leoanara's nose and she fought back a sneeze.

"What should go with the rabbit, do you think, Leonara? Cobalt requested garlic for the soup and some Mardielan mint for something of surprise." That was Daggerlone's top cooker she assumed. There were so many new names, numbing and impossible to remember. Leoanara decided she wouldn't even bother with trying to learn them now.

She peered inside the box and tried to hide her disinterest. She ate rabbit every day and was bored with it. "Perhaps we could choose cloves or coriander?"

"No coriander," the High Lady said, picking up what she wanted, pinching and placing the spices in Leoanara's open hands. "I've always liked the taste of Cobalt's mustard sauce. It goes wonderfully with rabbit."

"That sounds fine, High Lady Gilgar," Leonara responded, because it was polite, but this was the most boring part about being a lady: walking around and making sure things were of order and smiling pleasantly. So far, Leonara had met the butterer and the pantler, the cooker and his scullions, the steward and his apprentice, and Leonara's cheeks were hurting from faking her smile.

Later, Leonara and the Gilgar ladies sat in the Hall of Hearths by one of the fires (there were fifty of them). Only half the hearths were lit, making early winter warm. Leonara, Ritra and Aurel Gilgar set to working on stitching and embroidering and gossiping, a favorite pastime for most highborn women. The Gilgar women were no different, and Aurel kept flowing conversation with her daughter.

Aurel's gown was an inky blue samite, white flowers across her chest, large white trees reaching up her shoulders to the frilled collar, dainty roots meshing into the lace of her sleeves and gloves.

Leonara looked at the linen twine and yarns of rich colors and wondered how to choose to begin. *High Lady Aurel wears the white tree on her garments proudly, so I shall stitch something of the brightest gold.*

Leonara decided that she would work the three crossed swords of Hwaelin in pretty golden string onto a handkerchief. She entertained the idea of giving it to Sir Arne when she saw him again, perhaps at her birthday tourney, but she felt the blush creeping onto her cheeks and forgot that. She could give it to her father, but she knew she would do a terrible job of it if he was in mind. She should be thinking to give it to her future husband.

That idea made her gag. She decided, *The swords will be for me, gold swords to carry since I do not have real armor or weapons.*

The High Lady's needlework was impeccable, reflected in every raiment, and when Leoneara's fingers tried to mimic the swiftness and failed, she stopped her own stitching to watch. The Lady pushed her needle through and finished the tip of a pretty white tree atop a red bleeding heart. It was the sigil of the Whitemares, Aurel Gilgar's birth house.

"Never forget your home, Leonara."

"I never will. I must thank you for sharing your home with me, and I should hope that Daggerlone feels like home to me soon. This weather is a welcome blessing."

"Oh, dear, you know exactly what to say. You are as good as the best Hwaelins, but you know this will never feel like home to you. Your mother never loved Alluvel as her home, did she?"

At Leonara's silence, for she could not say anything kind that did not feel like a lie, High Lady Aurel tried to ask pardon for mentioning her mother but she exaggerated her apologies, and Leonara could not tell if she was sincere. Women were liars too, not just men. She made a noncommittal sound to the High Lady and continued working on her gold swords.

"Even to me now Daggerlone isn't like home," said High Lady Gilgar. "My cousin is Ornund's third queen, and she has told me though she lavishes in High Baeltaf, she does miss our Garlandfield. The canyon is unmatched."

Ornund had four wives and seven daughters. One son had been born to him, but the little prince died shortly after, like Leonara's own brother Keelan. It was known that the Whitemare Queen was loved well by Ornund for her beauty but was barren like her sister. Leonara wondered if the Midler family was cursed but could not think of a reason why they would be. Whitemares hadn't done anything terrible that Leonara could remember.

A knock, a servant entered with downcast eyes, and

Leonara did not look up. Gold through, and back, and through, and back the needle pierced and went. She was good at stitching, though not as good as a High Lady, and she was distracted.

"From Garlandfield Hall, High Lady Gilgar," said the bushy haired serving man.

"Thank you, set it there on the table." The servant did without ever making eye contact with the High Lady. *Am I as meek as a servant when I don't look at her?*

Leonara looked up when the man left and saw High Lady Aurel and Ritra both staring at her; Ritra looked back down to her rose patterns, but the High Lady cleared her throat.

"They pity me," Gilgar said, "some servants and all the low and little people that dare look up to form an opinion. They pity me because I could not give my husband an heir, and because you are here to do it. I suffered years, did so much for Brimtone, shite of a Dominion, but they see none of that. Your greatest accomplishment will be pushing a Gilgar son out of you, Leonara, and they could forget the rest."

That will not be my legacy, it will not be all I am. They should pity me if anyone, Leonara thought. *I'm the one who has to suffer now.*

Daggerlone's servants did not seem to pity the High Lady, rather they feared her. The servants at Alluvel had not feared her mother, but then again, maybe they had, and Leonara just did not pay any attention. She knew how oblivious she had been before, and the way Maisie scurried like a mouse with her eyes downcast made her wonder. Her mother's webwork of faithful ears was a fearful thing. Leonara did not want people to fear her, but perhaps High Lady Gilgar wanted that. Perhaps Leonara's mother did, too. *So, should I want for that? Would it make a difference in the end if people pitied me or feared me or did not think of me at all? I would still be here doing my duty.*

"I do not think the servants pity you, High Lady."

The High Lady laughed. "How much do you think it matters what they think, other than that it wounds my pride? They are only little people, after all, wild beasts waiting to tear us to pieces, looking up so high to me that their necks could break. Still, I tell you, pity is the weapon of the weak."

"And what is the weapon of the strong?"

"Steel," she said. Leonara looked around to all of the Brimmen steel swords that lined the walls between the hearths, two at a time crossed in Xs.

"You have it," she told the High Lady.

"And so will you. Do whatever you must to make sure they don't pity you any more, Leonara," she said, standing to retrieve the letter the servant brought. "As a woman, once they pity you, you lose some of your power. We are not given much to start, and once you lose the smallest bit, others will notice and try to take more."

Leonara listened to what High Lady Aurel said of a woman's power, and thought that considering her age and lack of agency, she was doing all she could. She had instructed Maisie to build a network of secret listeners in brothels and inns here just as there were in Kieln and had stolen some of the gold out of her dowr chest to fund it. It was something she thought her mother would do.

"I think I have had enough needleworking today," said Lady Ritra, standing. Leonara nearly forgot she was there as quiet she was, but there was something disturbed in her face. "I am going to the temple to pray until dressing for supper. Would you like to come with me, Leonara?"

"No," her answer came quicker than she could stop it. "But thank you, I am still quite interested in needleworking."

High Lady Aurel stared into Ritra's back as she left them.

As Leonara's needle led gold string, she thought of her brothers, and wondered where in Doom they could be. She'd heard every postulation and wicked story. She'd thought of even more herself. But still, she couldm't believe they were dead. She would feel it if that were true; she would know if they were gone forever. She told herself everyday. The needle pricked her, and a pearl of blood came.

She looked over to the High Lady who was standing at an angle to read the letter from Garlandfield Hall. *From her family,* Leonara thought.

She pricked herself again, and it hurt worse than the first time. *Bumbling today.* She could sit still no longer.

She rushed through the words, “May I take your leave, High Lady? It could be that I feel a headache coming on.”

“Of course, do go and rest. Shall I send Doctor Erik to you?”

“No, thank you. That’s unnecessary, I just want to lie down.”

Just to be alone in a room with no one to bother her or speak to her. Now, she did not have to share a room with Ritra. She had the room her father slept in before he left with all his men.

Sir Baynard was there at the door, carrying his sword and dressed in his full armor. He was left behind to be her personal guard and took the job very seriously, escorting her everywhere.

He smiled kindly when he noticed her walking toward. “Keep your chin held high, my lady,” he said. “Your brothers will turn up in good health, I’m sure of it. You’ll see Kieln again before summer comes.”

Of course, he knew all her reasons for mourning.

“Do you think it, Sir Baynard?” Leonara hated how helpless she sounded, but knew the old knight wouldn't care. He knew her as a whining babe at her mother’s breast, and he was too courteous and dear to mind her childishness. She was a child more than she was a woman.

“I do, my lady. Do not be discouraged.”

Sir Baynard Torde believed he was a good knight.

Blessed with his title by High Lord Fjorn Hwaelin, for whom he squired long before the Fourth Great War. Baynard was well in his years now, approaching six and sixty, and always feared the gods and maintained his Crestdays, protected those he believed innocent, and he served his liege without hesitation.

Until now, that was. Now there was much hesitation.

He believed Tagnar a good man however obdurate. The High Lord fought in their Great War young and clean-cheeked, watched the older Hwaelin men die before him, and found the courage to become a great commander at only six and ten. Tagnar Hwaelin managed to keep his wits in the Dreadwood, and near the tarpits hours before the battle. Many good men flung themselves into the molten tar when they came out the other side of the forest, but Tagnar came out stronger. Daemons made him more than a man. Beast of the Dreadwoods, many called Tagnar Hwaelin. The Beast led them to victory and took Veiltar from the North. Baynard, old as he was, never thought to question his High Lord since.

But to give his only daughter to Cragin the Craven? Baynard could not fathom why his High Lord would do such a thing. He understood the necessity of Brimtone's allegiance and Gilgar's men, but there could have been another way of going about it. There could have been a hundred other ways, so he saw it.

He stood outside the little lady's chamber and wondered why High Lord Tagnar could not just marry Lady Ritra like Lord Jonnere should have done, but of course the High Lord was in mourning, and he wanted his alliance before summer. When Tagnar left, he wore a solid red mourning doublet, plainer than fit his status, and the circles beneath his dark eyes were more pronounced than they ever had been. Baynard knew, Tagnar Hwaelin wanted a more valuable wife than a Gilgar. Perhaps an Osbur princess to solidify his claim.

Baynard tried to think of something else that could have been done, but Cragin Gilgar was a High Lord without an heir, a greedy man, and Lady Leonara's dowr was of forty thousand suns, linens and beddings of the finest Fair Island silk, forty acres of country and a small castle in the county of Goldcrown. This was the second best offer Tagnar could make to gain all Brimtone's weapons, to make sure the Osburs received no more.

But to give his only daughter to the Craven?

Craven Gilgar earned the name when he turned around and

refused to enter the Dreadwood during the Fourth War. He had been a young man, just like Tagnar, but filled with cowardice or self-preservation. Gilgar's father, who had been High Lord before him, died before they went into the trees. Young Gilgar adamantly refused and rode back to Daggerlone with some three thousand men. Years after, better men still called him Craven, Baynard among them. *If he had gone into the trees, he'd be dead now,* Baynard knew it. *If he were dead, poor Leonara would not have to suffer him. She could have his young nephew and be lucky for a chance at contentment. But no, she must marry the Craven for Tagnar to have Brimtone.*

The idea of it would have been enough to send the lovely High Lady Tisinda to an early grave. She would not have allowed her Island daughter to be humiliated in such a way. It was her memory that led Baynard to volunteer first among Tagnar's men to stay in Brimtone and guard Leonara; it was for his departed lady of secret smiles.

The gods are cruel, but they are just. You are one man in the many.

They were words of aidaires spoken in temple, spoken down from the mouth of the Good Thyne. And now the words were habit, a self-impressed reaction long turned involuntary for when his thoughts drifted to High Lady Hwaelin. He thought he might try to stop that habit now that she was gone. Thinking of her could only hurt himself.

Sir Baynard Torde was honorable, and despite the smiles Tisinda Hwaelin gave him and the tears she shared, he held the Knights' Code of Honors to the eleventh. He kept her confidence and shared in her grievances, had spoken soft words for her comfort though he never overstepped—but how he had wished! He could never have her, but Baynard had been contented with living within her dwelling, guarding over and protecting her. Then he was unable to do so.

But how can a man protect a woman from herself? He did not know, and it haunted him, as did a thousand unanswered questions. *How could I have saved her? What could she not tell me? She told me so much.*

He did not think she was so grieved, had not realized that her drift of attitude was not just a small bout of seasonal sorrow. It had gone beyond that, and he of all people should have seen. He was supposed to guard her and protect her.

She did not want protecting, he reminded himself. *She said that she was capable of protecting herself without shield or sword.*

How do spiders keep themselves safe? Tisinda once asked him.

She lied, or she was wrong. Her webs could not save her.

He had thought Tisinda the best liar. She had kept her secrets from her husband for years. Everyone knew she had spies, though no one knew who they were, nor could they find them out. Everyone knew she had wild ambitions, though she never said it. She was like a spider— small, dangerous, with a mind made for creating intricacies.

The fourth code of the High Order was to never speak dishonestly, but Baynard lied to Lady Leonara. He did not think Jonnere was out there living. He knew Tagnar's first son well and knew Jonn would do anything his father commanded to be seen as worthy of his inheritance and title. Baynard had not seen Jonn Hwaelin since his mother's death. The young man had loved his mother, and was hurt worst by the loss of her, but Jonn was a man who understood duty. His brother, less so, was still not a man to run away from pain or a fight. Baynard thought a fight likely led one of them out of the highcastle that night.

And where goes one, there, too, the other. They always chase each other's tails.

Baynard thought of Mittrik trying to start fights at his own birthday tourney like an absolute belligerent before he ran the joust. Baynard could not remember the reason for the fighting now, but it was two Rainfroy men against the younger Hwaelin. At first it was only taunts. It could've been anything that set Mittrik off, a particular wrong word about his sword or his horse or his precious hair. Baynard watched from afar as the older Hwaelin intervened and calmed both parties in time, before the younger pulled his sword. Jonnere Hwaelin had always been a boy ready for the game of appeasing kings and lessers.

Tisinda's maid passed Baynard to enter Leonara's chamber, humming to herself. She was a quiet one, but Tisinda didn't keep incompetent people around her, so he knew she was not stupid. The fact that the maid was so quickly close to Leonara was proof enough that she was smarter than she appeared.

Two years ago, the maid gave Baynard this sly look, and he had known that she knew of his love. He wondered if Tisinda told her maid, but dismissed that thought. Tisinda wouldn't tell his secrets, or any of her own. The maid was only perceptive. He decided to hate her but found he was not the kind of man who could hate a woman for so little a thing.

Still, Baynard didn't like her, and he didn't trust her. There was something shrewd and ratlike in her look that worried him, and she walked around the castle a great deal for such a sizable woman. Always occupied, that one. He wondered if she should be so near the little lady and decided he would take special attention to the maid.

Maisie walked, with nimble knees, on her softer-than-felt shoes across the wood of the lower floor's corridor, the one that took her out to the yards and by the pantries and kitchen. She hoped not to stir any ghosts. Hoped to go unnoticed by the living, too. She dallied, listened, and worked in the while. Quiet-like, to observe and not be observed. Maisie heard a lot today— done a lot, and she was proud.

Rose must've been right scared of heathen ghosts and their virginal sacrifices because she rid herself of her virtue shortly after arriving, to a highborn if any. The knight's name was Sir Willam Thedge, son of a rich lowlord whose house made their money from the Brimtonian steel trade, protecting the roads, and overworking their serfs.

Rose told Maisie that Sir Willam wanted appointment to the Higher Order. Blushing, Rose said he had the softest hair and prettiest blue eyes, and that she wished all her babes could look like him. Rose said she would be lucky to get with child; he never finished inside her and said he wouldn't keep any bastards. Rose didn't believe him. Maisie told her to count the blessings gods would grant. No one needed more knight's bastards. These were the worst class of men, Maisie found, those that felt cheated of greatness before birth.

Maisie heard other things about Willam Thedge, and by all the accounts of people not being bedded by him, he was not kind or gentle. He was quick to anger and slow to sense, and they said he had a good time beheading people for the sake of justice. Poachers, especially, who just wanted food for their children. *High Knights never claim bastards, and that's what he's after,* Maisie would think and worry, and then she'd think of all the rumors. Ones the same color as Arne Osmonde, killing his bastard son ten years ago to keep his named sword. That could be hearsay, but Maisie knew for fact Honorable Arne had killed a Kielntown whore four years past. She knew it as fact, she did.

Despite reputation, Rose would claim, "Willam loves me, I know it. He is my Gerdwill, I'm his Rosette. He says so. He sings me the song as I sleep. He'll win the joust and build the cutest, smallest underling castle for us. He will. You should hear him sing."

Men quoted songs when they wanted a woman, but Rose could be sure he wouldn't always want her. He was highborn, and said he wanted the High Order, and Rose was a little girl's chambermaid. Just because he was currently Errant did not mean he would never ascend or marry, and he would marry his own. *Won't claim any bastard, no matter his fate, and then what would happen to poor Rose?* Maisie tried not to think on it and distracted herself with the busy work.

When supper was over, Maisie sought out Lady Leonara to inform her of all she learned.

Firstly, the task of uncovering what kind of woman High

Lady Gilgar was. Lowladies of Brimtone thought less of Aurel Gilgar, because she was a Midler. According to the servants, she was a stern figure who hated error and enjoyed finding faults, but she was as generous a High Lady as they could wish for. She had been short tempered since the kitchens burned down five Sisters' passes ago, but she let the top cooker's wife give birth in one of her own featherbeds during the construction, so they admired her. She was religious, very devout, and after the burnt kitchens were rebuilt, she had the masons stay on to build an addition to Hetten's temple within Daggerlone's walls: a private space for praying to the demigod, Caeth, Hetten's first son.

There was also the establishment of Lady Leonara's spy network throughout Brimtone, which was a very easy thing for a little lady to demand but harder to put together without anyone noticing. Maisie had gone into Dagger's Town twice looking for potential ears. Not one looked promising, so Maisie began looking at the little orphan children that crowded the streets. They were the easiest to buy, which meant that any child in town could already be listening for someone else. She would have to be careful who she hired, and then she would have to go out into farther towns and do it all again until trust was earned by others. Maisie wanted someone she could trust with it all. *Maybe I can train Rose up. Teach her to shut up.*

It is the sort of thing Woolringer did for me, Maisie thought, thinking of how high she'd risen since recruited. It was possible High Lady Hwaelin already had ears here, but they had likely run to someone else to sell their secrets once she died. Still, some might be around Brimtone and be of use to her. *How will I find them?*

She passed Old Baynard Osmond, and walked into Leonara's room.

Leonara sat before a wide silver dusted looking glass, smoothing back her pale hair with the golden and sapphire comb she had brought from Alluvel. Maisie waited to open the door completely so that she may listen to the child sing, though the lady did not have a lovely voice. The song she sang wasn't like cradle songs or tavern songs, or temple songs Maisie heard in Rour. The rhythm changed after every verse and continually grew in speed.

"Where's my Oasis? Where's my trove?

I am here," said a man
The man that answered she,
was a rich man, good man,
very, very sure man
He wished to lead her to the sea.

Her feet go far, and her gowns are clouds
Her feet will fall, and waver into shrouds
So too the man who married her
Her feet should ne'er have carried her
In the blood she waits, in the sun she cries
Before Deadriver claimed her, she climbed"

"That's an odd song," Maisie said as she closed the door all the way and stepped into view of her lady. Little Lady Hwaelin blinked at her. "The words seem a bit unpleasant. What's it about?" Maisie asked.

"It's a Fair Isle song about a rebellious lady and her many lovers. My mother sang it to me before she died."

"It's got a catchy sound. I kept my ears open for words about your father's plans in Eiselver, as you asked, m'lady," Maisie said gently, stoking the fire. Lady Leonara, now at full attention, turned around so she went on. "And I've also been listenin' about what kind of woman High Lady Gilgar is, according to the servants and low ladies whisperin' from the feast since we arrived, but today I heard somethin' quite interessin' about her."

"I think I'd prefer to make up my own mind about High Lady Gilgar before I hear what little people think of her, but do not forget what they have said. What have you heard of my father?"

"He goes to Midhold to speak with northern lords about the warring on the Coldrock, and then he plans to ride to Eiselver to renew their alliance so that food can go north to Aze's men. He's giving Aze and Dorgrey gold for the war. I heard that some Brimmen knights think it's about more than that, and many aren't happy he's siding with northerners to have his way. He's been in talks with the High Lord of Mardiel, it seems as well, and a scullion from that Dominion say he's in your father's pocket and every Mardielan knows it, but I don't trust kitcheners with anything. I do know that Doctor Petrard sent birds west before we left, so it could be true."

"Did you read those letters?"

"I did not, m'lady." She tried to, but they had been written in code and Maisie could not understand it. The High Lord and his doctor had begun writing in code a year ago, and that is when High Lady Tisinda got truly suspicious. Maisie knew that the High Lady had solved the key to decode their letters, but she was not privy to know exactly how. "Would you like for me to read everyone's letters from now on, Lady Leonara?" Maisie already did.

"Read every letter you can. Do you know what all this means, Maisie?"

"No, m'lady," she lied.

Lady Leonara sat atop her featherbed and let out a breath that dropped her shoulders to her lap. Folded over, her face rested in her hands. "It means my father is going to start some bloody war, and he needs allies. He needs Brimtone, their steel, men, and he needs Eiselver's lands of good harvests. He needs the north after all their battling is done I suppose, and only that is why he needs me here."

"There's more, m'lady."

"What else could there be?"

"Gilgar's half-wit fool," Maisie said, "Tiptoe, he's a spy, and not so stupid as he plays, I know it. I've caught him more than twice since we arrived, listening where he shouldn't be, listening to you. He was creeping in secret on the dwelling's own doctor in conversation with High Lord Gilgar, and then I caught him spyin' on you and Lady Ritra. Only one of the times did he catch me, too, and he smiled right at me with smarts. Outside Gilgar's private room."

"All servants listen at doors. That doesn't mean the fool's a spy," Leonara said, so innocently Maisie almost laughed.

"He is," she affirmed. "I'll uncover who he listens for, don't you worry. There's at least five spies in every castle, m'lady, twice as many in a highcastle. At least ten, one for every Dominion, and likely more. One of my jobs for your mother was to find the spies within Alluvel and feed them misinformation."

"What kind of misinformation?"

"Whatever your mother wanted."

"Thank you. I am learning to be suspicious of everyone, fools and maids especially. And learning how to spread lies, and how little I know of people outside Alluvel. I barely knew the people within its walls. Is there anything else?"

Maisie denied that there was, and Leonara sent her out.

Left alone most morns, Leonara broke her fast in her chambers instead of eating in the Hall of Hearths with the rest of the highcastle. Maisie sometimes chewed a morsel in front of her, but it was uncomfortable to force the maid into conversation. Leonara preferred solitude now anyway.

In Alluvel, the High Lord's family would eat their two daily meals together privately in a small yet ornate dining hall, and on occasions her father would invite a lowlord and his family, or host a lucky miner, captain, shipman, or fisher who had caught something magnificent. In Daggerlone it was not so.

Growing up, Leonara was only entertained by singers on special days, a Crestday every so often, birthdays always. After her kitten died when she was a girl. Her father said anything else was extravagance and frivolity, and extravagance was not how the Hwaelins lived. Hwaelins did not need to flash their wealth for people to know there was plenty. They were the name of wealth by which everything else compared. Rich as a Hwaelin, proud as a Hwaelin, people swore by such an old name. Their colors were gold and gray: gold for the mines in the south and west, dark gray cast like the iron mined in the east of Kieln.

Cold as iron, warm as gold. Her father said that of her once approvingly and with much affection. *I hate him,* she would remind herself whenever she thought of him.

At Daggerlone many of the higher servants dined in the Hall of Hearths as well as the lordlings at court and the High Lord's family.

Suppers were not like the private meals she had at Alluvel as a girl, where her brothers would argue, her mother would smile, and her father would say something wise. Meals in Daggerlone were loud and filled with laughter and music and everyone got their fill four times over. Leonara thought Gilgar wanted his whole dwelling to be as large as he. There were the lowlords of Brimtone, seven of them, the underlords who were too many and too proud for Leonara. At meals, there was always the one fool, Tiptoe, the supposed spy, and other singers and jugglers and poets came from all over Baeltaf.

It was something that would delight most ladies, she thought, to be in constant merriment, to see knights and lords always dressed in their finest.

High Lord Gilgar loved to listen to the lutes as he ate, but Leonara was just annoyed by them. The singer sang loud songs about love stories that made her jealous, and some days he would sing older songs about Hetten's demigods, songs that Mittrik would have surely liked. Mittrik used to grab a lyre and join the singers when they came to Alluvel. She could not help but roll her eyes at the descriptions of the gallant knight and his pretty lady, which the bard sang, "was blessed with hair pale like snow, and eyes that outshone the Sisters' glow." It was a song about a Fair lady clearly meant to flatter her, but it was not a Fair song. It wasn't quick enough, it wasn't mysterious enough, it wasn't anything. It bored like the rest of her days in Daggerlone.

The family Gilgar ate without ever saying a word to one another upon the dais, scraping their forks against their plates and not looking up until Leonara excused herself. Sometimes Ritra would talk to her, but it was about things of which Leonara knew very little: what was popular to wear in High Baeltaf, betrothals of people who she had never met, rumors of Ornund's court, poetry that she had never read. It made her feel stupid, and she did not like that, so she tried not to speak much to Ritra.

Tonight, Leonara felt like she might throw up the mustard sauce, so she sipped on water instead of the red Mardielan wine. *My father needs me here to win a war,* she reminded herself often of what was important, and it made her feel less stupid. It was important that she do her duty and she do it gracefully. It was an awful, terrible, nightmare inducing duty, but she would try with every last bit of goodness she had to be graceful.

High Lady Aurel seemed to sense her discomfort as Leonara smashed a fig tart over and over and over with the blunt of her knife, unable to eat it.

Patting the corner of a napkin across her lips, the High Lady said, "I am sure you are glad to miss the winter hails in Kieln. They will begin soon, I think."

"It does not hail in Brimtone?" Leonara had never known a winter without deadly hailstorms that kept her locked in the highcastle for many boring months.

"Maybe it does further south, but here we have some heavy snows usually near winter's end," said Ritra, "but the winds will lift you off your toes some days and make everything cold as ice. That's why it's nice to have the Hall of Hearths."

I could actually be out in the snow, perhaps. Imagine, full winter and being outside. There'd be falling flakes *of snow, I could build snowcastles, build a snow lord and lady to keep it.*

No, stupid, Leonara corrected herself. *High Ladies don't build snow people. Children do.* She shook her head. *But wouldn't it be lovely?*

"Do you enjoy drawing, Leonara?" High Lady Aurel asked.

"Erm—drawing?"

"Or painting. I know some ladies that like to paint flowers or landscapes in their available time. Lady Snurer's drawings are rather beautiful, the few I have seen. She designs dresses this way, too, for her dressmaker. I have asked her to design my next gown, in fact."

"No, I don't paint gowns, my High Lady."

"Nor do I. I ask to learn more of you. I see you reading much about the highcastle, and I am trying to discover what else it is you do. Do you enjoy music?"

"Yes, I do."

"Isn't our Tiptoe delightful? Singers come and go, but we keep our Tiptoe here. He was my father's fool before coming to Daggerlone, my lovely dowr fool. Do you play the harp, perhaps?"

"No," she answered. "I mean, he is delightful, but I do not play any instrument well. I wanted to learn when I was young, but my mother did not like the sound of the harp, and my father told me my time could be spent learning more valuable things."

"Your mother did not like the harp?"

"She preferred Island stringed-instruments like the sijern. She could play it very well, actually. Only my father said it sounded like whining metal."

Aurel smiled. "I also wanted to learn music when I was young, but my ears aren't for it, my fingers better with needles, and Ritra had no interest in it. She's deaf for song, an uncommonly bad voice, unfortunately. There are many harpers that come through here. Perhaps one could instruct us all. You, Ritra and me."

"You learn to play songs and entertain?" Gilgar looked up from his plate. "Hahgh!"

"You're never too old to learn something new, my love."

"I don't care to learn," said Ritra.

Aurel laughed. "I expected that of you. I'll learn to play your favorites, dear, and we'll have no use of Tiptoe."

Light bells jingled toward them.

"What I hear?" the fool said. "Pray, ask of me a song or say, a game to play, a dance or mock spelling, whichever you prefer, to prove I am worthy of my place at your Dwelling."

He is someone's ear, Leonara thought. *Who could employ him? Probably the High Lady, he is her childhood fool, though it could be anyone. I don't know enough yet to be suspecting.*

"Oh, do say the happy story of Caeth's first trial in his quest," requested Ritra. "No more than that, though. His later trials are not so light of heart and you do them so sadly."

So, Tiptoe did merrily, dancing when he spoke as Hetten in the heavens commanding, strumming his lyre and acting out with kicking legs Caeth coming against the sea monster.

And then he finished his rhyme to sing a song Leonara had never heard, one about a lord's bastard-turned-pirate who fell for a Lady of the Pearls and ran away to the Forsaken West with her. It was vulgar and more for the men along the hall than anyone. Leonara liked it better than anything to do with Caeth, and could not help but think Mittrik would laugh at the verses.

"A Fair Island song for you, Lady Hwaelin?" Tiptoe asked when he finished.

"Do you know any?"

"I should, I was born on the Isle to a band of Fair singers," he said. "Do *you* know any?"

Leonara and the fool stared into each other. *Can he not lie? Is that what he means to tell me? He is unable if he was born on the Isle. Even this could be a lie. All men are liars. Maisie said not to trust him, she said he spied on me, but she does not know of triewthblood. He could belong to Aurel Gilgar, but he might be my uncle's ear. Or one of my mother's, or—*

"I prefer something of the Mainland, Tiptoe," said High Lord Gilgar. "None with words for now. I would like to hear my guest's voices in conversation."

Leonara couldn't think of it now. She would know for whom he listened. Maisie would find out soon enough.

It was later in the evening, as Maisie was about to help her out of the sleeves of her gown, when one of the High Lady's maids came to Leonara, and the night pronounced itself different from all the others.

"M'lady," the serving girl said. Leonara did not know her name (and was sure she would not learn it) but had seen her walking and working with Rose. She was as young as Leonara, perhaps younger even. "High Lord Gilgar asked for you to meet him and his High Lady in their chambers."

That servant led Leonara there once she adjusted her gown and splashed water on her face. Her room was on the same floor as the grand chambers of the High Lord, just around the corridor. She didn't need to be led.

The door was not opened for her, instead the servant knocked and then left quickly. Leonara only thought it peculiar for a small moment, but then she was asked to enter.

The room was very dark. A four-poster featherbed took up the left wall and much of its center, and High Lady Aurel was in it, half dressed, covering herself with a blue sheet. Gilgar was standing beside his hearth, pouring wine into cups.

High Lady Aurel's shoulders and arms were darkened by blue bruises and swollen bite marks where scabs were fresh and viscid, and on her neck, there were other bruises greening and yellowing into the porcelain shade of her skin. It looked like a small animal had gotten ahold of her, had been with her for days, but Leonara knew the truth. She was not a stupid child. The marks were from the animal of a man who stood in front of her now, who stared at her with a wine stained smile and sweat on his brow.

"Dear girl, come inside and shut the door."

"Cragin," Aurel said, "love, ah— beg you let her leave."

"Shut your mouth or I blood it again."

"Leonara, do go, we swam in wine and—"

"Shut your mouth!" he bellowed over her. Leonara retreated,

but he caught her with his eyes. "Now. Relax, my lady Hwaelin. Let's have you stand by the fire, girl. Get warm. I want words with you."

Leonara closed the door behind her, caging herself with the predator. If this was a dream she wouldn't obey. But in this life, she always did. If she dreamed, she'd turn around, run through the wall, into her father's arms, or her brothers'. She would jump out the window to wake. That's where she looked, out the window to a black and gray night. She avoided Gilgar's hungry glare.

Instead she crossed the room, eyes never acknowledging him, never his wife trembling in her bed.

Leonara saw that Gilgar had taken the golden fox, Queen Leonara's fox, out of her dowr chest and placed it atop his table by the wine, cheeses, and bread. The fox didn't looked right there, but nothing in the room looked right. The pelts of the featherbed disheveled, dust filmed the furnishings, the chamber pot smelled of something foul as if a servant had not cleaned it in a week. The fire that was lit in the hearth barely glowed, the brazier in the corner fed the room with little more light. When she dared look, Cragin's eyes were pure black in the shadows, and his wife's face was fearful and more wrinkled than ever. Over all, the fox's ruby eyes judging with indulgence.

Leonara did as she read in *Subtleties*, and spoke into herself what truth she needed as she stood by the light. *My father needs Gilgar to win his war. That means I need him. If my father tries and fails... if he does not procure the crown, when winter leaves the Raglands for spring, I will surely be killed by the Osburs. I need Cragin Gilgar just as much as my father. I will be a High Lady.*

"Are you feeling well, High Lord Gilgar?" Leonara asked.

"Very well. Very warm. How are you feeling?"

Cold, she thought, as claws of ice scraped down her back, and her skin sweat despite it. "I do feel tired. It is late."

"You're right, it is," he said. "Come here then, girl, let's have a look at you before you go."

He got closer and snatched her face in his meaty fingers. When he spoke, he got so close that she could smell the warm stench of wine on his words, the sweat beneath his clothes. "You are a pretty thing in proper light, aren't you? You'll get better, I hope. Fair looks breed strong, that's for sure. Hair like corn silk, eyes that glow like the songs. Almost. Now let's have a good look," he said, and it was a command somehow. His change of tone, his awful face held a threat, and something in her sank. The sharpest panic, but she told herself to be brave.

To leave.

"High Lord, I'm... very tired. I should return to my chamber. Good Night." She removed herself from his grasp and tried to sound as confident as her mother always had, but she heard her own failure and fear.

He grabbed her again, stroked his hand along the sleeve of her arm and hooked his thumb into where her dress met the collar. He gave it a tug, and a bit of her shoulder exposed.

"No!" she cried out and pushed his hand away. "You can't."

Leonara saw him lean away, for an instant relieved, and then he slapped her.

Her head turned by the force of it, and she stared at the floor. She could hear the sound of his palm against her face even after, was sure she would always remember the sound; her right cheek stung, her jaw was sore, and a distant bell tolled in and out of her ears. Tears came, and she could not stop them. No one had ever struck her. No one dared.

"Don't fight me," he whispered, drawing his whole body closer. "Don't fight, girl, I only mean to have a look at you."

He turned her around harshly and began unlacing the bodice of her dress, mumbling to himself as he did. Words she didn't understand.

Leonara kept looking at the floor, at the tiny wet spots where her tears fell on the wood. He jerked her waist, her collar fell, and he reached around her. A sound came out her mouth as his hand cupped her chest over the gown, and it sounded distant to her own ears. She tried to speak again, for fear that if she didn't, her voice may go and naught return. *I might scream. I should. Baynard will come.*

She inhaled, and then she heard two deep *dud-thuds*. Leonara turned to see Gilgar crumble to her feet with a clattering. Above his body, High Lady Gilgar stood, and in her shaking hands, the golden fox, paw dripping blood scarlet as its ruby eyes.

Sour remnants of supper flooded Leonara's mouth. She held her throat taut and kept everything down, and she held her breath in anxious waiting. Sure he would rise any second. But he remained face down.

He'll get up and kill us both. It would be too perfect for him to die now, life is never perfect. The Sisters make it so.

She stared and breathed through her nose. The air smelt like the light metal of blood. She could almost taste it on her tongue. Gilgar lay on his stomach, eyes closed, and his blood was beginning its trail across the dark wood beneath his head, puddling around to look like a crimson pillow. She watched as the rise and fall of his back slowed, then stopped, and the fabric of his underclothes dampened to a darker gray.

High Lady Gilgar moved Leonara's hair from her back to tie up her laces. Aurel was breathing heavily. Her breath smelled like the mustard and the honeyed wine. Leonara felt paralyzed. *Could she really have killed him? Could he be dead? He couldn't... She couldn't have. It's too easy. Or not easy at all, one of us will hang for this. I will hang for this.* Me, *not the Dominion's High Lady.*

"Do not speak a word to anyone until I come for you, do you understand me?"

Leonara stared on at High Lord Gilgar, and now it smelled of blood and piss, mustard and bile, and she realized the fat man was truly dead. Mittrik had told her that in battle men shat themselves when they died, and she had told him he had never seen a battle and wouldn't know. *Could he—*

"Leonara! Do you understand?" the High Lady asked louder, and this time she lifted Leonara's chin, and that did startle her.

"I—yes, I do," she said.

"Go to your chambers and bar your door. Only open it for me. Go!"

Leonara ran out of the room, turning the corner again, bumping into the wall. She ran the corridor and barreled straight into Sir Baynard before she finally took in a breath.

"My lady, are you well?" Sir Baynard asked, taking in her teary face, her gasping, the tousled state of her collar and hair.

She ignored him, pushed past him to run into her chamber, shutting and barring herself therein. Her knees gave out, and she leaned her back against the rough wood of the door. Her hands hid her face. She realized her mouth was bleeding. *From where he hit me. He's dead.*

"My lady?" Sir Baynard called, pounding the door hard, and it shook the wooden boards against her head. "Leonara?"

She couldn't answer. She could cry and clutch her knees. She could think over and over with every jolt of Baynard's knocking, *What do I do? What do I do?*

"Why are you crying?" Ritra asked from a wall of shadow.

Part 4
Canyassor II

translated from the Second Book of Amina XXIII.1-5

"There is no wisdom in [truelight], only unbridled power. Wisdom is somewhere else, and I wonder if wisdom is what the vines seek as they collide. 'I do not have it,' I tell the vines, but it could be out there amidst the People. Maybe what [truelight] seeks is not here, with us. Maybe we are just one Rock of many more, and our Rock finds itself cursed for unbalanced nature. Maybe [truelight] seeks nothing. Maybe there is no curse, and that would be my joy. If only there is [truelight] and [void], but I am without that other and can see the bright above the rest. What relief a shadow might be, but what pain, too. Pain regardless, whether the shadows come or not. I ask only God, 'For whom do I pray, for myself or my brother? Do I pray for his salvation or for my peace at the end?'

12. A DECISION OF SELECTION

Bakéz waited before the black window in the room of the mapped floor, a dark cast likeness of himself looking back from the opaque square. On the other side of the window was the blue sky, but no color filtered through. He was waiting to speak with the Masters of Ku'du. Across the Sweet Sea, in Ku'du's capital of Shul Rahga, there was a great meeting hall and a black window that was four times the height of any giant. There, the Ku'dur Masters would convene and all would place their blood against the glass and call out to this specific black window.

As a member of the ruling family, blood ritual was forbidden as ordained by First-One. Though the connection made through a black window was not quite a blood pact, it was close enough for the devout. So, Bakéz waited for the Ku'dur to make the connection with their own blood, untempted to give up his own. So much of ruling is waiting, that was what Zyonhir would tell him. Bakéz would not consider himself largely known for his impatience but when few knew, the Rock did.

Whether black glass was true magic or not, he was intentionally unsure, and mostly didn't care. His ancestors legalized black windows in the Blessed Lands in the first turns of their rule. If he started questioning older policies of Teviona, so would the whole Rock.

An image pieced together on the black window, and Bakéz stood ready as all ten Ku'dur Great Masters became clear and colorful. *Ten Masters. They've already replaced Sus'Laki.*

They all bowed with the same stiff movement. Unison. Ku'dur, like Eerim, needn't speak to communicate, but spoke in the Blessed way for the meeting.

"Tyanien Bakéz," said one of the Masters. "Bliss upon you."

"Bliss upon you all," Bakéz greeted. "I am glad that we are all here in good health today. The warriors tasked with entering the Wilder—"

"First this news of the Hwaelin brothers' last inquiry, I think," interrupted the only female Master. "Truly, am I to believe neither of them knew about this assassination plot? Not one thought prior to this attack is incriminating? That there was no magical practice before their excursion to Canyassor?"

According to Zyonhir, Bakéz must believe just that. They were put to inquiry and their answers found them guiltless. "You can't expect a possessed Biler to fight enchantment," he argued. "All we can do is send them back to Baeltaf. Your council has already agreed-"

But obviously this Master dissented. "Do you have a good reason that they are still in Talosa today then? Free? And Mittrik Hwaelin? Left unenchanted, is he so ignorant as well? Or are they smarter than your inquirer's questions?"

"I needn't remind you, your ancient council put forth the questions, good Master." *Tyanien shouldn't have to call anyone their Master.* But politics was a charade of tradition. "We don't kill people who commit crimes while under enchantment. Not in the Blessed Lands."

"We did agree to send them back to Baeltaf, and to ban their return," said another Ku'dur Master, in a distinguishingly pleasant tone. They all looked too similar, copies of the other, with their private eyes veiled and their uniform horn shape. "On sadder news, your mission into the Wilder Wood is being declared a failure. The war is over. Your war is over, and most Radicals are gone, thank the Mother. The ones left on this side of the trees will be dug up, I trust. The ones who left...We don't know where they ran and won't unless we ourselves follow. The Wilder Wood has them all now."

"Has even one of your warriors returned?"

"No one has returned, Tyanien Bakéz. No Radicals, no Ku'dur, lost like any other that dare try cross the Wilder Wood, I'm afraid," said one of the Great Masters who attended Tyonar's union celebration. Who witnessed his fellow Master murdered. "A loss expected yet no less tragic."

"I am sorrowful to hear it," Bakéz said. He suspected the Masters of Sus'Laki's murder, but for a moment.

He crushed the thought.

Cursed himself, and thought of what he should. Only his duty. He remained present in the meeting. With the news that over one thousand Radicals managed to flee into the Wilder Wood.

Dead Radicals would soothe, and now he could only hope the strange stories from the other side were true. Not many otherkind could survive beyond the Wood, if any kind at all. "Thank you for the time the Great Council has spared to speak with me and inform me of the mission."

"There is more, however, that we shall speak of, good Tyanien," said the Ku'dur at the center, who had replaced the Pretender's father.

"Tidings of a truly hideous nature have reached us, Tyanien Bakéz," said one with a deep voice, one who had lived three hundred turns and served on the Great Council for over over one hundred. “We have been told that there are better ears listening for the Blessed Lands in three Dominions of the Biler lands, and that these ears have allegiances to the Teviona family.”

It was a crime against the Civil Accords and against the Treaty of the Separation. If it were true… But it wasn’t. Bakéz looked to the crop of judging eyes.

“This cannot be, I assure you.”

“Certainly, we do not give merit to such flagrantly fabricated rumors.” The Master's tone said otherwise. “We only wished to inform you they exist.”

In this world of eyes and ears, rumors were weapons, calumniate in some cases good as killing. It was not true, though. Bakéz would know of such a thing. He kept eye contact with them all as well as he could, thinking, *And how do you people know? Where did this false truth begin?* He was thankful that his thoughts were his own, alone in this room. *Clearly they have ears listening beyond the Line of Separation, like every other western realm. But I can’t just accuse the Great Ku’dur of breaking law. Their truths will be clean as the river, and I’ll look the fool.*

“Thank you for bringing such reports to my attention, good Masters. I assure you, this is all some kind of farce. The Blessed Lands have always been open and have never dealt in secret surveillance.”

“Yes, of course, Tyanien Bakéz,” said the woman. “If other rumors of such a nature come to us, we will be sure to inform you.”

“Thank you,” Bakéz said again, but he hated to do it. This woman did not believe him either, her upturned lip made that clear. “And thank you all for the time spent in meeting with me.”

“Until the next, good Tyanien,” said one Master, then all the Great Masters bowed and said the same.

Slowly the row of Ku’dur faded and Bakéz was left staring at himself again, frowning.

Zyonhir came to eat second foods with him as per their routine, but Bakéz no longer felt hunger.

"I spoke with the Great Ku'dur Masters this morning," he said after his brother ate most of his fruit and bread.

"Did that go well? Are Ku'dur on their march home with the escaped Radicals?" Zyonhir had never held out hope.

"No, they are lost to magical trees, of course. It was a miserable meeting. The Great Masters had much to say, or rather much to accuse us of," Bakéz said, fidgeting about the table of fruit and breads and grains, trying to gain an appetite. "They heard that we have ears listening for us in three Biler Dominions."

Zyon nodded. "Five."

"What do you mean 'five'? You don't deny it?"

"No, that would be pointless. Everyone will know soon enough. A treaty was signed with the Prince of Mennu Zepey. The ears officially belong to the Eerim secret service and Mennu, though the Blessed Lands are funding most of their mission. It is our objective they follow, through Mennu's laws of surveillance, and one of the Eerim spies *is* born on Blessed soil so someone must answer to us."

"Zyonhir, how could you do this thing now, after CoБmak and before we have even taken our place?"

"It is the perfect time for it, actually."

"It is illegal," said he, the older. The leader. "People are entitled to privacy, that is in the Law."

"Yes, but since what is considered *private* changes with every passing reign, it isn't a very good word. No one knows what privacy is supposed to look like. The Law works to keep faith between peoples, between them and the governance, and in these days no one has faith in privacy, brother. They trust that we will keep them safe from hunger and war and disease. They do not trust conjured illusions of secrecy. Anything else is a lie. Anything can be discovered and anything fabricated. So, why must we keep up this pretense?"

"The Law, brother."

"Yes, the Law. I will speak to that, but are you not a little curious about what the better ears have heard beyond the Line of Separation?"

Bakéz tried to control his anger. "Of course, I am. But shouldn't at least my truths be clean?"

"The father of these Biler lords is beginning his campaign across their midlands, we knew, but has signed a betrothal contract for his younger daughter. Rooj Rhinere knows it and is planning to go against the Civil Accords by not reporting the child's marriage. The girl was born in Waterhaven and is not yet fourteen."

"That girl is a daughter of a Biler lord. We have no jurisdiction. The Civil Accords mean nothing to Bilers, they did not sign them and know nothing of them."

"But to Rooj, to the Fair People? The girl was born on the Fair Isle, and therefore is afforded every right the Accords guarantee. Her mother was wise to give birth to her daughter there. It ensures that she cannot be forced into a marriage and cannot be married at all before the age of seventeen. Despite all this, it seems Rooj Rhinere, or perhaps more accurately his son, has supported the marriage and has sent gifts of silver and salt. We now send inquirers to the Fair Isle with these Hwaelins, and then we can also get to the truth of this matter with the Hasyal in Rooj Tisinda's letter."

It was an excuse, Bakéz realized, to send a child of Amina and ask the right questions. "Rooj Rhinere broke the Accords once with his own daughter, and that was swept under the tide easily enough. You think this time it shall be any different? Do you think Rooj Rhion will be any more reasonable of a man?"

"I do, for a few reasons." Zyonhir's calm was more destructive than Bakéz' anger.

"Zyonhir, you are not stupid. We cannot make waves in Baeltaf and tear down their traditions, their marriages and laws of contract. Opposing Fair Isle is not how we will start my rule."

"It is the Fair Isle who have wronged. With them, this

game is played if the Line of Separation stays intact. I have no interest in starting anything with Bilers. We have too much food on the plate as it is."

"So," said Bakéz most wearily, "we have better ears in the Biler lands, and you think the Rooj will not see us playing this game dirty. How can we be so hypocritical to attack another continent's laws and culture when we cannot even adhere to our own?"

His brother smirked. "The Rooj won't make trouble about these ears. They can't have clean truths now, they've worked across the Line for centuries. Marrying little girls away to garner support is not their tradition, it is a crime. This Biler girl is barely older than Janila, Kez. These men are vile, and it would be blessed to kill them. For self-serving men like Bilers, this is a crime that is too easy to commit, but unfortunately starting war with the lords of Baeltaf, or the Rooj, is not my intention. The girl's betrothal only exists because the young Hwaelin lords have gone missing and are thought dead. With their return, the older will marry High Lord Gilgar's only daughter and that will be the end of it. The girl will be set free from contract."

The city became louder in Bakéz' ears, his brother's voice distant.

"Are you so sure?"

Zyonhir kept eating. "It was the original agreement between the Lords of Kieln and Brimtone. Cragin Gilgar would prefer his only daughter to be a queen, and for her son to be a king, rather than be married to a child."

Bakéz regarded his younger brother carefully. "A child he believes comes with the richest lands in all Baeltaf if her brothers are dead, the only relation of a man who plans to make himself king. She may be the best available conquest in their kingdom, and as much as we joke, the High Lords of Baeltaf are not all idiots."

"Yes, but the Hwaelin brothers are not dead. They are here. They will leave as I arranged it."

"They were supposed to leave yesterday, little brother," Bakéz said, forcing calm. "We will not have ears listening for us in the Biler lands. This is a terrible thing you have done to me. Worse yet, to send them to a place where the existence of better hearing is forgotten and unknown? How can a Biler fight otherkind? Jonn Hwaelin got away with *murder* with that same excuse. Our enemies will surely use this against us. It goes against what these lands were built upon: integrity and openness. The Blessed Lands, and every leading family that has ruled have made oaths of honest politics and open minds. We have made oaths not to spy in secret on any! Not to sign secret treaties! *They hate me already!*"

Zyonhir blinked. "They don't all hate you. Other leading families have broken oaths without consequence, the Jarey certainly and every one before them. The hawks left this palace covered in their shit and we Teviona are still cleaning, but we will not be judged like them. Judgement will be on our side. We must peck with our own beaks until then, sadly. Everything I have done is in the records, but has been well hidden."

"Zyonhir, tell me you lie. This will ruin us before I am cloaked."

"Maybe I lie. Try not to think about it. Think that this is how politics has always been navigated between otherkind. And if it is true, it is my mistake alone, and perhaps father's. He os filled with pain draughts and may not be aware what he signs, but is too proud to give up his cloak. It took little from me. He trusts me too well, but my truths will hold in court, I promise you. Therefore, I did it before your cloaking, brother, so you could be exculpated, and your truths are still clean. In time this will be brought to light, of course it will, but I believe in my decisions. This is for the good of the Blessed Lands. Your position cannot be taken from you, and you determine mine. This is not a mistake, I tell you. And maybe I lie. Nasty habit of mine."

"This is not the Blessed way."

Zyonhir scoffed at him. "Every other nation has ears

listening and spies operating beneath available truths. Why are we the only ones held to such a standard of transparency? We, Teviona, are left deaf while any Confederate can buy a cheap ear. How is that just? You must believe in a God that ordains such nonsense. I must do what is best for us."

Justice, Honor, Loyalty. These were the words of Riambo. Bakéz' could feel his white hot anger glowing, because they could not do this and use the words of their mother's blood as reason, and Bakéz could not excuse it as the future Great Leader; but Malak came in then with such perfect timing, easy smile on his face; and he realized his younger brother must have been waiting outside the door. Listening.

"You sent for me, brothers?" Malak said, all too cheerful.

"I did," said Zyon, eyeing their brother with unguarded suspicion. "What were you doing yesterday? The day before?"

Malak shrugged and continued smiling in his dimpled way, like his mother, and Bakéz watched Zyon fight frustration. Zyonhir envied Aadarae; he often said that he wished he could get truth out of all their siblings without effort.

"Well, I could question you about what you weren't doing," Zyon continued, standing to face Malak. Malak was taller, with their father's broad build; his heavy arms declared him a warrior. Zyon's arms declared him a scholar, but he was always the more intimidating. It was his golden eyes, Bakéz thought. "I won't ask because I already know what you weren't doing. You weren't watching the Bilers in their cells, you were parading them about Talosa. After Jonn Hwaelin murdered a Ku'dur Lord."

"The Pretender's father, I know. I was there. Was I supposed to rot in the dungeon with them?" He made a worried face. "My mistake."

"Malak, enough," said Zyonhir. "You were supposed to arrange their flight home days ago. As soon as the Ku'dur Council gave permission. What was more important than following orders?"

Obviously their younger brother resented Zyon's choice of

words; his face pinched, and his eyes were then critical. "I did not realize you ordered me. You proposed it to me like a request."

Zyonhir laughed. "It does not matter." He turned from them to stand beside the windows. "I am sending you to Sharann to meet with the royal parliament that is convening a people's court. You are the only Tyanien that hasn't met with them. Show your support, give a gift to the royal family, parliament, and to the commons. Don't think of Janseyu's disgrace. Then, when that is done, you go to Iri. You are good at talking to Eerim, so talk down the price of tariffs."

"Sending me away, so soon before Rae's Selection?"

"You will return to see her union, Malak," Bakéz reassured him. "Do this and do not complain. Our father agreed that you should go. It is not a request."

Malak nodded, and looked to Zyonhir, stared a moment too long. He turned and stomped out of the room. All Teviona, even his own children, looked the same when they did that. Spoiled palace brats. Himself included. Zyon sat back in his chair, unperturbed.

Malak had always been hot-tempered, but had grown contemptuous since Coбmak. The loss of his dearest friend, Bakéz' own cousin, Riambo Rajen, affected him more than he let on. Rumor had been Malak and Rajen were lovers. Bakéz didn't know his brother's truth. Malak proved angriest with the decision to send Aadarae and Pyaren to the Southern Wilder Tower to kill Laki. Because of that decision, Pyaren lost a leg and Rae lost... everything.

"I know I agreed to send him, but I wish we could try to make our siblings happy in our limited power," said Bakéz.

"If you still think we have the power to make anyone happy, you are a stupid man."

I might be, only because I must be, he thought, mind of Blessed People, conscious of the golden look of planning that burned in his brother's eyes.

And resolved not to think of it again.

The Select Son of Leu called Teia to a meeting in the Academy before training that day.

His name was Select Hésof Inyalo, the oldest judge on the Select Council. He was well studied in the energy of waters; he wrote the book on its molecular structure after the advent of microscopes strong enough to see water hearts. He was intelligent, cold, and walked like he was born to the position of Select Son, but he was very old, beginning to hunch with his stepping. He was a proud man, and while he tried to hide it, Teia noticed how the pulse of his lifewater was weaker than when she was a girl. His arms were thin, and it was obvious it had been many turns since the man tried to wield anything larger than a wave upon sand. A descendant of Leu born by the tribe of her fifth son, Esiel, and all children of Leu were stronger than the other wielders, but the man had let his muscles turn soft within him.

To Teia, the man was a reminder to never turn soft, to always push her sixth sense even in her fading years. She would be like the first Seawoman that way. She would always be able to command a sea. She'd be gray and strong.

More than all that, Select Hésof was an annoyance. He was a judge, sure, but he liked judging Teia far too much. Her position in the palace as ward of Great Leader Iial made her life feel like an unending trial, three thanks to Hésof.

"Select Son," Teia said calmly, three times beating clenched fist over heart, and he turned to look at her with keen, dark eyes. She avoided those eyes and looked instead to the stone of Leu on his circlet. "I hope you are well, Master."

"I am trying to be, as we all are always. You did take your time sweetly in coming to me."

"Look out a window, Master, and see I am here just before dawn. I hope this is not a long discussion. I do not want to intrude on your first prayers."

"I am thinking of Selecting you," he said, taking her in with a scrutinizing up and down. "The Selection is fast approaching, and I have been indecisive for some time, but no longer. You are my first choice, Leuanien Teiabel."

Her heart dropped and her lifewater flooded with a feeling like liquid fire. "Why?"

He kept silent for far too long, and the iciness in her lifewater overtook the fire and hardened that resentment she always carried for the man.

"Tell me why, Master."

He nodded. "It has been three cycles of Selections since one with direct descendance to the Leuanien clan has been appointed to the Council. Your name has weight in these times."

"I am not the only Leuanien at the Academy. There are at least a dozen others with direct descendance and the Leuanien name. Two, my own family. What of Cata?" *Who hates me*, Teia thought, *best not have her on the Select Council where she would be in charge of my fate.* "Or better Danitza. She has the right temperament for it. She wants it."

"It is an honor to be Selected, child. And you are just a child, remember."

Teia dipped her head. She was not the right choice. Her cousins were both older, both had come to the academy from Leurai. They saw Teia as a rival, despite her attempts to convince them otherwise, and both women lived to be demonstrated before the masters and before the Select, to prove their worth when the time came. They'd forgone marriage for the chance. *They might hate me forever if I am Selected now without ever having worked for it.*

She looked up to the robed man, and again focused on the gem instead of his small watery, black eyes.

"I do not understand why you would choose a child, Master. I have never chosen to study judgement, law, or politics for the purpose of not being Selected. I am unfit and unprepared." Teia also hated the idea, but this she would not tell the elder.

"Am I not residing Select Son over all descendants of Leu? Do you think I am unaware of what you chose to study?"

Teia looked to her feet again and tried not to clench her teeth together when she spoke. "You have made it very clear that you are aware of everything that I do, and you have often told me how much you disapprove of my actions and general behavior. It makes me wonder why you would think I can make an appropriate Select Daughter for our people. Will you tell me, or shall I read your reason in the illegal papers?"

His face was solemn and hard, and then shifted into something pensive and softer, so much softer it was startling. She had not thought Select Son Hesof had a soft face, only soft muscles, but there it was imploring her with tenderness.

"Tyanien Aadarae needs friends where she can find them if she is to make real change on the Rock," he said. "And you know more about the nature of the waters than I think even you realize. You are consistent, aggressive, though you yield when you must. You follow your path willingly, diverge where you can, and when rain comes, and you are tested you never fail to take control. You are steadfast to your own person most of all— just as the sea, just as the first Seawoman from whom we descend."

He is complimenting me with such sincerity. Quite a shock. *Can I argue with him*? She tried to think of a way she could. Any way. She stood there scrambling for words in awkward, angry silence. *Nothing, I have nothing. If Rae is Selected, so must I be.*

"It is an honor to be considered," he said to her silence.

"Thank you for such an honor," Teia was able to say, but nothing more.

The Select Son put his weak hand on her shoulder. "You will be great someday."

I am already, Teia thought. *I was made for greatness like the seas, born into it. I am descended from great captains. That is who I am. Not a judge, to be judged. Never this.*

She left in a haste, trying to find rhythm in her breathing, something normal and constant, but her breath was choking her. She went to the private training hall that Rae used, knowing she would find her there at this hour.

Rae was working on strength training already, hanging on the climbing bar beside the eastern wall. Her form was a welcome sight to Teia. Rae used her weight to pull herself up the wall, to remove the horizontal bar from its notch and throw herself higher, the bar clanking into the higher notch, and so on she went until she was at the top. When she reached the highest level, she pulled herself up to straddle the bar and look down at Teia.

"My muscles are already tired, but I still want to fight today. I have anxiety to expend," Rae said, and Teia nodded. Rae was always anxious.

Teia breathed deeply as she walked across the floor and began stretching her arms and wrists, focusing on a faint tug in her sense from the rushing aqueduct across the room and readying herself for the fight. When Rae truly saw her, the smile on her face vanished, and she dropped to the floor with a spark at her bare feet.

"Do you want to talk or train... or anything else? We can sneak into the city to have a drink. Three-One knows I could drink."

"I want to train," Teia answered decidedly.

So, Rae put on her sandals, because she hated fighting with bare feet and claimed the feeling of truelight in her bare soles ached too much, and they stood on either side of the room, preparing themselves for their game of battle.

Teia used three stiff limbs to bend water, her right foot balancing her, her muscles tightening and burning out her concerns. She focused on *du*, beyond herself.

Not a drop would spill from her grasp today.

It was all but impossible to fight against Rae's manipulation of truelight; water could not block it or disrupt its path, neither could air or ground or flames. It sliced through all matter, unnatural as it was. Most of Teia's energy wasted dodging and jumping, her game offensive only when Rae let it be. When Rae gave truelight purpose to heal, it numbed Teia. When Rae gave it purpose to harm, it burned.

Teia had been giving it her all, but was astounded at the whoosh in her heart as her sense picked up those two small drops across the floor. Rae's blood. *No, that's not right.*

It was. *Du* never lied. Rae touched her bloody lip and Teia closed her eyes. *What's wrong with her?* She hadn't given up her lifewater to an opponent since the war.

"What was that?" Teia asked, not looking but *feeling* the deeply split skin and blood of Rae's torn lip.

Rae lifted her hand, Teia opened her eyes, and a glow blocked the lower half of her face from sight. When Rae withdrew truelight, the only evidence she had been injured was the blood on her fingertips. She retreated toward the western wall, the exit door.

"Distracted," she said.

"Yes, us both," said Teia.

"I need to rest. Will you give me time?"

"And anything. I will wait here." She kept shock and worry out of her voice but wondered if it was evident in her eyes; Rae hesitated before turning out into the corridor.

Left alone, Teia decided she'd throw daggers at a straw dummy that she imagined as the Select Son of Leu, as the dark haired Biler, as Sfar'Laki. She thought that would make her feel better, but didn't like the idea of an Eerim hearing her thoughts if one happened outside the open door.

She threw the first dagger and realized as soon as it left her hand that it would land too low on the target. She reached out to the stone of Leu that edged the blade, felt it connect with her like a hook pulling at her skin, just like du. Her hands warm to it, and compelled the dagger to change course. The blue tip raised and it stuck dead in the center of the straw man's chest, the second dagger lodged beneath the first. It did not change her mood; she still felt bitter and heartbroken.

Teia never wanted to be anything other than Captain of a great ship, or better to be placed before a whole fleet to command, like her mother and her grandmother and so many foremothers. She wanted to find and chart seas and only be at land when she had to be. She would never be granted that as a Select judge. She would not be permitted anything for herself. A thought would never be her own again, living to rethink the thoughts of judges passed.

And so Teia took her time alone to dance with water like the blind dancer from the union day, or as close as she could get because she wouldn't ever be a true dancer. She was a warrior.

But she loved dancing like all else she could not have. Too much, not enough.

With so much desperation it hurt.

She put all her anger into the flow from her arms and outward into the energy, and she felt each individual water heart thrum and kindle her feeling, moving rapidly, heating, and then, just as Teia breathed in and tensed all her frustration, the water hearts froze to ice, expanded solid and held their near crystal form, interlocking like the rigid bonds of stone. She exhaled, and the water came to life again, fluid and cold, swirling above her with the curling motion of her wrist. She heaved the water above her head, and her arms shook with the weight, the pressure of release flooding her blood.

Rae talked quietly to herself when she returned to the training hall, carrying three large books, two considerably older and bound in simple hide, the other of thick woven Canyai make and adornment; several long, rolled maps were clenched between neck and shoulder, almost falling from her arms. Teia stopped dancing and became curious. She drew up ten Standard pounds of water to her from the nearest vat, wove it above her in ten fingers.

"What do you have there?"

Rae said, "So much, and you might think I am insane. The scientists used to say it, and I could be proving them right. Come and see."

"Are you ready to go again?" Teia asked, flicking five little droplets onto Rae's face, making sure to not get any old papers wet.

"I am done fighting, come look at this now."

Teia dropped the water back into the vat and walked toward the weapons display where Rae was dropping her large maps and scrolls. She was speaking before Teia got there.

"One of the scrolls in this last Eastern tome mentioned a binding of papers that was found in what was left of the Rising Wood, and it was taken to the Biler king in the year 8564, well, at least by my best estimate. Some man named Sir Balamy of House Redcreed found it during the last excursion into the newly blackened trees, and took it to the Glittering Temple in the Bones of High Baeltaf," Rae rattled off as she opened the Eastern binding onto a table of daggers and carefully flipped through the pages. She pointed to a brown, near crumbling page. "That house has since achieved Higher status in their lands, but that is not my point. Here, it mentions *The Sinners' Almanac and Verse* that Sir Balamy found and here, in this song by a traveling court performer, it calls something the *Witches' Works* and says the words brought 'the great heavy black' to the realm's lungs and heart. I am thinking it refers to the same writings."

"Sinners' Almanac… As in the Saints of the Rising Wood? As in their book?" Teia liked history better than most subjects she had to study, and had read of the group of Tachirka rebels that had lasted in the Rising trees after the Separation. They had waited and then made sacrifice to strike the Biler lands with an unholiest of plagues. Those great killing spells had roamed the east for nearing ten years of death and rot, both people and crop fields wiped out and later scorched. The Tachirka's plagues rivaled even Sfar'Laki's dreaded death smoke. Teia was surprised to hear that Bilers got their hands on it.

Rae nodded, a contagious excitement in her eyes. "Most likely, I think. If the book gives a detailed script for a plague pattern like that, it might give us some idea how to help my father, how the plague might be affecting his organs."

"So, will you go to the great temple of the Biler lands to find it?" Teia smiled, and turned to open the largest of the maps, a detailed image of the Biler kingdom and all the great landmarks and dwellings were drawn by a Fair Islander, a man who signed his name below as M Beii. A powerful family name on the Fair Isle.

Teia ran a hand across the gray color of the Bitter Sea as it led to the shores of the east. *Yes, yes. Three-One, in all, please guide her there. Save me. Design her path with consideration of me.* She looked at Rae. She may have needed a push, and Teia was ready to give it. "Please tell me that is our plan, Tyanien. You mean to get this book."

"Bakéz and Zyon will insist I send someone in my place. This Selection is important for them and their rule."

"You said it, it is your place to get this book. I am sure they will suggest you stay. It didn't go well the last time they insisted you do something, though. You are a Tyanien just as much as any of your siblings, a better one if you would ask me, Aadarae. They cannot command you in anything yet. This is the time for action and autonomy before they are above you. Though I see your face looking to me, it shows you have already decided what you will do."

"I think I have."

"You dare listen to them again? After they failed you?" It might have been a biting question, but Teia did not care now. Someone must speak truth about her brothers' failings as leaders, someone must give Rae the courage to make her own choice for her life. Since the time Teia first met Aadarae, when she came to Talosa to be the Great Leader's ward during her mother's voyage, Teia had listened to the youngest daughter speak of being a covert healer like it was the greatest dream imaginable. They had been so young then.

Rae never wanted a crown on her head; she wanted a commoner's shawl, long, heavy skirts and a corset so she could heal in secret throughout Dominions abandoned. And perhaps Fehatsi would insist that such desires remain dreams, but Teia thought Rae deserved better than that. *I deserve better than that,* she couldn't help but think.

Rae released her raw lip in her contemplations, and there was a decision in her posture. "No. I mean, I don't think so, I don't think I can. I don't want to be Selected, but it is more than that. I just… I have a terrible feeling about it. Feha said it would go away, but it won't. I don't think I am meant to be Selected. I think that is wrong."

"So, what will you do?"

"What I must. I will go east."

"And I go with you, of course," Teia said, placing a hand atop Rae's glowing one. Her lifewater felt like the fierce sizzle of oil in a pan, and Teia's heart leapt.

Three-One thank you, thank you, thank you, she exalted silently. *Neither of us will wear thin metal crowns so heavy and labor our lives under scrutiny and congresses. And even if the spellers' book is not in the Biler worship house, we will not be here to see the sacrifice or the shocked faces of the people in our own. We will not be seen by them. I could cry for this happiness. I wonder what Fehatsi's face will look like when we tell her.*

"Of course, you will go with me," Rae gave back, drawing in less truelight, but still she could not contain it all, and her eyes poured over the map with such hunger. There was not truelight in her eyes, but there was fire.

Passion.

"My lyaren, my friends," Teia's head snapped when she heard Fehatsi from the outer hall.

"We are here!" Rae called back.

Fehatsi looked annoyed when she came into the room, and Teia thought it was rather early to be so annoyed, even for her. It was not as though *she* was woken early to be told that she would have all her dreams taken away and be Selected for a lifetime of public service.

"Happy afternoon, how were lessons, they were fine, you trained hard, Master Paserín cracked the whip, alright. Now," Fehatsi said, coming to stand before them. "I must speak plainly. I am unhappy that these Bilers have been walking around the palace freely these past eight days. As if they are not suspected criminals. As if Jonn Hwaelin didn't kill someone. Malak took them down to the animal houses the day after the union, and they have gone to Ashakai's Mouth and to the station of the trains. Tourism! How does that happen? I thought they were to leave after the union. Next, someone will tell me they are extending their time here to see the Selection."

Rae was still eyeing the scrolls on the weapon table, and did not look like she was listening. "I don't know," she said. "It must be an oversight. Bakéz and Zyon have much happening."

Too many oversights on their end, constant oversights, but at least this time it could not end in the death of thousands, Teia thought. *Just one Ku'dur Master.* "I am confused," she said to Fehatsi. "Do you want Rae to spend time with the Bilers, or no? She stays at a distance by your orders."

"By my advice," Fehatsi corrected and huffed. "These men are foreigners, and they are Rooj still despite the rest. Rooj are good at keeping their truths clean while moving the pieces. They have little other choice, and Fair blood is ambitious. Rooj rises, that is what they have engraved in every stone. These men do not have to have intent or knowledgeable thought to be part of a Fair Island scheme. The Rooj are likely using them for something."

"Fair People are not so much smarter than us. Your prejudices limit you, Feha," Teia said.

"Worse, they limit others," Rae added, flipping through another set of flattened, bound scrolls.

Fehatsi sighed and clasped her small hands in front of her. "Yes, that is my meaning. I want to limit the Bilers, where they can go and what they can do. We should limit them all the way back across the Line until Bakéz opens borders. If he does. It is past an appropriate time for the Biler's return."

"I agree with you," Rae said, looking up and smiling so brightly. "It is time for them to return to Baeltaf, and I intend to go with them."

Fehatsi did not disappoint, there it was: that shocked, horrified expression. And, yes, the stuttering. Teia could not help but chuckle. She contained it quickly enough, for her younger friend seemed lacking for air, her mouth closing and opening as she decided upon which emotion to settle. After several intentional breaths, Fehatsi chose anger.

"Teviona, be serious! What could you mean? Are you using sarcasm now?" Fehatsi asked, although she knew that Rae hated sarcasm—or rather knew Rae was very bad at it, which was one and the same for the youngest Tyanien, who could do most things easily.

Rae said, "No. I am going east to the Biler lands. More specifically, I am going to the great temple at their capital to steal an ancient speller's book that might contain the script for the Biler Plagues of 8554."

"No." Fehatsi shook her head violently, the many thin coils of her hair whipping her brow. "No. No, you are not abandoning the Selection to travel east, and no, you are not going to ruin any chance of peace between Baeltaf and the Blessed Lands by sneaking into and stealing from their holiest temple. No!"

Rae nodded, and though her face was sad, her voice was sure. "I will not be Selected, and I will be going to the Biler lands to do all that. Sneaking and stealing."

"Our kind of fun," Teia interjected.

"No, Rae. Second-One, save us, she has gone mad!" Fehatsi's anger turned to Teia. "And you are just allowing this disastrous plan to unfold? You are letting her have her way?"

"More like encouraging her to have it." Teia smiled. "She is our Araeboril, and my path in life is to follow her. If she says that being Selected is not for her, I will not tell her she is wrong, and I think you are rather bold to say so. It is wrong enough to disagree with your Tyanien, but with the Araeboril, Fehatsi?"

"No, she may disagree with me," Rae said, "but this is not so spontaneous as you may think, Feha. I have known I shouldn't be Selected for a long time. I told you, last turn, of the dreams and my apprehension. The dreams have not stopped. They have gotten worse. But I have a good feeling about the *Sinners' Almanac and Verse*. Look and read here. It could help my father, and it could be in the Glittering Temple. These Bilers might know something of these magical spells we've forgotten. I know that the Bilers did not come here by coincidence but for bliss and a provision of goodness."

"Not every random occurrence is bliss ordained by God for *you*, Aadarae. Coincidence exists, despite your faith. Last turn, what we talked about, your dreams— that was horrible grief. Of course, you don't want to be a Select Child. You have never wanted to burden yourself with the duty the title Select Daughter carries, and now the Bilers have brought a convenient way of escape," Fehatsi tried her best to convince them, her face contorted and uncomfortable. Teia could feel the anxious perspiration on her friend's brow, her hands, beneath her arms.

Rae straightened and said, "Do not presume to tell me about burdens of duty. I know my own words. I do my best to live by them, that has always been true. But you are right that I do not want to be Selected, and I will not be. This anxiety is more than a bad feeling, more than turns old grief. I know grief, and I have known it since I was a child. I cannot heal my father without understanding how the plague works. Sfar'Laki gave me memories of his pain, not memories of how the damned smoke was conjured and what went in it. The Biler Plagues of 8554 are the closest thing in history to his smokes and tricks, and I am following the trail."

"How do you know this spellers' book is still in Baeltaf?" Fehatsi asked. "The Bilers destroy what they don't understand. You think they would keep a book of dark magic?"

Her face fell as if she really had not thought of it. "I don't know, but this is the only lead we have. My father will die soon if I don't find something. This isn't a debate, lyaren. I have decided, and I won't send someone to do this for me. It has to be me."

"See? This isn't about your father, this is about you!

Madness. You are the *most* stubborn! I feel such fear knowing that I cannot ever change your mind," Fehatsi said.

"Not in this instance."

Fehatsi stared, and stared, and a battle went on between her pleading brown eyes and Rae's defiant green. Teia watched. As they warred silently, Fehatsi's face lost expression, waiting and waiting. Teia could feel tears pooling in them both, neither backed down. Rae's expression hardened, final and unquestionable in that hardness, and Fehatsi could no longer stand against the strike of Teviona.

"Shit," Fehatsi said and closed her eyes and blew out of her nose loudly. "Tufaned shit. Rae, this is crazy even for you. The most reckless thing you have done."

Teia reminded her, "North Achka '08? That was reckless."

"No," Fehatsi said. "This is worst of all."

"I understand," said Rae.

"Oh, good, at least you understand. So, what would you have us do now?"

Their Tyanien smiled weakly. "Go to your father and tell him of these plans, and I will go to Daijirek and my father. We must not tell anyone else. I do not want the whole Rock, least this whole palace knowing about the journey. My mission is to be as discreet as possible. I will convince my father and master that this is a good plan, and you shall have to convince Rehonan, Feha. Let him be in charge of getting the Bilers on a vessel to the Fair Isle as soon as possible, getting us all on it. If anyone can arrange it smoothly, it is the Korr."

Fehatsi's laugh was forced. "Thank you, Araeboril, for such an easy task. I will just request an air vessel and crew from the tufaned Korr. I am certain that he will be pleased to help his only daughter cross the Line. I will get us the largest vessel, too. A Plane Breaker. Just you wait. I will ask for it, do not worry." Fehatsi enjoyed her own sarcasm immensely. She glared at Rae before turning on her heels.

"She is very angry," Rae observed, looking back to the map.

"She will recover from it quickly," said Teia. "She always

does."

"She should not have to. I know while I feel a wrongness in being Selected, it is wrong in many ways to abandon that life. It affects more than me. I will apologize and make it up to her eventually, but I just… have so much on my mind, Teia. Things I cannot manage to say aloud, or else they become true."

"Then speak nothing of that. Speak commands to me. What can I do for you, my Tyanien?"

"You can begin making your goodbyes and gathering our things, doing whatever else I do not remember. There is much under that instruction. I need to go speak with my father, and I think he will send us with some warriors for protection and more than the standard allotment of provision that the Select Council would give. I will say goodbye to everyone, go and see both Detunae, and go to the library to select which healing texts to bring."

"And speak with your master." Teia wondered how the Select Son of Amina would react, what the wisest elder would say to his favored. *Can he deny her? No. Who could?*

"Yes, also that which brings me most dread. He will be very disappointed in me, and I must feel it."

"Are you disappointed in yourself?"

"Very much."

"Don't be," Teia said, sure. "Trust your instinct, and you must trust Third-One in you to guide you where you go. You are the most devout believer I know, so you can trust yourself. I follow you and you follow where the truelight takes you. I know it is taking you to Baeltaf."

Rae's jaw clenched. Her tears didn't fall, but Teia felt them. "Thank you, lyaren."

When the Select Son of Amina opened the door into his study, Tyanien Aadarae was there with her back turned to him, lit finger guiding over the titles along the books on the wall.

"Have you been waiting for me long, child?" he asked.

She still didn't face him. "Not a concerning length of time. I kept myself occupied while I waited and tried not to listen in on your conversation with Master Cyenae."

He chuckled. "I am sure you did. Have you found anything very interesting? You should go to the Academy to see what they are doing with your proposal for colorblindness in false eyes. It is promising. Experimental, and it will take more research, but there is something good coming from those Biler experiments."

She turned her body to him, but she looked at her sandals, stare unfaltering, toes wiggling.

"Do you believe Amina was a true prophet?"

"Yes. Amina was a prophet, as were all the First Children."

"Do you believe that *everything* we have written by her is valid prophecy?"

He understood what she was trying to ask but chose not to acknowledge it. She would have to ask him plainly to get that degree of honesty from him.

"Tyanien, I believe that the First Texts are so inspired and well-guided in their choosing that we must believe their value outright. The First Children were all prophets, but prophets may be affected by faults or evils from the third plane. We know that even blisses granted by Three-One can be corrupted within ourselves. We are still animals. But Amina was a prophet, Tyanien Aadarae, as you are in many ways."

"I am not a prophet."

"Aadarae—"

"I am not. There are no prophets in our time, or at least, I am not among them. No one hears First-One's voice yet. I don't. Please, you must believe I am not any such thing. I would know if God spoke to me beyond Third-One's guidance."

He nodded, but she was wrong.

"Do you know that I am the second Araeboril?" she asked him.

Her doubt did shock him. "Yes, I do. You know it, too."

She looked up. "I never asked if you did believe in the end times and those prophecies. You know which I mean. I did not want to know the truth before, and you warned me against asking questions when the answer was unwanted, but now I need to know. What we want does not matter. Do you believe a Hasyal, wielding void, will bring the end times soon?"

He said, sadly, "Yes."

"So, you believe they are now working against me?"

"Yes."

Her look morphed into one so angered and pained, sudden then gone. Soft again. A false face a Takircha could admire. Daijirek wondered what went through her mind. At last her hands stopped moving, stopped sparking, and she said, "I cannot fight a war if I do not know the enemy. I will not start a war against shadows, looking over both shoulders in constant fear."

"'The first enemy to defeat is within yourself,'" Daijirek quoted the first book of their mutual descendance. "Amina had much to say about the Other, about the second coming. We know it is a time of war, deception, and trial."

"And the Rock has always been there. I would never blaspheme the First Texts, there is value in those writings. They are inspired, but the Books of Amina… well, I would not say there is much in them to help me. She cannot advise me against an unknown threat as this, if it does exist. How do we know the second wielder of void is out there? How do we know they will bring the end times, and that they aren't just a person as frightened as I am? These are all just legends and stories to me though I am part of them. The Hasyal could feel the same. How can I find the Hasyal before they find me if they do want me dead? Why did Sfar'Laki believe he was the Hasyal, and why did he believe that he must kill me to save the Rock from its end? We still cannot make sense of that, of anything the Radical's believed. Where did their beliefs start? Could it be true? Is that why Xonieren tried to kill Amina? Are we all being tricked?"

At every question, the words *I don't know* pulled up Wanúm's throat, but he said nothing. He could not answer, so he shook his head and ran a weathered hand down his beard.

"How can I defend myself against something abstract, Master?" She added. "We know nothing. Prophecies do not predetermine my life or choice, or who I am. I may be in a war against some faceless evil. Maybe or maybe I am not. Before I killed Sfar'Laki, he told me he was the chosen Hasyal, that he believed his purpose was to run a sword through my heart and bring healing to the Rock. Radicals believed in him, for whatever reason we do not know, and they believe I must die by the Hasyal's hand. Enemies may wear the same face and keep trying, until the true one makes a claim. I cannot kill them all, I will not. I cannot."

"'The time of the next is made of frauds,'" Daijirek recited, "'in the end even truths will be unknowable. In the end times, pretenders are undetectable, and everyone believes a lie as kingdoms totter. The truedark gains a foothold on the Rock, and the people rejoice. A system of roots go unseen. There are creatures beneath the ground that wait to strike, not as fearful as those waiting in the sky beyond outer spaces, and void and truelight live together unknowingly before the congregation begins."

She finished the verse with him. "'And the truelight, its second wielder, will try to find a home and will strive for every good thing and love all as I have.' You quote more dreams to me, Master, but you never quote the verses where Amina dreams I will die and fail."

"There are many interpretations—"

"There was only one interpretation before I was born, and people feared the end was upon us. You were clever, and you ordained what would be preached, anything to stop mass panic. But it is written, 'The next wielder of truelight will not accomplish the task set forth. Only suffering is the bride, and all will be lost for her. Near the end, you will hear the voice of First-One and still be brought to destruction. Void overcomes at the end, and you will mourn because you saw it coming and could not do one thing.' You believe Amina was a prophet, but I will not believe in any prophecy. How can you?"

"With faith. Amina could not know everything in absolutes, Tyanien Aadarae. Her dreams were like warnings to us, sent from Three-One to set a fire beneath our sandals, but we have control over our destinies."

"They are only dreams," she said. "Forgive me, Master, for disagreeing with you, but I do not believe Amina was all that people think she was. I know I am not. I know that I control my destiny more than writings from a woman who lived thousands of turns ago. Amina did not know me. If I believed what she wrote, I wouldn't be able to face a day."

"The dreams of the first Araeboril are more knowing and powerful than those of normal beings," Daijirek told her. "You claim that you are not a prophet, you may not be, but Amina claimed she was."

"At times she thought it was true and could speak her truth. That doesn't make it so! I know that as well as any," Aadarae said, and her face turned back to distress and pain, her finger points twitched and glowed.

She looked at him again and her expression screamed guilt, and for once in so long, she looked so much like the broken girl of Wanúm's own dreams. She was never good at keeping secrets from him, or so he had always thought before the truth came out about her affair with that child of Hahnae, the empath apprentice. That secret she kept from him for turns. Wanúm did not need to be an empath to know that Aadarae was overcome with the burden of a new secret. Her look now was reminiscent to the pitiful look of a beaten animal, and something else, a fear so evident and so very horrified that it spoiled his blood.

"You look like you are about to confess to a murder. Speak at once, Tyanien," he said.

"Master, I have... dreams. I, you see, I," she stammered, then took a deep breath to steady herself. "I have been having dreams like before. Like when I was a child. Since the union, every night in my dreams I am alone in a black space, and I watch as the Rock is cloaked in fire and then darkness. None of it touches me, but I can feel it. There is screaming, and that darkness and that is all. And there is no truelight there. None. Never. I don't know how to describe how that feels, a place without anything. I have never seen a place without truelight, but the dream is so real. I only hear two things, the screaming and a voice that comes just before I wake, and it says the same thing every night."

His lifewater still felt curdled; his gut swirled sickly and the muscles of his diaphragm seized. "Do you see the Hasyal in your dreams?"

She shook her head, no.

"Tell me what the voice says."

She shook her head. "I will, but I am no prophet. Dreams do not—"

"*What* does the voice say?" he asked more harshly.

"'The Blessed Lands will perish for you. Stay and see, you lead darkness to the heart. Flee from your home or die with it.' And then it laughs and says, 'You will die no matter what you do, but flee.'"

"What are you thinking?"

She prattled with nerves. "I need to leave. I am no prophet, but my dreams mean something. My fears manifest. The enemy is unknown, and I am not. I am too much known. My name, my face is easily recognized almost everywhere. They have painted my face on walls and reported my life to any person with ears. I have never been afforded any kind of privacy, and what of the Hasyal? What privacy is afforded the nameless across the Line of Separation in the East? Or across the Wilder Wood in the West? I cannot know until it is too late. I cannot fight an enemy I do not know. If I stay, if I am Selected, I lead the Hasyal here. I lead them to Talosa if I sit on the Council. I cannot do that, Master. I have to leave, or a darkness destroys the heart of the Blessed Lands."

He nodded, understanding, realizing how wrong they were from the start. If only he could go back and do so many things differently. "What would you do instead? Where would you go?"

"I ask you to let me heal covertly in the Biler lands. Give me a three turn leave, as most healers you send and let me *heal.* That is the only purpose I have right now."

That was not true. Her purpose was much greater. But she said, so she believed the words. *She believes her purpose is to go east and heal covertly, who are you to deny it? Are you still such a proud man?*

Wanúm was not, he would not be again. "I will agree to this, Aadarae. A three turn leave to go across the Line, sanctioned by the Selected."

Though he could not lie, she looked like she did not believe him. He felt hope within her, and grief. "You will allow this?"

"I will," he said, not quite believing himself. "Because you say it is what you must do, and I have learned that you will always find a way to have your way, and your way is greater than mine. You will naturally seek out the correct path. There is nothing I could do to stop Three-One's plan for you."

She enveloped him in a hug and gave him three thanks, a kiss on his cheeks and forehead, and then half a dozen more thanks for good measure. She radiated joy, gratitude, and mostly truelight, her veins tethered to the energy like she was painted in strokes of a silver dripping brush.

"I feel such relief from you," he said when she stepped away. Tears fell from her smiling face.

"Remember you feel a fraction."

"Where do you go now?"

"To my father."

"You came to me first." The Select Son was surprised.

She smiled brighter. Truelight dimmed. "I thought it would take more to convince you, and now that you have agreed it will be that much easier to convince him. It would be even easier if you spoke to him, Master. He listens to you."

"I will speak with the Tyano."

She went to leave but stopped before walking out the door.

"Do you think I will win? Do you believe I am capable of winning against one who wields void?"

Despite Amina's last prophecy... He fought a pull on his tongue. "I hope you will win," he could say. Her departing breath defeated, he felt no hope in her but prayed she felt his strongly. Her face broke Wanúm's heart.

Alone in his study, he thought of all her many questions and one loud other. If not her, who in all this plane was he to Select?

Dry season blew unbearably hot, even in the mountains near nightfall, and even for Santir who'd lived in Talosa nearly half his life. He missed sea breezes, and the salt baths of his childhood village, he even missed the snow of North Achka this time of year. This heat might kill him. He thought the winds wielders should send better, cooler wind along to the capital and almost prayed they did. But he felt wrong praying to his God of pure love for good wind when his heart was bitter and quiet for anything else. If Klo lived, he would pray enough for them both.

Yeroen rested, claiming thirst and fatigue, but Santir expected he was feeling the later-day affects of his drunkenness. Yeroen, like many Canyai, didn't know when to stop celebrating. But Klo had quoted the scriptures enough at Santir that he knew by heart: there was a time for celebration and a time for work, a time for sowing and a time for reaping. A time for joy and a time for grief.

He wouldn't wait for joy coming.

Santir took his blade and hacked the overgrowth back into the jungle, taking every frustration out on the grass. Yeroen spat some of his water onto the leaves, then drank more of it with loud slurps.

"Don't throw that on me," Santir said, cutting more tall grass.

They had started cutting the path's overgrown green together at dawn, but Yeroen abandoned the task and now had his back against the house steps. Playing with the water from his clay jug. Taking sips of it midair, he hummed.

"I hadn't thought to," Yeroen said, swallowing more water, curling the rest above his hand.

"I will believe you if you don't throw any of that on me. You take very long rests. Grab your blade. Or dry more of this grass for me."

"I have a strong thirst."

It was then that both men heard the distant song of the tevi bird from the south. Santir turned to face the sound. He felt his back wet with Yeroen's water. In the span of Santir's shocked breath, Ambos sprang into the clearing with Rae on his back.

"What are you doing here?" Yeroen asked, jumping to greet her as Santir recovered.

"I am here to collect, and the debt is your promised company," Rae said, falling off of her seat. "We leave to the Biler lands tomorrow night to find something that might help my father and all plagued. You were right, and I was wrong, Detunae."

"I love when you say that!" Yeroen shouted. "I told you, didn't I?"

"You did," Rae said, rolling her eyes and looking to Santir, who felt stupid, wet, and excluded.

Yeroen kept laughing. "Yes, I did! Do you think I could be a seer? I might have taken your blood."

Santir saw Rae smile, mischievous, and then she used her shoulder to shove Yeroen to the dirt. It did not stop his laughing.

"Did you see that coming?" Rae asked him.

"No, but I should have," he answered, and finally Santir interjected.

"One of you, explain to me what you are saying," he said, sick. "Did you say you are leaving for the Biler lands?"

"I did," she said. "Yeroen is coming with me. He did predict this, but could not yet know my reason. To shorten an extensive explanation that I have given five times today already, there is a speller's book, and the plagues that it afflicted on the Bilers are similar to those conjured by the Radicals. I will retrieve it, and with some help, a cure can be found. I hope."

She spoke truthful nonsense. "You are not going to be Selected?" Nonsense.

She looked down and ran a hand across Ambos' slick fur. "I will not be here for the day of Selection. I will be in the capital city of the Bilers healing and searching for the spellbook."

"What are your commands for me, Araeboril?" asked Yeroen.

"Gather little belongings, what you can carry. Say your goodbyes and be ready to leave for maybe a turn or more. I don't know what else you need to get in order."

"My affairs are in order here. I am almost perfect now. I will be at the palace before first light."

"No, get your rest and sleep as long as you can. It will be the last night of home's comforts for a long time, so enjoy it. Just be at the palace by late night tomorrow."

"No, stop," Santir said. "You are deciding to leave just like that? Rae, you can't. The People will be devastated."

"I know, and it causes me pain to think of that, but I am leaving," she said with big, hopeful eyes.

"Why are you looking at me like that?"

"You must know that I want you to come with us, Santir."

His response was immediate, before she could ask him if he wanted to go. "No."

"Please. It will be time away from here," she said, unbothered. "It is an escape if you need it, a mission if you don't. We had plans to see all the Rock, and this is something close to those dreams."

"You dreamed to see it all with Klo, Tyanien Aadarae, and he is not here, and I am not him."

"I know it. What does that matter?"

"I... it's all that matters."

"You have always been my friend."

"I have seen more of the Biler lands than I ever wished to see, and I won't be involved with those ridiculous nobles any longer."

She grimaced— bared teeth like an animal. "You have been to the Biler lands before, so your experience makes you more valuable to my mission. I might need your help. I do need it. I do."

"I doubt that. Standing alone, you could take on ten thousand Bilers with their painted armor and swords, but I doubt there will be war when they see you. I imagine, for your love, they will fight, because they don't yet know how free that is given. You will have any nobleman there to escort you to courts and parade you in front of whoever you wish to know."

"That is your answer to me?" she asked, clearly shocked that he would deny her.

"Yes," he said quickly.

"What will you do here? Will you participate in more illegal trade?"

"No, I don't know what I will do, but I am no criminal."

"You don't know. I don't understand why you would stay here if there is no obligation. Have you thought of your plans?"

"No, there isn't, and I have a plan, sort of, and I have thought of it very little," he spat, throat hurting. "I do not need another obligation to say no to you. I can say no."

"Will you go back to working under Ilarel in the city?"

"No, I haven't seen him since the war ended. I'm not an apprentice. I can work on vessels by myself."

"Will you do that?"

"I don't know, Rae." He wanted to scream, Stop questioning me! Just go!

Go, already.

"You are saying you would rather stay here and do nothing than come with me and your brother to the Biler lands. Why?"

"No!" Santir coughed out, finally yelling. "Enough tufaned questions! *I owe you nothing*!"

She was shaken by his volume, though less than he. Yeroen,

face affected in awkwardness, resumed cutting the grass along the path, much more effectively than Santir had done since he could dry the weeds in one motion, then water the dirt behind him.

"Forgive me," Santir said to Rae, "Tyanien, I didn't—"

"No," she interrupted. "Forgive me. I will not ask your reason for wanting to stay, but I do wish you would come with me, Santir. I am leaving for a place unknown to me, for Three-One knows how long, and I would like to have you and Yeroen close while I can. It is fearful of me, a weakness, but it is true that I am weak, and I am wary. It isn't the far west like you dreamed for, but it is something new. It is a kind of adventure."

You know nothing of my dreams, and I, nothing of yours. "I am honored by your offer, but my place is here, Tyanien."

"If that is your truth, live it. But I will miss you."

"And I, you. Goodbye, Tyanien Aadarae," Santir said.

She couldn't be more shocked; she'd counted on him following. Always following her. "Goodbye. Tomorrow at the Beautiful Gate someone will be waiting for you, Lietuenant Detunae," she said to Yeroen, with all the authority of her birth, and he responded with the appropriate, "Yes, my Araeboril."

Ambos, the horrible, ever-loyal beast, growled at Santir before they took off into the trees.

Good, she leaves, he thought. *It will be better for me without her. I can make peace with my ghosts and abandon this love for her. This hatred. Klo will forgive me, and so will Three-One.*

Yeroen shook his head and left into the house without saying a word, the work far from finished. Santir hated that his brother could feel the water burning in his eyes, leaking, cooling on his skin.

13. BACK TO BAELTAF

From Blessed Lands, they would fly to Fair Isle. From Fair Isle, they would board a ship at the port closest to Waterhaven, and leave the Hwaelin men wherever. Teia was more than excited for the sea voyage, having never been on a water ship herself.

Rae ended up forgetting a good deal, so Teia had plenty to do. She made sure they had enough stones of their descendance, enough weapons (though Fehatsi would never forget her arrows), and Teia made sure Ambos knew of their plan. The laijeiri was most upset to return to his place of origin, yowling non-stop all day. Rae also forgot to say a goodbye to Mouwat Giana, Kloennian's poor mother, but Teia thought this might be intentional and said nothing about it.

Presently, Teia and Fehatsi bustled across Rae's room packing clothing, deciding what little to bring. Rae would insist they dress like common folk when they arrived in the Biler lands, little good it would do to make them blend amidst them. They couldn't take much. For Teia and Fehatsi, it was time to say goodbye to their finest things. Their Tyanien was somewhere else, and while Fehatsi fretted, Teia knew that Rae would turn up when she needed to.

"I feel I am forgetting something," Fehatsi said as she came out of the washroom wearing something Teia had never seen. She took Fehatsi's hand and spun her around to admire the fine silk work and golden twine of the bodice.

"Aya, I like this very much. Is it new?" Teia asked. She spun Fehatsi around again. "It looks Quo'Orinthian."

"Good eye. Yes, a gift from that Eerim, Elihai, who lives in Riam and writes to me so often. He sent it to me to wear on the union day, but I had something better made. I thought to wear it now, considering I will not get another chance for three turns in the Biler lands."

"Yes, they would burn you on a pyre for such a dress beyond the Line. Does he believe himself a contender for your heart, this Elihai? I didn't think you cared for him."

"'To want love is seeing your house's candle from a distant hilltop. To be loved you must be the flame there waiting. To love is to burn and lose your home in the passion.' I would not consider myself belonging to any of these. I do not burn with Elihai. I enjoy receiving dresses from admirers, and he knows my mind. So, he can't say I led him on."

"'Candle from a hilltop?" Teia rolled her eyes. "Eerim proverbs bore everyone, Feha. Unoriginal blabber. You write that Eerim too frequently. Good thing we are leaving and will be without correspondence. How did the Korr take the news of our holy departure?"

"Surprisingly well. Too well. He told me that if Rae believes it isn't Three-One's will for her to be Selected then she shouldn't be. He said that if she is leaving the Blessed Lands to go east, then I must leave the Blessed Lands and go east with her. He said we must trust our Araeboril's *intuition*. Intuition—he called it that, for the first time. He always called it impulse. 'Every Tyano has their Korr,' he said to me."

Teia held back a laugh, but the smile couldn't be contained. "That is surprising. I had imagined more yelling and refusal."

"Us both. It doesn't feel right, does it?"

"Your father's non-reaction?"

"No, obviously that's shocking. I meant leaving the Blessed Lands in such haste feels wrong. Flying off in the dead of night makes it feel like we are doing something we should not."

Teia shrugged. "You say it feels wrong to leave, Rae says it feels wrong to stay. I am excited for a ship on water. I've never been on one."

Fehatsi smoothed her dress and shook her head, going back to the bag she was packing earlier. "You are always on her side over mine."

"Yes," Teia responded. "She is our Araeboril, and you are just my friend. My closest friend, but still."

"She will be our Araeboril one day, but now? Amina was not born into the title, Teia. Right now, Rae is just a girl running from a union she doesn't want because she still loves a dead man."

"Fehatsi—"

"No. It might be that you do not yet understand that every action she commits is not Three-One's will, but she is slipping. She is failing."

"She isn't—"

"How long have we known her? She is panicked and was traumatized by all that happened in that tufaned tower, traumatized by losing Kloennian, and now she refuses to tell us all what she thinks. But others know. She's been making mistakes for two turns because she's frightened, and now more reckless than ever without Klo to ground her. She thinks the world might end. You've read the illegal papers, don't deny it."

"You sound like you are the one frightened," Teia said.

Fehatsi sighed and finished tying her pack. "I am, because I understand that Rae is running without thinking, thinking without caution, and I understand that you and I have no control over what happens to us. For her we forsake all freewill. We go east without a plan. Without anything. Do you think we won't be discovered when they see our skin? Do you think Bilers will be as kind to sojourners as we have been? We are going to search for a missing speller's book three hundred turns old in a kingdom stuck in times past! That is all frightening to me."

"I could believe your truth is the real one, Feha," Teia said, "that you are right and our Araeboril isn't, and she is panicking and running away without other thought— I still think we should help her do it, not as her Korr or her guard. We are her lyaren. I cannot speak for you, but helping Rae run from an undesired union falls under my responsibilities. And I can handle racist Bilers."

"Maybe," Fehatsi said, "but something in my gut persists to

bother me. It feels sinister."

"See a healer."

"Be serious."

"I am serious, lyaren. You do not get to question a Tyanien's authority because of an upset stomach."

Fehatsi whispered, defeated, "I know. You think I don't know? It is impossible to have a conversation with you concerning this when you follow her blindly, with such little caution for yourself."

More than enough caution for myself. If not for this, I would be a Select Daughter, Teia's thought brought a twinge of guilt.

She said, "With as many as there are against Rae, a few blind followers cannot hurt her."

"How wrong you are, lyaren." Fehatsi wouldn't cry the tears in her eyes— spit pooled in her mouth— Teia could only feel her plain distress, but not see it.

Rae came to her room later, not speaking but looking as though she wanted to. Fehatsi treated her with silent anger, and Teia could not get out of her head enough to say anything. So, the three of them sat in silence in Rae's windowless room ignoring each other until Azún Kanila's presence was announced to them. The Tyano's General, and the only known man born with sense for two natural energies, flames and winds.

The warrior came in dressed ready for battle in coiled armor, weapons on his hips and arms, head smooth and unpainted. Before anyone said a word, Azún knelt on both knees before Rae.

"Tyanien Aadarae," he said, "I am granted permission to cross the Line by Great Leader Iial. I am here to serve you and fight beside you if you allow it. Take me up as one of yours. Wherever your feet go, mine will follow from this day until your mission, whatever you decide your mission to be, is accomplished."

"Oh, Kanila," said Rae to the older man. "Bakéz would have you stay. Has he not told you? He wants you to be his General."

"He told me. Are you rejecting me, Tyanien?"

"No. Rise, my warrior. We go with Three-One. Bakéz and Zyon will be angry if you leave with me."

"Yes," he said, standing. "Leave them to me. My position will not wait for me, but I don't care."

"I am glad you are coming with us, my warrior. It does make me feel safer."

Kanila stood prouder hearing it. "You have every sense behind you now. The Great Leader was worried about you traveling to the lands of the Bilers, Tyanien Aadarae. Those men are absolute savages. For me, it will be an honor to kill for you there."

"We will not kill Bilers," their Tyanein was quick to say. "I plan to heal them."

"So, you give up being a General to go with us?" Teia asked of Azún, wishing it wasn't so. With Azún Kanila on Rae's guard, Teia was no longer the superior. She would have to answer to the dual wielder, just as she always had in the Academy. On every field of battle. This journey felt less and less like an escape.

Azún stared at Rae. "To follow Araeboril," he said, and Teia saw that he, too, was blind.

"Roll again," Zyon said, rapping his knuckles on the table.

Bakéz picked up the three die, shook his cupped hand with bottomless hope and tossed.

"You have had rotten luck today," said Zyon as they fell to nothing.

"Only today?"

A hesitant knocking came.

Bakéz questioned, "Who is out there?"

"Your sister, Tyanien Aadarae," a servant announced her to them, and Aadarae's muffled voice behind the thick door could be heard, "Just let me in. I must see them."

Zyon sighed. "Yes, let her. We stopped speaking of important things a while ago."

Aadarae always smiled when she entered a room, just as she was taught as a daughter of the greatest ruling family. She wore simple clothes, farmer's clothes covered in dirt, like she had been running around the city trying to go unnoticed.

"Brothers, stop what you are doing since it is so unimportant," she said. When Aadarae entered a room, she also had a frustrating habit of saying, Pay me all attention.

"I am about to win," said Zyon, looking pointedly at the die in his hand, "and I am honestly not prepared to suffer your exuberance this early. Can you come back later or maybe tomorrow?"

"I am hurried to speak. You must listen now. But go ahead and toss your turn, brother."

Bakéz, who was in less of a hurry to lose the game, welcomed her interruption.

"No, no. What do you want to speak of, little sister?" he asked.

"I do not know how to begin. There is much happening. Zyon, when was the last time a master instructed you in a Biler history lesson?"

He paused, and his face looked uncomfortable as his mind grabbed an answer. "I... many turns ago when I had twenty-two. It is impolite to ask sudden questions that pull on distant memory, Aadarae."

She took a seat atop their table, in between them, and took the die from Zyon so that she could roll them between her hands. "Impolite it may be," his sister said, "but it is good for you. It wakes you up in a way, Daijirek often says. You might remember something of the Biler Plagues of 8554 from your lessons, and the Saints of the Rising Wood in Baeltaf."

Zyonhir nodded. "That is what the church of The Mother has declared them. Before 8689, they were called the Bloody Red Spellers."

"I did not know that. That sounds proper dramatic for the time, though. Did you know that, Kez?"

"No," he answered.

She smiled and rose from the table, let the die fall, and they landed on faces that would have lost her points in a game.

Zyon's brow knitted over his Riambo eyes. "Why do you bring up Biler Plagues, little sister?"

"I meant to bring up the spellers' book used to create the Plagues of 8554."

"Why?"

"I need to find it, the *Almanac and Verse of Plagues,* it is called by one old Biler account from their king's court. It is mentioned in the song of an eastern bard, and the first time in the record of an excursion into the remnants of the Rising Wood after they burned and regrew. The last time it was mentioned by a poet, it was in the Glittering Temple of their sun god. It could still be there."

"How did you find all this information and record?" Bakéz questioned. "Not from any written thing in our stores."

"In a way, I sent for it," she said, face all of feigned innocence. "In another way, I did not do exactly that. I mentioned some of it to you days ago, of books from the Biler lands and the false eye theory I proposed. They are working on it in the academy. I am told it looks promising."

"Aadarae, tell me," ordered Bakéz. "Tell me all of it."

"The brothers Detunae retrieved four old texts for me, three from the library in a sun god worship house, and one they found in the library in the highcastle of the Dominion called Kieln."

Zyon's whole face elevated with his angered chest. "They stole from the home of these Biler nobles they smuggled here? By your orders?"

She nodded, having the grace to look guilty.

"Did you order them to bring the Bilers here?" Bakéz asked.

"No. I only wanted Biler books because of the plagues, I didn't want noblemen. But you see," she said, "my sources are good, and my mission could be feasible. I am going to try to find this book and use it to create a cure for the plague. The book might have the answer, and it is in the Biler lands."

"I would send one hundred armed wielders to the Biler lands before I sent you," said Bakéz, feeling every betrayal against him, not only hers but Zyon's as well.

"You do not have authority to send anyone across the Line," Rae reminded him, like a slap. "The Great Leader grants permissions and only the Selected Children of Amina can send missionaries and healers, and I am a healer."

"The speller's book for the Biler Plagues could be burned," said Zyonhir. "Had you thought of that?"

"I had, actually," she said. "I know that it is possible, and likely since Bilers love burning sin, but if it isn't burned, it could help our father. It could save him, Zyon."

"His plague has progressed too far," Zyon said sadly. "You cannot save everyone, Aadarae."

"You both continue to make sure of it."

And what could they say to their savior? While she was winning the war, they were losing the greatest battle. They had been hasty with stationing their warriors in the field, they had not first secured the village entirely, and they had trusted the wrong people to help them do it. Eerim traitors. If they had been more intentional, more suspicious— if they hadn't tasked other men to be so— they could have prepared for a Radical attack. They would have known it would come from within, had they asked the right questions. They could have stopped it. Everything can be known with enough influence, Zyon said after the loss.

"Forgive me," Aadarae said, and that made it all the worse. "It is me that feels inadequate, and it is certainly not your doing. You say I cannot save everyone, Zyon, but I feel like I can save no one at all. I do not think I could live with myself if I didn't try to cure our father in anyway I know how, and this plan is all I have."

"You call it a plan? I have yet to hear anything that constitutes a plan," Zyonhir chided her. "All I have heard is that you intend to leave. You must realize that you are behaving like a nonwielder, grasping at nothing to save our father. He is already gone."

What selfishness. There is no hope for our father. You are only trying to save yourself, Bakéz thought, desiring to break his silence.

He said, "So, you think you will travel to the East, wear a collared dress and curtsy before some Biler king with these nobles beside you? You will try to convince Biler lords of peace? Convince them to give over a book of plagues, even!"

Rae laughed at him, clutched over in a fit of giggles that reminded him of a child. She laughed more as a woman; as a child she had been quiet. Tame.

"No, no," she finally breathed out. "I am going as a *covert* healer, of course. Just as I have always wanted. I will put on a shawl and some heavy frocks and travel on the back of a turnip wagon, or whatever, and I will go to the Glittering Temple and find the *Saint's Almanac* and take it in secret. I have no intention of standing before a court of Bilers and letting them try to judge me. Oh, it is difficult to imagine, but that is very funny, Kez."

"Is it?" *Just as you have always wanted. Selfish, selfish child.*

"Yes, though the way you are looking at me tells me that you don't find it funny at all."

"Aadarae, after these Bilers leave the Blessed Lands," Zyon tried to reason, "then we can have this exact discussion, and you may feel more inclined to let us send skilled people to do this thing for you after the excitement and passions have faded. I thought we were in agreement that you must be appointed to the Select Council. It is exactly what our family needs in the pass of power. I understand this book of spells is important to you, it is thereby important to this family, but we can find it without you leaving. We could let Teia lead a mission to sneak this book out of their lands if it would make you happy."

She shook her head. "It is not a thing to debate now, brothers. The details are done. I have decided to go and to give up the Selection. Daijirek is already seeking a new Select

Daughter. He has approved my request and given me my three turns leave as a healer, and Bapo has given me a guard of two warriors plus my party of three."

"Are the Detunae brothers going with you?" Zyon asked.

"Only Detunae Yeroen."

"No. He will not go with you."

"He will. He is. They're preparing the vessel now."

"Select Daijirek agreed to this?" Zyon stood from his seat and began pacing.

"Yes, and Korr Rehonan."

"You will not listen to us at all?" asked Bakéz.

"Not as you speak to convince me to stay. I am going."

You are not her Great Leader yet. Bakéz almost shouted. "You tell me as a courtesy?"

"I tell you as a goodbye. I leave this very night with the Bilers."

Bakéz could have laughed if he wasn't so angry. *And even then. She is our Araeboril. We will all fail by her.*

"Then goodbye, sister," Zyonhir said and hugged her. It was a kind, *uncomfortable* hug. Zyon wasn't affectionate, but Aadarae returned his embrace with enthusiasm. He was the one to break away first. Zyon said, "May Three-One pour blisses on you and keep you safe. Take care of yourself and return home to the Blessed Lands once you have found the Saint's book or after your three turns. No longer than that."

"I will return once I find it, or when I discover it is gone," she answered, then looking to Bakéz. "I will be home as soon as I can. I don't believe our father has three turns."

The corners of the room were red in Bakéz sight. She was abandoning him in his rule. The Blessed people were kindest to her, loving to the highest degree and forgiving of any impropriety, and they saved no love for him or Zyonhir. His sister was taking away a valuable shield from their family. She knew they would be open to many sorts of social and political attacks without her, and she was not concerned by it.

"I have made my goodbyes to many and so many more

I must make. Goodbye and every bliss be upon you, Kez," Aadarae said, looking hopeful.

"Goodbye." He didn't want to hug her. He was failing, too much happening he could not control. He did not make a move, and neither did she.

Finally, she left them and closed the door, and Zyon rolled the die. They landed on triple fives.

"That ends the game."

Bakéz sought Third-One in him for patience, for any shred of godliness that would be granted him. "Our father is not in his right mind to agree to this. She will abandon us to fend off the sharks of politic on our own."

"As you and I have always been. She goes out to swim, I think," said Zyon. "Her sensitive heart will be horrified by what she finds in the Biler Dominions. I have no doubt she will stir chaos wherever she goes. Her leaving Talosa may not be so bad as you think. Trust me."

Trust you! That did make Bakéz laugh. *Who to trust among brothers and truthspeakers?*

Zyon sensed the irony and smiled. "Trust that you may not see Aadarae for three long turns. Can you imagine a reunion after such a goodbye?"

Bakéz was grateful that his brother was not a child of Amina. He asked awful questions.

Nearly three weeks in the Forsaken, both Jonn and Mittrik were covered in painful, itchy marks; they looked ailed with the pox, which Jonn feared at first. He dared not pray for health while in the Forsaken, or the gods might judge him more harshly. Perhaps killing a daemon atoned some of this wretched sin.

He asked for a healer, but was told by every westerner that he would be well with a pepper-scented salve. But Jonn felt like he might scratch himself to death if he didn't choke on the smell.

If he were to die while Forsaken, should he not pray?

Like Caeth pleading to be given a second life after failing so miserably in his first. The gods listened then and did not condemn. But Caeth was Hetten's son.

A healer came to both Jonn and Mittrik eventually, gave them more ointment for the pain, but did not seem concerned at all for their condition. No doubt healers here were used to seeing these bumps. This green land seemed to be in the middle of a plague of insects. There existed biting bugs everywhere, and it seemed each's purpose was to cause pain and to drink on blood like fae. Jonn had counted over one hundred red bumps on his skin, and Mittrik claimed to have twice as many. The brothers sat in their rooms and scratched at themselves miserably, waiting to go back home as travel plans were made without them.

Jonn wasn't surprised when he learned that the People of Fair Isle knew about the magic of the Forsaken West, nor was he very shocked when he learned his mother had known and visited Canyassor once before she married, but he was more than shocked to learn of his sister's betrothal to the High Lord of Brimtone. Tyanien Malak had told him all of it. Jonn was also told by the dimpled man that preparations were made for him and Mittrik to be flown to Waterhaven in one of their flying ships, and then go by way of good, *normal* ship to Kieln. Jonn was anxious to leave, to go back and fulfill every duty to protect his sister. Anxious waiting in the Forsaken, where not even his thoughts were safe.

Jonn imagined Leonara there in Daggerlone, suffering through conversations with the Gilgars. He imagined her utter fear at having to marry such a man. She must think him dead or the worst kind of coward. His sister deserved better, a long and diverting Courting, a kind man who would love her for more than her name, a man who would protect her. A man she could love, a handsome knight like she always wanted.

Jonn asked to be taken home *now* — please, *immediately* — after hearing all the news, but had been informed of their departure for the following night.

He wasn't surprised to see Mittrik disappointed. Since Jonn told him the news of their sister, and the plan to leave, he had been walking ruts, embittered face.

"Father is mad for what he did, signing Leonara's life over to the Craven," Mittrik said. "It's madness."

"Father must think we are dead. He needs Gilgar's support, and is desperate," Jonn said. "Do not be so upset. When we return, Leonara will be freed from that wretched contract of intent and all will be well. I marry Ritra Gilgar, and you continue doing whatever you were doing before this." *You could start start thinking of our family first, you could mature.*

Mittrik was profoundly affected, though, by this world of magic. He spoke plainly, honest like he had never been. "I don't want to leave," he said and finally stopped pacing.

Jonnere knew it from the moment they arrived. "This magic is not meant for us. I know you have a lust for this place, that you do not want to go home, but we must."

"I know we must. But why would I want to? It will be a devastating winter for the common people, for us, too. There are wars being fought in Baeltaf," Mittrik said it all in a solemn tone, flexing the hand that he had broken as a child. "A war already between northern Dominions with no end in sight, and Father is planning to start another, bloodier in the south. For the bloody realm."

"Yes, he is." Jonn nodded. "But it is our war to fight."

"You knew of this? All his plans?"

Jonn scowled and looked down his nose to Mittrik. "Of course, I knew. I'm his heir. They're *my* plans, too. You think father would keep me in the dark about his war? He trusts me. Why do you think I traveled through marshlands constantly the past six Sister's Greetings? You don't think Father could have sent Arne all the way to Hailspring if it was just to collect the levies and settle down Bluers? I've met with the lowerlords, their underlords, meeting petitioners there and readying men to gather and march through the Raglands. It will happen in less than a year's time, but blood will be shed as soon as the

Osburs realize our intention."

"The Raglands?" Mittrik asked, quiet, and Jonnere stopped. His brother's eyes had gone wet, like a little boy.

So, he is the one in the dark, he realized and was glad. *Completely. He knew nothing of our constant planning. Father didn't trust him, never told him of it, and he could choose to ignore what he didn't see. He had to have chosen blindness to not see what we were doing.*

"Yes, that is Father's plan, to lay siege on High Baeltaf, to break the Sword of Pride against Ornund's own neck. With Gilgar's men and the northern lords, we can block off aid from Tunure, and High Baeltaf could be taken by the south."

"The Keep of the King is impregnable."

"Not if you have men on the inside."

Mittrik turned so Jonn couldn't see his face. He stood in the corner of the room, like a child. "And Father does?"

"Egan Norr, Lord Chamberlain, and more. He has the Sea of Whales thanks to the rest of the Pearl lords standing by him. They have three thousand ships that will sail into the capital's bay as we move up the coast."

"He wants to be our king," Mittrik said, wheeling around. Jonn watched his brother's face change. "But he's willing to do anything, give over family and honor for it. Leonara's betrothal is proof of his determination. He'd sacrifice any one of us."

"He does this *for* us, to end Ornund's growing weakness and ridiculous taxing." *He really didn't know.* Jonnere was surprised to feel sad for his brother. *But now he understands what we're risking. Good, so that he will do what's right.*

"He is desperate," Mittrik added haughtily, "you were right, and Mother knew something of him we do not know. He killed her. I feel it."

"I didn't— I," Jonn stammered, as if for a moment he had forgotten,

She was dead

lost forever

But how could he forget?

"He didn't kill her, Mittrik. She hung herself. She was a sad woman, she'd never been happy. The conventions of High status, losing a child so young, the rains, it endlessly depressed her. It killed her."

"Rain didn't kill our mother. He did, just as you said the night we left."

"I was grief-stricken, Mittrik, I was *drunk*. I was not in my right mind."

"But you were not wrong, and now we go back to Baeltaf to fight for him? Are you not shaken by the very thought, fighting to make for ourselves such a king of all Baeltaf?"

Or the thought that one day I should be your king? Jonnere thought it must be both.

Their father was a killer, but he'd make himself king, he'd would crown Jonn in equal glory. What his father did mattered less than what he would do for them. He tried to convince himself for the thousandth, millionth time. If Jonn could muster trust, ignorance… if he could just fought for Tagnar now. Stranger impossibilities turned true in this new world (elves, groles and such evil), so Jonn could, for now, argue Tagnar's innocence.

Jonn could argue, even when he didn't believe it. He must.

Or Mittrik might never come home. What was the other choice? Where would the crown fall if Jonn didn't side with his father? Not on Jonn's head, but on a Dawnburst or an Aze, or worse— it would never fall off Osbur's fat brow.

"He didn't kill her." Jonn shook his head, repeating, "He didn't kill her. You're wrong."

"And you want to be king? You never told me," Mittrik said.

"It was not something I wanted until Father told me it was within our reach, and now it's been the one want of mine for a year."

Mittrik laughed unkindly. "You're more ambitious than I knew. Why should you be king?"

"I would be a better king than any Osbur."

Mittrik sneered. "A bigger house and polished throne isn't worth all this. Would you sacrifice Mother and Leo like he's done?"

"Do think less of yourself," Jonn answered, loud again. "Or more of me. I have to answer every cursed question of these westerners, but not all of yours, Mittrik. In this new world, that has not changed. I love our sister as much as you, don't question it. As does our father. Dawnbursts and Osburs are stealing from us, and they have all this deserved from the north. A better time should come. They are at their weakest, and we are gaining allies. Our family belongs ruling, and we'll unite the northern and southern Dominions for it. One day, you will be High Lord of Kieln, a great knight, and I will be your king. That's why we make sacrifices."

"Hetten help… you sound like him."

Jonn turned away. Mittrik had always longed for adventure and glory, more than anything else. The splendor of this world was a delight, so much sweeter than the blood of war, and the glory of battle was one Mittrik did not want to know. He claimed to, but Jonn knew what Mittrik faked. That courage. That swagger. He was soft in the heart for pretty girls and songs, liked swords only for showing off, liked lances for the joust, but he did not have the stomach for real war, for the killing of innocent men. He wasn't ready to make sacrifices for cause and glory; Mittrik wanted these handed to him. In this, Jonn knew he was more of a man than his brother stuck in fantastical boyhood. Jonnere felt ready to do anything. Beyond fantasy. He was above any western prophecy, he told himself.

That following night, with swords and cloaks on their backs, Jonn and Mittrik were brought to the throne hall before embarking on a flying stone. Jonn thought it was to receive proper goodbyes from the royal family, but only three Tyanien were there to see them. The witch and her brothers that were twins, Janseyu and Owéttan.

The sight of a spiritcub made Jonn's lungs constrict tightly beneath his ribs. Mittrik stopped him from retreating. His next breath hurt as much as the first. Little as the beast was, it could steal his soul. It sat on the seat of the white throne, a king itself, licking its forked tail like any other cat would, but even from the bottom of the steps Jonn could hear its purring like the rolling in of autumn thunder. Jonn had heard the stories of the Dreadwood, of the men that lost their minds therein, of the others that were taken up by unholy evils. The spiritlion, like any daemon, was another beast that wanted his soul.

Only now Jonn discovered that the three youngest Tyanien, the witch and the men who looked so like her, would be going to Baeltaf with their own personal guard of mage warriors. Shock did not encompass all he felt.

"We will get a chance to fight again," the scarred Tyanien said to Mittrik, who seemed pleased by the idea.

"I hope you don't cause trouble now, Lord Hwaelin," the woman named Teia said, her eyes moving suggestively to the dagger at her thigh.

In the presence of so many mages with sharp objects, Jonn tried to appear relaxed and act the part of a High Lord. Of a king. "No trouble. But you are going to Kieln like this, with your soldiers? You will stick out quite plainly amongst us, dressed as you are." *Looking as you are, darkly marked by your magic and sin.*

The witch princess smiled happily. It meant to ridicule him. "We will be covert as the healers *already* in Baeltaf, Lord Hwaelin," she said. "Once we reach the shores, you needn't worry for us."

Jonn was not worried for them. About them, yes. *These westerners will disappear into the country, and then what? What can I do about it?*

But if the mages did not disappear? A jolting, wonderful idea.

Sin, surely, but most sin could be pardoned for just cause. *If I helped them and they helped me?* This might be the great opportunity he needed to take his father's war, win it. He could have crown and vengeance both. *Better they do not go in secret. Just seeing such magic would cause Osbur's army to drop their weapons and flee nine ways. If we have them, if we only have her, who would dare fight? What could Tunure and all of Osbur's army do against us?*

Against me?

Santir saw his current enemy's face through the metal bars of the Beautiful Gate. He wished not for the first time that he'd been born with the extra sense of his father. If only he could feel *du*.

Santir wished to reach in and hit the guard, but the space between each bar was too narrow, the decorative curving bars prevented even a finger. But how good would it feel to slap the gateman? Despite lacking a fighter's skill, Santir had a fighter's spirit, like his brother.

He had no time. It was late night already.

"I am her friend," Santir said, and it felt like the thousandth time. "I am speaking the truth, I have been here before. I have dined at the garden table with Tyanien."

"Go home," said the gateman.

"No, I will not. I am Detunae, you must let me speak with Tyanien Aadarae now," Santir said again, slamming a hand against the gate.

The palace guard shouted, "Stop that!"

"Let me in!" He slammed his hand against the gate again.

"No one enters the palace today, young man. Lieutenant Detunae is accounted for. You can't see marks beneath armor, but I am a child of Rionae and I promise I will burn you to boils if you touch the gate again."

"You don't understand, I was invited by the Araeboril herself. I am Detunae Santir, the younger. Tyanien Aadarae wants me there."

The gatemen laughed.

"She does! She leaves for Fair Isle tonight with the Biler

nobles, and I am meant to be on that air vessel."

"How do you know that?" The gateman sounded concerned at this, and suddenly Santir could feel heat from the other side of the gate; the man of flames ignited.

Santir had, too. He hit the gate as hard he could, ignoring the burn of his hand. "I told you! I am her friend! Leave me out here thinking as I am, and everyone on the Rock will know where she goes and how. Get a child of Amina, let them ask my name."

"Detunae?" It was Tyanein Malak coming down the great steps, and Santir could see his face clearer as he got close. He looked worse than Santir had ever seen him. He wore his royal clothes of brightly spun colors, but he looked too small for them. He was thinner. There were dark circles under his eyes.

"Tyanien," Santir said and dipped his head, embarrassed at once, taking the smallest step away from the bars of the Beatiful Gate.

"It is alright, open the gate for him," Tyanien Malak said to the gateman, who rushed to follow the order.

Santir could have cried, could have hugged the Tyanien, but they were never friends. Tyanien Malak was courteous and kindly enough to offer to escort him up to the air vessel dock himself.

"You are not traveling with her, Tyanien?" Santir asked. It surprised him, he had assumed the fifth Tyanien and the doubleborn all to go east with Rae. Santir thought Tyanien Pyraen would go if he had both his legs. Of all Rae's brothers, Tyanien Malak was the most protective of his family. He had threatened Santir, Yeroen, and Klo on countless occasions. Each time was colorful, and the Tyanien made sure to use more words than necessary, big words that the simple men could not understand.

Malak said, "No, I am not. My brothers think I will be of better use in the Confederation, and I might agree with them."

Santir had been in the palace no more than five times during his friendship with Rae, and that was certainly not enough to make him comfortable. Tyanien Malak did not look at Santir once while he led him up the three hundred steps, or when he led him through the palace, and the walk was long to the northern tower where all royal air vessels docked. He was not taller than Santir, but Malak turned up his head to look up so that he could seem larger.

Men like Tyanien Teviona Malak did not enjoy looking at simple men like Santir. They looked forward for any advance, inward to praise themselves in their gain, but rarely downward. Such men stumbled easily, his mother would say, but they were the men who ascended. *Not even the Araeboril's prayers can save such men*, Santir thought as he stepped toward his fate at the top of the northern tower. *I should pray.* He hadn't in so long.

"Be well, Detunae," said Tyanien Malak as he turned to leave.

"Will you not come to say goodbye to her, Tyanien?" Santir asked.

"I have. For you, I will ask this, however. Promise me that you will do everything to keep her safe, Detunae. You would do anything to save her, yes? You will die for her if she needs your life?"

Santir suppressed the riotous laugh that came. "My Tyanien, she does not need others to keep her safe. She is the Araeboril. I'm no warrior or wielder to protect her. I am a mechanic of simple birth, and she is powerful enough to face any danger. I am grateful she asked me to come at all."

When Tyanien Malak looked at him again, all compassion was gone, all sham of kindness, too. He was the proud, arrogant man Santir wanted him to be, the man that was easy to hate. Hate was the greatest sin, but Santir wouldn't care if the Tyanien wouldn't.

"I was worried that you were of that mind," said Malak, "and you laugh. Be gone from my sight and do not get in her way, little Detunae. Why she chose you, I will never understand."

Me either.

Malak did not leave down the steps, but stared at Santir with quiet rage, and though he had not the right color eyes, Tyanien

Malak had the malignant self-righteousness beholden in the strike of Teviona. Santir had to prostrate, bow. He turned to walk out the tower door and into open warm air, Malak's glare hot on his back.

He stopped caring about Tyanien Malak once outside on the tower platform. The vessel hovering was the largest Santir had ever seen in person. It lit the platform with a fake oval of daytime. The fastest aircraft model produced by the Talosian academy, and the people appropriately called it the Plane Breaker. The loading ramp lowered to let the crew enter with cargo, and he heard the sound of airshoots starting. First like brass trumpets, loud and announcing glory. The air shoots of Santir's vessel sounded like a fat man snoring, but the Plane Breaker's air shoots sounded like music and a hundred nenchai roaring. He'd worked on military vessels during the war, but he was never allowed near a Plane Breaker. Only master mechanics were permitted near such great vessels.

She was sharp and would never be confused for a stone by a stupid Biler. It resembled a proper ship more than anything, with a tail like a large whale's, but it was sleek, curved, and glorious. The firestones from its bottom thrusters heated the ground even where Santir stood, and the wind from it snapped his clothes around him. As much electric machine as contained nature, the Plane Breaker was the fastest military grade ship of three levels— the lowest level for cargo and barracks, the deck taking up the entire middle level, and another set of cabin rooms on the highest. Enough room for at least two hundred soldiers and their officers. Santir wondered how many people Rae was bringing with her. Not two hundred, surely. But then again, the Araeboril was traveling across the Line.

"Santir?" Rae called, and he saw her there halfway up the long ramp that led to the decking level. She was immediately running, toward him, followed by her lyaren and his brother. Only Rae looked surprised to see him. She ran, but no one else did. Santir knew they were upset. He knew they had to be; he had been mad at himself for so long, and unforgiving.

"You are here," said Rae, "with a bag."

"Are you here to say goodbye, Detunae?" Fehatsi asked when she stood in front of him.

"No, obviously I am here to go with you." Santir knelt before Rae and looked into her eyes, the plea spilling from his wet lips. He was crying. "Forgive me for— for everything, for not accepting your offer before. For how I behaved. These past two turns I have not been a good friend to you. I still ask that you please, please take me up as one of yours, Tyanien."

Her face split into a happy smile, and then he was in her arms, hugging her back tightly. "Santir, thank you! Three-One, thank you! To your feet, my warrior!" And she pulled him up off the ground, but didn't let him go. "You are good and loyal. I have always thought that of you. We go with Three-One, all of us, how it should be. What made you change your mind?"

Her voice unsure, but Santir didn't need to think before his answer. "Klo. He would go with you if he could, and he would be the angriest if I didn't go. When we meet in Paradise, I want to be on good terms."

Rae nodded, and he thought something like relief was there. Santir wasn't an empath, but he was her friend. He knew her faces. Most of them. Right now, Rae looked like she could fall apart.

He looked around, at Riambo Fehatsi and Leuanien Teia, his own brother, and the Araeboril all smiling at him. They were going together, a family like once before. Almost. With these smiles behind her, Rae would not fall apart, and neither would he.

Santir felt Rae was the kindest, most forgiving person he knew when he walked up the ramp of the air vessel and saw it close. A child in a sweets shop aboard the deck of the Plane Breaker, walking around the great panel scribes, the recording devices, hands running acrost the electric frame's gloss. Inside, the vessel had a sound like a beetle's buzz, deep within every wall. The view out the glass from the decking level was better than the view from Klo's mountain. From here, at the top of the northern tower of Talosa's palace, Santir looked out to the flower circle, the sky eye, the river of Ashakai that split into three, the train tracks, out to small vessels flying across the starlit backdrop, tower houses titupping the clouds. Talosa, as beautiful as it would ever be.

"The Bilers?" Santir remembered and asked where they were.

"Packed away somewhere," said Yeroen. "I told you I had a plan half formed in bringing them home with us. It worked out in the end, as it does. They are not such terrible men."

That, Santir doubted. They were still born without blessing, of Rooj. Santir still didn't love them, though that was holy command. They were Bilers, after all. His brother was trying harder than ever to live every act of selfless love, as commanded by Three-One, for Rae. *Though Yeroen fails in everything else, he follows that first command, to love openly and without hesitation. Since truelight burned him, he doesn't need to try.*

"Look at it, little brother," Yeroen said with a reassuring thump on his back. The greenest trees black in the hills, fading into gray cloud as the Plane Breaker ascended. "Look at Talosa like it will be the last time."

Santir looked, but he knew it would not be the last time. Perhaps it was just wishful thinking, since he doubted it was Three-One in him that gave assurance. It had been a long time since he listened to Third-One. Godliness present within him? He doubted. No divinity would want to dwell in his soul as it was.

I'll be better, he promised himself. *I'll try.* Santir looked out and wondered if this could be the last he saw of Blessed Land. He could die in the Biler kingdom, anything possible. *But I will come home again,* something told him. *Rae won't let a Biler kill me.*

It wasn't Third-One in him, but hope in her was close to faith in God and would be enough for now.

Or so he thought.

Everyone on the airship must have heard the tortured screaming. Mittrik heard the female cries through the plated metal. Distant, shrill— horrible, desperate, but when he went for the door, it was locked to him. He now did feel prisoner, and tried to push on the door with all his strength as one muted scream turned into the indiscernible shouting of many. Jonn and he banged on the door but the screaming stopped, or maybe it was only that the banging sound of many boot-steps drowned all else.

The boot-steps and chaos turned into more distant voices, and Mittrik sat on the bedding propped against the wall, knowing he could not do one thing. The room of the air ship was small, and the walls were gray and empty like a Kielnish sky, nothing to distract him from frightful imaginations.

Eventually, the door opened, and Riambo Fehatsi walked inside. Mittrik would never tire of seeing women in men's trousers, their legs carved out clear and shapely.

"Hwaelin lords," she said. "I heard the door pounding, but it must remain locked for security. Please forgive us for any discomfort. The flight will not last much longer."

"The shouting? What's happened?" Jonn asked.

"Nothing to worry you. I have come to inform you that our original plan to travel with you to Baeltaf has changed, Lords of Hwaelin. We will not travel east with you. My Tyanien and her guard must travel elsewhere."

Mittrik faltered, see Jonn's face flash disappointment. Hwaelins couldn't hide that emotion well.

Fehatsi said, "Your family on the Fair Isle has been informed that they will be receiving you and will make the preparations for a ship back to Kieln. We will wish you farewell at our landing. It has been a true pleasure, my lords."

"And what of Rae?" Mittrik asked before she could leave. "She desired to go to Baeltaf and heal. She told me that."

The woman's eyes hardened, and her lips pursed in a way

that reminded him of Nexitha, and arseholes, but quickly she slipped on an easy smile. A dangerous smile. "Tyanien Aadarae made the decision against Baeltaf. She decides where this vessel flies. We all follow her orders."

"Where will she go?"

"Forgive me, Lord Hwaelin, but that is to be known by Tyanien Aadarae's company and the Captain."

"And is she alright? We heard that screaming. Was it her?"

"She is well. She is on the control deck with the Captain discussing the change of course."

"May I see her?"

"Lord Hwaelin," the woman sighed, "Tyanien Aadarae will never be willfully unkind to anyone, despite a contract with honesty which makes just the opposite true in most children of Amina. She's never met someone and not been filled with compassion and empathy and wonder and love. It's not within her, therefore I am left with the task of being unkind." She sighed again.

Mittrik stared at the woman's dark face. "My lady?"

"Let me be most clear, Mittrik Hwaelin. You should not think to be near Tyanien Aadarae. Try not to think of her. I know that you have important duties once in Waterhaven, sufficient distractions from this. The Tyanien is resting now and will wish you farewell when we land. Good Lord Hwaelin —" she turned to Jonn, and Mittrik felt properly quieted by her. "I meant what I said about desiring peaceful relations between our two lands. Our people deserve it. Your people deserve trade and good weather. If you ever wish to discuss opening the Line of Separation, or if you wish to write to Tyanien Bakéz, I am sure that your Fair grandfather can aid you."

"Do you answer for her?" Mittrik cut in before Jonn could respond. "For Rae?"

Riambo Fehatsi rolled her eyes. "You have been answered, Lord Hwaelin."

"That's not good enough for me," Mittrik said, and then he walked past her, out the open door and down the tight corridor, turning left at the end. Jonn called after him, as did Riambo Fehatsi, but he did not turn around. He could only look ahead.

He passed shuffling men at work in the dwindling light, some who carried boxes, others who carried swords, but all looked at him like he did not belong. He took the first right and it led to a steep stairwell, more like a ladder.

Rae sat alone on the bottom step, her head in her hands.

"Rae, are you feeling well?" Mittrik asked as he knelt beside her. The narrow walls pushed them together, and he was nervous like he never was with women.

"No," she answered, looking up with an exaggerated breath, and it was soft and warm on his face. "In my life this is worse than I have felt in a long time. Not the worst though, so I should be thankful."

"Were you screaming?"

"Yes, forgive me if I woke you. I had a dream."

Mittrik nodded his understanding. "I am sorry," he said. "It must have been a very terrible dream."

"Yes."

He didn't think she'd speak more unless he asked.

"Why have you decided not to go to Baeltaf? I thought you could see a joust, like we said in the trees."

"I hope to one day, and you can win as you said you would. But I am listening to my dream, and it told me to go to the far west."

"Farther west than Canyassor?"

"Much farther. Canyassor is very central, but I suppose that's what everyone thinks of home, and we do make most maps. *Adrissor* is what Canyai call the place beyond the Wilder Wood. Unknown Lands. Hardly anyone comes back from beyond those trees. My father's first wife never came back. Real magic is beyond that boundary. Not one soul in the past forty turns. By the southern border of the treeline, there is a tower. I must first go to the tower, where I killed the Pretender, but I am sure my path leads me to Adrissor."

"The true unknown? And it will be very dangerous, I imagine."

"Yes. It has always been this way, though I denied it." She clutched that white stone necklace at her throat, the little bird in flight, long feather tail spread. "Many healers have crossed the border of the Wilder Wood, and none have returned. Only a handful of explorers in all our histories have crossed the Wood twice, never a human. Thousands and thousands of turns, and what the few survivors brought back is unlike this world."

Mittrik tried to imagine such a place, but knew he could not, as he could not have imagined anything he'd seen in the West. He had to see it himself.

"I always wished to venture and discover worlds unknown," he said. "If you would have me, I would go with you, lend you my sword as you need it, to see this wildest west."

"You wish to discover two unknown worlds. That is ambitious, Mittrik Hwaelin." Finally, the corners of her mouth lifted so that Mittrik's heart all but spun. "I want to admire that, but I am unsure if I admire ambition."

He smiled, too. "Will you take me?"

She looked at him with eyes more promising than any future he would face in Baeltaf, and he had to hold his breath. "Can I trust you for true?"

"Yes," he said, glad for his answer. "Yes, always."

Her eyes did not change, as if she did not believe him, but she nodded. "If you wish to join me, I will not tell you no. But I warn you, I have no idea what comes next. I know nothing of what is beyond those trees beside what is legend. I will not turn you away because I need all the help my god will grant me, and I am fearful."

He took her hand in his own hand, the hand she healed. "Do not worry. We can discover the farthest unknown together, and we'll live through whatever danger."

She removed her hand from his; the action stung. Her thumb stroked along the wing of her carved bird necklace and stopped so it covered the emerald eye. Then she excused herself and left him.

Jonnere stood waiting for Mittrik in the corridor just outside their windowless gray box, the door held open with his leg. He looked reluctant to be trapped therein again. His face was everything Mittrik feared. There, the disappointment of their father, their mother's cold eyes, riled in anger purely belonging to Jonn. Mittrik's stomach flipped.

"Are you so lost in all Forsaken magic?" Jonn asked, crossing his arms on his chest. "Truly Doomed, are you?"

Mittrik shook his head, not understanding. "You know I don't believe in any gods or forsaking. I didn't think you did."

"I know you, what you're thinking without you saying it. I needn't be an elf. I've known for some time, longer than you perhaps. It should not surprise me that you would rather chase a woman than follow me. It's always been your way."

"Jonn—"

"But to chase *that* woman? A *witch*, for Sisters' sake!"

"You don't understand. She's not just a witch. She's more than that, caught up in a greater story than mine. You saw her magic, like lightning held before our eyes. How she moves... like nothing else. Everything we've learned is just stories, and she is real and right before me. She is greater than demigods and heroes of Old."

"She is, or you are? You've always had this sense of greatness, inherited it as I did. She may be a hero, but we are just men. We are fortunate to be lords of Baeltaf. Our lives are there, our family. Are you not bound as I am by blood, honor and at very least enterprise to our house? I want greatness just as much as you do! We go back, win our war. Be better than legends ourselves."

"It doesn't have to be your war, Jonn."

"*It always has been*. Don't you understand? There's no choice here. Think with reason," Jonn pleaded.

Mittrik could see his brother's heart breaking, but his own heart felt whole of excitement, promises of magic. "I have thought, of little else in fact, and the opportunity of what waits before me is…it's—"

"Greater than what lies behind you?" Jonn supplied. "You might share in a bit of *her* glory, or carve out glory all your own and have your name be remembered in Baeltaf forever. As a conqueror, as a knight, Mittrik, and Kieln's High Lord. Is that not what you've always wanted? If you go now, what will you be remembered as?"

"I don't know," Mittrik said. "But you're right, there is no choice. I cannot turn away from this new fate afforded me. I am meant to see this world. Magic, everything else, I am meant to witness."

Jonn gazed long with the harsh eyes of a better lord, color of salt and sky, then he turned on his heel, dragging a hand down his Fair, grieving face. "Yes, perhaps you are meant for that. Perhaps you will do exactly that and be happy. Happiness you follow, never me. Then be it so. I will not try to stop you."

Mittrik wanted to apologize, say he was sorry, but it would not be truly felt. He wasn't sorry.

"Thank you," he said instead.

Jonn clenched his fist, and for a moment Mittrik thought he'd have to let Jonn hit him. But his brother just said, "I deserve more than your thanks. You're leaving me to fight alone."

"Jonn —"

"Mittrik. You said all you must."

Mittrik suddenly did feel remorseful, imagining his brother on the battlefield without him, and almost changed his mind, but then he remembered the look of lighting spun between a woman's fingers. Of that lightning alight in his bones, of fires and seas that bent to men. He remembered how it felt to be healed by a witch and fly on wind, to mount a spiritlion and look down at a strange new world, and he must keep going.

One day he will forgive me. That made Mittrik feel better, though he wasn't close to forgiveness yet.

Not wanting to be alone with his brother enraged, Mittrik decided to wander and think. His feet led him out to where Rae had been, but she was not on the stairs. He climbed the steps to the decking level, as people called it, where men with animal masks worked before gray tables in silence. The two brothers who brought Mittrik west stood tall and silent near the glass, looking out of the transparent window.

Yeroen smiled when they met eyes, so Mittrik took encouragement to stand beside them.

"I hear you go west with us, Biler," the mage said. "Good choice."

"You think so?" Mittrik asked.

"Greatest honor to follow the Araeboril, to know her. To be known by her is to be loved. Few would turn down such a gift, more would kill for it."

The mage's brother laughed. "To be known by her is to be caught in her net. A special kind of curse, her love. None of us had a true choice, and we must make peace with that."

"Santir," growled the mage, and then Mittrik could not understand the rest of their conversation, so he looked out of the expansive front glass, out to gray-golden sunlight that colored the sea beneath.

Her love.

Heavenly bodies seemed like three coins hung in the orange-colored morn, a large gold chip skimming sea between twin silver pieces fading. The Sisters and Hetten overseeing his choice. He would see their faces shining on him as he rode east toward Fair Isle and left his brother, and all through the evening-fall as he flew west toward the unknown. They would look on at him the whole while, judging.

Judge me, if you're real. I'd be Doomed. But you're not.

He clenched his fists.

You're not.

And I've never felt such freedom. I've never been more excited for my life.

"How long until we reach Fair Isle?" he asked the brothers. *When do Jonn and I separate, for how long?* There was no answer for his unspoken question, hanging over him like a thundering cloud. The cloud, heavy and deafening to Mittrik, did not affect the westerners beside him. Their sky must look clear and golden as it was, standing together.

The mage spared a toothy smile. “At this speed? By third hour of light we arrive, I bet.”

So, Mittrik began the longest morn of his life.

Part 5
Unknown Lands
West of the Wilder Wood

translated from the first tablet of the Dead Cadence
"Sing to the broken arriving.
Hollowed flames respond.
Sing to shadows and see how they bid for you.
Bleed and see how they fall."

14. DREAMS OF THE EAST

Past the great trees of legend, hopefully only forty kilometers beyond its most western edge, in the wilderness, a man named Wen was plagued with dreams. They bade him to the wasted trees his mother spoke of, spoke to, and he listened to them as he'd listened to her. These dreams came from somewhere beside himself, not within him. No use denying their power now, and how he tried. For years.

A torture nearly every night, most painful and vivid when he strayed off course. He had not strayed in almost two years. Now, Wen closed in on his target, determined. Only forty kilometers, he hoped.

Tonight, he lay on his back in a forest, face marked by streaks of blood. Not his own. His chest was bare, a brandished mark of overlapping circles over his sternum. He ran his fingers across the familiar mark. In every dream, it was on him. The place was too quiet to be real, but the pounding in his heart grew steady in fear, as if he had just run a great distance to arrive here.

The trees loomed over him. He felt their scrutiny and their hatred; he felt their life. They surrounded him, closing in and bending over each other, crowding to get a better look. They whispered with their leaves, in the rustling by the wind, and they had no compassion for him. They were his father's court, they were his brother and sister, they were trees. *Traitor,* he almost heard, and whom had he betrayed?

There was a woman dancing just behind the trees that were not true trees, but now reflections in crystal of living branches, and he called for the woman to stop, to turn around and face him. *Lai?*

LAI!

But she ran.

The branches reached out and tried to grasp her with knotted fingers. He reached, too, but as the trees touched her skin, their branches burned to ash. He feared he might burn if their skin touched.

Still, he reached.

He had to keep up with her, and his feet would not move. She left him with the trees. As he left her with the enemy.

"Come to us, child of the west," voices rang behind him, harmonic and beautiful like music, but not like music in that they were empty and detached of any life or emotion. These were not the voices of humans or any other kind that Wen knew. "Come to the tower and be made. Be set upon your purpose. You are ready."

And all too quickly, there was a deep pain in every piece of him, burning and writhing; so deep it was, and he could only wait for it to end.

Wen opened his eyes and the sun was barely rising. His back ached but that was common. Chey stood by a dimming fire of burning dust, staring at him with faulting expression.

"What?" Wen turned around, angry. He kept Chey's movements in the corner of his eye.

Your screams woke me, Chey signed, and Wen turned to face him. *I know you are cursed, but I am a man who needs sleep.*

Wen said nothing. *I'd been screaming again?* He looked to the flat lands behind them. Too much noise was no good thing. *Attracting some kind of life here to us, life then death, as it follows. Damn these dreams.*

The dreams were his burden for over ten years, though he

could remember having strange dreams even as a boy. He had been following his dream's instruction for the past three years, and they called him eastward to the edge of the world.

Wen sat there and tried to finish waking, the pain of his dream fresh and real under his skin. Chey rolled up the blanket he had slept on, making quick work to pack and saddle his highhorse. From his own pack, Chey retrieved a bit of burnt fish and bread for them to have before setting off. Wen drank the last bit of water in his skinflask, remembering the dryness of the deserts behind him, thankful for the humidity in the air.

Look west, Chey signed.

Wen did and immediately cursed. Razers coming in one of their great mechanical rovers, the metal painted blood red. From what he knew of Razers, it was blood. Changling blood, witch blood, elf blood. The rover moved across the desert too quickly. Wen and Chey could not pack up and leave fast enough. Wen had his xosper, an animal not built for speed; they were bred for endurance in the deserts. Chey could run on his humped highhorse, but Wen knew he would not leave him.

The rover rolled toward them on its tracks, twin links of the great wheels leaving deep impressions in the soft sand, tracks universally avoided. The two men waited, listened as the world rumbled.

The machine stopped fifteen feet away, the dirt of its approach caking Wen's nose. Out of the opened hatch climbed three men with covered heads and then another kind slithered to the sand. The humans were of one of the desert factions of Ghondul by their striped dress and turbans; the Ligarthien was naked, like most reptilians, with his crude weapons hung from thick leather straps crossing his chest and looped around his gray arms, five glass vials obviously full of agent black tied around his middle. Witch poison.

"Setsa aliud," one of the human men said, a morning greeting of the Ghondul. By his tipped accent, Wen guessed the man was from Sibmah or the villages beside.

"Setsa aliud ava," Wen said. He asked them why they

stopped and what they wanted.

"We were just coming this way and I smelled the smoke of your fire, and then we saw it," said the Ligarthien, his tongue coming out to taste the air. Wen never liked the sound of reptiles trying to make human words. It sounded like someone speaking with water in the lungs, like drowned men trying to breathe, like a human dying under a sack cloth. Their kinds' mouths weren't for words. The Ligarthien asked in the language of the Blue, "Where do you go?"

"We are making our way to Ur. How far is the Sick River?" Wen asked.

"You cannot get there from here. Other roads behind could have led you, but this is the one road that does not lead you back home, Empirian."

A threat, Wen smiled. He knew they were close to the river, they must be (Wen had looked at a map only nine nights past), and all roads eventually ended in the Emperor's city anyway. There would always be a road back home though Wen would never take it.

"Oh, poor devolved cousin," said the lizardman to Wen's xosper. "To be ridden by one with soft-skin. Humiliating... pitiful. I would sooner die. Would you like that mercy, cousin?" His next words sounded like growling, a giant's deep snoring, and then one click of his pale tongue.

The xosper backed away and hissed; the Ligarthien laughed and his tail twitched, loosing dirt and scattering rocks into the ashes of their fire.

"No? Good for you, cousin, I was only asking. I'm glad you still have pride. Your people are known for this, yes, Empirian?" The reptile turned to Wen. "Known for your pride and great conquests, the once ever-expanding Blue. Though there have been few conquests these past years."

"I thought we were known for our better looks among humankind."

The Ligarthien flicked his tail once more. "Whoever told you that lied. You look like a proud man, though. Like a wealthy man without his wealth, in fact, young Empirian."

"I am proud. But it is for my youth and for the size of the equipment I carry below my belt, I assure you, not for any wealth I ever had."

"If you say. Does your large equipment make up for your gunt's? Did they cut off your staff and rocks, too, gunt?" the Ligarthien asked of Chey, tongue clicking. "I hear the slave masters do that to their little witch boys in the Deep South."

Wen stepped closer, wary to get in between the reptile and Chey, who could hold his own ground, but Wen was the only one who might stand a chance to talk these men away. Wen almost wished they would try and fight, but he knew the power of a wish. "If you are truly such a knowledgeable, traveled scale," said Wen, "then you would know by the symbol on his left cheek that he is not from the South, but that he was born in the Blue Empire. You'd know by his other cheek, he is a free man."

"Free, oh? *Hka-hka-hka.*" The Ligarthien smiled the best smile he could manage with his wide mouth, showing his sharp, short teeth. He spoke low from his throat, feigning so only Chey might hear, "Did you feel free when the coppers were exchanged, and they burned your right cheek to char? *Free*—is what he says you are, gunt, what the not-rich man says. Do you believe him? *Hka-hka* Do you think I do?"

Chey smiled, but Wen was sure nobody could tell.

"Pretty haft," the Ligarthien kept talking, gesturing to the obsidian dagger Wen carried, wrapped in cloth at his belt. The men by the rover walked closer to them.

"Many women have told me the same," said Wen, stepping to distance.

"A mighty nice blade, I bet. It looks old and valuable. What is your price?"

"It is priceless to me," Wen said. "I'll sell you the xosper instead, I won't have need of it soon."

"I think not, but no, thank you. I want the blade, and that is a pity for you, Empirian. I only offer to buy once."

Wen stood back and prepared himself. "Why offer when you always meant to kill me and steal everything?"

The reptile laughed in his garbling sort of way. "I told you I am well-traveled. Picked up some manners, politeness for greeting and eating and the rest. Your kind enjoys pulling manners over your animal, ignore the rest. You like to think it sets you apart though every kind has ritual. This is not stealing, Empirian. We are all animals trying to eat and live our best. If only you had a chance to learn that."

Chey unsheathed his dagger, spun it casually in his hand while staring down the human men, now too close. From here Wen could smell the stench of the Ligarthien's breath, too.

"Tell me," Wen started, slowly unbinding the dark, glass-like blade, holding it up in the dawning sun, "in all your travels did you once hear about a slave fighter named the Blood Fist? A tongueless gunt who traveled through every pit in the Blue, and then well beyond into the Ghondul, in nearly every pit of the desert factions killing for sport. He could half a man's face, any kind, bone and sinew, with a single blow of his left hand. Lightning crashes there. Without a weapon, he always won. This gunt is that very pit fighter. Do you think you can survive against such a man?" The obsidian blade held up was deepest black, but when Wen moved, it caught along the sunlight and turned bright white, at another angle it was purple.

By the twinge of fear in the Ligarthien's eyes, the change in his stance, Wen knew that he recognized Chey's name.

"Four Razers against one blueblood with a tipped tongue and one tongueless Bloody Fist? I like my chances." The Ligarthien was slyly moving back toward his men, all with their ghijaers ready and reflecting the sun at their backs, almost blinding Wen. Their features all were shadows. "I have bet against every kind of living thing, and here I stand alive. Here is a pit fighter, there was a mudwitch, a waterwitch, another hundred missionaries, *hka pity.* Your gunt is dangerous, but what are you, Empirian, that I could fear?"

He tilted, right then left, his sun-lit-white obsidian, Wen moved out of the glare to make his own threat. "The lucky bastard who kills you."

Chey acted quickly, hurling a dagger into the closest man's neck, then diving toward the next with his scythe held wide toward the reptile. The first thing Chey did was use the staff of his scythe to break all the glass vials against the Ligarthien's own chest before he could get a chance to use them. Chey, like almost all witches, was affected by the chemical and needed to make sure that it was not used against him.

That left the two human men staring down Wen. He was faster than the first man that came at him, and was able to block the first deal of his blows. Fighting two men was always harder; the second was much faster than the first. He stayed back and waited for one of them to make a mistake, the slower man, and then Wen cut him down.

From the corner of his eye, Wen saw the Ligarthien drop and Chey throw his scythe to the sand. Chey liked to insult men by killing them with their own weapon. It was more effective than words could ever be.

The man cut upward and sliced the side of Wen's leg, and he cried out before thrusting his blade forward, missing the man by a hair. Again, they crashed against each other, and Wen pushed back, but he felt the sting in his leg. He felt the blood on his ankle. Adjusting his grip, he put his strength into every strike, and he was able to cut the man's arm deeply. That staggered him, and Wen used it to his advantage.

But then hands shoved his ribcage, the distance cleaved between them, and the Ghondulian sprinted, knocking him to the ground. Wen was on his back with sand in his eyes, and he tried to shield himself, taking deep gauges to his forearms, until the other man got the better and knocked Wen's dagger to the sand.

Wen looked up to the Ghondulian, not quite believing he could die here and now, so close to his destination. *At least the dreams will stop. Dead men don't dream?*

The Ghondulian dropped his weapon as Chey's scythe sprouted sharp and red from the front of his chest, crying out before Chey jerked quickly and cut the man from abdomen to throat. Wen lay motionless, covered in his warm blood.

He pushed the split man off his body and onto the dirt, very out of breath. Wen walked beside the dead scale, spat there beside Chey's feet and scowled.

They're dead. Why are you upset? Chey asked, bowing to rip the jaw off the dead Ligarthien and add his to the collection of bones on his belt.

"I said I was going to kill the scale. Did you not hear?" Wen asked, still shaking from the fight, thinking on how he almost died.

I heard, but you were busy.

"My word means something. If I tell someone I'm going to kill him, I'd like to do that. Don't you think?"

You're not fast enough. Get over it.

"You know I won't. Come help me with this wound, then."

With all his remaining coin, Wen had paid for Chey's freedom four years past after watching him kill ten bigger men in the fighting pits of Naujal. He conjured lightning to break apart men's faces. Wen never regretted the decision. The two had lived off what they could steal and find and trade as they made their way farther east. At this point in their friendship, Wen thought the ex-pitfighter was invincible. He knew Chey thought it of himself. In their shared self-aggrandizement, they were the same.

Chey tore a piece of cloth from his own blanket, poured some of their white liquor over it and gave it to Wen so he could tie it around his bleeding thigh.

Neither of them went near the rover, which still hummed like a cicada in the sun. Some other lowlife scavengers would find it and move into the shell— take over its magic. Wen was surprised to see Razers this far south, but he should not have been. Razers were everywhere east of Dy scouring, raiding and pillaging, raping and slaving for their homes. There were as many factions of Razers as there were factions in Ghondul, likely many more.

Chey tapped Wen's shoulder when he was done rifling through what the dead men had on them.

Your style is lazy, predictable. That will kill you faster than your mouth. That Razer had you. Stop fighting bad.

"I can't die if I wanted to, but maybe you're right," Wen said, nodding. "His blade almost cut my leg off. I would have bled out before I could see you avenge me."

Hope that wound does not rot your blood as we get closer to the Sick. What a miserable way for you to die, blood poisoning, after everything we have faced.

"You don't think it will be blood poisoning? How do you think I'll go? Never, like the blood-tellers say? I always thought I'd go in my sleep next to a beautiful woman, happy and tired."

Lie. You don't think you will ever die. It's one reason you're half mad.

"Oh, please. You know I don't trust every eyeman's fortune. Tell me how you think I'll die."

Chey's hands were descriptive. *Some other bastard kills you while you dream your wild dreams. I hope you die fighting, not lying on your back. But you're probably right. Might be that beautiful woman beside you slits your throat while you sleep. When you die, you won't see it coming.*

"When we die, what do you think comes next?"

We, Chey's hands moved between them aggressively, we *will not die together. You will die first, then this journey ends for me, and I go back to the Blue. Find my mother if she lives. Your insanity will not be my death. Trust that I am a man greater than that. Your craze will only kill you, and likely soon as we approach your magic trees.*

"I hear you, but I was asking a question. What comes after death?"

Do I look like a corpse? Less than you. Living men cannot know.

"Are you afraid of the trees?"

Afraid as you. I heard stories.

"You keep saying, with very little detail. You are a terrible storyteller. Or maybe you are like me—I have heard nothing about the other side worth repeating."

Evil.

"We have that on this side of the trees."

In abundance. Wen thought it would be different outside the Empire, but he was wrong. His brother was not the most evil of men, like Wen once thought. Evil was inherit in every man. There was evil within himself, planted in his chest.

"Chey, you must promise me something before we move to cross the treeline."

Promise?

"If I die, don't take my bones back to the Empire. I cannot go back," he said, "even in death. Promise me you will leave my bones where I fall, that you will not take them back to the Empire no matter the reward."

Much gold to promise away for the relief of one dead man. Do the dead care about their bones?

"Do I look like a corpse? Promise me. Please."

If you die, I promise I will let the vultures and the worms have you. I will take your ring, your blade and collect all the gold the Empire will give me for their missing prince. I can find some other man's bones.

"Good, the ring should go back to my father. And the dagger — it was never mine to keep. If I die, return it to my mother. She is sure to have dark purposes for it." His mother said it was a blade of ancient prophecy.

Do you think your brother would spit on your bones and curse you? Chey asked, then signed vaguely of Wen's mother and her power. *Is that why?*

Wen laughed and said, "Maybe he would, but that is not why. I'm sure my brother has cursed me with everything already. The ring and blade should be enough for any reward, and it should go to you. You've saved me enough times to deserve it all."

Obviously. You kill the next Ligarthien. This got you emotional.

I hate when you're emotional.

"Thank you," Wen said. "I appreciate it."

Wen's only possessions were his father's ring and his mother's blade and the stubborn xosper. He sold every other valuable possession when he ran east, and that had not been much. He and Lai had left with two xospers, a purse of stolen jewels, and enough food strapped to their sacks to last them a few weeks.

Wen's brother had taken everything but one xosper and the purse of jewels ("Out of love and pity," Wue had said). The jewels went quicker than Wen thought they would. It was six years ago when his funds ran dry, only one year after he ran, so Wen tried to find work in villages as a farmhand, but he was no good for it. Everyone dismissed him at first mistake with their crop. Wen was a bastard prince, not a laborer. So, he fought for money, killing for money if it paid well enough. Mercenaries could always find play in Ghondul if their luck in the Blue dissolved. He would get settled within a town or community, or band of men, then his dreams would break him, call him out, and he would move eastward. Then he'd drink and try to settle, only to dream and break again.

The very next day Wen and Chey caught sight of the Sick River, a mossy, red-brown string frayed across the plain. Following the water south, they would arrive at the place called Ur, the last stop along the Sick that fed into the Flaming Sea. Beyond that?

Wen didn't know, but he had to find out. Had to get there.

And he was willing to sacrifice every last thing he had for the dreams to stop.

I don't like being this far south, Chey signed to Wen as he set down his paddles. Chey felt anxious, more than usual, his skin prickling. His arms were sore from hours of dragging the hooked sticks through that muck and murk which led into numerous floating villages along the Sick. *Heard stories, people getting tangled with Merses. Never ends good for humans. You row. Reeks down here like shit.*

The small redwood boat tilted from side to side as Wen took the paddles and did his share. The boat had belonged to a smarmy, annoying man at the mouth of the wide tributary called Halloom (this is what Wen called it and Chey trusted Wen in these matters). The boat owner, bald and big nosed, had done the usual: spoken only to Wen and eyed Chey with contempt and revulsion. Chey had been refused a ride into Ur, since the man claimed gunts left a smell that lingered and weren't ever allowed on his boat. The annoying man said it cost three marks a soul to get to the city, but only Wen was permitted and would have to pay an extra mark for his "lifestyle." Chey had killed him quickly, before the thin voice could squeal. They had left Chey's humped horse, and Wen's xosper there; Wen said they could not take them to the dream tower. Chey knew it was pointless to argue.

"There are no Merses in Ur," Wen said. "Just like the Empire, they've got witch slaves to keep attacking tides back, and most Merses stay under, in the Deep Under."

Could be. But I've heard stories. Breeds of Merses can hide in any shallows this far south, and they just wait for people. In patient bubbles.

"Almost all Sea Merses stay deep down nowadays, and they don't come to surface, except some say in Limars. Those are the ones with sharp teeth and sharper minds, the ones to worry about. A River Mers, though, yeah one of those could be anywhere I suppose." Wen shrugged as if the thought didn't bother him. "But we went through all of Canan and Dejiir and didn't see one. And who would drink the Sick? There are not even fish in the river, not for kilometers around the city. It's more than unlikely that we will see any type of Mers, and if we do—we'll make it up as we go."

Chey clapped his hands. *You're stupid and live without a plan. Your only plan, 'go east, to the tower, trees.' You think of nothing else. Can a Mers kill a man in a blink, swallow his lungs before a man realizes he's trapped?*

Yes, but a man can kill a River Mers, Wen motioned. "And I have a plan. Sort of."

You mean I could kill a River Mers. What kind of Mers wait beyond the trees in deep water? Chey gave back then thought to himself, *and I don't think you have a plan. Not a good one, at least, little prince.*

"You could kill any River Mers with little effort, I would put my marks on you. But have you ever heard of a human killing a Sea Mers? Please... no chance. If you did succeed, if that is even possible, doubtless the Guild of Merser Deep would rise from spume to avenge the flayed fin."

How much salt water belongs to the Guild?

"I don't actually know, if you can believe that. All of it not touching Empirian shores, if I was made to guess. Could be more. What if the sea is bottomless?"

Chey rolled his eyes. Wen had grown up in the Emperor's palace, had been instructed by wise men and scholars his whole life, and knew many things that Chey did not. Wen often drawled on and on about topics Chey knew nothing of, not caring if he listened. He had learned much since the runaway prince bought his freedom in Naujal.

Chey had dreamed of becoming a learned scholar when he was a boy. He would watch the scribes at work on the inker's street, pay close attention to their precision and glaring focus as they flicked a wrist over a word, dotted a page and carried on in upright posture.

He'd sit straight and pretend to write words in the sand. Chey had not been taught reading or writing, but he saw the fine craftsmanship and diligence it took to be a scribe. Perhaps if he had not ever asked a question, his mother's master may not have sold him off for discard; his mother had warned him against it many times. If he had never questioned, he might have been taught sums so that he could aid in household affairs. That was all a non-magic Empirian slave could hope to do if he did not wish to clean streets, harvest, or collect grabaldulls from rivers. But Chey had forgotten his mother's warnings just once, and that was all it took for him to be found out as the worst kind of witch.

He had asked a baker if there were gallit seeds in the loaves he bought, because he remembered his mother's master hated them. The baker had hit him, told him there were no seeds, and sent him away. That night, guards came into the place where his mother and he slept, cut out his tongue as she screamed, and they took him, sold him to pit masters all on account of being a gunt. That was the last time he had seen his mother. He had been a boy of six.

As a man, he did not care for Wen's stories. He heard better in the cells outside fighting pits, and hadn't much liked those either. But he liked any story as a boy, every one.

Chey's mother told him stories about a dead, loving god that would come back to life and save them; about a race of people, designed by that god, to save the weak in the meantime; about a redemption so sweet the slaves would whisper their songs. She told Chey stories about a man that had been his father, a gunt from the east who did not live long. From other children he heard many stories that he would pretend to write out in the sand. As a boy, his mother's master taught him in parables, trying to make it easy to remember his lessons. He loved stories then.

In the pits, wild stories spread more common than lice. Some claimed to have seen a fishman from the mysterious Guild of Merser Deep. Others made deals with an eyeman to never lose a fight (poor deals, if they'd spoken earnest). Chey had not believed anything the other fighting slaves said, but he remembered how one had described a fishman: horrible dead eyes and blank faces, swollen lips and webbinged fins, rows of teeth like a shark. Another man claimed that fishmen can disappear into thin air like ocean mist, but that the smell lingers for days. All exaggerations of someone else's garble, at best.

Something, both cynical and naive that he repressed,

reminded him that those stories of Merses could be true (some of them), but at this point, it didn't matter to Chey, even as the river widened. He didn't determine their course. And Wen, a prince, had never seen a fishman. He told Chey that fishmen liked to keep their mysteries, and did not let many live to speak of their encounters. Not even the Emperor of the Blue had seen one.

In the Deep South, they branded gunts' foreheads with overlapped crosses so you could recognize them before they opened their hollow mouths. A man and his son, both their foreheads marked, were standing and working on the side of a large floating raft of bundled and bound reeds, their master's hut behind them. Their net deep in the water, Chey wondered what kind of catch they would get, since supposedly 'there were no fish in the Sick.' From the trail of purple smoke coming from the hut and the sweet and bitter smells that flooded the close air, Chey guessed that their master was a witch doctor.

He called out to get their attention by clapping his hands, and then clapping his right hand against himself. The way Chey communicated with Wen, the disgraced prince, was very different than the way he was able to communicate with these men, even though they were from such a different place. The Tongueless had their own way and he had learned it traveling as a boy. It wasn't only the signs that were different, but the mannerisms, the positioning of the fingers that were so important, and honestly something a man like Wen could never hope to understand.

Chey could be less deliberate, too, with others like him. The movements were faster, closer to their bodies, and made to be less obvious than the kinds of movements he spoke to Wen with. The man and his son looked up and greeted him in unison, a polite kind of greeting with genuine smiles. It looked good for them; they had no tongues, but their lips still looked normal and curved up how they should, unlike his own. The men who cut him had been careless or especially cruel. He would never know for sure.

The man told him, *You know when you come upon the city, go down the river you cannot miss it. Only way.*

He asked them where they could find food and rest once they arrived there, and the man gave him detailed instructions on how to follow the river, and then go down a maze of narrower canals to find the inn called The Heart of Ur.

Thank you, and your day be well, Chey signed to the man and his son.

Wait! Wait! The boy's eyes were wide; his hands moved fast. *Be careful of the snakeweed in the water. Traps your oars. The mangrove is thick by the Heart,* the son signed.

Thank you.

Be safe, brother, signed the father.

Dread, too, when their eyes met and held that told Chey this man was very afraid of something. He felt it like a stone in his own stomach. Fear in himself, like it was his own. The fact that the man was a Deep South slave was reason enough to live in fear, but that was little to what Chey felt. The son did not feel it; the son smiling, Chey could feel his happiness. The boy still had the normal amount of fear present in a slave, Chey felt that. Always, they all did. He smiled, and the kind man returned a better one with his unmarred lips.

Chey could feel other gunts' emotion, but he never asked another gunt if they felt his. He did not know which idea he preferred: that he was alone with his gift, or that others could feel from him the same. Right now, the other gunts would feel his tiredness, and his fear, sizzling like oil-fry on random spots along his skin with every push South.

Prince Wen stayed silent for most of the day, of everyday. The prince was more tired than anyone should be. Cursed dreams kept him in constant unrest.

Before meeting the prince, Chey had heard stories of *Ish Wen*. He had heard that Emperor Ish Kha's bastard son had run away from his duties because he was shamed for something—ambiguous and in every story different.

Chey knew the truth, though.

Wen had loose lips after a fourth flagon, and had told the story wearily one night, years past, when they both sat in the desert on either side of a small fire. The prince had loved a girl, the daughter of a verderer he had met while hunting, and she had loved him. Lai, her name was. He had been fourteen years old, and she was not much older. Knowing the Emperor would never approve of them, they ran together and made it all the way to the Mount of Blackbase. Wen may have been a bastard, but he was the legitimized and titled bastard of the god-man Emperor. He deserved more than love accordingly; he deserved a woman with a powerful father and a rich inheritance.

There at Blackbase, Wen's brother, the Crowned Prince Wue, along with his honor guard caught up to them. They killed his lover, and Prince Wue gave Wen two choices: fight the guard and die, or flee the Empire and never return. Wen's younger, trueborn brother always hated him and reveled in such an opportunity to dispose of him. Wen didn't say they took turns with the poor verderer's daughter before they killed her, but his tortured eyes betrayed the memory.

At a glance, Wen did not look like a man who knew such grief. He walked like a wealthy man and smiled with inflexible assurance, like prosperity would always find him, surest swagger to his steps. But Chey knew most nights Wen cried, and the dreams were his greatest enemy. He pitied the prince. He thought the young man was more than a little deranged, and his future bleak. Haunted men never lived long, half entombed already.

As old as he was, Chey had cared for few people, but after years of travel, he would say he cared some for the prince. Chey would be fifty soon, an older age than most pit fighters ever reached. He wondered if he would still be living if the prince hadn't bought his freedom, and decided he would because he had always been the best.

15. SONGS IN THE WEST

Ur was a different kind of city than any Chey had seen, and he'd seen more than four dozen as a pit fighter. After traveling with Prince Wen for so long, he'd seen a great many more than that. Ur was like none of them. There was not one house of stone, all moss and grass and thatch, clay tile above few.

It was obvious when they arrived to Ur, when the paddocks no longer scattered far apart but squished tightly together, and they no longer supported small huts, but instead carried large wooden buildings. Other, taller homes were built on stilts, but all the wooden homes seemed wet and wilting, bent in illness and decay toward the center of the river. The rooves of the houses arched over them as the boat slid through the Sick. Some swamp-dwellers looked out their windows to them, others drew the rough cloth drapes. Every half kilometer, on either side, a canal would open, and he could see the smaller houses and hovels piled behind the main river road.

They got lost, but Chey found a group of helpful, tongued slaves working in the smelly shallows of the river. The men had given him directions to the Heart of Ur and had called him *Zaka Nuu*, Full-Face, for the marks on either of his cheeks. Chey liked the term; it was better than gunt anyhow.

The Heart of Ur was not an inn, but neither men would complain. Ladies were almost naked, there to please; some men undressed as well but Chey ignored them. The building was of three levels, the bottom wide and open and made to watch the women that swung from silk draperies suspended by the ceiling.

By the door, a man played a longbowl badly, drunk off a good lay and whatever they brew here. His eyes closed, he sang off key. Wen scowled theatrically before he snatched the instrument from him. The drunk opened his eyes to protest but when he saw Wen dressed in his Imperial marked armor, he dropped his face and went back to drinking.

Wen plucked along the wooden longbowl which had only four of its strings, and it produced a hollow twanking sound. He sat at a table, hummed quietly as he played. Chey sat, too, leaned back, interested at the lustful displays around him and also not interested enough. He was horribly tired. Too tired to want, but he liked what he saw. His eyes enjoyed what they could, of beautiful women in sheer dresses, sweat shined breasts. One pair dressed in dark blue came to them.

"Halmua bua va'vir," *A pretty song, that is,* the courtesan cooed as she sat on Wen's lap, spreading her legs so that her fringe skirts fell to cover her center. Her chin was dotted with the black circle symbol of the slave courtesans of the Deep South. Her lips were red. Her face was veiled above her eyes, and Chey wondered if they were brightly colored or hollow. He would have to pay handsomely to discover what was beneath the veil, but by her confidence and the fact that she had chosen the prince, Chey guessed she had eyes. "Id sortó, tharkani?" *Where do you come from, master?*

"A'Impro," Wen told her, *Empirian,* smiling and palming her rear. He took a finger and ran it along her plaited raven hair. "Bua ea uus yaad erthuum shish mini." *A song my mother sang long ago.*

"Halmua iea uus?" *Was your mother pretty*?

"Sa. My mother is a queen," Wen said in the Blue tongue and gave her a squeeze. The courtesan laughed, unaware Wen never lied about his mother.

"All good mothers are." The dark-haired woman leaned her full chest into his face, slinking the light fabric loose from her shoulders. "Tell me, please, master. What does an Empirian man do on this side of the isthmus? Business in trade? Killing for hire?"

"You are from the Blue as well," Wen remarked.

"I am from your dreams, sweet face."

The prince's smile wavered, then turned all the more eager. "So, tell me, beauty, do you know how a man can get to the mystical treeline that opens east? How to cross it?"

"I do. I know lots, and lots of things," she said, sardonically grinning and trailing a finger across Wen's jaw. "You could just walk up to the treeline and try to cross. You could try, but the natives will kill anything that enters without permission and you might starve before you get to the other side. I've heard you can't eat a thing in the forest, or you're trapped forever. Not that the trees provide much."

"And how does one go about getting permission?"

"A simple way. Another drink? Let me pour." And she did so dramatically. Chey leaned back with his cup, thankful that she was kind enough to pour for him, too. She threw an arm over Wen's shoulders, not minding the armor or blood, saying, "The natives worship real and strange gods, ones that come out of the living roots and judge for themselves. You can't pass over to the east without permission from them."

"From the real gods?"

The courtesan nodded. "One of them, at least. You look different than most that come this way. Is this the farthest you've ever traveled, sweet tharkani?" She licked her lips and started mussing Wen's hair.

"Yes, but Ur is east as it gets. Almost south as it gets, too, on this side of Dy."

"Ur is the last stop on this side of the world. People come from all over to be judged by the tree gods. The way to the treeline and judgement place is easy, but going in and out, who knows? Who comes back to tell it?" she asked impishly from her place on Wen's lap. "Three ways, three towers." And she held up three long fingers tipped in purple dye. "The closest tower is the one in the south near here, but it has been abandoned to ruin."

"Yes, that is the tower I seek. How do we get there?"

"The Fallen Tower, you mean. That's what we call it now, but oh, you can't go there, Sweet Face. It's cursed now. It blew up, fell to dust and ash one night two years ago, out of nowhere. I remember the whole sky turned white and terrifying. The gods of the Wood don't meet with men there anymore. You'll have to go to another of the towers to meet them."

Wen nodded and drank deeply, absently running a hand across the courtesan's thigh.

She asked, "Why do you want to cross, Master Sweet Face? I would hate to never see you again."

Chey watched as Wen tried to think of a good lie. He had to know the whore did not want to hear about the insanity of his dreams. "Adventure," he said, shrugging. "I heard wild eastern tales from missionaries."

"How lucky. I've never met a missionary with a tongue. To get to the Tower in the Middle, on humped highhorse you go north on the Spice Road for," –she gently tilted her head side to side as if considering—"two moons pass, and then go east after you pass the walled city of Suwam. The tower is near there, the villagers will show you the way, and the gods of the natives decide if you are worthy of crossing."

"And the cursed tower? How close is it from here?"

"Only two days and nights down the Sick. It opens to the sea, a cliff-shore, and the tower is there, all the magic trees just behind the ruins. It was a sight, before. Some men would take me there on their boat."

Wen nodded happily, then decided to pay the woman and use her upstairs for more than directions, while Chey sat and drank, watching the dancers swing around him. It would be wisest to get up and leave, turn back for the Empire, but no. Chey was loyal, and Wen paid for his freedom and saved his life more than once. He wondered if that meant he would always be something of a slave to the prince, protecting him, at his side. He didn't like the sound of that, downright hating the prospect of saving Wen's royal ass from whatever lurked beyond magic trees. Chey focused on the dancers. If he were smart, not loyal, he'd leave and never look back. Perhaps he could.

We came all this way, I have followed the worn prince this long. I am many things, but not a coward or deserter. I cannot leave him as simply as I cannot leave my right arm behind. I should kill my goodness, it will kill me first.

More than enough time had passed when Wen came down the stairs, enough for Chey to second and third guess his decision.

"I found you a woman who can't refuse you on sight." Wen nodded behind him where another veiled girl, shorter and lighter, stood timidly. She had yellow hair, pretty thin lips. "She said her eyes had been a brilliant green once, and I told her you're dumb. She doesn't see, and you don't speak. It's a match made by the divine."

No, by you.

Chey shrugged, then gulped down the thick mead.

"That's the attitude. I'm divine. Remember, son of a god." Wen gestured to himself as the blind girl led Chey upstairs. "One of them, at least. Enjoy her while you can. Who knows if they have courtesans east of the trees?"

Chey laughed. Despite his over-extended life, he didn't know much, but he knew whores were everywhere and anywhere there was eagerness with coin. Sex would be sold, even if it looked something different across the trees. Mankind would never be depleted of exploiters for resources unending, and that would always be a truth.

And if there are no men, no women, only monsters beyond?

"No, *no*!" Wen shouted, and then spit the taste of mead and sex into the sludge of the Sick. "Our boat!"

They stood at the edge of the tussock that held the Heart of Ur.

Stolen. That's will of balance at work. Magical law. Wasn't our boat, truly, was it? Chey looked unsurprised, his ugly mouth turned into a careless could-be-smile. No doubt elated for this; he had been dragging his feet for the past hundred kilometers. Wen wished to hit him.

"Yes, you're a very clever man, Chey. Thank you."

What now? he asked.

"Well, that's not so clever. We steal another damn boat, obviously," Wen said, hot and tired. *What now?* he signed back, mocking. "Magic will grant me this."

In two short minutes two Ligarthien came out of the brothel and walked to the edge of the paddock where their skiff was tied, a slave boy sleeping inside. Wen slit one Ligarthien's throat from behind before he could warn the other. Chey handled the second scale, and they let the little slave go free. He would likely be captured, but he might get out of Ur before it happened.

When the freed boy ran into the Heart, Chey ripped the jawbones from the Ligarthien, and loosened the knot of his belt.

"Your waist looks cluttered," Wen said. "You didn't even kill that one."

Chey looked down to his belt of bones, and then untied one of the browned human jaws and tossed it into the water, extending his arms to ask, *Is that better?*

Wen nodded and laughed. "The more scale jaws you collect, the more human jaws you'll drop."

Chey signed, *There are four times as many Ligarthien on this side of Dy, and they're all thieves.*

Wen laughed again. "True, but we are the thieves here."

Here, this time. Ligarthien fear me not because of bones on my belt, but for something in my eyes. You do not have this something in your eyes.

"Plenty of sand, though. People fear you because you're an old, clearly marked pit fighter with a poor sense for accessorizing. What do your eyes tell them that's so special?"

I kill, I enjoy it every time.

Wen didn't laugh. "You're boring me, Chey. To be honest, you started boring me a long time ago in the desert."

You freed me to protect you, not entertain you. If you want entertainment, buy a flute or another whore.

"Perhaps I will. If she could kill for me and row through the night, she'd replace you entirely."

But the first night on the Sick, Wen refused sleep and paddled the boat instead. For years he had been fighting sleep on the nights he could, even if it made his days more miserable. The second night on the river, tiredness struck him suddenly like a hammer against a gong, wailing, causing his eyes to burn. Chey ended up rowing double for Wen's tiredness and did not waste the opportunity to curse him for it.

When he laid back and closed his eyes, Wen began to dream again.

This dream was the same as many before, but different. He was marked by the overlapping circles, and he was so afraid. He anticipated that pain. There was the dancing woman, as always with her back to him.

But there were no trees that hated him. He and the woman stood on mountain covered in snow, looking below to a world of absolute nothingness. Empty space, gaping. She toed too close to the edge, and when he reached to pull her in, she fell from the peak. He couldn't move fast enough to save her.

"You are mine," thundered one voice resonant of an Empirian gentleman. Not a voice like Wen's, or any like he'd heard before, not like the cruel voices in his dreams. "You will find me."

Wen sat upright, awake. Tears in his eyes, he refused to let them fall. Chey didn't stare, still paddling in the dim mist of morning grays, humblest yellows, the oars moving brown red water behind them in great strides. The water no longer smelled of rot.

They'd reached the sea. Wen looked up to see the cliff from his dreams. He saw, in the distance, the hazy outline of the tower on its precipice alone, slant, decrepit. The tower looked ready to fall off the cliff. As they came around another bend, he could see it all better, all of it worse; the upper levels crumbled to ruin and dust. Behind the broken tower, an army of black and leafless trees as far as he could see, following their path even as the cliff became hills. As the hills became black mountains.

You've got me now, whoever's called. I am here. To kill you, or die trying, Wen promised. *I can't dream forever.*

EPILOGUE

Shadows moved toward the center of the cave, drawn to an unstable black flame, swaying alone in the first hearth of many. The cave was empty, but the shapeless forms grew. Dwellers of this Rock who knew of this place came in times of desperation and called it Zor Uannieth, or Ground for the Seekers. The shadows who met here called it nothing. Ministers of the dark, they called themselves because they lost all right to their names. They were many of a great host of ministers to self and to every downcast thing. While not beings of the second plane, this was their battleground.

"Ours is approaching an age, sister. Is it not time to reveal ourselves and show our child the truth?" rasped his voice. "Spoiled soon."

"We want spoiled," a dark mass hissed as it entered hollow fire. "You have much to learn. Did you gain no insight from the first or second? Let the Hollowborn believe the only truth is the life we created for a while longer. We lift no veil so that there is only that seen reality and those tangible things. Our child must believe our masterful lie. That will be truth forthright to proceed."

"And do nothing as the trees work their own misdeeds? They edge the line of freewill with their manipulation of dreams and restlessness. They have communicated with the Hollowborn, with the opponent, and with thousands of sleepers strung like puppet dolls."

"Let them! The trees know what they do, nothing more. If Rock dwellers can cut the trees down, what do we have to fear from such ephemerals? I care not for the trees and their bloody plans, only that we succeed in our planning."

"The Hollowborn needs souls to follow. Believers for suffering."

"And they'll come. Suffering does. This time is better, can't you feel it? That guilt, *mmm...* Feel it. It's rich. Nurse that despair. Let the void's dominance grow, and when we reveal the absolute truth, the Hollowborn will fall with a horde. The sowing is longer than you may expect."

"And it will be sweeter," he whispered to the flame. "Generations I've waited for the end of this Rock, to taste its blood, abomination. This, the vilest of any I've seen. The Enemy gives unnatural gifts to these amphibians."

"It will happen in due time, my wretch. We wield our blade, but their weapon is sharpened. Trust that the Hollowborn will come into cursed hands, for there is still sacrifice and suffering in wait. We'll have our gate, I promise you."

"Yes, to swallow this damned Rock whole and move on to the next. I grow weary of waiting for the downfall of such a place."

The hollow flame darkened. Its edges grew. "Patience now, brother. We struck too early last time, and the Hollowborn's compassion failed us. Xonieren was weak, and Amina was strong. Each time we learn more of this place. This third time our influence is greater. We are wiser. I am."

The shadow released a hideous laugh that crackled unlike the fire. "I am wiser —believe it—and hungrier."

GLOSSARY

A

Amina- in Canyassor's written history, the first Araeboril

Ammi- in Canya meo, an endeared word for one's mother

aidiare- a priest of Hetten, god of light, trained by the Glittering Temple

Aurel Gilgar- High Lady of Brimtone; wife of High Lord Cragin Gilgar and daughter of Lord Whitemare of Garlandfield Hall and Woodswake

Araeboril- in ancient Canya meo, Truelight Bringer, the one born with power to wield truelight

Sir Arne Osmond- a lord of Baeltaf and knight of the High Order; second son of Lord Halbert Osmond of Mirkwik, lowlord of Hailspring; knighted by High Lord Tagnar Hwaelin for his dwellings

Arnund Osbur III- King of Baeltaf from 675 A.C. to 686 A.C. son of Tormuld Osbur; ***deceased***

Sir Artur Kensgood- a lord of Baeltaf; second son of Lord Artur Kensgood of Sharpspear's Motte, lowlord of Sharp Point; knighted by King Ornund Osbur II for Tagnar Hwaelin's dwellings

Azún Kanila- by descendance of Yett, a wielder of flames and winds; Leading General of offense and protection for Tyano Iial of Canyassor

B

batíseral- in Canya meo, the term for a person poor enough that they are exempted from citizen's tax and allowed to glean from a richer man's field to eat

Bapo- in Canya meo, an endeared word for one's father

Biler- common word for a person of Baeltaf

Sir Baynard Torde- a lord of Baeltaf and knight of the High Order; third son of Lord Unbur Torde of Mineswail; knighted by Idgar Hwaelin for his dwellings

Bruse Nagan- son of Olav Nagan; the King of the Free North from 675 A.C. to 679

C

Cairo Tayer- an Eerim with the better ear; the Lord of Bogu Etka, a Master of the Eerim Council

Caeth- fabled demigod, son of Hetten and Emilla

Canyassor- the Blessed Lands

Chey- “Blooded Fist”, a freedman of the Blue Empire; a sensor of truelight

Cragin Gilgar- High Lord of Brimtone

D

Daijirek Wanúm- Select Son of Amina; descended of Amina, a sensor of truelight

Derrik Osbur- High Lord of New Galligrey

Detunae Santírek- second child of Detunae Antoren and Detunae Haba

Detunae Yeroen- by descendance of Syornan, a wielder of waters; first child of Detunae Antoren and Detunae Haba

du- natural energy of water

E

Egan Norr- Lord Chamberlain of High Baeltaf, counselor to King Ornund VI; Lord of Limper Island

Eleina Osbur- Queen of Baeltaf from ; wife of King Tormuld and a daughter of House Dawnburst of Tunure; ***deceased***

Sir Elrik Ragnhild- a lord of Baeltaf and knight of the

High Order; knighted by Ilingar Hwaelin

F

Fajak Seirmona- by descendance of Emín, a wielder of lands; advisor of harvests and supply for Tyano Iial of Canyassor

First Children- the children of Ilidrian and Malia, the first born with senses for the energies who populated Canyassor, married the surrounding islands and became the Canyai

In order of birth:

Leu- the Seawoman, first born child of Ilidrian and Malia; wielder of waters

Emin- the Groundbreaker, second born child of Ilidrian and Malia; wielder of lands

Jeyen- the Breath of God, third born child of Ildrian and Malia; wielder of winds

Yett- the First Flame, fourth born child of Ilidrian and Malia; wielder of flames

Rionae- fifth born child of Ilidrian and Malia; wielder of flames

Ashakai- the River Daughter, sixth born child of Ildrian and Malia ; wielder of waters

Hahnae- the First Empath, seventh born child of Ilidrian and Malia; wielder of lands

Fetixol- the Favored Son, eighth born child of Ilidrian and Malia; wielder of winds

Synornan- Captain of the Western Seas, ninth born child of Ilidrian and Malia; wielder of waters

Tandilyen- tenth born child of Ilidrian and Malia; wielder of flames

Natinae- Losa's Champion; eleventh born child of Ildrian and Malia; wielder of waters

Byelro- twelth born child of Ilidrian and Malia; wielder of lands

Xonieren- the Cursed, thirteenth born child of Ilidrian and Malia; wielder of truedark

Amina- the Truelight Bringer, fourteenth born child of Ilidrian and Malia; wielder of truelight

G

Geffrey Auber- High Lord of Midhold

Good Thyne- the spiritual leader of the faith of Baeltaf

gunt- an Empirian slur for truth-pullers

H

Hasyal- in Canya meo: *Other*, refers to the coming wielder of void who will set the End Days in motion

hak- natural energy of flames

hekt- in the Blue Empire, the class of slaves who possess magic

Hesóf Inyalo- Select Son of Leu; by descendance of Leu, a wielder of waters

Hetten- Biler god of the sun

Hollowborn- Western word for the Hasyal

I

Ish Kanh- Emperor of Sogua Lan, the Blue Empire; known by his people as "the Godman"

Ish Wen- second son of Xian Kanh, Emperor of the Blue Empire

J

Jonnere Hwaelin- a lord of Baeltaf; son of High Lord Tagnar Hwaelin and heir to Kieln

L

Leonara Hwaelin- a lady of Baeltaf; daughter of High Lord Tagnar Hwaelin of Kieln

Leonara Osbur- Queen of Baeltaf from 660 A.C. to 665 A.C., wife of King Tormuld III; ***deceased***

Léu- see First Children

Léuanien Anjalá Mazo Teiabél- wielder of the waters, a child of Léu; only child of Captain Léuanien Anjalá Anira

Line of Separation- marks the divide between the isolated Biler kingdom and the rest of the Rock to the West

lyaren- in Canya meo, a friendship greater than blood (m. yaren)

lyosháno- in Canya meo, little sister (m. yosháno)

M

Maisie- chambermaid of High Lady Tisinda Hwaelin

Mashákuen Cyenae- Select Daughter of Amina; sensor of truelight

Mittrik Hwaelin- a lord of Baeltaf; son of High Lord Tagnar Hwaelin and second heir to Kieln

modaire- a priestess of the Sisters, goddesses of chaos and jealousy

Moima- Canyai tradition observes every fifteenth day as a holy day of rest

Mouwat Kloennian- descended of Hahane, a wielder of lands; son of Mouwat Edanir and Mouwat Giana; killed in the Battle of Coбmak in the Rock turn 8911; ***deceased***

O

Olav Nagan- King of the Free North from 640A.C. to 673A.C.; died in the Battle of Bitterwell; ***deceased***

Ornund Osbur VII- King of all Baeltaf's Eleven Dominions, son of King Arnund Osbur III

Other- see *Hasyal*

R

rae- in Canya meo, truelight
Rejadora Kelatni- leading investigator of the City Guard of Talosa
Rhinere Rooj- High Lord of the Fair Isle
Rhion Rooj- a lord of Baeltaf; son of High Lord Rhinere Rooj and heir to the Fair Isle
Riambo Fehatsi- second child of Riambo Rehonan and Riambo Yelma
Riambo Rajen- first child of Riambo Rehonan and Riambo Yelma; killed in the Battle for CoБmak in the Rock turn 8911; ***deceased***
Riambo Rehonan- Korr of Canyassor, second to Tyano Teviona Iial
Ritra Gilgar- a lady of Baeltaf; daughter of High Lord Cragin Gilgar of Brimtone
Rose- a maid of Lady Leonara Hwaelin

S

Sfar'Laki- the Pretender; bastard child of Sus'Laki, a former Master of the Great Council of Ku'du; conjured the plague of 8909 and the plagues of 8910 and began the War of the Radicals that lasted until 8911; killed by Teviona Aadarae in the Southern Wilder Tower; *deceased*
sectar- a unit for measuring distance in Canyassor, roughly
shiar- natural energy of winds
Sisters- goddesses of chaos and jealousy represented by the twin moons
sor- natural energy of lands
Sterke- Alden Sterke, blacksmith of Alluvel
stones of descendance- stones that hold within them

centralized stores of energy, the five types being: firestones, airstones, waterstones, landstones, and stones of Amina

degenerate stones- stones that have lost most of their storing power over time

pure stones- stones of energy found in nature that can be activated by nonwielders but cannot be disactivated by nonwielders, making them unstable. These stones have the greatest longevity and can be tuned by any wielder born of its energy

refined stones- stones of energy, made artificially from the seeds of the pagalug by a wielder of specific descendence; refined stones cannot be activated, used, or tuned by anyone but those born of the specific descendance by which it was made and these stones have a varied amount of strength

Sus'Laki- Master of the Great Council of Ku'du; father of the disgraced Ku'dur, Sfar'Laki

T

Tagnar Hwaelin- High Lord of Kieln; third son of High Lord Idgar Hwaelin

takki- Canyai currency equaling 1/25 of 1 silver Standard and 1/100 of 1 gold Standard

Talia Rooj- a lady of Baeltaf; daughter of High Lord Rhinere Rooj

taro- Canyai currency equaling 1/10 of a takki

Teviona Aadarae- tenth Tyanien of Canyassor and daughter of Tyano Iial and Onatae Dianis; wielder of truelight

Teviona Bakéz- first Tyanien of Canyassor and son of Tyano Iial and Onatae Fehana

Teviona Dianis- Onatae of Canayssor from 8884 to present; Canyassor's Mother and wife of Tyano Iial, born daughter of family Marrén

Teviona Fehana- Onatae of Canyassor from 8882 to 8888; Canyassor's Mother and first wife of Tyano Iial, born daughter of family Riambo

Teviona Hanala- sixth Tyanien of Canyassor and daughter of Tyano Iial and Onatae Dianis

Teviona Iial- Tyano of Canyassor, second of his name, son of Tyano Ídran and Onatae Nelara

Teviona Janila- a princess of Canyassor; first child of Tyanien Bakéz and Teviona Kwalí

Teviona Janseyu- ninth Tyanien of Canyassor and son of Tyano Iial and Onatae Dianis

Teviona Kwalí- born daughter of family Vilavel; wife of Tyanien Bakéz

Teviona Malak- fifth Tyanien of Canyassor and son of Tyano Iial and Onatae Dianis

Teviona Nelina- third Tyanien of Canyassor and daughter of Tyano Iial and Onatae Fehana

Teviona Owéttan- eighth Tyanien of Canyassor and son of Tyano Iial and Onatae Dianis

Teviona Pyaren- seventh Tyanien of Canyassor and son of Tyano Iial and Onatae Dianis

Teviona Suni- an Eerim with the better ear; born daughter of family Rkeknak of Eron; wife of Tyanien Tyonar

Teviona Tyonar- fourth Tyanien of Canyassor and son of Tyano Iial and Onatae Fehana

Teviona Zarso- a prince of Canyassor; second child of Tyanien Bakéz and Teviona Kwalí

Teviona Zyonhir- second Tyanien of Canyassor and son of Tyano Iial and Onatae Fehana

Tiptoe- fool of Daggerlone
Tisinda Hwaelin- High Lady of Kieln; wife of High Lord Tagnar Hwaelin and daughter of House Rooj of the Fair Isle
Tormuld Osbur III- King of Baeltaf from 658 A.C. to 675 A.C., son of Arnund Osbur II; killed by an arrow through the chest in the Fourth Great War; *deceased*
truedark- muiove, one of the two unnatural energies; the energy that filters into the middle plane from the third plane; commonly called 'void' in the the eastern language of the Rock
truelight- re, one of the two unnatural energies; the energy that filters into the middle plane from the first plane
Truelight Bringer- see Araeboril

P

pane- a unit for measuring distance in Canyassor

W

Woolringer- an informant of Tisinda Rooj who recruited Maisie the chambermaid

Y

yaren- in Canya meo, a friendship greater than blood (f. lyaren)
yosháno- in Canya meo, younger brother (f. lyosháno)

X

Xer'Bowзn- a Great Master of the Council of Kudu
Xonieren- in Canyassor's written history, the first and only Hasyal

EXCERPT FROM THE NEXT IN THE SERIES, *HOLLOW BORN…*

The steward of Waterhaven was a small man, agile though he must have been nearing fifty turns, so small that from behind one might mistake him for a boy. He kept thinking on counting his steps, numbers, *numbers* drawling on, so Huesh assumed the man was simple, obsequiously simple. Simple and Fair, short and slim, narrow shoulders and clean face, with hair and eyes nearly white. *Fifty and four, fifty and five, fifty and six, fifty…* and so on, so boring. He led Huesh to a room in the East Tower.

It was not Rhinere Rooj who greeted Huesh, however. It was his son, the much less likable Rhion. As soon as he was in the room, Huesh's head throbbed.

Lord Rhion kept a guard of seven Takircha soldiers projecting false skins, all looking like large men, dressed in plate and mail, all carrying Biler styled swords. They stood close to their little lord.

Eerim could not hear the thoughts of a projecting Takircha. All that Huesh could hear from them was the struggle to maintain the illusion. He heard seven versions of grunting and moaning and groaning beneath their falsehood, but no words, and their red eyes betrayed none of their discomfort. They were seasoned Takircha, ones who could put on skin as easily as putting on a cloak. Their falsehood protected Rhion Rooj.

Like a shield, they surrounded him, and they were so loud that Huesh could get nothing from the Fair man. This was a common western tactic to keep one's thoughts private, but to Huesh, right now in this meeting, it was infuriating to find. Since when had Takircha been crossing the Lines and serving eastern noblemen? Who were these changers?

"Graceful Lord Cairo," said Rhion Rooj, not stepping away from his guard. "I hope your trip was pleasant. You were not expected, but I am so pleased to see you."

"Your father isn't pleased enough to see me? I have come a

long way, Lord Rooj, and long trips are always unpleasant."

"My father is in deepest mourning for my sister, Lord Cairo. You may have heard of her death. She was his favored child. I hope you will forgive him, but he refuses to see me most days."

"That as is?"

"As is. Let me have a servant see you to a room, good Master. A great room and hot bath on a balcony with a view. A warm body I could also send your way. Perhaps you would feel more inclined to speak with me once rested."

"No need for any of that." *Arrogant human, but I like him a bit more. I hate him, but I must respect him now.*

Rhion smiled. "No? I heard you attended the Teviona wedding, and I imagine it was much a celebration, and a tragedy. But Eerim drink and shout with joy across the Rock for one of their own to have a Tyanien's ear."

"It was, we do, but I have a room on my air vessel, and there I will sleep as it flies. I leave now for Achka, to my home by the River of Swans as your father cannot walk down a few steps to see me. Let your father know that is where he can reach me, and he would be most prudent to talk through mourning." *I shouldn't say prudent.* Pwudent *isn't as nice a word on human ears.*

"I will tell him." Rhion smiled.

Huesh tried to pry, tried to listen within Rhion past the screaming of seven projecting minds. A worthless effort. Their loud struggle more than distracted, it *disrupted.* It was uncomfortable to be near. Like sharp nails against a school board, like birds squawking before battle, pain like water stuck sore in his ears. From Rhion all he could gather were brief images of the Oasis, one word: *regret*, and if Huesh wanted for either, he only need look out a window. From Rhion's face, whatever he was thought, he thought smugly.

What a man for an easterner! Intent on keeping secrets, more than his father. He must have many. They must be great. Riddles and false words are easier to decode than false skins, and I thought this would be a good day. What a man... Rooj might win the short game yet... how hilarious...how terrible that could be. The Council's ears will be rapt for me.

BR Payne’s website, where you can find the author's social media, character profiles, and soon the music for the song of Deadriver, performed by the author and REGALJASON

www.ingramcontent.com/pod-product-compliance
Lightning Source LLC
LaVergne TN
LVHW010223110826
845148LV00022B/1265

9781737963905